FOREVER

FOREVER

THE LAIR OF THE WOLVEN

J. R. WARD

THORNDIKE PRESS
A part of Gale, a Cengage Company

Copyright © 2023 by Love Conquers All, Inc.
Thorndike Press, a part of Gale, a Cengage Company.

ALL RIGHTS RESERVED

Thorndike Press® Large Print Romance.
The text of this Large Print edition is unabridged.
Other aspects of the book may vary from the original edition.
Set in 16 pt. Plantin.

**LIBRARY OF CONGRESS CIP DATA ON FILE.
CATALOGUING IN PUBLICATION FOR THIS BOOK
IS AVAILABLE FROM THE LIBRARY OF CONGRESS.**

ISBN-13: 979-8-88578-864-9 (hardcover alk. paper)

Published in 2023 by arrangement with Pocket Books, a Division of Simon & Schuster, Inc.

Printed in Mexico
Print Number: 1   Print Year: 2023

To true love, in all its forms.

GLOSSARY OF TERMS
AND PROPER NOUNS

ahstrux nohtrum (n.) Private guard with license to kill who is granted his or her position by the King.

ahvenge (v.) Act of mortal retribution, carried out typically by a male loved one.

Black Dagger Brotherhood (pr. n.) Highly trained vampire warriors who protect their species against the Lessening Society. As a result of selective breeding within the race, Brothers possess immense physical and mental strength, as well as rapid healing capabilities. They are not siblings for the most part, and are inducted into the Brotherhood upon nomination by the Brothers. Aggressive, self-reliant, and secretive by nature, they are the subjects of legend and objects of reverence within the vampire world. They may be killed only by the most serious of wounds, e.g., a gunshot or stab to the heart, etc.

blood slave (n.) Male or female vampire

7

who has been subjugated to serve the blood needs of another. The practice of keeping blood slaves has been outlawed.

the Chosen (pr. n.) Female vampires who had been bred to serve the Scribe Virgin. In the past, they were spiritually rather than temporally focused, but that changed with the ascendance of the final Primale, who freed them from the Sanctuary. With the Scribe Virgin removing herself from her role, they are completely autonomous and learning to live on earth. They do continue to meet the blood needs of un-mated members of the Brotherhood, as well as Brothers who cannot feed from their *shellans* or injured fighters.

chrih (n.) Symbol of honorable death in the Old Language.

cohntehst (n.) Conflict between two males competing for the right to be a female's mate.

Dhunhd (pr. n.) Hell.

doggen (n.) Member of the servant class within the vampire world. *Doggen* have old, conservative traditions about service to their superiors, following a formal code of dress and behavior. They are able to go out during the day, but they age relatively quickly. Life expectancy is approximately five hundred years.

ehros (n.) A Chosen trained in the matter of sexual arts.

exhile dhoble (n.) The evil or cursed twin, the one born second.

the Fade (pr. n.) Non-temporal realm where the dead reunite with their loved ones and pass eternity.

First Family (pr. n.) The King and Queen of the vampires, and any children they may have.

ghardian (n.) Custodian of an individual. There are varying degrees of *ghardians*, with the most powerful being that of a *sehcluded* female.

glymera (n.) The social core of the aristocracy, roughly equivalent to Regency England's *ton*.

hellren (n.) Male vampire who has been mated to a female. Males may take more than one female as mate.

hyslop (n. or v.) Term referring to a lapse in judgment, typically resulting in the compromise of the mechanical operations of a vehicle or otherwise motorized conveyance of some kind. For example, leaving one's keys in one's car as it is parked outside the family home overnight, whereupon said vehicle is stolen.

leahdyre (n.) A person of power and influence.

leelan (adj. or n.) A term of endearment loosely translated as "dearest one."

Lessening Society (pr. n.) Order of slayers convened by the Omega for the purpose of eradicating the vampire species.

lesser (n.) De-souled human who targets vampires for extermination as a member of the Lessening Society. *Lessers* must be stabbed through the chest in order to be killed; otherwise they are ageless. They do not eat or drink and are impotent. Over time, their hair, skin, and irises lose pigmentation until they are blond, blush-less, and pale eyed. They smell like baby powder. Inducted into the society by the Omega, they retain a ceramic jar thereafter into which their heart was placed after it was removed.

lewlhen (n.) Gift.

lheage (n.) A term of respect used by a sexual submissive to refer to their dominant.

Lhenihan (pr. n.) A mythic beast renowned for its sexual prowess. In modern slang, refers to a male of preternatural size and sexual stamina.

lys (n.) Torture tool used to remove the eyes.

mahmen (n.) Mother. Used both as an identifier and a term of affection.

mhis (n.) The masking of a given physical

environment; the creation of a field of illusion.

nalla (n., f.) or nallum (n., m.) Beloved.

needing period (n.) Female vampire's time of fertility, generally lasting for two days and accompanied by intense sexual cravings. Occurs approximately five years after a female's transition and then once a decade thereafter. All males respond to some degree if they are around a female in her need. It can be a dangerous time, with conflicts and fights breaking out between competing males, particularly if the female is not mated.

newling (n.) A virgin.

the Omega (pr. n.) Malevolent, mystical figure who has targeted the vampires for extinction out of resentment directed toward the Scribe Virgin. Exists in a nontemporal realm and has extensive powers, though not the power of creation.

phearsom (adj.) Term referring to the potency of a male's sexual organs. Literal translation something close to "worthy of entering a female."

Princeps (pr. n.) Highest level of the vampire aristocracy, second only to members of the First Family or the Scribe Virgin's Chosen. Must be born to the title; it may not be conferred.

pyrocant (n.) Refers to a critical weakness in an individual. The weakness can be internal, such as an addiction, or external, such as a lover.

rahlman (n.) Savior.

rythe (n.) Ritual manner of asserting honor granted by one who has offended another. If accepted, the offended chooses a weapon and strikes the offender, who presents him- or herself without defenses.

the Scribe Virgin (pr. n.) Mystical force who previously was counselor to the King as well as the keeper of vampire archives and the dispenser of privileges. Existed in a non-temporal realm and had extensive powers, but has recently stepped down and given her station to another. Capable of a single act of creation, which she expended to bring the vampires into existence.

sehclusion (n.) Status conferred by the King upon a female of the aristocracy as a result of a petition by the female's family. Places the female under the sole direction of her *ghardian*, typically the eldest male in her household. Her *ghardian* then has the legal right to determine all manner of her life, restricting at will any and all interactions she has with the world.

shellan (n.) Female vampire who has been

mated to a male. Females generally do not take more than one mate due to the highly territorial nature of bonded males.

symphath (n.) Subspecies within the vampire race characterized by the ability and desire to manipulate emotions in others (for the purposes of an energy exchange), among other traits. Historically, they have been discriminated against and, during certain eras, hunted by vampires. They are near extinction.

talhman (n.) The evil side of an individual. A dark stain on the soul that requires expression if it is not properly expunged.

the Tomb (pr. n.) Sacred vault of the Black Dagger Brotherhood. Used as a ceremonial site as well as a storage facility for the jars of *lessers*. Ceremonies performed there include inductions, funerals, and disciplinary actions against Brothers. No one may enter except for members of the Brotherhood, the Scribe Virgin, or candidates for induction.

trahyner (n.) Word used between males of mutual respect and affection. Translated loosely as "beloved friend."

transition (n.) Critical moment in a vampire's life when he or she transforms into an adult. Thereafter, he or she must drink the blood of the opposite sex to survive and is unable to withstand sunlight. Occurs generally in the mid-twenties. Some vampires do not survive their transitions, males in particular. Prior to their transitions, vampires are physically weak, sexually unaware and unresponsive, and unable to dematerialize.

vampire (n.) Member of a species separate from that of *Homo sapiens.* Vampires must drink the blood of the opposite sex to survive. Human blood will keep them alive, though the strength does not last long. Following their transitions, which occur in their mid-twenties, they are unable to go out into sunlight and must feed from the vein regularly. Vampires cannot "convert" humans through a bite or transfer of blood, though they are in rare cases able to breed with the other species. Vampires can dematerialize at will, though they must be able to calm themselves and concentrate to do so and may not carry anything heavy with them. They are able to strip the memories of humans, provided such memories are short-term. Some vampires are able to read minds. Life expectancy is upward of a thousand years, or in some cases, even longer.

wahlker (n.) An individual who has died and returned to the living from the Fade.

They are accorded great respect and are revered for their travails.

whard (n.) Equivalent of a godfather or godmother to an individual.

ONE

Advance Genetics Lab
Walters, New York

A volcano erupting in the open jaw of a shark.

As Lydia Susi leaned into the monitor, one half of her brain identified the image for what it was, a PET-CT scan of the chest of a twenty-nine-year-old male with extensive stage small-cell lung cancer. The cross section, which cut the patient's rib cage in horizontal slices, showed the tumors in the right lung, which seemed bigger to her, and two new masses on the left side. Given that this was both positron emission tomography with F-fluorodeoxyglucose in conjunction with computed tomography, the growths were well visualized, but also appearing as hot spots given the highly metabolically active abnormal cells.

It was a very clear and helpful diagnostic picture of a dying man's respiratory landscape, and yet, her Ph.D. in biology aside — as well as forgetting about the last six months of looking at similar images — she was nonetheless struggling to stay connected to what she was looking at and what it all meant: i.e., that the traditional immunotherapy, just like the chemotherapy, hadn't worked.

"Daniel . . ." she whispered as the doctor beside her cued up the next cut and continued to drone on.

Instead of properly processing any of the information, her brain continued to treat the slideshow as a Rorschach test of avoidance, her thoughts skipping away from the grim news to pull random pictures out of the oblong frame of red-tinted shadows and yellow-and-orange clouds. It wasn't stage four cancer run amok, no, absolutely not. It was a first-generation video game, where you could drop a crudely pixelated soldier onto an alien planet and use the boulders of tumor growth to take cover behind while blocky monsters chunked around and tried to eat you. No, wait, it was a plate in a psychedelic buffet line, with only the baby new potatoes part of the Grateful Dead entrée having been spooned on. How about Jackson Pollock, in his little-known oncology period? Sofa slipcover pattern? Bowl of fruit.

The visual extrapolation that finally stuck was that of a volcano, her mental cracked-up-Krakatoa seated where the spine formed a little triangular notch on the bottom of the chest cavity's slice, the ghostly point of the vertebra seeming to launch an eruption that was tinted with that angry Kool-Aid red and the comic strip yellow and the autumn hearth orange, the whole of it contained within an outline that reminded her of that scene in *Jaws,* when Chief Brody goes to Quint's to hire the contractor to kill the shark.

All those boiled, open jawbones hanging around, their graceful contours like the shape of the rib cage.

Here's to swimmin' with bowlegged women.

"I beg your pardon?"

Lydia looked over at the white-coated doctor who'd been talking at her. Given that the man was staring over in surprise, she'd clearly shared that little ditty about genu varum out loud — and what do you know. She hadn't properly processed him, either. Trying to remember his name, she failed, and if she had to describe him ten minutes from now, she knew she'd suck at that, too. Then again, he had anonymous looks, his thinning brown hair side parted, his unremarkable eyes myopic behind rimless glasses, his facial features functional rather than attractive. With his surgical scrubs hanging loose on a thin, nonathletic body, it was like his IQ was so high, his brain co-opted all of the available nutrients and calories out of his digestive tract before they ever got a chance to fill him out.

The one thing she did know about him, and that she would never forget, was that he was a brilliant oncologist.

"Sorry," she mumbled. "Please continue."

He pointed to the screen with the tip of his Montblanc pen, the little white star on the top making the rounds of the tumor growth like a fly trying to decide where to land. "As you can see here, the primary site has increased by —"

"Yeah, yeah, she knows that already."

As the booming voice cut through the narrative, Lydia thought, *Thank God.*

Turning away from the monitor, she clung to the eyes of the man who marched up to them. Augustus St. Claire was unlike every other researcher and clinician. Standing well over six feet tall, with an Afro and a wardrobe that consisted solely of t-shirts from the sixties, he looked like someone who belonged in Jimi Hendrix's band. Instead, he was the leader of this privately financed facility that was exploring medical advances well under the radar of the Food and Drug Administration.

Today Gus was wearing a well-washed H. R. Pufnstuf number, the pattern seafoam green, the background mustard yellow, the name done in those trippy, melt-y sixties letters.

"I'll take care of this," he said. "Thanks."

The other doctor opened his mouth to argue the dismissal. No doubt he was the type who had succeeded at everything academic and professional in his life and was more used to people welcoming him into discussions, especially if they were about life-and-death medical issues. But when Gus stared him down, he clipped that black pen with its icy bathing cap back into the pocket protector on his white coat and ambulated himself out of the boardroom.

The glass-and-chrome door eased shut, and for a moment, Lydia looked through the bank of floor-to-ceiling panes that ran down the front of the space. The underground laboratory on the far side was so vast, she couldn't see the end of the facility, all the workstations and equipment in shades of gray and white, all the people who bent over microscopes, and put liquid into

21

tubes, and frowned into the screens of laptops, in bright blue and white blocks of scrubs and doctor coats.

"How long's he got, Gus."

Even though she knew. Still, some stupid desperation on her part tossed the question out into the air, the fishing expedition for some kind of hope, any kind, guaranteed to come up with an empty hook.

Guess she had internalized these new scans, after all.

Gus went around the long black table with its stable of leather chairs. There were projector screens at both ends of the room, and she imagined the scans being reviewed here by the senior staff. They were not going to be surprised. Small-cell lung cancer, especially in its late stages, was an absolute bitch.

"You want something to drink?" Gus said.

Down the long wall of the room, a layout of sodas, sparkling waters, and fruit juices had been arranged on a credenza, everything from the labels on the branded bottles and cans, to the crystal glassware, to the ice cubes in their refrigerated dispenser, lined up with OCD precision, a platoon of libations reporting for duty in the war against dehydration.

"So do you want anything?"

"No, thanks," she replied.

Gus helped himself to a room-temperature Coke, popping the top of a can and pouring the Real Thing down his throat like he was dousing a fire in his abdomen.

Lydia waited until he took a break halfway through to catch his breath. "I want to know how much time. And enough with the I-don't-answer-questions-like-that and every-patient-is-different bullshit. We're way past that point now, and you know it."

She turned back to the view out into the laboratory. All those brilliant minds working around the clock, trying to create a future that wasn't going to come fast enough. At least not for the person she cared about.

As Gus came across to her, she braced herself, but all he did was glance over his shoulder at all the drinks like he desperately wanted to bring something to her.

Crossing her arms, she nodded at the laptop on the table. "FYI, I will launch this thing at you if you try to offer me an orange juice."

"Vitamin C is important for a good immune response."

"Then let's infuse Daniel with twenty gallons of Tropicana. How's that for a protocol."

Gus finished his Coke, and when he put

the can down, there was a declarative sound to the impact. "I'd say two months. Tops. He tolerated the immunotherapy like a champ. The chemo as well. He's extraordinarily healthy, except for the cancer."

Other than that, Mrs. Lincoln, how was the play.

And "tolerated"? That was not a word she would use to describe the way the man she loved had had to endure the brutal side effects of all the courses of drugs.

"Is there anything else we can try?" She put her hand out. "Except for . . . well, you know he doesn't want Vita-12b."

"I told you, I'm not going to argue with him about his decision."

"You're a better man than I," she muttered. And yet could she blame Daniel?

"Here's the thing." Gus picked up the can and brought it back to his mouth, a hissing sound rising into the silence as he tried to find another sip in the empty. "He should be able to choose whether or not he wants to be a guinea pig —"

"I've *never* said the choice wasn't his —"

"— but now that we're out of conventional options, maybe he changes his mind. Or maybe he doesn't."

Drowning in frustration and sorrow, Lydia ripped the tie out of her hair. Then she recaptured everything she'd just freed and wound the loose bun right back up.

Sometimes you just had to do something with your hands. Other than throw things.

"Daniel has to make the call soon, though, right? I mean, he's as good as he'll be today —"

"Actually, he's going to rebound some now that the immunotherapy's going to be stopped. As I said, he's a healthy man in his prime underneath it all, and we've always been on top of his symptoms and complications. And we can do CyberKnife on his liver again and put in a stent if we have to. The bone mets in his spine and hip are what they are, but they haven't gotten much worse. Of course, his lungs are the real problem. Bilateral is a bad new development."

No, shit, Dr. St. Claire.

Lydia pulled out one of the executive chairs and all but fell into the baseball-mitt-like seat. As she stared at the laptop screen, she wanted to cry, sure as if she were already at Daniel's wake. She wanted to weep and gnash, pound the glossy table with her fists, stamp her feet, kick the glass wall, throw the computer so hard that it splintered into a Dell-branded jigsaw puzzle. But you only fought what you did not accept, and as a numb helplessness started to wrap her in cotton batting, she realized that she was finally putting down her sword.

How had it come to this, she wondered. Then again, if the pair of them were walking down the aisle together, her in a white dress, him all tatted up in a tuxedo, she would have had the same sense of confusion. Awed, rather than awful'd, of course.

"Do you tell him or do I," she said softly. Then she looked up sharply. "And if it's going to be a doctor, it has to be you, not one of those other . . . well. Anyway."

"Not one of those über-compassionate, windup toy researchers? I'd be touched by your request, but they set a low bar at the bedside, don't they." He held up his forefinger. "They are exactly who you want in the lab, however."

"I believe that." Lydia shook her head. "I need to go tell him. Probably best coming from me."

"You want me to be with you?"

"It's not going to be a news flash."

When Gus got quiet, she glanced over. The man was staring off into the distance between them, his eyes not really focused, like he was reviewing the case for the seven millionth time in his head and looking for something, anything, they could try.

"It's not your fault," she said.

"Sure feels like it is on my side." He fired the Coke can across the space, pegging the wastepaper basket at the far end of the credenza like it was a basketball rim. "I'm going to grab a break. You can always text or call, 'kay?"

"You, taking some time off?" She tried to smile. "Unheard of, even if it is ten at night."

"I'm going to get shit-faced, actually. Care to join me? You can invite that boyfriend of yours."

"I'll take a rain check, if you don't mind."

"Fair enough. And remember, call me. Day or night."

As he headed for the exit, she murmured, "You're a good man, Gus."

He stopped with his hand on the door. As he looked over his shoulder at her, his dark eyes were grave. "But not good enough to save him."

Before Lydia knew what she was doing, she was up and out of the chair. When she embraced the doctor who had been right on the front lines with her, there was a split second — and then he hugged her back.

"I'm sorry." He cleared his throat. "This is not the outcome we want."

A moment later, they parted, and he squeezed her shoulder before leaving. Out

27

on the far side of all the glass, he made his way down the rows of workstations — and the other researchers stole glances at him, like he was a rock star striding through a public place, a unicorn among mortals.

The back of the t-shirt had a series of faded dates, like Pufnstuf was on tour. It was hard to know whether the top was an actual vintage one or something created to look period. Knowing Gus, it was probably the former. He seemed like the type who would blow off steam by collecting relics he'd hunt-and-pecked for.

Returning to the laptop, Lydia went through the chest images again, looking at the clear evidence of disease progression. There were other locations on Daniel's body that had been scanned, but she had no interest in going through them, at least not right now. If there was nothing more to be done, it didn't really matter how much things had advanced in his spine and hip. In his liver. The only good news was that there was still nothing in Daniel's brain. The doctor with the anonymous features had led with that announcement, as if it had been preplanned. Or maybe it was just alphabetical, "brain," starting with *b,* before "hip," "liver," and "lung."

"Dr. Walter Scholz. That was his name,"

she said absently as it came back to her.

Lydia closed the laptop.

When the best case was that you didn't have cancer in your brain — yet — that pretty much said it all, didn't it.

She needed to go find Daniel.

And tell him it was over.

Two

A-b-ab-abthth-thaat's all folks!

As Porky Pig's sign-off Looney-Tune'd around Daniel Joseph's head, he poured himself a couple fingers of whiskey, and then tried to get the top back on the liquor bottle. As the cork-seated disk skipped around the open neck, he thought back to two months ago, when the tremors had started. The neuropathy in his hands was the kind of thing that had arrived without preamble, the side effect of the chemo like a houseguest who'd moved in without invitation for the holidays.

And was apparently staying through 'til New Year's.

What he remembered most about the initial salvo of this particular concession of normal functioning was his frustration at its appearance. The trembling had kicked in at dinner one night, when he'd been trying to get a forkful of peas to his mouth. When the

30

little fuckers had jumped off the tines and made like green casino dice on the plate, he'd rolled his shoulder and realigned the angle of his elbow. That had done nothing to help on his second try — and over the next couple of days, the extent of the disability had revealed itself. Each new discovery, from struggling to text on his cell phone or put the cap on his toothpaste or lace up his boots . . . had royally pissed him off.

Ah, the good ol' days. When he'd had the energy to spare on shit like being cranked over something he couldn't change.

Now? He wasn't much older, but he was definitely wiser. Or tired-er, as the case was. So yup, standing at the counter, he just sat back and watched the jittery show, feeling nothing at all. It was simply one more thing to endure, and, given the à la carte menu of physical crap he had to deal with, not worth getting worked up about.

And hey, who needed an electric toothbrush now, right? Fuck Oral-B.

When he finally hole-in-forty-seventh'd things, he added some soda and turned away from the little setup of squat crystal basins, bottles of Seagram's, and the amber anchor of his favorite brand of whiskey. In the midst of the professional-grade kitchen, he'd come to think of the modest stretch of alcohol and accoutrements as his personal bar, a pocket of cocktails in the midst of a setup Gordon Ramsay would have gotten a case of the hot cross buns for. From the Viking wall ovens and sixteen-burner gas top, to the pair of Traulsen refrigerators and the three deep-bellied sinks, you could feed an army out of the square footage.

And as he thought about the owner of the conference-center-sized house, he reflected, not for the first time, that C.P. Phalen was the only private citizen he knew in the continental United States who could really live up to that hyperbolic vernacular: "army." As in uniformed, professional, armed men in squadrons who were a point-and-shoot for whatever she wanted. There were no women in the ranks, and after having watched C.P. in action for the last six months, he had a feeling it was because she liked to be the only female anything in the room. But whatever, it was her gig, and like everything else on the estate, went by her rules.

Bringing the liquor to his mouth, he took a sip and knew he was going to pay for the tipple later. His digestive track was iffy on a good day, the rotating wheel of constipation, diarrhea, nausea, and vomiting the kind of game show he played on a regular basis. But fuck it. Sometimes, he just had to mimic the habits he'd enjoyed before his own personal time bomb had gone off. The rogue experiences were always more appealing in theory than fact, but they were a compulsion he needed to scratch, even though he knew things were going to turn out badly.

Shoring up his energy, he started for the sliding glass doors that opened out onto a terrace the size of a soccer field —

And made it about five feet.

The walking cane he'd begun to use was back where he'd left it, leaning up against the stainless steel cabinet, the hook of the grip linked onto one of the pulls. For a split second, that old familiar fury at how much he had lost hit him, but the flash of anger burned out fast because he just didn't have the resources to hold anything for very long, whether it was an emotion or something as basic and physical as his balance.

Or even a rocks glass.

Shuffling back over, he locked his hand around the crook, and fell into what had become his new-normal of walking, the cobble, cobble, cobble together of swinging legs and arms kind of seasonal given that it was November: Gobble, gobble, gobble.

Maybe he should have put pumpkin into

33

his Jack Daniel's.

At the slider, he hung the cane on the wrist of his left hand and opened the sheet of glass. Minding the lip at the base of the frame so he didn't catch a toe and die facedown on the flagstone in a shatter, he stepped out into the cold, moonlit night.

Upstate New York was beautiful in the fall, but it was no longer autumn, the chill in the air having gone from the nip of a golden retriever puppy to the chomp of a Belgian Malinois — and nature had responded accordingly. On the far rim of the meadow behind the mansion, everything was off the tree branches and browning to a crinkle on the ground. Funny, with time running out, he was noticing the seasons more.

The spring, the summer. Now the fall. Would he see another snowfall?

He thought of the scans that had been done on him. He had the feeling Lydia was getting the results right now because she'd made some deliberately offhand comment about going down to the lab "for a quick sec." Like she had any other reason to take that elevator deep into the earth? No doubt it was a pregame for when they broke the bad news to him, but like he didn't already know? He was living in his body. He knew his breathing was worse, and when he sorted through the symptoms he'd been dealing with, he was pretty damn sure that some of the fun and games was the cancer getting a further jump on him rather than just side effects from the pharmacy's worth of shit they'd been pumping into him.

Closing things up in his wake, he looked past the discreetly lit terrace and winterized pool to that ghostly tree line. It was about a hundred yards away.

It might as well have been a matter of miles.

Going on a catty-corner angle, navigating by the heavens' blue light, he eighty-year-old'd it over the cropped grass, all of which had turned a uniform brown, none of which was disturbed by any weed growth. C.P.'s lawn was kind of like him, medicated for better performance, although in its case, the metastases were kept at bay.

Maybe he just needed some Miracle-Gro.

Halfway to goal, he took a breather, bracing himself on the cane, opening his mouth, panting in a way that, as recently as the spring, would have only come from a full-out sprint. Glancing over his shoulder, he considered giving the security detail a little wave. The estate was up-the-ass with high-tech infrared cameras, no privacy to speak of inside or outside or anywhere — but he didn't think anyone was going to come rushing after him like he was a toddler who'd wandered off. He'd been doing these after-dark wanders for the last couple of weeks. If someone had had a problem with them, he'd know about it by now.

Did the men who watched him hobble off feel sorry for him? he wondered. Was he a cautionary tale to all of those who were where he had been as recently as April?

He'd been a highly trained soldier, too. He'd had weapons and strength and cunning — and a secret mission. Granted, he'd worked for the government, and been sent here to wipe out C.P.'s lab . . . but then just like the way his body's cells had betrayed him, he'd learned that all was not how it seemed on the surface.

And now that laboratory was fighting for his life.

Like a camera lens being focused, the house in his rearview suddenly registered with clarity. The massive stone structure was gleaming in the soft illumination of its security lights, the multitude of windows and doors covered with a reflective film that meant there were one-way mirrors all along the various elevations, nothing but the dark, barren landscape projected back at him, all that white furniture and art hidden from view.

The people, too.

As he scanned the glass panels, he wondered who might be looking back out at him and his conscience squeaked a protest somewhere below his conscious thoughts. What the hell was he doing, sneaking out to the woods again? Especially considering what he was bringing with him.

Turning back around, he kept going, and when he finally reached the trees, he penetrated their ranks in a random location so he didn't create a trailhead that might show in the daylight. And then, as he continued along, he did what he could to leave the foliage undisturbed. Just like the whiskey and soda in his hand, and what was in the pocket of his jacket, this whole covering his tracks thing was a holdover from his old life, the one he had lived for twenty-nine years, five months, and twelve days.

A gunshot wound that should have been fatal had been the gateway to what was actually going to kill him — or his knowledge of what was cooking under his surface. That cough that wouldn't go away? The one that sometimes came with a little blood? The tiredness? The weight loss?

Not allergies, as it turned out. Not his bad

diet, his lack of sleep, or the stress that came with keeping Lydia from becoming collateral damage while he executed his mission.

When the docs at C.P. Phalen's had X-rayed his chest to assess the damage . . . that was when they'd seen the cloud in his lung. The secret his body had been keeping from him was out, and the second era in his life had begun.

Daniel had to go slower now that he was in the woods, and it was hard to believe that there was a downshift below "snail's pace," but there it was. As a buffering fog set into his mind, his disorientation in what should have been a familiar landscape made him panic, everything suddenly looking foreign even though he could see quite well, the trees forming no pattern that he recognized even though he'd been tromping around in here for at least two weeks, the ground cover an obstacle course he couldn't remember how to get through.

Getting his phone out to use the flashlight seemed like a lot of work, especially because he wasn't sure how more illumination was going to help his —

He was saved by a broken branch.

The inch-thick, five-foot-long maple shooter had been split by a pair of hands, the messy crack in the wood no longer fresh, the angle pointing in a direction about seventy-two degrees to the right. A little farther on, he found another that was propped in the juncture of a birch, and as he kept going, he crossed paths with a third.

He'd left the arboreal arrows because chemo brain was real, but also because working a plan, even if it was as simple as designing an orientation system that covered only a hundred and fifty feet, made him feel like he wasn't completely useless.

And there it was.

The fallen tree had been an old one back when it had still been up on its root system — not old-growth old, but its thick trunk had suggested a good fifty years' worth of four seasons, and the proliferation of branches at the top made it seem like it had been healthy for a good, long period. Something had happened that had cut its life short, however, and as he came around to where it had broken free of its base, he shook his head at the ragged scarring that was obvious even in the moonlight. There was rot in the core, some kind of black staining of the wood in an invading pattern, maybe a fungus? He wasn't sure. He'd never been into nature much, except as it provided coverage in situations when either he needed to defend himself or because he hadn't wanted to be seen.

Glancing over his shoulder, he remembered him and Lydia getting stalked through a forest just like this. They'd hidden up in a deer stand, and he'd known better than she had the whys of it all. Dropping down from their perch, he'd attacked the aggressor, taken control of the man, and then told her to head back out to the main road and get the sheriff — and after she'd left, when he was sure she wouldn't see or hear anything, he'd put a gun with a suppressor on its muzzle to the head of the threat to her life. Pulling the trigger, he'd stripped the body of weapons and hidden it in a shallow cave. When he'd returned to where he'd killed the guy, he'd looked up to the heavy gray sky and asked for rain to give things a little wash just in case any small-town lawmen decided to go CSI on the scene.

But that wasn't because he'd been worried about murder charges. Back then, Lydia hadn't known what he was, and he'd wanted to keep it that way.

He hadn't known what she was, either.

Returning to the present, it was a relief to pivot and plant his bony ass on the fallen tree. Reaching into his pocket, he took out a black pouch with a corroded zipper.

Inside? Two things. Well, one object and a group of things.

The root cause of his own black fungus, as it were.

After he put his Jack and soda aside on the bark, he shook out a cigarette from the red-and-white pack, the paper tube with its packing of tobacco and blunt, buff-colored terminal, at the very core of his health issues. Putting the business end of the coffin nail between his lips, he remembered the first time he had broken his post-diagnosis nicotine quit. It had been two weeks ago. He'd wandered out of that stone fortress of Phalen's, a fresh cellophane pack in the pocket of his coat, his just-need-to-clear-his-head lie still floating in the air back at the big house, the anxious eyes of the woman he loved more than anything else boring into his back as he'd hobbled to the woods.

Like maybe she'd known what he intended on doing.

The fact that his hand didn't shake as he brought the lit Bic to the tip seemed to suggest that some part of him had a suicidal impulse. And the inhale went okay, the familiar suck and swallow of smoke a reflex, the soothing sensation that came over him a Pavlovian response, his central nervous

41

system already anticipating the effect of the nicotine even before the chemicals changed his internal —

The exhale did not go well. A coughing fit hit him like a linebacker, his diseased lungs flat-out rejecting the smoke. Choking, gagging, he knew enough to keep the liquor off to the side even though there was a temptation to try to ease things with a sip. The irritants of smoking and alcohol were a one-two punch that was going to drop him, and as he finally caught his breath, he didn't need the results of all that nuclear medicine testing from this morning to know what was going on.

The second treatment option of immunotherapy hadn't worked any better than the chemo had, and now he had exhausted all conventional avenues.

Like a complete jackhole, he tried the inhale thing again, and on the exhale, he turned the cigarette around and stared at the lit tip — while he wondered why, if he was willing to smoke, he couldn't get on board with the experimental drug C.P. had cooked up in her lab —

When he started coughing again, he tried to get control of the bronchial spasms. As they got worse and worse, to the point where he began to cough up blood, he tripod'd, tilting over his thighs, planting his palms on his knees, holding himself at an angle so his lungs had the best chance of expanding fully in his rib cage. He had to time the sucks of cold air with breaks in the hacking, his face flushing from the workout, a sweat breaking out under his jacket —

It should have passed by now.

Usually, it was over by —

In the back of his mind, a flare of panic went off. He was too far out for anyone in the house to hear him, and though there were security cameras out here in the acreage, there was no telling whether anyone was monitoring them, with no imminent threat present.

With a fumbling hand, he went for his phone, and as he dropped it, his watery eyes refused to focus and he thought . . .

Maybe this was it. And how stupid. To come here away from everything and smoke in the cold and die.

Just as his sight started to go dark and his head spun, as his body began to list to one side, as he considered the horrible idea that he would be found out here in the woods, a frozen block of cancer, dead for a dumb reason —

He caught a full(ish) breath. And another. And a third.

As the coughing jag sputtered out into nothing more than sporadic huffing, he did not try it again with the cigarette. He just watched the thing burn, the stalk of ashes distorting on the end like the finger of a wicked witch. When the cinders fell off because of the wiggly rabbit ears of his fore- and middle fingers, he bent down and got his phone from the bed of leaves at his feet. Wiping the screen on his jeans, he stared at the dark face of the thing — and remembered a plan he'd had months ago.

It had been a good plan, a plan to help Lydia after he was gone, a way to connect her with her community. And he'd been really frickin' urgent about it all. Unfortunately, medical tests, medications, and side effects had wiped him out, and then bad news after bad news had eaten into not just his time but his energy, too. The slog through the various protocols had been a blur and also an eternity, the days and nights flying by at the same time he trudged through them, the end result being that spring, summer, and almost all of the fall had passed without him following through on what he'd intended on doing right after he'd been diagnosed.

And maybe there was another reason he hadn't met up with that mysterious contact.

In a quiet, secret place in his heart, one that he didn't even let Lydia into, he had hoped that it would all work, that the drugs would do their thing and kill the cancer cells, and he'd be around to participate in her life.

And protect her if she needed it.

Nope.

After all the volunteered-for suffering of the remedies, on top of the not-volunteered-for shit of the disease, he was now here, a bump on a log, unable to smoke or drink, having wasted most of his good quality of life on all kinds of lottery tickets that had scratched off big fat nothings.

But he was alive for this moment and he was done fucking around.

Bringing the phone up, he steadied his elbow on his knee, opened the device with facial recognition, and navigated to the note section with his palsied fingertip. The number he'd received from a clandestine contact back in April was right where he'd left it, the last entry he'd made, the only entry he'd made.

Initiating a call, he made a fist with his free hand and coughed into the thumb end. One ring. Two rings. Three rings. Four —

The recording of a deep female voice cut in: *You've reached the voicemail of Alex Hess. Leave a message.*

Just as the *beeeeeeep* went off, he saw a pair of eyes staring at him from the tangles of dead underbrush that surrounded the clearing.

Bolting up from the fallen tree trunk, he over-pitched himself into a stumble, and with no cane in his hand, his loose-jointed body landed on his knees.

So that he was on eye level with the predator who had stalked him in the night so silently, so competently.

The female wolf had beautiful gray and white and brown fur, and in the moonlight, she blended into her surroundings, the dour palette of pre-winter grisaille camouflaging her position. With her head down low and her ears back, she clearly could have killed him if she wanted to, one good lunge all it would take. But instead of attacking, she retreated quick as a blink, her lithe body executing a tight turn, her paw placement so precise there wasn't even a rustle as she took off.

Fuck, he thought.

"Lydia!" he called out. *"Lydia . . . !"*

THREE

Market and 18th Streets
Downtown Caldwell, New York

Against the gritty soundtrack of Caldwell's nocturnal symphony of distant honks, sirens, and shouts, Rehvenge swept his full-length mink coat back and knelt by a face-down body that was still warm. Given the single bullet to the back of the skull, he didn't need forensic training to know that the hit had been a professional job, and before he rolled the dead male over, he glanced around the back alley. The buildings on either side were windowless, one of the cross streets was closed off because of a water main issue, and there was barely enough lateral room to squeeze a car through. You couldn't get more privacy if you'd put "No Trespassing" signs on the bricks.

"I figured we'd call you, you know?"

He looked over at the male civilian vampire who'd rung the bell. The guy had been using Rehv's sportsbook business for a while now, and he was a good bettor, regularly putting money on teams and spreads that didn't work for him, always paying on time, never causing any trouble. And piss-poor picker aside, he was clearly doing well for himself — or had won the sperm lottery: He was dressed nicely and his white Tesla, which was parked about fifteen feet back, was pristine as a hundy right off the Federal Reserve's printing press. Likewise, the female vampire standing next to him was a pick-me-girl cliché, breasts mounding up over her tight leather corset, her leggings spray-painted on. The smudge on the side of her red-painted mouth suggested she'd also been on her knees on the ground recently, although that was probably a metaphor.

"We were at Club Basque," the male confessed, like he was talking to his parent. "We saw him get into trouble and get booted. But we didn't follow him, and we certainly didn't kill him. We just happened to come here because . . ."

At this trail-off, the guy put two palms forward, all I'm-totally-innocent, like he was thinking Rehv was jumping to some kind of Colt .45 conclusion. Whatever. Mr. Slim-

Cut Slacks with the European tailored jacket, Bally loafers, and rule-abider vibe was never going to be at the top of the list for hired-hand enforcers.

As a siren sounded out close by, Rehv turned the victim over. The instant he saw the face, he had to keep the cursing to himself.

"We figured, you know . . . oh, *God* . . ."

Strangled coughing cut off the civilian's conversation, and wasn't that nice.

"This is not my problem," Rehv announced as he got to his feet.

The male's eyes went back to the corpse's face, like he was trying to nut up with the visual — and what do you know, he had to look away again and gag.

After a couple of swallows, he choked out, "B-b-but it's one of us."

"So. Why does this have anything to do with me?"

"I thought, well, maybe he hadn't paid you or something. I was just trying to . . ."

"Protect me?" Rehv rolled his eyes. "Thanks, but I promise you, if I have to issue a correction to one of my clients, the body isn't going to be found by anyone."

The civilian put his arm around his stomach like things were rolling in there. Then he glanced at his girlfriend. Sidepiece.

Rando. Whatever she was to him, the female wasn't sparing him or the dismembered dead guy a glance. She was locked on Rehv, her heavily lashed eyes low-lidded with intent like she was ready for a sexual upgrade.

Don't hold your breath, sweetheart, Rehv thought.

"What if humans find it?" the male mumbled. "Isn't that bad for the species?"

Rehv made a show of checking his Daytona Rollie with the rainbow dial. "Won't be an issue in another seven hours — six and a half if there are no clouds. Daylight is the best cleaning service there is."

As the male deflated, his good deed not as good as he'd thought it was, Rehv had to ask, "You said you were at the club and you saw him?"

The male nodded earnestly. "He got into some trouble with a human woman in the bathroom, and when he was kicked out by the bouncers, he was throwing punches. Big commotion, but it was handled. We stayed another forty-five minutes and then . . . found him here."

Rehv shrugged. "Look, I have to go —"

"It's the second one," the female purred, and when he glanced across at her, she deliberately ran her fingertip over her lower lip. "That's right, there was another."

"Where?" Rehv demanded. "When."

The male pulled some more head bobbing and took over the talking, clearly the hand-popper kid in the front of the class who had to get the A. "About three weeks ago. It was also close to dawn. Same thing, except it was a male who'd gotten in trouble at Blasphemy."

Rehv closed his eyes briefly. "You left that body and let it burn?"

"Yes. I mean, what am I going to do — we, I mean."

"Join the club." Rehv waved off toward the electric car. "Just go, okay."

"Thanks." Like the guy was assuming that Rehv would handle things. "I've been feeling badly about just leaving the other one. Oh, and um . . . what's the spread on the Eagles next week?"

"Call me later."

The female lingered for a split sec as her BF headed off for the Tesla, as if she were giving Rehv a chance to ask for her driver's license or something. Maybe her bra size. When there was no bait taken, she gave him a rear view and a half as she went over to the road Roomba.

When the happy couple were gone, he went back to ground, so to speak, even though the close-up didn't change anything. The male was still dead, and under any other circumstances, Rehv wouldn't have given a shit. He could imagine exactly the kind of "trouble" the bastard had gotten into with that woman in the loo, and assholes deserve what they got.

The problem was all in the eyes, as they say.

Or in this case, the no eyes.

Both peepers had been removed from their sockets, although not in a sloppy, messy way. There were no straggles of an optic nerve or parts of the sclera left behind; the meat had been scooped out cleanly, all melon-baller-tidy, like a spoon with a deep cup had been wielded with excellent skill.

"Damn it, Xhex. What are you doing."

He knew the answer to that, and it was a devastating one.

Taking out his phone, he pulled her contact up and initiated a call. When it wasn't answered, he wasn't surprised.

He didn't leave a message. But he knew where to go.

Club Basque
Market Street and 27th Avenue
Just another night in paradise.

As Xhex looked around the dance floor,

things were going well when measured against the extremely low standards set for behavior at the club. Nobody was actually having sex, doing a line, or playing pound-per-pound push-and-shove. Now, there were a couple of throuples who were in the but-for-pants brigade, whatever clothing they'd slapped on their naughty bits the only thing stopping penetration. And she was very sure if she'd pulled a stop-and-frisk on the two hundred humans grinding to the Euro rap soundtrack, she would have liquidated all kinds of illegal assets out of pockets and cavities.

But there was no reason to get invasive.

She checked her watch. Nice. Another four hours and she could go home.

John Matthew had promised to be waiting for her in their bedroom, and she'd been specific about what she was looking for. And it did not involve any clothing, job-related discussions, or third parties.

"Do you want me to handle closing to-night?"

She glanced over her shoulder. T'Marcus Jones had come up, and he was, as always, calm, collected, composed. He was one of the few humans she trusted to keep their heads straight no matter the situation — which was why she'd brought him over from

Blasphemy when Trez had opened this fifth club two weeks ago.

"That would be great." As all kinds of naked images of her mate played across her mind, she refocused on the crowd. "And at least they're behaving now."

T'Marcus lined up with her and crossed his heavy arms over his chest. "Nothing like showing 'em what happens when they don't."

Xhex opened her mouth to say something — and promptly forgot what she'd been about to come back with. As some kind of warning crawled up the nape of her neck and knocked on the back of her skull, she jerked around. Then covered up the paranoid twist by nodding at one of the bouncers who was stationed by the bar.

When she pivoted back to the dance floor, her skin prickled, and that was when her instincts really came alive. The disturbance in the air was subtle, not the kind of thing that anyone else would have noticed. Then again, she'd picked up on it not because her hearing or her eyesight was good.

This was probably not good news, she thought.

"I'll be right back," she told her second-in-command.

"You okay?"

"Peachy. Thanks."

Cutting through the crowd, she was bumped into by a guy, and instead of throwing him out of her path, she nudged him aside. And when a woman asked her for directions to the bathroom, she paused and gave them. Then one of the bartenders rushed over with his finger wrapped in a dish towel because he'd cut it opening a beer bottle. She sent him on to the first aid kit in the manager's office and told him to get to the ER because he was going to need stitches.

Finally, she was at the club's easterly exit, the one by the storage rooms that were locked.

"You might as well come in," she said at the reinforced steel door.

There was a split second of pause — and then the male who opened the heavy panel with his mind made his appearance.

As usual, Rehv was wrapped up in his floor-length mink, a *symphath* burrito who was trying his damnedest not to leach any body heat if he could avoid it. Tough goal for Caldwell in November, but then he was also fully dressed underneath, with a dark gray suit and a black silk shirt and tie. His mohawk had been recently trimmed, so the horizontal stripe down his cranium was even shorter than usual, and his amethyst eyes seemed extra bright in the low-watt glow of the service hall.

"Who's dead," she asked grimly. Because that tight expression on his face was hardly bearer-of-good-news shit.

"I think you've got the answer to that."

"Excuse me?" When he didn't come in, she put her hands on her hips. "Are you looking for an engraved invitation? Or do you just want to play doorstop."

By way of reply, those purple eyes narrowed on her, and she knew exactly what he was doing. But instead of getting all thought up about him going *symphath* on her, she just got good and relaxed in her shitkickers and let him do his thing. He was going to scan her grid anyway. Arguing with the motherfucker was a waste of breath.

"You mind coming in?" She indicated the hall around them. "You'll be warmer, for one thing. For another, I'll be warmer. But fuck the weather, you're about to set off an alarm that we don't need to deal with, thank you very much."

Rehv stepped into the corridor, and the door eased shut behind him. As the lock was returned to its secured position, the *symphath* in her flared up in response, but she didn't give in to the payback scan. At least one of them could remain polite.

As the silence stretched on, she glanced up at one of the ceiling fixtures, which was out. *How many half-breed* symphaths *did it take to change a light bulb? Answer: None. Because they'll just manipulate an army of humans to do it for them. Or vampires. Or Shadows. Or . . .*

Wolven, a voice in her head whispered.

No, we're not going there, she thought to herself.

"Are we done yet?" She motioned over her head. "You finished checking I'm okay, or shall we stand around for another hour while you diagnose me with shit I already know about —"

"Xhex."

"Yup." When nothing else came back at her, she shrugged. "What you got? Come on, I have work to —"

"You can't be out killing our kind. Humans? Fine. Messy, but you know the drill —"

"Excuse me?" Xhex lifted her brows and leaned in a little. "What the hell are you talking about."

"I got a call about another piece of your handiwork. I don't need it, and neither does anyone else. You keep dropping Trez's patrons around Caldwell and it's going to land on Wrath's front door. I don't give a shit if they're getting silly —"

"Stop right there." Xhex put her dagger hand up. "I have no clue what you're talking about, and you better get your facts straight before you come in here and start throwing around unsubstantiated accusations —"

"The victim's eyes are missing."

"So? Maybe he was an organ donor."

"Xhex. I warned you in the spring —"

Raising her voice, she mowed over the convo. "I'm in charge of security here, not corporal justice. If someone fucks around, they're tossed and that's where it ends as long as they don't go stupid on me. What happens outside this club isn't my problem, and people can find their graves just fine without my help."

"Please don't do this." Rehv shook his head. "Don't try to lie to me."

Okay, if this were anyone but him? Talk about losing eyes. Limbs. Internal organs . . .

"I'm not doing this." She crossed her arms over her chest. "You can just read me for confirmation —"

"I would, but your grid is fracturing, so there's nothing to fucking read, Xhex."

She opened her mouth. Closed it.

58

Rehv's voice softened. "I warned you this spring, but like you don't know what's happening to yourself? You need to be honest here, and not with me."

April's little funfest of nightmares and mental scramble came back like a bucket of chum hitting her head and dead-fishing down her entire body: She instantly remembered all those days of waking up in mid-panic, not knowing where she was or who she was with.

That fucking lab. Even after all these years, it was still with her. Then again, if someone was used as a pincushion by a bunch of humans in white coats, it was hardly the kind of thing anybody "got over."

"I have no problem being honest," she said. "What I don't like is somebody crashing my party when they don't know what the fuck they're talking about."

"You never followed up on that contact I gave you —"

"The fuck I didn't. I agreed to meet the guy. I went up to Deer Mountain. I sat at that summit, in the middle of the night, and he never showed. Afterward, he never answered my messages and I haven't heard from him again — so unless you have Dr. Phil on speed dial or any other bright ideas, will you quit making it like I'm falling apart

— and, once more with feeling, I didn't fucking kill anybody tonight."

Rehv rubbed the top of his head, his broad hand passing over the stripe of hair. As he switched his cane from one hand to another, he looked like someone he loved was dying in front of him — and the show of emotion was so shocking, it dimmed her pissed-off a little.

"Fine," she muttered. "I was feeling rough back then, but the mood just drifted off — and I will take this relative peace and quiet, thank you very much." She shrugged, then glanced over her shoulder. "Ask the boys around here. Like, tonight, some a-hole was hitting on a woman in the bathroom, and I just kicked his ass out. He hadn't crossed any physical lines with my patron, he was just a leech. And you know what? When he swung at me? I didn't even nail him in the nuts — I'm about to give myself a tolerance sticker."

"That's the male who was killed. Someone saw him here in the club — and knew you kicked him out."

"So maybe they stabbed him." When Rehv frowned, she threw up her hands. "Look, what do you want me to say?"

They stared at each other for what felt like an eternity, the thumping backdrop of the club the soundtrack to all the tension.

"I even gave someone directions to the fucking bathroom," she exclaimed. "I've turned over a new leaf, and if you don't believe me, that's on you. Talk to John Matthew. I'm not waking him up in the middle of the day anymore, I'm not — why am I doing this. It's not my job to make you feel better about where I'm at."

"But your grid —"

"Annnnnnnnnd maybe you're reading me wrong. But like your opinion, that's none of my business or my problem —"

"Yo, Alex? You got a sec?"

Twisting around, she'd never been so grateful for an interruption by one of her staff. "What's up."

Although who cared. She'd chew her own leg off to get away from this *symphath* intervention.

Her bouncer spoke up louder as the music changed. "Bruno's passed out on the floor of your office with blood all over his hand, and I dunno whether we should call nine-one-one or not."

"Coming," she called out over the din. After the guy walked off, she looked at Rehv. "If there are dead vampires showing up in alleys, talk to the Brothers. And if they're missing eyes? *Lys* is a readily available weapon, and I haven't used mine in a couple of years. So we're done. Thanks for stopping by and fucking my vibe."

Rehv switched his cane back and forth again. Then he rubbed his eyes like he was tired. "I'm just worried about you. And I'm not wrong about your grid."

She walked up to the male. "A piece of advice? Not that you want it. Go back to the training center, find your mate, and spend a little time with her, if you know what I mean. You're teed up about this, and the concern is great, blah, blah, blah, but I'm okay. Not dwelling on my past has turned out to be a far more effective strategy than confronting it. Go figure."

She gave him a pat on the shoulder that felt as patronizing as it no doubt came across; then she walked away. The sense that she was leaving drama behind was a relief.

The idea that the King of *symphaths* might be the one losing his fucking mind?

That was downright terrifying.

FOUR

There were pluses and minuses to everything in life. Take first-floor bedrooms, for example. Con: If someone wanted to break in, it was easier. Pro: Fire safety.

Along that easy access angle came the benefit that, if you were a wolven, who had just shifted to go out into the darkness to find your mate — only to discover that he was sitting on a log in the forest, trying to give himself even more lung cancer . . .

You didn't have to go through a house the size of a football stadium, all birthday-suit naked with tears rolling down your face, to get back into your clothes after you changed back again.

As Lydia resumed her human form, her body reassembled itself in a smooth morphing that had little in common with the *An American Werewolf in London* or *The Howling* gory-style torture. The second she was back up on two legs, with nothing but bare skin to insulate her from the elements, steam wafted off of her, the body heat created by her racing retreat from the forest evaporating into the cold air. She also lost about fifty percent of her hearing and seventy-five percent of her sense of smell — but all that was incidental because she'd lost one hundred percent of her mind.

Although that had nothing to do with the shifting.

Shivering, she went over to the sliding door, and as she reached out to put her forefinger on a sensor, she caught sight of herself in the reflective glass. Her hair was longer than it had been for years, the sun-streaked blond ends grown out dark from so much time indoors, the ragged tips down below her shoulders. Her body had always been lean, but now it was scrawny from her having only picked at her food for months. Her face was hollow, her eyes pits of emotion.

She looked like a different person. Then again, she had been transformed.

With a shaking hand, she put her fingertip on the reader, and when there was a *click,* she opened the slider and stepped back into her bedroom. *Their* bedroom —

Why in the hell is Daniel smoking? What the fuck is wrong with him. Why in the hell is Dan-

64

iel smoking —

That refrain had been going through her head since she'd seen him hiding in the woods with a literal coffin nail all lit up, but it wasn't the only repeater: *What the hell does it matter.*

The latter was even more devastating.

Closing herself in, she went over to the bed. Standing next to the salad of messy sheets and comforters, she stared through her tears and tried to figure out whether she was heartbroken or mad. Then she segued back into whether her emotions mattered. Which they didn't. Parsing out the nuances in the shit stew she was in when it came to her feelings was like getting upset if he was smoking: Nothing was going to change the trajectory they were both on.

Wiping her face with her palm, she picked a pillow up off the floor and thought back to the beginning of their relationship — when they'd just been dealing with people at the Wolf Study Project being killed, and bomb threats, and her getting stalked, and, you know, easy-peasy stuff like gunshot wounds, poisoned wolves, and embezzlement. Back then, there would have been good reasons for bedding to be in disarray. Happy reasons.

Erotic reasons.

65

Closing her lids, she remembered the first time Daniel had kissed her in the kitchen of her little rented house. She could picture him so clearly, leaning into her, their mouths meeting for that electric moment, the contact soft and explosive.

She had known then, deep inside, that he was going to change her life. And she'd been right. It had just not been in the ways she'd expected at the start.

Standing naked over their bed of chaos, she thought back to the way they'd spent the night together. The black satin sheets were in disarray because he'd been sick twice, both of them scrambling for the bathroom each time, him because he was worried he wouldn't make it, her because she was worried that it was so much more than vomiting.

He'd always had side effects that were worse than the cancer, the symptoms draining and distressing, the unknowns and complications slipping underneath the umbrella of doom to rain on their heads. It was a constant scramble, and so of course their relationship had become all about his health. They were always on the front lines of his body and what was going on inside of it, always monitoring and assessing every twinge and each grand mal issue — and then, on top of that, were all the protocols, the scans, the plans. The failures.

Dear God, always the failures.

Turning away, she went to the pile of clothes that she'd taken off before she'd left. She'd folded them carefully, even though they weren't worth much, because establishing even a small amount of order seemed important. The layers went back on sequentially: underwear, socks, pants, shirt, sweater, down-filled vest. That last one was probably unnecessary. She had no idea where she thought she was going.

The next thing she knew, she was making the bed as if she expected some agent from the Federal Bureau of Mattress Control to assess the effort and decide if she should be put in jail for felonious sheeting. When everything was smoothed and tucked, and the pillows back at the headboard, and the extra duvet folded at the foot, she stepped away and double-checked that things were even on both sides.

Then she marched into the en suite loo, got her Clorox wipes container out from under the sink, and began yanking the damp white sheets out of the top. As she returned to the bedroom proper, the fresh linen scent blooming in the overheated, stuffy space was fresh air's poor relation, but it was better than nothing. With Daniel's neuropathy, he was always cold, so they'd been running the furnace in this part of the house since before Labor Day — something she didn't like, but was more than willing to put up with for his comfort.

But the fragrance wasn't the point. She had to disinfect surfaces that were not infected.

Because . . . reasons.

Moving throughout the black-and-white room, Lydia wiped everything down, from the lacquered chests of drawers, bed stands, and seating area, to the flat-screen TV mounted on the wall, to the framed mirror and the jambs around the doors. She left the oil paintings alone, the abstracts that matched the black paneling covered with glass that she was worried the wipes would leave a fog on. And anything that had fabric she also gave a pass to.

After all the effort . . . she felt little satisfaction and needed something else to do.

Closet. Walk-in closet.

Even if her wipes were fairly useless, surely there had to be something to fold in there. Put in a drawer. Hang up, stuff in the laundry bag, line up shoe-to-shoe.

Emerging into the windowless enclave, she

ran out of steam as the motion-activated lights came on. At a good thirty-by-fifteen feet, the closet seemed as big as the house she'd rented in Walters, and the space was kitted out with custom-made black-lacquered cubbies, bureaus, and compartments. There was also a section of shelves to put shoes on, and a center built-in with enough drawers to stash a dozen wardrobes the size of Lydia's. Overhead, a pair of rock crystal chandeliers provided glowing illumination, and under her feet, the black carpet was plush as a mattress —

And there it was.

All the way in the back, tucked in as if it were a dirty little secret, her single suitcase was a narrow, bright blue panel that reminded her she was a guest in this massive mansion — and that her stay was going to terminate when Daniel . . . terminated.

"So are you going to put that luggage to use?"

At the sound of his voice, she closed her eyes. And before she could think of anything to say, or even turn around, his harsh breathing registered. Pivoting, she looked at him in alarm. His knit hat was off-kilter, his face bright red, his mouth open, the wheezing so pronounced that she snapped into nurse mode, even though she wasn't one.

"Sit down," she said as she lunged for him. "Come here —"

He batted at her hands and took a step away. Lost his balance and dropped his cane. Stumbled and fell into one of the empty compartments where suits should have hung on matched hangers. His body nailed the back panel loud enough to echo, and for a moment, he just went still. Like he was a brittle object, broken.

"I'm okay," he said in a weak voice.

When she tried to help him out of the nook, he shoved her hand to the side again. And then they just stayed separate, him conforming into the base of the sectional, her sitting back on her ass on the thick, luxurious carpet. The fact that they were surrounded by empty segments where things should have been seemed apt.

God, his breathing sounded so bad.

Lydia pulled her knees up to her chest and rested her cheek on them, her head turned away so she was staring at her suitcase. Why had she bought one that was such a bright color, she wondered numbly. That was not her style.

"I'm sorry," he said roughly. "About the smoking."

She took a deep breath. "What you put in your body is your choice."

"If it makes a difference, I can only handle two draws on the damn things. Then, you know, the coughing takes over."

Every time Lydia blinked, she saw the image of the tumors in his lungs, glowing on that laptop.

"So what were the results," he asked.

"Not good," she said. "Gus can give you the details."

"He doesn't have to. The fact that you aren't yelling at me says it all."

There was a rustling, and then a series of coughs — and it seemed the height of cruelty that the choking sound, that combination of gasp and wheeze, was what made her want to scream at him. What did that say about her?

"You can leave," he told her. "Or I can. This whole thing has been . . . bullshit, really, and you can get out —"

"I can?" She looked over at him sharply. "Explain to me how that works — and no, it's not about filling a suitcase and driving off. You think you're not going to be on my mind anywhere I go? There's no escaping you."

When he winced, she cursed. "I didn't mean it like that."

"You just told the truth. That's all — and I don't blame you. If I could run from me, I would, too."

As she tried to think of what to say, her focus lasered on him, in a way that suggested she kept most of his physical details dimmed these days because it was just too painful to catalogue the changes. Now, though, she couldn't avoid anything about the way that his torso curved into an awkward S, the cabinetry behind him dictating his position, his body too frail to do anything but conform to its environment. And then there was his face, so pale now as to have a gray cast, the dark bags under his eyes a combination of exhaustion and malnutrition.

For a split second, an image of him from the first time she saw him barged into her mind. He'd come for an interview at the Wolf Study Project, and as he'd appeared in the open doorway of her office, she'd stumbled over her words. He had been so tall, so broad, his face glowing with health, his dark hair so silky and thick, his eyes a fiery hazel. Now, he was like an older, hard-lived relation of that other man, a stranger who shared many of the features and all of the coloring, but none of the youth and vibrancy.

With every fiber of her being, she wanted to go back to the previous him. She wanted to feel his strong arms around her, and smell his clean, fresh scent, and know that, come nightfall, she could look forward to the two of them getting into bed and messing things up in a good way.

"I'm not leaving you," she said roughly.

"You should." He shook his head grimly. "You really need to."

Incompatibility was a divergence in Robert Frost's forest full of roads, wasn't it.

Daniel was not a poetry guy, but everyone had read that little ditty about the yellow wood, the two roads, the pairing off. Back when he'd been in his old life, on the very rare occasion he'd thought about affinity between two people in a relationship, he'd always assumed that it applied to matters of personality, habits, and values. Like, introversion and extroversion. Geographic location, jobs, marriage priorities. Kids. Religion. Cap-on, cap-off shit when it came to Crest.

For example, when he'd met Lydia, his Plenty of Fish profile, if he'd had one, would have been a real party: Introvert with extensive weapons training; no-roots drifter working for a shadow arm of the U.S. government; never, ever interested in taking a wife. No future plans, other than an expectation that he'd be executed in his sleep at some point.

Lydia had been a surprise in most ways, and a shocker in a specific one, but there had never been any issues with them getting along. They had been of like mind, and very like body, at the beginning. Now, though, they had diverged, and he was taking the road less traveled — and yes, it was making all of the difference. Unfortunately, his one-laner was a kick in the ass that came with an early grave — and the reason there was no more traffic currently on it was because the chances of someone his age getting catastrophic cancer was a lottery win in the worst possible sense.

The urge to apologize to her again for getting sick was like his cough, a returning spasm in his throat that he knew wasn't going to be eased for long. Still, he swallowed the syllables as best he could because he knew actions, not words, were what mattered when you were making amends, and his immune system was just not up to the task of curing him. And neither were all the drugs he'd been taking.

"I think you should speak to Gus again about Vita-12b," Lydia said in a low voice. When he started to shake his head, she cut in, "If you can smoke, you can be more

74

open-minded about it."

Her eyes, those beautiful whiskey-colored eyes, stared across at him so intensely, he felt like she'd taken his shoulders in strong grips and was shaking him.

"It's our last option, Daniel."

"No, it isn't." He made an attempt at sitting up again, but his torso, wasted though it was, somehow weighed seven thousand pounds. "The last option is to let go."

She gasped a little, and tried to hide the inhale with the back of her hand. When she recovered, she whispered, "Don't say that."

"The truth is what it is." He eased even farther back into the cubbyhole he'd fallen into. The position twisted his spine and torqued his hips, but relieving the discomfort wasn't worth the effort it would take to straighten himself out. "Whether we talk about it or not, I'm dying, and we need to face that."

"But you could just try Vita —"

"You remember how much fun we had last night?" He glanced out the open doorway of the walk-in to the bed that had been made — no doubt by her, even though C.P. Phalen had all kinds of staff. "God, it was so fucking romantic, you holding me over a toilet as I threw up bile. Really great. Was it good for you? I know I saw tears in your eyes, and yeah, sure, they were from joy. On my end, I was tempted to quit in the middle, I really was, but I persevered for your pleasure because that's the kind of man I am —"

"Daniel."

He closed his eyes and cursed. "You know, I remember when you used to say my name in different ways. Now, it's just that one way."

"Will you *please* just talk to Gus one last time?"

Daniel looked down his body. He was wearing an old pair of his cargo pants, not that he needed all those pockets for anything. The waistband was very loose, a requirement given how much his stomach bothered him — and something his weight loss conveniently provided — and beneath the cinch of his belt around the bones of his hips, his thighs and calves no longer filled out anything of the legs. It was like he was wearing someone else's bottoms, and really, wasn't that the truth?

"You know —" He coughed a little, and then stayed quiet for a couple of seconds afterward just in case the spasms bloomed into another round of respiratory Pilates. "I can't remember the last time I had a meal that didn't taste like metal. Or slept through the night. Or wasn't consciously aware of my body's every twitch and jerk."

"I know it's been hard —"

"I've been stuck with needles, cut open, and stitched up. Filled with dyes and put in machines. Stared at and prodded by strangers. I've been wired thanks to steroids before the chemo and up for days, and then so tired that blinking was like sprinting a marathon. I've had more antibiotics than a Walgreens stocks during flu season and I've worshipped toilet bowls like it's a new religion." He lifted one of his hands and let it speak for itself when it came to the shaking. "You want to know why I smoke out in the woods? It's like wandering through a museum of my old life, and I like the exhibits even if I no longer own the paintings. I'm just trying to reconnect with myself before I fucking die."

Lydia seemed to collapse into herself. But then she rallied with a refrain that made him want to scream: "C.P. Phalen said it might cure you."

"She's not a doctor." He tried to mediate the harshness in his voice. "Gus, who is one, tells me they don't know what it's going to do to me."

"You could just try it —"

"Lydia," he cut in. "You have *no* idea what

77

this has been like. I don't doubt being on the sidelines sucks, but you haven't lost your faculties —"

"Oh, no, you're right. I'm just losing the man I love by inches. It's a goddamn cakewalk for me."

He looked away. Looked back. "How much time did Gus give me? Six months? Nine?"

When she didn't meet his eyes, he swallowed a sickening feeling. "Less?" he choked out. "How much? Jesus Christ, Lydia, of all the things to keep from me —"

"A month. Two, tops."

Daniel closed his eyes again. He'd had a feeling they'd get to this point eventually, their roads going left and right, hers toward more intervention, his solidly to *no mas.*

"I'm done with the treatments," he said. "I've rolled plenty of dice and only managed to waste what good quality of life I might have had." He pointed to himself — and pointed out what seemed like their only thing in common. "On my end, I'm losing the woman I love by inches, and I just want a chance to reconnect with *you.* Vita-12b is a novel agent, unproven outside of lab slides and computer models, and I am not willing to squander what little wellbeing I have on a hypothetical. I'm just not going to do it

— and this choice feels like the only thing I have control over."

There was a long silence. Then she exhaled and all-four'd her way over to him. When she took hold of him and eased him into her lap, he mostly kept the groaning to himself, and as he stretched out on the black carpeting, he did what he could to get comfortable, dragging his arms and legs into a position that ached less.

This was just so absurd, he thought. There was a bed probably fifteen feet away. But that was too far for him.

His eyes watered, but he refused to let things devolve further with the misty shit. "I would do anything to change this. For you. For us. Anything."

"Then talk to Gus," she said hoarsely. "One last time. If you get weaker, you may not even be a candidate anymore and then there's no going back. Please — and afterward, I promise, I'll never bring it up again."

As a wave of exhaustion crashed into the shores of what little energy he had, Daniel kept the cursing to himself — but then looked over at her blue suitcase.

When all this was over, she was going to have to go on without him. And her memories of him and how this ended were the final gift he could give her.

"All right," he said. "I'll talk to Gus."

The tension that eased out of her gave him a surge of strength, a shot of resolve.

"Thank you." With a gentle hand, she stroked his back. "Thank you . . ."

Memories of the beginning of them returned, and he smiled. "Remember when we used to joke I had no sense of humor?"

She sniffled, and then laughed a little. "I was the one who said you had one. You were the guy who thought you had a congenital comic deficit."

"Spoken like a true biologist." Daniel gathered her hand in his own, her trembling stopping as their palms and fingers merged. "Well, I can't think of anything unfunnier than this."

"Is that a joke," she said roughly.

A bad one, he thought to himself.

Then he recalled how she had once laughed. "Knock, knock."

Another sniffle, and then she wiped under her eyes with her free hand. "Who's there."

"Boo."

"Boo who?"

Daniel eased over onto his side and squeezed her hand. Looking into her glowing whiskey eyes, he said sincerely, "Don't cry. I'll always love you . . . even when I'm gone."

As her tears intensified, she took a shuddering breath. "You were supposed to do a punch line that fell flat. Not one that leveled me."

"Well, as cheesy goes, it's just north of a dad joke." He coughed and tried to hide the sound by talking through the grab of his throat. "But I do love you, Lydia Susi. And I always will. Even if my body gives out, that's the eternity I'm going to give you, 'kay?"

His beautiful wolven nodded and then pressed her lips to his. Which was what you did when you had loads of words to communicate . . . and no voice with which to say them.

"I love you, too," she choked out.

FIVE

In the center core of her mansion, in a study that doubled as a bulletproof panic room that was capable of withstanding a chemical weapons attack as well as one involving conventional bombs, C.P. Phalen hung up her secured landline, but kept her hand on the receiver. Feeling as though she should do something, anything, she released her hold and turned her leather chair around to the floor-to-ceiling, reinforced glass wall behind her desk. Nothing to see, given the hour.

Not like she would have been able to focus on much, anyway —

"*Hello.* Anybody home?"

With a jerk, she twisted back around and grabbed the front of her throat. "Jesus!"

"I'm not trespassing." Gus St. Claire thumbed over his shoulder. "Your door was open, and I've just said your name three times in a row. My next move was to start

82

singing — a travesty you've saved us both from enduring."

C.P. blinked. And in spite of the fact that her head of research and development was speaking English to her, she had to sift through the four languages she was fluent in to figure out which one to reply with.

Gus put his hands on his hips. "So you've been told the results, huh. And about how he's not changing his mind about the trial."

As her eyes shot to the phone, Gus went over to the bar that was set up underneath her favorite orange-and-yellow Mark Rothko.

"Oh, my God, Phalen," he said over his shoulder, "I would love a fucking drink. Thank you. You're a great hostess, anybody ever tell you that?"

With a theatrical show, he spooned some ice cubes into a squat glass and doused the collection with enough Herradura Suprema to put out a good-sized fire. He drank at least half of the tequila on his way to sit in the chair on the opposite side of her desk, but no problem. He had the prescience to bring the bottle with him.

Setting down the fountainhead of his refills, he crossed his legs ankle to knee.

Swirl. Swirl. Swirl — *siiiiiiiiip.* "Ahhhhh. Top-shelf as always. Hats off to you, Phalen.

You've got excellent taste."

C.P. Phalen cleared her throat. Then . . .

"Not much to say, huh." Gus took another long drink. "Don't blame you. Yes, testing Vita-12b in vivo is our next step, but I'm not going to force Daniel to do it. Ethically, I am his treating physician and that relationship has to come before — hello?"

She tried to focus as Gus waved a hand in her direction. "I'm sorry."

"Look, we'll find our patient. It's just not going to be Daniel."

"Not him." C.P. nodded. "You're right."

Tilting to the side, he poured himself another healthy serving. "I told you last week, I still think we should reach out to some national programs. MD Anderson. Mayo. Cleveland Clinic. Everyone knows me and there are ways of being discreet —"

"No," she said as she snapped to attention. "It will get out. Those patients are registered into systems that track, you know that."

"Then what are you suggesting. All this work has been for nothing?"

She watched him finish what was in his glass, and then pour a second refill. "Are you driving home?"

Gus raised his glass. "I'd tell you my Tesla will do that for me, but that's a bad joke, isn't it."

"You can't drive drunk."

"Who said I'm leaving? And no, I will not perform any official duties in the lab. My plan is to take this bottle with me when I go — and you're going to let me have it because you give me anything I want around here. I'm going to go to my office and finish it while I play *Call of Duty* until I pass out. I'll be sober by tomorrow morning — and yes, I even have a change of clothes down there. Ya welcome."

"Thank you."

As his brows dropped down over his dark eyes, Gus shifted forward in his seat. "Phalen."

As her eyes shot back to him, she wasn't aware of having looked away. "What."

"When we started this — when you hired me for this job — I was in charge of the labs and the science. You provided the money and the privacy. We both agreed that we'd take it all the way, and you told me that the runway to patient trials was clear. So here we are. We're at the runway and you're putting up roadblocks. For a woman who's dodging the FDA, I'm surprised you're trying to play neat and tidy all of a sudden. I can get us the clinical partners, and you know better than anybody that money buys silence — plus if you're worried about adverse outcomes, I will personally ensure the safety of the subjects."

C.P. rubbed the back of her neck. "I need a little more time. I'll get you your patient one —"

"And what about after that? Patient two? Three? Ten?" His stare glowed with all kinds of no-bullshit. "Even if Daniel volunteered, we need others."

Glancing down to the floor, she pictured the lab. All those scientists, doctors, researchers.

"Goddamn it, Phalen . . . you didn't actually believe we'd get here, did you. What the hell did you think I've been doing in that facility of yours?" He knocked his glass on her desk to get her attention. "This is my life's work. I'm not going to give up . . ."

Gus's voice drifted off. And then he collapsed back in the chair with such force, he splashed some tequila on the carpet. "You're selling us, aren't you."

C.P. shook her head. And then said remotely, "I do have three international partners who are interested. One of them could, in theory, take Vita and pipeline it through their R&D using our data. European approval for clinical trials could occur, and then we could leverage that to get

86

through the US barriers —"

"You're fucking selling her." He held up his palm before she could respond. "And of course you've had conversations already. I know your reputation. It's about money for you, not the science."

"First of all, how about you not put words in my mouth. Secondly, how'd you like a bona fide clinical trial? There are your patients — as well as a pathway to FDA approval. Unless you thought we were going to sell her on the black market? The ultimate end game cannot be covert."

Gus frowned and looked at his glass as if it were a crystal ball. She knew what he was thinking.

"You're going to have to give her up at some point." C.P. shrugged. "You've grown her up well, but she's going to have to go on her own."

Staring across her desk, the lack of clutter on the slick, shiny surface made the lacquered piano-black top seem like it was a portal she could fall into, a black void ready to swallow her.

"You're going to have to let her go," she repeated.

There was only the slightest catch to her voice, and she was proud of that. Funny how for all her own life's work, all the money, all the businesses, all the political maneuvering, this one moment of composure, in front of this particular man, seemed like a culmination she had been working toward.

When Gus finally looked at her again, the expression on his face was remote. And then his lids lowered a little.

At first, she thought he was going to get aggressive. But then his eyes went on a wander, traveling down to the top of her silk blouse.

As a flush of heat went through her, C.P. brought a hand to the mother-of-pearl button. Which was ridiculous. Like she expected the fastenings to spontaneously flip open?

He lifted his stare to meet her own. And then he abruptly got to his feet and returned to the bar with the glass and the bottle. He put them out of alignment with the display and came back to her.

Gus pegged her with his forefinger, like the thing was a gun. "You're either lying to me or you're lying to yourself. You've decided to sell, and I want to know where she goes."

"I have made no decisions about anything, and in any event, I can't promise you —"

"You're going to tell me because you owe

me that. It could be another five years before she comes back, and that drug is my baby, no one else's. Not even yours."

"And if hiring you isn't my decision? Then what. Are you going to retaliate? Expose me? You've been just as illegal as I have in all this."

"But I have less to lose."

As he turned away and headed for the exit, she said sharply, "Don't make an enemy out of me. Neither of us will enjoy what happens next."

At the doorway, Gus paused and glanced over his shoulder — and for the first time, she saw the man, not the scientist. He was as tall as she was, which was saying something as she was six feet, two inches in heels. With his Afro adding even more height, and his shoulders being so broad, he was an imposing presence. This was not a news flash. What was a surprise was that for this moment, he took up so much space not because of his intellect . . . but rather because his hooded eyes and body were registering for the first time.

"I'll say that right back at you, Phalen. You will include me in your plans, whether you want to or not. That's where you and I are — and if that pisses you off, it's okay. I won't be in your face anymore after you sign her over."

In the wake of his departure, C.P. pivoted around and stared out the window again. As her mind threatened to dissolve into chaos, she remembered what she'd seen on the security feed while she'd been on her phone call. Daniel had wandered out to the forest there a little while ago — only to come steaming back across the meadow in the wake of a beautiful wolf with a stripe down its back.

Or Lydia's back, as the case was.

Reaching behind her, she hit the release under the desk, and as the monitor and keyboard elevated out of their hidden compartments on the surface, she faced them. With a sense of disassociation, she accessed her secured email, and called up the results of the scans that had been sent to her about twenty minutes before her call. She had to force herself to be objective, and it was a while before she was able to be.

It was such a shame, really.

Without a miracle, the patient in question was going to die. And there was nothing she could do about it.

Six

The following morning, Daniel woke up to the scent of hot coffee. As he opened his eyes, he was astonished to be in bed — not because it wasn't where he had started the night, but rather because it was where the dark hours seemed to have ended. The last couple of days had begun not with Folgers in his cup, but his head in the bowl.

"Hi."

He rolled over onto his back because it was easier than trying to sit up. Lydia was standing at his side of the mattress, dressed for work with a mug in her hand.

"Hi," he said.

"I'm heading out." She took a sip. "I just wanted you to know."

"Okay. Did you have a shower?" Stupid question. Her hair was wet. "I mean, you did."

What the hell was he saying? His head was so damned fuzzy.

91

"You were sleeping really hard." Lydia glanced down at the collection of pill bottles on the bedside table, the huddle of orange cylinders with white tops and labels the kind of thing that made his stomach roll on reflex. "Did you take some Ambien during the night?"

"No." He stretched under the covers, his joints aching at the strain. "I didn't."

"What about the oral-morph, though?"

"Oh, well. That. Yes."

In the back of his mind, he edited the conversation, changing the discussion from that oral suspension of morphine he took like water to what Lydia expected to accomplish during the day at the Wolf Study Project — maybe a quick review of her meetings, the winterization of the trails, perhaps a bet on when the first snowfall would hit the mountain properly. Then he dubbed in him reporting on . . .

Well, he didn't have a job. And his old one had not been the kind you conversated to your wife about, anyway.

Not that she was his wife.

"— Daniel?"

"Sorry. What did you say?"

"Do you want me to call Gus for you? Or a nurse?"

Closing his eyes, he fought the urge to

scream that he didn't want anyone showing up in their bedroom unless they were on-site to fix the fucking Wi-Fi. He was so sick and fucking tired of —

"No," he said evenly. "I'm fine."

"Okay." She took her cell phone out of the back pocket of her khaki trail pants. "My ringer's on, all right?"

Her hair was loose around her shoulders, but that wasn't going to last. She was going to pull it back, probably on the way into work. The blond streaks had really grown out at the crown of her head, the new longer length not a style, but more because she hadn't had any time to get it properly cut. In her WSP-branded fleece and white turtle-neck, she was outdoors professional, down to her Merrells.

"You taking an SUV?" Which was another stupid question. "I mean —"

"C.P. says she doesn't mind."

"I'm sorry you hit that deer."

"It could have been much worse. And technically I swerved to avoid the buck. What I hit was a boulder."

"Right, sorry. It was a while ago." When her expression subtly shifted, he frowned. "What?"

"Nothing. It's not important —"

"Tell me." His voice was sterner than he'd

93

intended. "Please."

"It's not important —"

"Lydia, at this point, there is so much unsaid between the pair of us, I'd really appreciate it if you'd just spit something out. Anything, really."

She opened her mouth. Closed it. That agreement he'd made about revisiting the experimental drug for her wasn't sitting well, and they both knew it. No matter how many times he told himself it was just a conversation, with a guy he trusted, who wasn't forcing him in any particular direction? He still didn't want to fucking do it.

Lydia cleared her throat. "I, ah, I totaled my car just last week. It wasn't that long ago, in a calendar sense, I mean. But that doesn't matter."

"Oh." He rubbed his scratchy eyes. "Right. I remember now. Well, I'm glad you were okay."

What the fuck was he saying?

"Airbags are a miracle." She looked down into her mug. Then put it forward. "I would offer you some, but your stomach . . ."

"It's okay."

"Do you need help to get to the bathroom?" She nodded over her shoulder, like she was thinking he might have forgotten where the facilities were. "Daniel?"

"No, I'm okay."

His heart pounded in the silence. And when she started murmuring things about being late, he nodded and said things back to her, good, solid things, spoken in a good, solid voice, neither too direct nor too lax. A normal voice.

And then she was gone.

It took him a minute or two to realize she hadn't kissed him goodbye. And that made him pull the sheets way up under his chin, like he was a five-year-old in a bad windstorm, trying to be brave.

Disgusted with himself, he shoved the sheets down to his hips. He was naked, although not to be sexy. He got the night sweats, and generally speaking, it was more efficient to just throw off the covers and let the cool air work directly on the maximum amount of surface area. Looking down at his chest and his abs, he was amazed at how smooth everything was, his previous muscularity gone, his torso now like someone had iced him with cream cheese frosting, the pale skin rising and falling in waves over his bone structure.

With his shaking hands, he lifted the sheets off his pelvis. His sex was lying off to the side on his hip. With the rest of him having shrunk, the size of his cock was absurdly large and out of proportion. Even flaccid, it was still as thick as it had ever been, the blunt head a knot at the top that was no longer supersensitive.

The idea of touching the thing, of tugging and pulling at it, had as much appeal as digging a ditch with a golf club.

Cursing, he yanked the duvet back over himself. Then he looked across to the darkened screen of the TV on the opposite wall. The remote was on the bedside and he blindly reached for the only thing he'd been giving hand jobs to lately.

As the pixels, or whatever the hell created the picture, flared to life, the familiar setup eased him — oh, good. *At Home with Dan* was on.

To his surprise, QVC had proven to be very good company during the lonely days, the hosts morphing into colleagues — friends, even. He and Dan Hughes were especially tight, and not just because they shared the same name. He really liked the shows on home improvement, the ones that were about storage solutions and ideas about how to make spaces work better. He never bought anything, of course. One, because he didn't own a house. Two, even if he had a mortgage or was a renter somewhere, he didn't own enough shit beyond what fit into the saddle bags of his Harley. And three, his side hustle dying slowly kept him from making any disposable income, so there wasn't much in his checking account.

And going into his savings to fund hoarding instincts violated financial disciplines he wasn't previously aware of having.

But buying wasn't the point for him. In his out-of-control world, the illusion that he could mail-order a shelving system and turn everything around was as addictive as the idea that he could light up a cigarette or sip some Jack and somehow reach back to the days when he'd been blissfully unaware of his mortality. He also liked the countdown of how much had sold of what, as well as the QVC price cuts and sale prices and the whole three easy payments of $16.84 thing.

And then there were the hosts. With their relentless cheerfulness and their this-is-my-home-welcome-to-it stage sets, everything was so sitcom perfect, nothing ever going wrong, only the positive, the glass half full, the optimistic consumerism, being offered like a platter of sunshine on a gray day.

Plus they were going into the holidays. So everything was Tom-turkey delicious and red and green festive.

As good ol' Mr. Hughes's reassuring murmur caressed over the details of a desk

97

with a retractable keyboard tray, Daniel closed his eyes and had a thought that he needed to go empty his bladder. The fact that he felt no urgency at all might mean his kidneys were shutting down. Maybe that should bother him more —

His cell phone lit off with a shrill old school ring-a-ding-ding and he jumped. Slapping around the bedside, he got ahold of the thing, in case it was Lydia hitting something else — although at least this time, she was in one of C.P. Phalen's armor-plated SUVs that could probably crash through a concrete wall and still go eighty on the highway —

He frowned at the number and then quickly answered. "Hello?"

"This is Alex Hess. You called me last night."

On the other side of the connection, Xhex shifted her Samsung to her left ear and leaned back against the headboard of her mated bed. Almost immediately, she was distracted by the sound of the shower and glanced over at the partially open door into the marble bathroom. Between one blink and the next, she imagined John Matthew arching back and sweeping suds from his freshly cut hair.

Niiiiice . . .

Except then the labored breathing registered. The rasp was not subtle in the slightest, the kind of thing that even a human wouldn't overlook.

"Hello," she said with impatience.

Because she really didn't want to be doing this. Thank you, Rehv. After the male had pulled his doom, gloom, and loom back at Basque, apparently he'd felt the need to tee up this contact again. But she'd already been flaked on once by whatever asthmatic vampire this was. Or was it a human?

She didn't know, because the SOB hadn't showed. And surprise!, she was even less interested in playing games now.

"Thanks for calling me back," the hoarse male voice said.

In his background, there was the murmur of a TV, but then the chatter was cut off like he'd hit a mute button. The groan that came afterward suggested he was settling into a different position, wherever he was.

She tried to remember what Rehv had told her about the guy, but it had been how long? Six months? And back in the spring, she'd been on her way to some kind of existential crisis of her own so she'd been a little distracted.

"Look," she said, "I'm about to crash for

the day, so let's get on with this —"

"I understand you have some information about . . . Deer Mountain."

Instantly, she remembered ascending a trail, pine trees crowding in around her, the night so much more dense and dark than it ever was in Caldwell . . . as an entity like nothing she had ever seen before appeared in her path.

You have a disease of the soul. If you do not cure it now, it will destroy you.

"Are you still there?" whoever the hell it was asked.

"How about we start with an apology. I waited for you for an hour back in April — that view was nice enough, but not where I wanted to waste sixty minutes of my life."

"I'm really sorry about that. Something . . . came up."

"I'll bet. But no loss on your side — because I don't know anything about that mountain."

Or what the hell she'd seen on it.

There was a pause. "That's not what my contact told me —"

Coughing interrupted the flow of words, and it was a while before the choking was reined in. Naturally, Xhex twiddled her proverbial thumbs by recalling what that entity had said to her, the words nudging up into premonition territory, the whole interaction the kind of thing she had deliberately forgotten —

There is a path before you, my child. It will be long and dangerous, and the resolution of your quest is not clear at this time. But if you do not start . . . you will never, ever finish.

"I was told you could help me," the caller finally resumed. "That you knew things."

She cleared her throat. "You were misinformed. I don't have anything to say to you about Deer Mountain —"

"It's not for me. It's for my . . . well, she's not my wife yet. She's . . . searching for her community, and we have reason to believe it is on that mountain."

This was a human, she decided.

And didn't that make her even less interested in getting involved.

As the scent of John's conditioner wafted out of the bathroom, Xhex glanced again in the direction of the marble enclave. Clearly, things had progressed all the way to the end of his shower routine. The fact that he always did the same thing, in the same order, was like a metronome to cleanliness, a to-do list he checked off, and she liked that about him.

She liked everything about her male . . .

For no good reason, she considered how

she'd feel if he needed help. And what she would do to get whatever it was to him.

"What kind of community are we talking about?" she asked even though she didn't want to.

"She's . . . not like me."

"That tells me nothing, sorry."

"She's not like you, either."

As Rehv had been the reference, maybe Mr. COPD on the other end of the phone knew he was talking to a vampire. But maybe he didn't.

"She needs to be with her kind," the man said roughly. "She needs . . . to not be alone in this world."

Something in the tone made Xhex frown and sit up, her legs swinging off the bed. As the balls of her feet made contact with the antique Persian rug, she moved them back and forth, the feel of the wool brushing her callouses the kind of thing that she couldn't decide if she liked or not —

All of a sudden, another memory came to her. It was clear as a bell, and was accompanied by a feeling of dread: Vishous staring at her with those icy eyes of his, the Brother's voice low with warning as he'd told her he'd had a vision of her. After which he'd uttered a single word.

"Wolven," Xhex heard herself say.

No pause now from the man: "Yes, she's a wolven. And if you know what that is . . . well, I don't know how you fit into all this or what your connection is to that mountain. But I'm running out of time and I need help, so I'm willing to grasp at straws."

Caught in her own head, Xhex muttered, "If you're short on hours, you should have showed up back in April."

"I thought you said you didn't know anything about the —"

"I'm not interested in arguing with you." She needed to snap out of this: Not her problem. "And I can't help you because I don't know shit —"

"I'm dying. And I can't leave her alone in this world. I just can't. Please . . . help me."

Well . . . what the hell did she say to that.

Can of worms, she thought. This was a total can of night crawlers, everything a tangle of big, fat fish bait.

"I really don't know what I can do for you." Over in the bathroom, the water was cut off, the dripping loud, the sound of her mate flopping a towel around his body quiet. "Yeah, I did go up that mountain once. But there was nothing there other than rocks, trees, and pine needles on the ground."

"No, there are other things on that moun-

tain," he said roughly. "I've seen them myself."

"So then take your mate to the trail and
find them. You don't need my help." She
switched ears. "Look, I gotta go. Sorry.
Good luck."

She ended the call just as John Matthew
appeared in the bathroom doorway with a
towel wrapped around his waist.

You okay? he signed.

"Yeah." She put her phone aside. "It was
nothing."

As her *hellren* stared across at her, she
eased back down against the pillows. For a
moment, she felt entangled, but then she
just let that tension go — and the fact that
it was easy to segue out of the unease meant
the shit wasn't that important . . . and
besides, she was feeling better than she ever
had lately. More stable, instead of less.

Unlike certain other people. Who happened to have mohawks.

And maybe she was a bitch, but it felt
good to turn her back on the grind of
whatever bullshit destiny had tried, and
failed, to line up for her. April had been the
moment, and that was passed, she told herself.

"C'mere," she murmured as she motioned

for her mate. "I want to give you some-thing."

John Matthew's lids lowered, as if he were reading her mind, and right on cue, her *hell-ren* came across the antique rug on a prowl, his body moving with sensual intent. When he stood in front of her, his broad dagger hand went to the erection that had thick-ened up at his hips. Gripping himself, he released the terry cloth wrap.

Then he let things fall to his feet.

"That's what I want," Xhex moaned.

Turning onto her side, she palmed her mate's erection and pulled him forward. Opening her mouth, she had a moment of thanks for the fact that the grand antique bed they slept on, which was not ordinarily her style at all, was so built up with its carved head- and footboards that it placed her at just the right level.

Sucking John's arousal in deep, she closed her eyes and snaked a hand around to lock onto his ass. In and out, slow and steady, with his fingers spearing into her short hair, and his breathing getting heavy, and his hips pumping to the rhythm she set.

This was what she needed. The crap about her past in the lab, and what had been done to her during those experiments . . . and V and his stupid visions . . . and that mountain, which was not her business and nothing she was interested in . . . and Rehv with his issues? Fuck it all. Here and now and with her *hellren* was the only thing that mattered.

As John started to come, her phone rang. The sound, like the dying man who was probably trying to reach her again, was easy to ignore.

Destiny was a goddamn shit salad, and no offense to the guy and his dread disease or whatever was killing him, and his GF with the four paws and the silver-bullet problem, Xhex was not going to add any croutons to what was already in her bowl.

For the first time in her life, everything was okay.

She was *not* fucking it up.

SEVEN

At the end of the day, as the last of the light was draining from what had been a cloudy sky, Lydia pulled up to the imposing gates of Phalen-ville. She didn't have to wait long for the estate's security department to clear her and unlock all that wrought iron. Hitting the gas on the borrowed SUV, she proceeded down an allée of trees that locked her into what she had started to think of as the Jolly Green Giant's colon. The chute was the length of a football field, and there was no exiting once you'd started down the thing, no breaks in the lineup of all those matching conifers. At the end, things opened up and the stone house was revealed.

Funny, the sprawling mansion got bigger every time she saw it. Or maybe the size distortion was because she felt like she had to reacquaint herself with the grandeur every time she came back. Then again, when

107

you'd spent your life living in two- or three-bedroom houses, you suffered from building dysmorphia if you got an upgrade like this.

Inside, she could forget the scale. Outside, she could see nothing else.

Pulling around to the side, she came up to the detached garage, hit the opener, and waited for the third door down the lineup of ten to open. After she parked, she turned off the engine and just stared at the varnished wainscoting in front of her. Like everything else in C.P.'s world, the interior of what was — or should have been — a utility building was finished as if it were a living room. Or maybe a stable for champion thoroughbreds.

She needed to go inside. Find Daniel. See how his day was.

See if he'd done what he'd promised her he would.

A look down the cars that were parked and she tried to do some math to give herself a delay. With all the matching blacked-out Suburbans, the three Mercedes sedans, and then something that looked like a spaceship with wheels, she couldn't imagine what the value of the collection was.

"Lot of money in pharmaceuticals," she muttered.

Getting out, she hit the button by the door and stepped over the laser eye so she didn't impede the closing. Then she stopped. The garages were separated from the main house on the surface level, but connected by a subterranean tunnel. As she stared at the side entrance of the mansion, she pictured where it would take her: into the professional kitchen, where professional chefs would be making a professional-chef kind of meal for C.P. and herself . . . and whoever else was dining tonight, like lab staff or security.

Anxiety tightened her shoulders, and as she looked up to the sky, she searched the cloud cover that seemed to be thickening by inches with every lumen of light that was draining from the horizon. Darkness was encroaching upon the property, weaving out of the forest, crossing the meadow and making a bid for the house like an invader that meant to conquer. And yet the gloaming was beautiful, too, and she stayed where she was to watch the soft peach dim down until the very last of the sun's glow was nothing but a hint of pale gray —

A figure came around the corner of the mansion, stepping off the edge of the terrace and following the little flagstone path that linked the back lawn to the velvet-black asphalt courtyard.

The cane and the uneven gait would have given Daniel's identity away, but she knew him by his scent anyway. Her first instinct was to rush over, not because he was going to fall, but because she wanted to save him the effort of covering the distance — but he didn't like when she coddled him.

Collecting herself, she put a determined smile on her face —

She never did get to speak the falsely cheerful hello. A blaze of light hit her retinas, blinding her so badly, she put her forearms up as a shield.

"Lydia?" Daniel called out as she stumbled back.

The light faded as quickly as it had come, and in the aftermath, there was no reorientation to the darkness, no reason for her retinas to readjust.

Because it hadn't been light in the conventional sense.

"Lydia, what's wrong?"

Daniel was right in front of her now, the cap to keep his balding head warm the first thing she noticed. It was on backwards, and the detail of the sewed-on tag was an absurd thing to notice.

"I'm okay," she lied as she tried to focus. Tried not to think the flash was anything important. Tried to . . .

And yet is it really a surprise, she thought.

Her Finnish grandfather had always told her that if you wanted to see your future, you went out at the moment of first dawn, when the sun was just starting to warm the sky in the east. There, he had said, you would find what destiny was bringing you in a blaze of light.

And if you wanted to see your past . . .

Then you went out at gloaming. And waited for the same.

"Honest, I'm fine," she mumbled as she reached out and wrapped her arms gently around Daniel's narrow shoulders.

With a surge of emotion, she wanted to crush him to her. Hold him so hard neither of them could breathe. Bury her face into his neck and scent him until he was all she could smell.

Their goodbye was coming — and she had known that in the hypothetical. But the light she had just seen announced their parting as reality.

Daniel was more her past now, more than even her present. In spite of the fact that he was standing in front of her.

"Listen to me," he said urgently as his arms came around her with a surprising strength. "I talked to Gus. I told him I'll

111

take Vita-12b. I'll do it. I'll do anything to
not lose you, to stay here with you. I don't
want you to be left alone and I've still got
some fight in me, I promise —"

Lydia pulled back. "No, no, Daniel, I've
been thinking. You're right. I don't know
what it's like, what you've been through. I
can't ask you to —"

"But I want to. I'll do it —"

"You don't have to —"

Abruptly, he laughed in a burst — and
then started coughing. After things with his
lungs calmed down, he shook his head rue-
fully. "How is it possible that we got to the
same place, just at different times?"

Lydia closed her eyes. He was telling her
what she wanted to hear, what she'd thought
the only solution was, but she'd reconsid-
ered her desperation all day long.

More than that, though . . . the light just
now told her everything she needed to know
about what was going to happen next.
Especially if he had resolved to take Vita-
12b. When he'd been against it? She hadn't
seen what she'd just witnessed, even though
she got home every night at the same time.

There had been plenty of chances.

Jesus . . . that novel agent was going to
kill him.

"No," she said urgently. "No, don't do it."

"What?"

Lydia grabbed for his hands. "I was wrong. You're wrong now. Let's — no, we have to enjoy the time we have, okay? You're right. Another treatment's just going to make you sicker and we don't even know if it'll work —"

"I'll do it, Lydia. I can do it."

Reaching up, she stroked his hollow cheek . . . and wondered how she was going to live without him. The sobbing that came with that grim, sad thought was immediate and uncontrollable — and for the first time since he'd started the chemo, he was the one holding her up. Somehow, even with his diminished strength, he managed to keep them both on their feet.

Good thing, too.

She would have shattered like glass if she hit the pavement.

Up in the house, as C.P. looked down at the two people who were embraced in her motor court, her vantage point jerked back and forth.

Daniel and Lydia were easy enough to track, though, given that they were standing flush against each other, their heads close, their arms wrapped tight around the center core created by their embrace. And the image of them together, bracing against the storm they were in, made her rethink a little of the romantic crap she'd always turned her nose up at. That whole two-who-became-one platitude had never resonated with her, but tonight, the living, breathing display of unity struck a painful note —

"I'm coming, I'm fucking *coming . . .*"

C.P. switched her grip on the windowsill in her study's private bathroom and widened her stance because things were about to get even more bumpy. With her skirt up around her waist and her silk panties and panty liner pushed to the side, the blond guard who was drilling her from behind might as well have been a dildo.

Actually, he was one, albeit one that had a heartbeat and respiration rather than batteries.

"Fuck —"

The tempo increased in a sudden surge, and she needed to use the muscles in her shoulders to keep from banging her face into the glass. And yet still she watched as the couple down below separated from their tight clutch and Daniel wiped his woman's face with his shaky hands.

The grunt from behind her was punctuated with a locking penetration, and as she felt the guard's cock spasm deep inside her,

114

she was relieved pregnancy wasn't a problem even though they weren't using protection. She was infertile — and she wasn't worried about STDs. The regular health screenings she required him to take made sure she was safe.

What he did after hours was his business. What they did during? Was hers. And as the two would never mix, he got tested weekly.

With his orgasm over, the guard's breathing was harsh and heavy, and she remembered back a couple of months ago when she'd found the sound erotic as hell. Now, it was just like someone working out next to her in a gym, the two of them side by side on StairMasters.

No orgasm for her this time. A first.

As soon as he withdrew and collapsed back against the marble wall by the toilet, she straightened from the windowsill and rearranged her skirt. A quick check of her reflection was satisfactory. Not a hair out of place and her lipstick wasn't smudged. No kissing, of course.

They really were so damned compatible. She needed someone who could be satisfied with nothing but doing her from behind on her schedule — also somebody who never argued with the boundaries, touched her in any other way, and didn't share the details with anyone. On his side? He apparently just needed a heart and a hole. At least while he was working his shift.

"Was that good, baby?" he drawled.

With his eyes at half-mast, and that prodigious cock of his taking its own sweet time deflating, he was a male animal who was well satisfied with his performance — and very used to receiving compliments. But that wasn't where she went. Goddamn, she hated when couples called each other "baby." "Babe" was even worse. But they weren't a couple, so his poor taste in sobriquets wasn't her problem.

"Pull your pants up and collect yourself, would you."

He stroked himself with a lazy hand. "You sure you don't want another?"

She hadn't wanted the first one. But she'd been feeling untethered. Unfortunately, he wasn't the grounding she was looking for — and why the hell was she cold? It was seventy degrees in here, and technically, she'd just had some aerobic exercise.

C.P. stepped out of the bathroom —

"Shit! Again?" she barked.

Gus was over by the bar, pouring himself a Coke, not a tequila. And as she shut the door quickly, he turned around and toasted her with the Real Thing. "He's go-

116

ing to do it!"

Shaking her head to try to focus, she tugged the sleeve of her tailored jacket down. And smoothed her skirt on a just-in-case. "I'm sorry, what — wait, Daniel? Is going to —"

"Yes!" Gus came forward. "And I didn't talk him into Vita. He chose freely. He said he wasn't going to leave Lydia, and that was why. So please, don't sell right now. Give . . . me . . ."

As Gus's words ran out of gas, his eyes shifted off to the side — and then he walked around her and ripped open the bathroom door.

"Okay," she heard him say. "My bad."

Cursing under her breath, she crossed her arms over her chest and prayed that the guard had gotten the bottom half of his black uniform back where it should have stayed — and yup, as the blond emerged, he had not only covered himself properly, he didn't say a word. He just nodded at her, like they'd had a business meeting between her sink and toilet, and walked out of the study with his head level. There was even a *click* as he closed the door behind his departure. As if he knew she was going to appreciate a little privacy.

Gus lifted an eyebrow.

"It's not what it looks like," she said briskly.

"You're going to tell me he's changing a light bulb in there?"

C.P. went around her desk and sat down. "Something like that."

"With his pants off?" Gus put the full glass down on the bar. "Never mind. It's not my business. And hey, tonight your study door was closed and I did barge in. Now I know why and I know better."

For some stupid reason, she noted that he was wearing a Talking Heads t-shirt. Which seemed a little too recent for his normal tastes. When had "Burning Down the House" come out? Certainly not during the decade of peace and love.

"Were you about to say something?" he murmured. " 'Cuz by all means, I'm dying to hear it."

Closing her eyes, she exhaled. "Gus —"

"Actually, better that you spare us both." He headed for the exit. "Daniel doesn't want to wait. We're going to do a checkup on him tomorrow and start administering Vita as early as the afternoon. I'll keep you posted — and ask you again to hold until we see what we've got *in vivo* —"

"I never said I was selling," she cut in sharply.

118

"You're going to want to wait." He glanced back at her. "If the results are shit, you can bury them and still make a profit. But if our baby does what I think she will? You're going to make a boatload more cash, and we know how happy that'll get you. You can buy a hundred of those blond fuckboys —"

"He is a fully trained militia soldier."

"Is that what they're calling them now? I'm so behind the times." Gus tipped his head as if he were wearing a formal hat. "My bad."

And justlikethat, he was gone.

There was no click behind him, though.

She did learn that he had, in fact, closed the door, however, when she left about ten minutes later.

He'd just managed to shut her out in silence.

EIGHT

"No, I'm going to kill you."

As Blade, half-bred *symphath,* full-blown psychopath, spoke the words to the human, he drawled them out because all parts of this experience were to be enjoyed. By him. Then he briefly closed his eyes and breathed in. Talk about an aftershave. The bouquet of terror-sweat was laced with Arrid Extra Dry, Bounce fabric softener, and — was it Paul Mitchell shampoo?

Fancy for a scientist.

"W-w-w-why are you —"

He put the forefinger of his free hand on the male's lips as a rush of arousal thickened his cock. "Shhhhh."

The other side of all his ambidextrous was locked on the hilt of a solid-gold knife that he had fashioned himself from a bar that was 10K — so the deadly length was good and hard. Pure gold, like an innocent soul,

120

was far too soft to be of any use as a weapon.

And the tip of his proverbial spear was resting right on the belly button of the human. To the point where a little red spot had bloomed at the contact, the stain spreading through the fibers of the blue scrubs like an infection on skin.

Blade and his next kill were standing in a stark hallway that was located thirty-five feet below a cornfield, ten miles away from the nearest town, fifty miles away from the nearest city, and a hundred and fifty million light-years away from the likes of Philadelphia. Above them, a vent was blowing warm air, and stretching down the corridor, fluorescent ceiling lights glowed like little cloud banks that were tethered in place.

Off in the distance, voices were in volley, the back-and-forths dimmed by closed portals, the exchange of syllables the kind of thing that humans couldn't track. As a *symphath,* though, he heard everything. And he saw things, too.

The pasty little groundhog of a man in front of him was north of forty — going by the receding hairline and the paunch — but not by a lot, and his emotional grid was lit up like a Christmas tree: Thanks to Blade's bad side, he could burrow into the secret, private places of almost anybody, visualizing both their nitty and their gritty. And because of what he was, he never failed to draw off the negative emotions, the upset, the paranoia, the fear, all of which were represented to him in a three-dimensional, CAD-drawing-like effect.

Like the balloon in a comic strip, bobbing over their head.

As a mewing sound burbled up between them, Blade catalogued his prey. The scientist in the white coat had sweat running down his bloated face and bubbling over his upper lip, and his heart wasn't so much beating as flickering, the pulse at the carotid artery a tremble that was oh-so-close to the very thin skin of the throat. The features of the face didn't register very clearly; then again, there were other details that were a tastier meal for his mind.

"H-h-how did you get in here," the man stammered.

Blade smiled and did nothing to hide his fangs. And what do you know, his victim's wide stare locked on them.

"You have bigger problems than my entry." Blade inhaled again, and leaned in so close, they were practically kissing. "And speaking of penetration, pity I don't have more time. I'd enjoy getting to know you. Inside and out."

Whimpering now, the sound high-pitched and repetitive. Like the squeaky toy of a dog.

"Unfortunately, time's ticking," Blade continued. "Oh, and don't be complimented, by the way. I have very low standards. I'm positively indiscriminate about who I'll fuck."

Moaning. A weaving on the man's feet, as if the hyperventilating and the inefficient pump of his cardiac muscle were causing him to pass out. "Where did you come from . . . ?"

Blade stared into the black holes of the man's pupils. "Hell."

With a jab of his fist, he gored into the abdominal cavity with his gold knife, feeling the organs give way like fabric, the energy created by the contraction of his shoulder and arm muscles transferring down the hilt, through the blade, and into the loose bundles of the digestive system.

The gasp was right by Blade's ear, like a lover coming, intimate and just for the two of them.

"Look at me," he whispered as he eased back while leaving the knife in place. "Dr. Randall Hertz, look at me — that's it. That's right. Now, listen carefully. Your legal address is One-Oh-Nine Prescott Lane in Charleston, South Carolina. You have a wife, Susan. You have two children, Martin, who goes by Marty and is named after your father, and the other one is Mary. The idea to go with *M* names was your wife's."

Those eyes got wider as that face got even paler.

"If you give me the codes to the cages in the experimentation unit, I won't leave here and go directly to your house and slaughter the three of them wherever I find them."

"Please," the man breathed. "Please, don't hurt my —"

"You have tortured and killed males and females here. You have taken them from their families. You have injected them with drugs and subjected them to experiments for the last ten years. You have left this fucking shithole and gone home to your fucking mate and your young while they have suffered. You've slept like a fucking baby in your goddamn bed, and filled your belly, and enjoyed all the creature comforts during your breaks — while those in the steel cages with the wires and the IVs and the mother*fucking* implants and electrodes suffered. So considering all that, I'm presenting you with an opportunity to save your family that you do not deserve. Give me the codes."

It was, of course, all bullshit.

The first thing Blade had done when he'd come up behind the man, spun him around, and submitted him against the corridor's wall? Burrowed into that brain and retrieved the codes.

But that was the difference between vampires and *symphaths*. A vampire would have gotten what he needed, slit the throat, and gone along his way. A *symphath*? This emotional exchange was a feeding that was necessary. He consumed the surges of emotion, lived for the flares along the grid, hungered for that priceless instant before death rendered this man nothing but a wind-down of biological functions.

"Give me the codes," he prompted.

"S-s-s-seven-twenty-two-nineteen-eighty-one. T-there's only o-o-one."

Blade smiled. "Your birth date. How cute. But not very safe. You should have gone with something more unusual, and used a few of them. What if someone infiltrated this facility with an eye toward destroying what you've worked so hard for."

Down at the gold knife, Blade's hand was getting coated in warm, fresh blood, the tide lazy because of a lack of pressure and the erratic heart rate. It was almost like he'd come inside the man, his ejaculate making a reappearance.

Abruptly, he had to steady the scientist by wrapping an arm around the small of his back. As if they were waltzing. "Randy, let me ask you something."

Moaning. Fluttering of the eyes. Like the dying man was in ecstasy.

Blade gave him a little shake. "Randy, did you honestly think one of us wasn't going to come for you? After all these years, and all the different sites, did you really not think that, sooner or later, we were going to find you?"

With that, Blade twisted the knife.

Then he snapped off the hilt.

As the body dropped to his feet, and that ruby red stain instantly doubled in size, Blade dropped what he had gripped onto the chest. The black wrap of boxing tape made him think of how long it had taken him to attend to the weapon's grip, and he smiled, wondering what humans would make of such a dagger.

Except they weren't going to find it. When he was done here, there wasn't going to be anything bigger than the diameter of a quarter left, and more to the point, the lab's owners were going to be so busy hiding the remains of the site, no kinds of forensic investigation would be performed.

Such a shame. At over sixteen hundred

dollars an ounce, there was a pretty penny in the weapon, and at least if it spooked some human, he'd get some value out of its abandonment. And he would have taken both parts back with him, but he preferred to leave something of himself behind in his victims.

With grim intent, Blade stepped over his prey and kept going.

He knew what he was going to find.

But he hoped, this time finally . . . he would be wrong, and some of the subjects would still be alive.

NINE

"So you've changed your mind."

As Gus repeated the words Daniel had just thrown out at the guy, the good doctor mostly kept the disappointment from his voice. And clearly, this wasn't the first piece of bad news C.P.'s head scientist had gotten tonight. Even before he'd sat down at the table just off the big kitchen, he'd looked like he'd been hit by a truck.

"I'm sorry," Daniel said. Then he glanced at Lydia. They reached for each other's hands at the same time, and as she squeezed his palm, he let out a long breath. "I just . . ."

Gus held up both his palms. "I'm not going to argue with you. Don't worry about that."

"We've come to a mutual decision," Daniel finished.

Lydia nodded and brushed a wisp of hair out of her eyelashes. "We think it's . . . time to live instead of trying desperately not to die."

The doctor nodded and sat back. Then he clapped his thighs and rubbed the top of his legs, his torso rocking in his chair like he was frustrated but trying to stay cool. "I get it. Trust me —"

The clipping sounds were dim at first, but as they got louder, Gus dropped a cuss word. Or seven. "And here she is, Miss America," he muttered under his breath.

At that moment, C.P. Phalen entered the alcove, and as usual, her perfume was like the beat of her stilettos — a banner announcing her presence. Not that she needed the extra highlight. With those heels, her *Truth or Dare* Madonna hair, and that tended-to face, she was polished as her marble floors and just as cozy. Daniel had never seen her out of her wardrobe of business suits, and had long ago decided she'd come into the world looking like the evil villain in a Marvel movie.

"So I gather we're not moving forward," she said.

"No." He glanced again at Lydia. When she nodded firmly, he murmured, "I'm sorry."

Actually, the more honest statement was that he was confused as fuck. He'd had one

129

plan. Then another. And now he was back where he started with refusing that Vita-12b the lab had cooked up. For a military man with a strict sense of discipline, the flip-flopping was making him mental — and he was no happier with this resolution than he'd been with the other, go-for-it one.

He was still leaving Lydia alone. And sooner rather than later.

The difference was that at least now she didn't want him to keep with the medical pollution. She just wanted . . . to be with him.

Same page at the same time, finally.

Not that C.P. was happy about it.

The woman looked at Gus, who was focused on the Coke can he'd brought in from the kitchen. The guy seemed to run on the stuff, yet he was never twitchy, never the kind who bounced a foot under the table or tapped fingers. Then again, he'd probably last slept a full night through back in the nineties and was running on fumes.

C.P. pulled a chair out and sat down at Gus's left. As the man shifted his seat a little away from her, you didn't need to be a body language expert to see the rift between the two.

"Of course, you have to do what's right for you," the woman said in a neutral tone.

"Listen, we can leave," Daniel offered. "Lydia still has her rental house and I can get the care I need there —"

A pair of noes came right back at him.

"You will stay here," C.P. said.

"I'm not your problem —"

"I didn't say you were," she snapped. "You'll stay here because —"

"You're hoping I'll change my mind," he countered.

C.P. took a deep breath and held up her hand. "Daniel, don't take this the wrong way — but fuck you and fuck off."

Daniel had to laugh. "You know, I've always liked the fact that you're a straight shooter."

"Not as straight as you think," Gus said under his breath. "Well, except in the —"

C.P. shot him a glare that, under any other circumstance, should have blown the scientist out of his chair, through the wall behind him, and onto the terrace.

Gus just gave her one of her own eyebrows back at her. Then he seemed to — did he just hum boom-chicka-wow-wow?

As silence landed like a piano dropped on the table between the four of them, Daniel felt like he was in an MRI machine, trapped even as he wasn't tied down. Meanwhile, out in the kitchen proper, it was a case of

131

business-as-usual, utensils clanging on steel pans, chefs chatting, something hitting a saucepan with a hiss —

"Oh, my God." Daniel frowned. "Onions."

"I'm sorry?" Lydia said.

"I smell onions." He tapped the side of his nose. "It's funny. I haven't realized how much my olfactory sense has been off."

Gus cleared his throat and leaned into his forearms. "You're going to find a lot of things returning. The side effects from the immunotherapy will retreat quickly. You're young and otherwise healthy, except for the cancer that's killing you."

While Lydia recoiled, Daniel blinked at the images that came back to him. In the course of his clandestine work, he'd dropped all kinds of enemies, in all kinds of ways. With knives, guns, his bare hands.

None of his training was helpful in this situation.

Then again, cancer was hardly an opponent you went at like that.

"Sorry." Gus rose to his feet and slapped a hold on his Coke. "Didn't mean to be too blunt. Come to the lab tomorrow. I'll run some fluids into you to support your kidneys, and I'll take some bloods and see what we can rebalance. I'm not a juice-cleanse kind of guy, but there are things I can do that'll help you feel better."

"Okay. Thanks."

As Gus took off, Lydia covered a yawn with the back of her hand and Daniel got up — and though getting to the vertical involved his cane and some careful balancing, she knew better than to try to help him. Relying on that kind of assistance always made him terrified he would lose what capabilities he had left, even if, thanks to the neuropathy in his feet, he was always a drunk, even when he was sober.

Always on the deck of a boat, with only his eyesight to orientate him.

"Let's eat something in our room tonight," he murmured. "Come on. You're exhausted."

As she looked up at him, her eyes were drooping. So were her shoulders. "That sounds amazing."

Daniel stood up a little taller. It felt good to take care of his woman, even if it was only with the suggestion of a night in — and about time, too. She'd been his nurse instead of his lover for way too long.

He carefully turned his head to C.P. so he didn't end up going throw rug on her marble floor. "I'll tell Chef we'd like trays sent down."

As their eyes met, the way she looked back

at him was intense. Then again, she'd put so much into this drug she was developing, and after all the things she'd done for him, he didn't like letting her down. Especially because he had a feeling she had invested in him and his health care fiesta because she'd assumed when he got to the point where he was out of options . . . he'd take the only one that was left.

"I'm sorry," he said softly.

She just shook her head. Then gave him the oddest little smile. "Don't be. I get it."

When Lydia came up to the door of their bedroom, she was surprised as Daniel lurched forward and got things for her, pulling the panel open and holding it in place with what certainly passed as a flourish.

"If you go take your shower," he said, "I'll let in the food when it comes."

She moved past him, and felt curiously off balance, even though he was the one who had the cane. "I, ah, I'm sure it will appreciate the warm welcome."

"Only if it was raised right."

Flustered for no good reason, she watched Daniel shuffle over to their bed and sit down with a groan. As he closed his eyes and released a ragged breath, she knew that the only thing worse than being in their reality . . . would be returning to it from some fantasy that, with their joint resolve, he was suddenly going to survive. They were getting a respite, not any true relief.

And they'd just closed the remaining door they had.

As she thought about what lay ahead, a flush rose up her throat and she put a hand to her frizzy hair. Before she fell apart again, she said, "I won't be long. In case the food comes."

"Don't worry about it. I can get the door."

"Thank you." She shook her head. "I mean —"

"Take your time," he said gently.

For a moment, she tried to remember the last time she had felt seen by him — and not as in come-into-a-room-and-be-identified, but *seen*.

"I've missed you," she blurted.

Daniel opened his mouth as if to point out the obvious. Then he nodded. "I know. I've missed you, too."

This was what they needed, she reflected. He'd been right all along.

As the quiet stretched out between them, Lydia felt the absurd impulse to kiss him. Which shouldn't have felt strange, should it?

"I won't be long," she repeated awkwardly.

In the bathroom, she reached into the marble shower and turned on the fixture that was mounted on the ceiling. You'd think it would be the greatest thing, a "rain" effect that made a person feel like they were communing with nature. In reality, because you couldn't vary the angle, if you wanted to get the shampoo out of your hair, your nose was getting a fill whether you enjoyed drowning on an otherwise dry vertical or not.

Given the luxury she was surrounded by, it was hard to imagine she'd pine for her little rental, but as she suddenly missed that modest house like it had been burned to the ground, she wasn't stupid. It wasn't just about the cheap shower stall.

God, all the introspection lately was giving her heartburn.

Taking her clothes off and letting them fall to the black marble floor, she got into the shower before the water was all the way warm, and as she shivered, she thought about everything Daniel had had to endure. This was what was on her mind as she efficiently shampooed and conditioned and soaped, and after she was finished, she stood under the falling water, closing her eyes and feeling the tapping massage on her tight shoulders —

The moment the easing of her muscles registered, she yanked herself out of the relaxation.

Cutting off the water, trying not to think, she wrapped herself in composure instead of a towel as she went over to the pair of sinks. Even though she instantly got a chill, her skin goosebumping up all over, she brushed her teeth on autopilot, forgetting that it was dinnertime instead of bedtime. She only remembered this as she was spitting out her Crest into the sink, but then that was another way to commune with where Daniel was at, wasn't it.

Change of taste. Food no longer as appealing because it had —

"Lydia."

Jerking up from the black marble basin, her eyes shot to the mirror. Behind her, through the open door, Daniel had propped himself up against the headboard, and as he stared at her, he had the strangest expression on his face.

Without thinking about it, she covered herself with her hands and spun around. "Are you okay?"

"Sorry," he said as he looked down.

"I'm coming."

Grabbing a towel, she hustled over to the bed. "What's wrong? What do you need?"

"I'm fine." Daniel's hand lifted to brush her off. "I just need —"

Knock, knock, knock.

"Come in," she said over her shoulder. Then she lowered her voice. "I'll get dressed, hold on."

As a member of the staff brought in a rolling cart, she hustled into the walk-in closet and dropped the towel. Reclothing was done out of one of the drawer lineups in the center built-in, and really, it was just a swap-out of clean versions of what she'd worn as she'd left the estate this morning. She had been sleeping fully clothed lately because she kept expecting to have to follow Daniel down to the laboratory in a medical crisis.

A waft of roast beef and roasted potatoes shut down her hunger instead of piquing it further — and she braced herself before she could reopen things and step out. The staff member was gone, but two trays on pop-up tables had been placed on either side of the bed.

"Are you okay?" she asked Daniel, who was where he'd been, leaning back against the headboard.

When he didn't reply, she went over and sat down on the edge of the mattress by him. Taking the starched damask napkin from under a sterling silver fork, she flipped the square out of its folds and placed it over Daniel's chest.

"Do you want to start with some beef first? Or the potatoes?"

While waiting for an answer, Lydia started in with the cutting, making quick work of the slab of prime rib that had been cooked to a perfect medium rare. She made sure the pieces were on the small side, in order to reduce the choking risk.

"Here, let's start with the meat," she murmured.

Turning to Daniel, she pinned a smile on her face. There was a pause before he opened his mouth. But then his jaw lowered and she delivered the piece in between his lips.

"Good?" she said as she went back to the plate for another serving. "Good."

As he swallowed and she put another piece on the tines of the fork, she felt like she was doing something positive, gaining ground on the slippery slope they were sliding down. With so little within her control, this was a balm for her raw nerves.

A small step in the right direction. Even though it wasn't going to matter much.

In the long run.

TEN

Down in the Black Dagger Brotherhood's training center, Rehv emerged from out of the office and traveled on sure feet down the long concrete corridor. Passing by the weight and locker rooms, he arrived at the start of the clinic section, and he didn't need to knock on closed doors to locate his Ehlena.

He knew exactly where she was.

And he didn't announce himself with his knuckles because he knew she was alone.

Opening the door to one of the exam rooms, he stepped inside, and his *shellan* looked around her shoulder. She was across at the supply cabinet over the stainless-steel sink, restocking things with gauze packs. Dressed in surgical scrubs and Crocs, with her hair twisted up on her head and pinned by a clip, she was in her element as she stretched up to the highest shelf, pushing the white boxes with the red crosses all the way back.

Instantly, she turned to face him. "What's wrong."

Lowering his lids to half-mast, he drawled, "Can't a male come see his female on the fly?"

Ehlena laughed and put a hand to the base of her throat. "Always. But you can understand why I jump to a not-so-hot conclusion —"

She stopped short as he shut them in together and threw the lock not with his mind, but with his fingers. Slowly. So she saw what he was doing.

"I'm going to the Colony," he said in a low voice.

Her eyes drifted down his torso, going to his hips. His mink duster was unfastened, hanging in two swaths that exposed his dark red silk suit — and his erection.

"Are you," she said breathlessly.

"Yes."

He tossed his cane and stalked over to her, grabbing her body and yanking her against him. His mate's scent instantly bloomed, and her mouth parted as she looked up into his eyes.

Just as he was about to lower his head, she put her hand on his sternum, right over his heart. "Wait, why are you going?"

141

"I have to have a conversation with some-one."

Ehlena closed her eyes and shook her head. "Be careful up there."

"Always," he said. "I'm the King, remember."

At that, he took her lips, penetrating them with his tongue while he swept his hands down to her hips. The dopamine he took to control his *symphath* tendencies when he was in mixed company had one very bad side effect: He was impotent as long as he was dosed. But every time he had to go to the Colony, he needed to have all his faculties available to him.

Especially the ones that made him dangerous to others of his kind.

You didn't go into a battle without weapons, and the chemical castration of his evil instincts was a death sentence up there. Even if he was the ruler of all *symphaths*.

Picking up his mate, he laid her out on the examination table and wrenched her knees wide. Then he clamped his broad hands on her thighs and rode down the taut muscles under the thin scrubs bottoms. When he got to her core, he palmed her sex and arched over her, going back to her mouth. As he rubbed her, he felt the heat.

And nearly came in his fucking slacks.

"I have to be faster than I want," he muttered. "Goddamn it."

Shoving up the top half of her scrubs, he pushed her bra out of the way and latched on to one of her nipples, sucking, licking. Back down at her waist, he jerked the tie out of its bow and then tore the goddamn pants in half. He wasn't any nicer to her panties.

Before he unzipped himself, he eased back and took a long look at the female who was laid out before him, that loose pale blue shirt up under her armpits, her breasts exposed, her nipples tight, her legs wide open.

Her sex swollen and gleaming for him.

He wanted to go down on her. And even checked the clock on the wall, the one with the white face and the navy blue arms — damn it, he needed to get his message delivered STAT.

His hands were sloppy at his hips as he ripped his zipper down. And the second freedom presented itself, his cock jumped out, a reminder of how often it was on the back burner. As his slacks hit the floor and he freed the button on his suit jacket, the blunt head of his erection went right to her core, without any guidance from his palm — except he wanted to draw this out, even if only for a little. Wrapping a grip on his thick shaft, he thrust his hips forward and stroked her with his tip, up and down, up and down — and now a partial penetration.

That made her gasp and him grind his molars.

What a fucking sight, his female arching and twisting, her breasts swaying, her fingers going to her mouth.

As she sucked them deep, he entered her properly, the smooth, hot, tight hold submerging his whole body in white-hot lust. Planting his palm by her head, he bent over and started pumping. He went so hard and so fast that Ehlena had to lock a hold on both sides of the padded top to keep herself in place.

The orgasm was fast for her, but it was faster for him. Almost immediately, he came, but he didn't stop. There was no locking in — instead, he kept up the rhythm, the slapping sound of him pounding into her a metronome of his need for his female . . . his desperate, fucking need to mark her, to go to this place of passion with her. Ehlena was, and always would be, his one true home, his solace and his harbor.

Devotion was not a characteristic of *symphaths.*

But he was half vampire, after all.

A bonded male.

"Rehvenge . . ." his *shellan* moaned as she torqued beneath him. "Take my vein."

Tilting her head to the side, she offered him her throat — and he wanted to say no, but only because he wasn't going to want to leave her if he started in with the feeding.

"Please, Rehv — take my —"

Baring his fangs, he struck without any conscious thought, and oh, fucking *hell,* the rush of the taste of her, her blood going over his tongue, down the back of his throat, into his gut. And the power that came with it. On a sudden surge, his hips swung against her even harder, and he started coming again.

And then so was she.

Beneath them, the exam table, which was rated for a weight load of four hundred pounds, started groaning, and when a clapping sound started up — metallic this time, not flesh against flesh — he wondered what the hell it was, what had come loose.

Not that he cared. The only thing he cared about was his Ehlena. Fuck, he was coming another time —

The alarm that went off was shrill, and his eyes shot over to the origin of the intrusion. The computer. It was coming from the —

All at once, in mid-suck and mid-thrust,

his brain clicked into high gear. And Ehlena was right with him.

"Someone's coming in on an emergency," she said, the words vibrating under his mouth.

With a curse, he released his lips and licked the puncture wounds, capturing a last taste of his female. Then he lifted himself and caught a last, vivid image of her, undone and open, his cock buried deep inside of her, the insides of her thighs gleaming from all his come.

Then he snapped to attention, withdrew, and helped her sit up. After she wrenched her bra across her breasts and fastened it, he pulled down her top, and as she slipped off the exam table, she kicked her bottoms off and went to the built-in desk.

Punching a code into the keyboard, there was a pause and then the alarm silenced and the screen scrolled up with text.

"Who is it," he asked as he took out a handkerchief and wiped down his erection.

He had to grit his teeth as the sensations shot right into his balls, but he didn't allow himself another release. He needed to know who was hurt and how —

"John Matthew." Ehlena looked over at him. "And it's bad."

Rehv closed his eyes. "Goddamn it."

Shoving the handkerchief into one of the deep pockets in his mink, he pulled his slacks up in place. "I'll go get you fresh scrubs from the locker room while you wash up. And I'll call Xhex while you prep the OR."

She captured his hand before he went for the door. Her eyes were wide and anxious. "I love you."

With a nod, he pulled her in close. "You're going to do all the right things, you, Manny, and Doc Jane. He's in the best hands."

The next thing Rehv knew, he was out in the corridor, and for the briefest moment, he couldn't remember which direction he was supposed to go in. As he took out his cell phone, things clicked into place and he headed to the right.

As he strode for the locker room, he initiated the call.

And prayed Xhex picked up.

Dead.

They were all dead.

As Blade stopped in front of the bank of ten-by-ten-foot cages, he stared through the fine steel mesh that was installed over the steel bars. Two males and a female, all hanging by ligatures, their flimsy hospital gowns limp as their limbs, some of the feet still twitching above the drains in the tile floor.

Each of their heads were cocked slightly to the side, as if he had called their names and they'd heard the sound. All of their eyes were open and blindly staring at him.

"Help . . . me . . ."

At the plaintive entreaty, Blade looked across the lab space. The setup was what he'd come to expect, the work stations of computers, monitoring equipment, vials, and test tubes ringing the space, an examination table with restraints in the center of the facility, the overhead lights bright white and glaring.

The man he'd just shot in the chest was slumped by a drain next to where the experiments were performed. Where those vampires had been cut open, prodded, injected. Where the suffering had been so acute.

Convenient, really. The blood would just drip down into the plumbing system.

"Help . . ."

"You realize," Blade drawled, "that expecting a rescue from the person who shot you is not logical. And may cause me to provide you further attention."

He refocused on the cages and the steel mesh. Vampires couldn't dematerialize through that alloy of iron and carbon, and he wondered how long it had taken the humans to figure that out. It had to have been a rate limiter that was solved pretty damn quick. Those rats without tails were inferior in every sense of the word, so to keep their subjects captive, to work on the males and females, they would have had to sacrifice quite a few of their own kind before they were successful at imprisonment.

Walking closer to the bodies, he knelt in front of the middle one, his hand going down to sweep robing out of the way — except he wasn't dressed in his blood-red drape. Not tonight. For this mission, his clothes were formfitting, and upon his back, he bore a heavy pack that had not slowed him down in the slightest.

He lowered his head in a measure of respect. The female had been in her prime, at least going by age — but she was in bad condition. She had been starved of at least blood and perhaps food, leaving her arms and legs without muscle. Ulcers marked her skin, the raw patches red and infected. Sections of dark hair had fallen out on her head.

The other two were in similar conditions, but the female was what bothered him the most.

She was just like his sister in so many ways.

An image of Xhex flashed into his mind's eye, and he replaced the stranger hanging by her throat with his own kin.

And then . . . another memory. From the Colony, a good twenty-five years before. He was looking out the window of one of the shill buildings, the structures that had been built and maintained to look like homes so the humans in that isolated upstate town would not become suspicious.

His sister was being driven away in a van. Against her will.

Funny that *"symphath"* and "sympathy" shared so many letters. Because the former had none of the latter —

A tickle in his eye made him blink, and as his vision got blurry, he wiped at the sensation with impatience. Looking down, he saw a red smear on his fingertips.

The tears of his kind were bloody, which did seem fitting. And even though he was a half-breed, as was his sister, he considered himself closer to their sire's side of things.

A gurgle from behind him drew his eyes over his shoulder. The scientist was losing blood fast, the red pool under his body gleaming like Blade's irresponsible, undeniable expression of tears in the harsh lighting.

Good thing he had come here alone.

150

Weakness was to be exploited, and regret was, among all the levers that could be pulled in a person, the most devastatingly effective.

He should have been working alone all along. If anyone found out he had been creating messes in the human world, even if they were covered up by the *homo sapiens* themselves . . . if anybody discovered the reasons for his aggression, the complications would be swift and onerous. But when he had begun targeting these rogue setups, so buried among all the human industry, so carefully tended, their secrets so guarded, he'd been ill prepared for the number of them.

He had thus hired on humans, creating through mind control a false governmental agency that was as those farmhouses up around the Colony, an illusion that allowed him to function at a higher level in the midst of a bumbling, fumbling, lesser enemy. Except then, back in April, a fuckup had occurred, and it had been a lesson well learned. He had therefore reverted to being a solo operator, hunting for these illicit, under-the-radar sites and destroying them.

All in the name of a sister who hated him with very good reason.

He watched the scientist struggle for

breath, measured the change in color of the face . . . noted the tapping of the fingers on the floor, as if the man were calling for help on an invisible Morse code machine.

Shifting around, Blade looked up into the security camera. Then he reached over his shoulder and pulled out the nozzle that was vertically secured on his backpack. Initiating the flamethrower, there was a quiet *woof*! as the equipment came alive, a blue flame kindling at the tip.

He started with the female. He always started with the females, if there happened to be one or several.

How many labs had he destroyed? A dozen, perhaps. In the last twenty-five years.

The flame exploded out of the wand in a stream, and as it hit the mesh, the profile of the yellow blast broadened and quickly consumed the fragile screen. With the barrier gone, the fire reassembled itself, becoming more ray-like.

The burning flesh smelled like meat on a spit.

Blade watched for as long as he could. Then he closed his eyes. When the scent changed, signaling that the skin, muscle, and connective tissue had been consumed, he went to work on the other two. Meanwhile, in the background, on the floor drain, the human slowly expired.

When there was nothing left except for piles of smoking bones below where the bodies had been hung, he extinguished the flame. No alarm went off and no sprinklers rained upon him — a surprise given the heat, although the HVAC system had kept the air mostly clear. This meant either the sensors were broken or the monitoring was for shit.

Or it was a silent alarm and help, such as it would be, was on the way.

Likely the latter, which explained why no extinguishing had occurred.

He stared up at the security camera again.

It was important to make sure the owner of this shit show saw his face clearly, like in a close kill, where you were certain that your prey knew who their murderer was. When he was satisfied that his image had been captured sufficiently, he pivoted to go. The scientist was well and gone, and it was a pity, really. He could have tortured the man with some mind play.

Except he'd been too scattered to enjoy his favorite hobby as soon as he'd seen the bodies in the cages.

As he came up to the exit, he stepped over a pair of corpses. Security guards. After he'd entered the code to get into the unit, they'd jumped out and reached for their handguns. He'd made sure their efforts weren't wasted. Trespassing into their minds, he'd made them turn their weapons on themselves, those muzzles going right to their frontal lobes.

Bang, bang. Flop. Flop.

At which point the scientist had started screeching.

Blade had looked past the noise, while he'd shot the man in the chest. The vampires had already been hung — and he could only assume that some kind of internal alert had gone off and the executions had been triggered automatically: He'd been able to still catch the scent of their stress and fear sweat in the air.

Then again, he hadn't been particularly discreet in his penetration of the lab.

Out in the hall, there were more bodies — more guards in their dark uniforms and their still-holstered weapons. They'd swarmed like flies and been just as easy to swat.

On his way down here, there had been much conversation. Now? No voices. Just the whisper of the HVAC system, an occasional electronic beeping, and dripping.

The latter was from the guards. Lot of leaking from all the bullet holes.

Blade had wanted to stab them all, leave a dozen gold daggers behind. But he'd had to get to work. So he'd used his gun.

"Such a very, truly boring hall, really," he said as he looked up to a camera pod mounted on the ceiling. "Time for some redecorating."

Reaching around to the base of his pack, he took out his C4 charges and went for a wander, setting them at regular intervals of fourteen feet, waist height. When he got to the vent through which he'd gained access to the facility, he shook his head.

Those fucking humans were so stupid. They knew enough to wrap the cages in steel — but it never dawned on them to defend their precious torture chamber against infiltration from the ductwork. If they had thought to fortify their heating and cooling system with mesh? He'd have died as he dematerialized down here. But no. In their arrogance, they thought only in one dimension.

Funny, it had been the same in each of the labs. Then again, humans were the same.

Ducking his hand inside his jacket, he took out his cell phone. Each charge was set to the same frequency.

Before he triggered the light show, he paused as something occurred to him. In the last six months, since that fuckup on Deer Mountain, he had found only this one last lab. There appeared to be no others. God knew he had searched for them, using the same channels he always did, yet his endeavors had yielded nothing.

Had he come to the end of his journey? There were fewer vampires after the raids of four years ago, and those who were left were likely to be very, very careful with themselves: Harder to find, harder to capture. Maybe it wasn't that humans were getting more ethical, they were just running out of subjects.

That was, of course, the most likely explanation. And one that was going to stick.

Blade glanced at his phone and thought about what was going to happen next. Ah, the satisfaction of ruining these bastards' toy boxes of pain. And it was always a big time. Unfortunately, the aftermath was always rather anti-climactic, although certainly climate-tic. Invariably, the human news ascribed whatever damage there was to natural causes. Forest fires set by "lightning"? Sure, most of them were Mother Nature. But not all. And then there were other explanations the press came up with: Plane crashes in the mountains, UFO sightings, space junk crashing to earth? Sure, most of them were mechanical failure, weather balloons, and meteors.

But not all.

As he called up the detonation app, and started entering the code, he resolved that it was possible he'd accomplished his goal, eradicating the torture chambers that were established to further the dominance of the human race.

Curiously, the idea his work was done was deflating.

He just had that one up on Deer Mountain left to deal with.

And then he was finished *ahvenging* his kin.

In the split second before he dematerialized, he detonated his chain of explosives — and courtesy of his boom-booms, he was escorted out by a violent push of air and a toxic chemical stink.

He rather felt like his life's work was ending.

And couldn't decide how he felt about that.

ELEVEN

It was all a blur.

As Xhex ran down the training center's corridor, the gray cement walls, ceiling, and floor were like the interior of a gun's muzzle, and her body was the bullet. And like any slug of lead, she felt nothing of the experience of propulsion, neither the acceleration nor its origins in her legs nor the slamming of her heart or burning in her lungs.

But she was aware of one thing.

She smelled the blood of her mate.

With panic her fuel and dread her tailwind, she followed the scent of disaster to the clinic's operating room — and when she arrived at the closed door, she tripped and fell, scattering her limbs on the hard floor. Before anyone could help her up, she dragged herself back to her feet and pushed her way into the —

Beeeeeeeeeeeeeeeeeeeeeeeeeeeeep.

Just as she entered, the unforgettable

sound rang out, and her eyes flipped to the monitor behind John Matthew, who lay on the operating table covered with blood. The flat line was inching across the black rectangle at the bottom, taking over from the uneven peaks and valleys that represented his cardiac rhythm —

"Code!"

Xhex reached forward, as if she could do anything, but somebody held her back as Doc Jane jumped up on the table, straddled John's hips, and began chest compressions. At his head, Ehlena slapped a mask on his face and started bagging him.

"Pushing epinephrine," Manny announced at the IV site.

"What happened," Xhex mumbled. "What's happening . . ."

Without warning, her knees went loose under her and she went down onto the tile — and that was when everything came into heartbreaking focus. All of John's clothes had been cut off, and there appeared to be nothing wrong on the bottom half of him. But what did that matter when he'd been shot in the heart.

"Thirty," Ehlena said briskly.

"John?" Xhex called out as she watched his blood stain Doc Jane's knees. "John, stay here. Don't go . . ."

She looked at the monitor again. The numbers that represented his blood pressure were shockingly low, and that line remained flat.

"Sixty," Ehlena announced.

Is time passing? Xhex thought dimly as she clasped her hands together and brought them up to the front of her throat.

Sweat beaded Doc Jane's forehead as she continued with the chest compressions, her straight-arm, palm-over-palm pumping, replacing by force that which should have run by electrical impulse —

"Let's go outside."

The male voice was familiar and close by Xhex, but the recognition didn't come and she didn't glance at whoever it was. As another time stamp was called out, she was convinced that if she looked away, the resuscitation attempt would stop . . . as if her presence, her love for the powerful fighter who lay motionless in the center of all the effort, was the engine for the lifesaving attempt.

"One thirty," Ehlena called out as she kept bagging.

"Xhex, leave them to work — we need to wait in the corridor."

Who was talking, she thought numbly as she focused on Ehlena's hand as it fisted . . .

fisted . . . fisted . . . in the same kind of reliable rhythm as the pump, pump, pump up on John's sternum.

Abruptly, her hearing sharpened and everything got too loud: Doc Jane had on a necklace with a charm that was sliding back and forth on the links, a chiming, metal-on-metal shift releasing as it swung. The bag had a strangely dry blow-and-suck rhythm. Blood was dripping off the far end of the table, from the pool that had formed under his ribs. And then there was the alarm from the monitor, and Manny's heavy breathing as if he were joining Doc Jane's effort in spirit.

Likewise, someone was gasping right behind her —

"Two minutes."

At Ehlena's announcement, everything stopped. The chest compressions. The bagging. The movement in the whole world.

Xhex's eyes locked on the monitor, on that flat line. On those very bad numbers.

"Come on, we need to go —"

It was that male voice again, in her ear, and then strong hands gathered her from the floor and removed her from the room even though she pushed at them, fought against them.

Manny called out, "Pushing epi —"

161

As the door shut on its own, she knew that that antiseptic, tiled room, with its stainless steel instruments and medical equipment, was the last place John needed to die. He should be in her arms; she should be holding him.

Rehv's face got right into hers. "Look at me —"

"What happened?" She gripped the front of his fine silk suit. "How was he injured!"

But like the details mattered anymore? Details only counted when you could do something with them to change the outcome.

She looked around at the faces that surrounded her, ones she knew so well, ones who had brought her here from the club, who had come for her in person, a lineup she knew she never, ever wanted to see.

"How did it happen —"

"He took a bullet for me."

The anguished intrusion brought everyone's head around. Tohr was leaning out of the exam room next door, blood running down his face and coating his bare chest with a red sheen.

"We were in the field," he said hoarsely. "Chasing two shadows . . ."

Behind him, Xhex's *mahmen*, Autumn, appeared, her pale hand resting on her

162

mate's bloody forearm. As her terrified eyes lifted, all Xhex could think of was . . .

Motherfucker. They were both going to lose the love of their life tonight if John died.

Tohr was never going to get over this, especially given how much he had already been through.

The Brother wiped his face with a trembling hand. "We ran right into a drug deal going wrong. The three humans were shooting at each other — and the second they saw us, we became their targets. I was hit twice, and then John jumped in front of me. He . . . he took the bullet that would have gone right into my head. He just leapt up and . . ."

As the words were choked off, the look of anguish that came over the male's face galvanized Xhex. Before she knew she was going to move, she shoved Rehv out of the way and launched herself at the Brother, bringing him down to her level by the shoulders as she reached for her *mahmen* as well.

"Tohr —"

"Oh, God," he moaned. "He took it to save me. The bullet . . ."

As the fighter dropped his head onto her shoulder, Xhex dragged her *mahmen* in close and had a strange moment of release

— not from her terror, but certainly from her sense that, however much the Brotherhood and other fighters were hurting, the magnitude of her emotions separated her from everyone else: Now there was one other person who felt this tragedy as deeply as she did —

Autumn returned her embrace, the female's arms reaching around as much as she could of her mate and her young.

Make that two people who felt this as deeply as she did.

That single bullet, which had been so anonymous when it had left its muzzle, had somehow managed to target and wipe out an entire family.

Xhex turned her head and looked to the OR's door. She had an impulse to read John's grid, but she was too scared. If she sensed nothing at all? She just wasn't ready for that. And if she did read something? What if the energy she took from him was the tipping point that sent him over the edge?

No, she thought as she squeezed her eyes shut. Better to just wait.

As if her not knowing the outcome somehow forestalled what she feared was his fate. And by extension . . . her own.

As Rehv stood next to Xhex and her immediate family of only two, he shifted his mink duster to the crook of his elbow — and felt a raw hunger for revenge that nearly knocked him out of his ostrich loafers. The fact that he was off his dopamine sharpened everything inside of him, from his emotions to what he intended to do with them. And playing witness to the tight knot of suffering in front of him, the grief and fear, the powerlessness? Well, didn't it all make him a downright vicious motherfucker.

There was a good, goddamn reason *symphaths* were isolated from others —

Down the corridor to the left, V stepped out of the office's glass door. As the Brother strode toward the crowd that had formed outside the OR, he brought a cloud of aggression with him, his long strides, his black-leather-clad body, the expression on his face, all proclaiming him for the menace he was.

"I'll be right back," Rehv murmured to Xhex, even though he doubted she heard him.

Walking off, he met V halfway and thumbed over his shoulder. "Did you get

165

any visions about this? Did you see something about John?"

V put a hand-rolled in between his front teeth. "No. But what I'm shown isn't the universe's obituary section. I'm not privy to everything — in case you're looking for some kind of good outcome because I don't know fuck all."

"Oh . . . shit." Because that was such a useful word in a shit-uation like this.

"Look" — up came the lighter — "John's getting the best care. And I'd be in there with them if I hadn't had half a bottle of Goose earlier this evening —"

"He's coded."

V froze in mid-flick of the thumb. "Again?"

"Fucking hell. He already has?"

"Twice." The Brother followed through on the lighting, then talked through the exhale. "In the mobile surgical unit. And I think they're also worried about stroke."

Every time Rehv breathed in, the scent of John's blood magnified in his sinuses until it drowned out everything else, from the Turkish tobacco V was smoking, to the bleach-based cleaner that had been used a couple of hours before to clean the clinic's exam rooms, to the fabric softener that had been used on the robes Autumn was wearing.

Easing back against the concrete wall, he let his mink fall to the floor. There was no going up to the Colony now. Not until he knew how bad this was going to get.

As if flatline isn't a rock bottom? he thought to himself.

"I hate waiting," he muttered. "I'd rather just know. Life or death. Then we can deal with the aftermath, either way."

V shook his head. "It's the in-between that I worry about."

"I thought Butch was the only Catholic we had." More Brothers arrived, Phury and Z nodding as they joined the people waiting along the corridor. "And no offense, I could do without the purgatory reference considering what's going on. Let's not give Fate any ideas."

"Not what I meant. What's worse than death is alive, but only in a breathing kind of way." Vishous took another drag and then went over to a trash bin to ash into the basin's stainless steel tray top. "Strokes can be particularly devastating."

Great, something else to worry about, Rehv thought.

"By the way," V murmured, "now is not the time, but I have the answer to your inquiry."

"Which one," he said absently.

"The security feed from that alley with the dead vampire with no eyes — but it can wait."

Rehv took a hold on the male's forearm. "No, tell me now."

V shrugged. "Unfortunately, I got nothing. Yeah, there were cameras, but they'd been torn off their mountings. The monitoring system's file storage only had footage from just before the killing."

So Xhex took care of her tracks beforehand. Probably because she knew that V would get the feed.

"You did the right thing turning the body over to us," V continued. "We were able to ID him, get in touch with his family. We kept the remains at the garage, in the morgue there."

Rehv lifted an eyebrow. "Didn't know you had one at that site."

"Sad necessity." V frowned as his diamond eyes went back to the door of the OR. There was a pause; then he spoke quick, like he wanted a distraction. "Was there a scent at the scene when you got there? We did the cleanup just before dawn, and I couldn't track anything of significance."

Rehv shook his head. "Nothing. Whoever

did it was wearing gloves and was fucking tidy about the work. Hell, maybe they were in a hazmat suit."

He refocused on Xhex. She was nodding at her *mahmen* and drawing a hand through her short dark hair while she shifted her weight back and forth, a metronome of anxiety. Getting into her grid required no concentration. The damn thing was lit up like a Christmas tree, her emotions neon bright in their superstructure, their thought balloon hovering off to the side of her body.

The defect was still there, the graph-like squares collapsing in so that some of them, many of them, were no longer three-dimensional.

And this tragedy was going to finish the job.

"So you think it's her," V said softly as he exhaled. "You think Xhex took out one of Basque's illustrious patrons."

"Maybe."

"Okay, that's a yes." More silence. "But if she did, she had her reasons. You know how shit goes down at clubs better than anyone else. Problems need to be dealt with."

If only he thought she did it to keep the peace. "Yeah."

And now if John died? If she lost her mate, it would be a tragedy that was going to wipe

169

out everyone, especially her. If John survived? Then she was going to get caught up in the stress of helping the male recover.

Then again, at least he'd know where she was.

On that note, no one was leaving the mountain tonight — when it came to the Brotherhood and the fighters, that was.

In the back of his mind, he pictured himself going down to Caldwell and finding the drug dealers who had gone lead shower on each other and caught a couple of vampires in the crosshairs. All he'd need was the address of that corner Tohr and John had come around. The territories in Caldie were delineated with precision and defended like the gold mines they were, so he'd just have to show up, search the memories of whoever was there — and take care of business the *symphath* way.

The problem? And it was a biggie: John Matthew was a Brother, and the Black Dagger Brotherhood would be the ones doing the *ahvenging*. It wasn't just a matter of deference to their relationship to the victim; it was law, as in codified.

As a kindling fury nonetheless took root in Rehv's blood, and the large muscles in his body spasmed like he was about to do something, he had to walk away from V and the others. The next thing he knew, he was in one of the vacant patient rooms. After pacing around, he went over to the hospital bed. With an exhale of disgust, he shoved his hand into the pocket of his double-breasted suit and took out a syringe and a little glass bottle with a rubber top. After he tossed his jacket onto the short stack of pillows, he unsheathed the needle, drew up a serving of self-control, and put the belly of the syringe between his front teeth. Rolling up his sleeve, he exposed the blue veins at the crook of his elbow, and he didn't waste any time. He injected the dopamine directly into his body's highway system.

The effect was quick, a whoosh of numbness going through him, his balance taking a knock such that he had to sit down next to his jacket. As the pads of his fingers went numb along with his feet, the tide continued up his limbs and spread throughout his torso.

Goddamn, he was cold already. He needed to go back and get his mink so his lips and nail beds didn't turn blue.

This was *not* how he'd envisioned the evening going.

And he was not the only one.

TWELVE

At 7:01 the following morning, C.P. Phalen was shown into a conference room on the seventy-fifth floor of a skyscraper in Houston, Texas. Unlike most of the business environments she'd been to in the Lone Star State, the decor was sleek, the furniture modern and simple, the palette a blend of soft grays and cream. There was no art on the walls, no crystal dangling from ceiling fixtures, no gold leaf, marble, or mirrors.

"Would you care for coffee while you wait?" a voice inquired in a European accent.

She glanced back at the executive assistant. The dark-haired young man was probably mid-twenties, his suit was definitely Italian, and that accent was the result of a German being taught English by a Brit. Cologne was French. So were the shoes.

"No, thank you."

The kid bowed at the waist and exited by

backing up. The door was shut quiet as a whisper.

C.P. went over to the bank of floor-to-ceiling windows. The morning traffic was still moving pretty well on the highway, lines of cars paring off at exits to funnel out onto the surface roads, the parking lots and garages just starting to fill up. The urban landscape could have been that of any city, the skyscrapers and office buildings gleaming in the early sunlight, the strips of asphalt dull tracks that formed boxes around the real estate.

C.P. checked her watch.

She had flown in on her plane and landed thirty-eight minutes ago. The disembarkment and car ride over from Hobby Airport had taken twenty-one minutes. Then she had waited fourteen minutes in the SUV before entering this building, checking in with security, and riding up the express elevator, which skipped floors two through fifty-five. The pro forma greeting with Pharmatech's executive receptionist had taken three minutes, and then she had waited for only a couple of heartbeats for the executive assistant to bring her down here. The fact that there was staff on deck so early was not a surprise given how much work the company did with Japanese investors —

Behind her, the door opened, and in the glossy panes, she caught the reflection of the man who entered the conference room.

Pivoting back around, she said, "You're late."

Gunnar Rhobes, CEO of Pharmatech, shut them in and made a show of unbuttoning his pin-striped double-breasted jacket as he came forward. His suit was also Italian and so were his shoes. His attitude was gift-from-God.

"You were early," he said in the same accent as the assistant.

"I was on time."

Pulling out the leather chair at the head of the table, he sat down and crossed his legs knee to knee. Then he steepled his fingers and stared at her over the manicured tips. He was a lean man, but not because he was unwell. He was a triathlete, an internationally ranked amateur, even though he was how old? Forty? As a result, his already narrow features were whittled down to the point where he had hollows in his cheeks, under his jaw, and on either side of his windpipe. Adding to the austere look, his skin was leathery and prematurely aged, like he never wore sunscreen while he trained outdoors, and his hair was cut so short that it was but a shadow over his skull.

"So to what do I owe this pleasure, Miss C.P. Phalen."

"You asked for this face-to-face, not me."

"Did I? Perhaps your scheduling people were confused."

"They weren't, and stop playing games. It's boring. You have the data. You know what the price is. What are you going to do about it."

A brow rose. "Your arrogance is well known in our industry, but I find it a surprise nonetheless. Do you honestly think you can just demand whatever you want and someone will give it to you —"

"The protocol works. What's your price, Gunnar."

"It works in the *lab.*" His pale eyes narrowed in a way that emphasized his hawk-like features. "It's early days for you, Phalen. And you've been in the R&D business long enough to not let optimism and a profit motive cloud your judgment."

"What a relief for you, then."

The left eye twitched. "How so."

"There are many ahead of you in line, so you don't have to get tangled up in my delusion. Or did you think you were the only one who's interested in Vita."

"I am the one who can pay the most."

"Money isn't everything."

"Then why did you come down here to talk to me."

"Due diligence. I wanted to see if you were still the asshole I remembered." She tilted forward and lowered her voice for a beat. "You haven't disappointed me. Guess I'm one of the first women who's been alone with you to say that."

"Petty insults are beneath an intellect like yours."

"If it's so petty, why are you flushing like that? And I know what you've been saying about me behind my back. I'm flattered you want to come on my tits, but I'll turn down the kind invitation. Thanks."

During the pause that followed, she was glad to get the sexual shit out of the way. Misogynists usually led with either a you're-stupid or a cross-the-line-with-harassment move. Maybe now the two of them could get down to the substance.

"Tell me, Phalen," he murmured. "Why are you selling such a valuable piece of business?"

C.P. crossed her arms over her chest. "It's just one more drug in my pipeline."

"I think you're lying."

He was right, of course.

With a shrug, she said, "And you have an easy solution here. Don't make an offer. It's just that simple."

"You're punching over your weight." He mimicked fisticuffs. "And before you argue with me, I wouldn't have come to this meeting if I were you. Don't you know the first rule of negotiating? 'He who states his terms first loses.' "

"I have another meeting at nine. Give me a price and we can talk. Otherwise, I'm leaving."

Rhobes sat forward so fast, it was like his chair was spring-loaded. "MD Anderson can't be a buyer. You're too underground for them."

"You do know what Vita is, right? It's a radical new approach to immunotherapy for certain cancers. Have you read Anderson's annual report? Been to one of their events? They're not a diabetes center, you realize."

"Your Vita is untested. You haven't had it in a single patient's vein."

"Yes, I have. And the trial results are exactly what we expected."

Gunnar blinked, another one of his subtle tells. "Well, then you have a problem. How will a place like Anderson explain that you've gone into testing on human subjects. And if the results were good, why aren't they in your materials."

"They're proprietary."

"Like the formulation and molecular structure, right?" He whipped his hand through the air like he was erasing text he didn't like. "Anderson won't pay what I will. And they aren't going to want the complication you represent."

"And what complication is that? If it's operating under the radar of the FDA, you're in my sandbox, too, so don't get all judgmental on me."

"My labs are all very well-known —"

"Tuttle. Pennsylvania." C.P. smiled coldly as the man's face froze. "Yes, I know what's under that cornfield. So if your next tactic is blackmail? You muscle me, I'll just expose you as well, and we all know how you don't like the attention on your company." When he opened his mouth, she put her palm up. "And I know one more thing about the way you operate. What happened to those two vice presidents of yours? Suicide? Really? I'll bet if those cold cases got a couple of tips, particularly if the information turned up on the internet, the trails would get real warm, real quick. Have you seen *Don't Fuck with Cats* on Netflix? Amateurs can be even more dogged than the pros."

"Don't threaten me," he said in a nasty tone.

C.P. planted her hands on the glossy table,

and leaned into her arms. "Don't *fuck* with me."

The silence crackled between them, and she almost smiled. She was quite certain that if he could have, he'd have sent her right out one of the windows, and she took a deep breath of the hatred-stained air.

Straightening, she walked down the length of the table, not breaking eye contact. As she approached where he was sitting, Rhobes swiveled in her direction.

"I'm your only buyer, Catherine."

C.P. didn't pause. "No, you're not. And don't get up. I'll let myself out —"

"You're going to regret this."

She paused at the conference room door. After a moment, she looked back at him. He was still in that chair, but he'd sat back again and recrossed his legs, knee to knee. In fact, Gunnar Rhobes was looking so superior, he might as well have been standing up and looming over her.

"No, I'm not going to regret anything," she said. "You've got your first rule wrong, you see. The number one thing to keep in mind at the negotiation table is don't try to force the hand of someone who has nothing to lose."

Those eyes darkened. "So you've declared war, have you."

"We're both capitalists. Did you think this was a tea party?" She nodded at him and opened the way out. "Enjoy your day, Rhobes. None of us know how many we have left — which is the point of my research."

As she walked off, she got lost in thoughts of strategy, but they were interrupted by a drumbeat that made no sense — until a pair of suits came pounding down the hallway. The men didn't look at her, and as they shot by her, she glanced over her shoulder. With their jackets open, the flapping made it seem like they had pin-striped capes.

Lawyers as superheroes. What kind of DC Universe was that? And there was satisfaction in knowing that something was going wrong in Rhobes's world.

When she got out to reception, C.P. went to the elevator and called down for her car on her cell. Just as she hung up, the doors opened, and she caught sight of her reflection in the mirrored panels as she stepped in. Her blond hair was in a perfect swoop off to the side, and her face was unlined thanks to regular Botox between the eyebrows. Her uniform of professional garb was elegant as always, and her tall stilettos added to her height.

She was just as she wanted to appear.

Imposing and in control.

The image had been honed after she'd gotten out of graduate school and started working at Merck. Her hair was actually ash blond, a color that was not even brunette but a gloomy rain cloud gray, and without the bleaching, it was thin and had little body. Before she'd gotten Lasix, she'd needed heavy-lensed glasses, and a modest breast enhancement had given her flat chest some cleavage. She'd also voice-coached herself by watching Diane Sawyer broadcasts, mimicking that trademark low push of smooth syllables — and actually, Ms. Sawyer had been where she'd gotten the shade of blond from, too. Her first attempts had been out of a box and brassy as a doorknob.

And now here she was, a creation of her own drive, a culmination of personal evolution . . . proof that you could, in fact, be anything you wanted to be if you just worked hard enough.

Her father had been a plumber. Her mother had been a homemaker.

She had been an only child and relatively normal until she developed a Wilms' tumor at age four. That was what started her journey into big pharma —

Ding!

181

The soft chiming broke into her reminiscing, and for a split second, she couldn't think of what it meant or where she was. When the elevator doors parted, she shook herself to attention and disembarked into the gray-and-black marble lobby.

Her heels made a clipping sound that echoed up into the high ceiling. Ordinarily, she didn't go around outside of her home or her lab without security, but she had wanted to come into Rhobes's territory by herself to show she wasn't intimidated by him.

Besides, he wouldn't do anything really nasty here. Cameras were everywhere.

Her blond security detail, the one she was fucking, was waiting for her just inside the revolving door, this time in a black suit instead of a military uniform. And as he looked over at her, his eyes made a quick up-and-down that had nothing to do with bodyguarding and everything to do with what he anticipated doing on the return trip to Walters.

Would he have wanted her before the glow-up? she wondered. Without the money?

The answer to that didn't matter to her any more than he did.

With a strong arm, he opened the static

exit to the side of the rotating one, and as soon as she was through, another man in a black suit opened the rear of the SUV they'd rented from a local security company. As she crossed the concrete sidewalk, she imagined the small-town girl who was underneath the gloss schlubbing it to the vehicle. C.P. was proof that destiny was engineered, not a passive reception of some star-given series of calamities.

"Where to, boss," the driver asked as her door was shut and the two security men got in the front seat. "You said change of plan?"

She looked out her tinted window, at Pharmatech's giant glass penis of a sky-scraper. "The airport."

"No meeting at Anderson, then?"

"No," she replied. "I'm rescheduling that. I've got work to do back in Walters."

Settling back against the plush leather seat, she got out her laptop. Her hands trembled as she composed the email to Gus, forcing her to delete and start over one out of every five words. Good thing it wasn't a long communiqué.

Besides, he would be excited by the news.

They had their patient one.

Rhobes, in all his arrogance, had been right about one thing. It was time to put Vita to the test, and the drug was her fucking baby, too.

After she sent the email, she got her assistant on the phone. "I need my lawyer. Now. I don't care where he is on vacation."

THIRTEEN

Back at C.P.'s subterranean lab, Daniel was having a bag of saline, a B12 shot, and a blood panel for breakfast. Not exactly Wheaties, but in his condition, the three-course meal was definitely for champions. Or someone who wanted to have enough energy to tackle a flight of stairs at more than a snail's pace.

As he lay back in the hospital bed and stared at his bony ankles and his thick socks, he considered the merits of buying a new pair of pants. Like, sweatpants. $19.99. From Target. When he hadn't been sleeping, he'd looked them up on his phone — but felt like he was cheating on QVC.

And it'd seemed like a waste of a twenty-dollar bill.

"What is?"

He glanced past his floppy pant legs at Lydia. She was sitting forward in the chair she always sat forward in, her elbows on her knees, her worried face pinched like she had a spike in the center of her forehead. Next to her, the built-in desk with its computer and rolling stool was a doctor perch waiting for a white coat. Undoubtedly, the vacancy would be filled soon enough.

"Daniel?"

"Ah, nothing." Had he been speaking out loud? "Your head hurts, doesn't it."

Her brows popped. "I'm sorry?"

He pointed to the nape of his neck. "Tension headache, right? I can tell by the way your jaw is twitching, and you've got that pale thing going on."

With a flush, she eased back and rolled her shoulders. "Oh, I'm fine. Really."

At which point, the *Jeopardy!* theme started playing.

Closing his eyes, he cleared his throat and said weakly, "Lydia . . ."

There was a shuffle as she jumped up. "Do you need Gus? The nurse? Here, I'll go get them —"

By the time he lifted his lids and opened his mouth to tell her he wasn't stroking out, she was already leaning through the door and barking orders. No competing with that. He waited until she ducked back in and came over to the bedside.

"I don't need Gus," he said as she took

186

his hand.

"Better safe than sorry —"

"I don't need him!" As she recoiled, Daniel couldn't decide which out of the two of them he wanted to curse more. "I need you, goddamn it."

Lydia shook her head like she was trying to translate his words into a combination she could understand — and as she winced and rubbed the back of her neck, he wondered why he had to be such a dick.

"You have me," she said with exhaustion.

"No, I don't. I have a nurse who looks like you."

"Daniel."

The image of her covering her breasts in the bathroom would not leave his mind. Of all the side effects of the medication and the cancer, losing her while she was right in front of him had not been on any of the warning labels he'd seen. Then again, did the FDA screen drugs for that kind of shit? Nope.

And he couldn't blame her. Not only was he impotent now . . . given the way he looked, he wouldn't want to have sex with him, either. Could he fault her for not wanting him?

Maybe the truth was, he was just hurt. As much as he understood her reaction, it was still painful.

But sex wasn't everything, right? The commitment was there, he didn't doubt that, and so was her love.

"Or maybe I'm just a responsibility to you now."

"What?" Lydia rubbed her eyes. Her face. "What are you talking about? Look, can we not do this right now —"

The door to the exam room flew open and Gus jumped into the room. Today's t-shirt was a faded peach color and had "Harvey Milk for Supervisor" in two lines on the front.

"What's going on?" the doc said as he checked the vitals monitor on what was clearly a reflex — given that Daniel wasn't hooked up to it. Yet. "What's wrong."

"Nothing," Lydia said as she fell back into her chair by the desk.

Gus didn't look at her, but stayed focused on Daniel, his dark eyes narrowing like he was reading heart rate, blood pressure, and body temperature from across the room. The Coke can in his hand was a reminder that that enormous power plant of a brain seemed to run on carbonated caffeine and carbs that came out of a vending machine.

"I'm okay," Daniel said. Medically, that was.

Well, except for the cancahhhh.

Too soon? he thought to himself. *Yeah, probably.*

Gus did a back-and-forth as he cracked his Coke open. Then he took a drink like he wanted to give either of them the chance to change their mind.

"Well, anyway, I got your bloods back." Gus went over to the workstation and signed in to the computer. "They look better already. How's your eating? Your weight is low and I'm thinking we should add some Ensure throughout the day . . ."

The rest of the doctor-talk drifted away, becoming background music of no interest. Over on her chair, Lydia was nodding intently, still in that forward position, her eyes rapt as she focused on the screen. She was in what Daniel thought of as her uniform, trail shoes, loose Patagonia pants that were the color of a cream-and-sugar coffee, and a turtleneck in a heather gray that really brought out her eyes.

Her mouth was moving as she spoke. Then she licked her lips as if they were dry. Meanwhile, Gus was doing a lot of nodding and pointing to the screen, his blunt finger with its trimmed nail tracing over glowing lines of text and numbers —

Daniel's first clue that he'd decided to

189

leave was pressure on his mostly numb feet. Looking down, he was surprised to find that he'd shifted off the exam bed — and the next autonomous motion was his right hand going to his left forearm, where it peeled off the clear bandage that was anchoring the IV and took the needle right out of his vein.

He tied the tubing in a knot with his shaking hands in a sloppy fashion. The inefficiency was, as always, galling, but he didn't want to leave a mess on the floor for Gus or his nursing staff to clean up.

Neither of the other two people in the room noticed him going to vertical, and an uncharitable part of him felt like that was apt. They were so focused on the lab results, they weren't seeing him anymore, the physician/caregiver equivalent of nose-blindness to some kind of stink.

He thought back to standing with Lydia in the carport, the two of them embracing, coming to terms with shit — and then when they'd told Gus and C.P. what they'd decided. He'd felt like he and Lydia had an accord, like everything that had been a grind had gone smooth again. But that easy street hadn't lasted and that was cruelest thing about their situation. With time running out, they needed to spend the moments that mattered together.

Truly together. Not as partners in a catastrophe, each brave-facing it and dealing with their truths on their own.

Daniel was all the way to the door, and even opening things up, when the other two got up in a rush and reached for him.

"No," he said sharply as he took a step back.

Catching his balance on the jamb, he forced his voice to be even. "I've got to get out of here. I just — give me a minute."

"Daniel, let me come with you —"

"I'm sorry," he said to Lydia with a voice that cracked. "I just — let me clear my head. I don't want to be a shit, I really don't. I just . . . I need to breathe for a minute, 'kay? You listen to everything he has to say and fill me in when we're back upstairs."

From inside the exam room, Gus murmured, "Let him go."

"Take your cane," Lydia said urgently. "Here."

She ducked back in. Leaned all the way out again. "Please. Take this."

He watched from a vast distance as his hand reached forward and locked on to the metal shaft's hook. Then, before he said something he was going to regret, he nodded at her and walked away. Shuffled away.

Limped away.

It was a while before the larger laboratory sank in, all the researchers busy at their stretches of stainless-steel counters, so many white coats and faces hiding behind clear safety glasses, their nitrile-gloved hands reminding him of ads for the Blue Man Group that he'd seen in the New York City subway once.

Glances were discreetly sent his way, and he could feel their disappointment in him.

Or maybe he was dubbing that in.

As he continued along, he assumed he was going for a short wander. That he'd return to the exam room and pull his mind and emotions together. Instead, he found himself all the way down at the elevators.

Well, looked like he was headed back to the house.

When he hit the up button, the doors opened immediately.

Maybe it was a sign.

He stepped in, turned himself around, and punched the button marked "L." For "Lobby." When there was a shrill buzzing noise, he couldn't think of why —

Oh, right.

Fumbling in his back pocket, he took out his swipe card and did the duty with the reader. The doors shut. And up he went.

Not a staircase to heaven, as it were. But an Otis elevator to C.P.'s crib.

Then again, there was no eternal peace waiting for him at the end of this short ascension. Or at the end of his road, either. Funny how being an atheist had never particularly affected him one way or the other. That pragmatism stung, though, as he confronted the worm-food option that his refusal to believe in a higher power promised him.

Salvation might just be a fantasy he was going to need to embrace.

"Shit," he muttered to himself.

"He needs to blow off some steam," Gus said. "It's been a lot lately."

As the good doctor sat down in front of his computer again, Lydia's instinct was to go after Daniel and make sure he was all right. Whatever that meant.

Gus leaned over and patted the seat she'd been in. "He'll be back."

"Maybe he's gone to have another smoke." As she felt the man look up sharply, she shrugged. "He goes out into the woods and lights up. With a Jack Daniel's. I found him there last night. No, wait, it was two nights ago? I can't remember."

Time had ceased to be linear for her. It

was more a fruit salad of minutes and hours, everything mixed up in a big bowl of sadness.

Who knew that there was a vinaigrette that tasted like grief.

Gus patted the chair again. "Sit with me. Let's keep talking."

Lydia did what she was told because she couldn't think of anything else other than following Daniel out into the larger lab. But then what was going to happen? An argument in front of the researchers? Yup, that was going to go well.

And what exactly were they fighting over?

"So how bad is it between you two?" Gus nodded at his computer. "I have the clinical picture. How's the interpersonal one going?"

Oh, we're great. You know, it's a hard situation, but with love, two people can get through anything —

"We're just bouncing all over the place," she said. "One minute connected, the next . . . flying apart. There's no stride to any of it anymore. And the idea that we're wasting today doing anything other than holding each other or — I'm babbling. I don't know what the hell I'm talking about."

"Yeah, you do." Gus eased back. "You know exactly what you're saying."

"I want to change the channel on this TV show. How 'bout that."

"I totally believe that's true, too. Look, I'm a medical doctor, not a psych guy, but this will work itself out. You guys are adjusting to where things are and it's heavy shit. It'll come around, especially as he feels better."

"Temporarily feels better." She held up her hand. "Sorry, did that sound bitchy?"

"No, and no offense taken. Trust me, I know exactly where you're at as the one who's not sick. The wanting to be a paragon of perfection, give all the right reactions, do all the perfect things. And meanwhile, you're losing your fucking mind and scared to death."

"I guess you've seen this a lot in your patients, huh."

Gus moved the mouse around, making circles of the little arrow on the screen, and after a moment of watching the rotations, she was able to focus on the lab report. On the left-hand side, there was a listing of tests, in the middle was a column of values, and over on the right, blocks of color. Red, yellow, and green. She wasn't exactly sure what had been assessed, but she understood the coding. Everything was red and yellow. No greens. And Gus thought things were going better?

Or would go better?

He clicked out of the report, his email account taking over the screen as the last thing he'd checked.

"I lived it, actually."

Lydia blinked and tried to remember what they'd been talking about. Those traffic light tiles were distracting as hell, a road map of this trip she didn't want to be on promising construction delays at best . . . twelve-car pileups on the highway at worst.

"Wait, what?" She snapped to attention, as Gus's words sank in. "You've —"

"My sister was eight when she died. I was fourteen. It was fucking awful — and I made it worse. I was a total shithead to my parents. Been trying to make it up to them and to her ever since. So yup, I know exactly where you're at."

He circled the mouse again, and the list of emails bumped down as a new one came in. For a second he frowned, as if the subject or sender was significant. But then he kept talking.

"It's a pretty typical story," he said. "Lot of us in this field are survivors one way or the other — and I'll tell you, regret is one hell of a motivator. You either do something with it or it eats you alive from the inside out. And sometimes, it's both."

Lydia put her hand on top of his, stopping the circling. "I'm sorry for your loss."

"Thanks." His reply was crisp, and she wasn't surprised when he moved away from her. "Anyway, back to Daniel —"

"What was her name."

More with the mouse. And beneath Gus's rolling chair, his heel started tapping on the tiled floor.

"Anicia," he said. "She was . . . my younger sister. She was eight. When she died. I was . . . fourteen."

The words came out of his mouth, but they were more like a mantra than information he was sharing. And in the silence afterward, she pictured him in all different parts of his life, all different eras, repeating those same combination of syllables, the meaning definitive for him and also a blur now, after so many repetitions.

He seemed lost in the world of his familiar.

And it was helpful, although she wouldn't have wanted him to suffer.

"You know," he said absently, "I hated her sometimes. She was the focal point around which we all spun, whether we wanted to or not. I had dreams of being Kareem Abdul-Jabbar, you know."

She waited for him to continue. "And?"

197

"All those games I played. I waited to see one of them in the stands. Even for a quarter. Just five minutes of playtime, I didn't give a shit. I was a starter, you know. I played every game." He looked at her. "Mom was always at the hospital with her. Dad . . . did the best he could, but we still lost the house." Gus lifted his forefinger to make his point. "Do you have any idea how selfish that was? I was all bitched out because I didn't have an audience, and meanwhile my dad was getting four hours of sleep a night and losing ground, and my mom was having a big old fucking party watching her daughter scream her way through another bone marrow biopsy. Fun, fun."

"You had things you needed." Lydia looked down at her hands, twisting them in her lap. "Things . . . you wished for. Things you missed."

"She was in hell."

"So were you." Tears filled her eyes and she brushed them aside. "You weren't being selfish. There was no room for you in your own life. That was the problem."

He was quiet for a while and a couple more emails came in. Then he released a long, slow exhale.

"Here's all I know for sure." Gus held up

his forefinger in that way he did. "Life's meaning is nothing more than the intersection of Murphy's Law with our random catalogue of dreams — while we hurtle through cold space on a rock and wait to die ourselves. So make the shit count where and when you can, Lydia. You're going to have to live with what happens in the next month or two for longer than you'll be going through it. Trust me, the aftermath is worse than the during. Make every second count now with him."

"I'm trying to. Daniel's on my mind every second of the day, all through the night. All I think about is —"

"But you need to still feel him. As a man, not as a patient. Let me be his doctor, so you can be his partner. I got the clinical side of things, okay? And one last thing. It's too late to save yourself. Pulling back from him now isn't going to make the goodbye any less painful. You're already in this with him."

"I'm not pulling away. I haven't . . ."

Last night, she thought. In the bathroom. When she'd covered herself . . . as if Daniel were a friend. Or a stranger —

Lydia got to her feet in a rush. "I've got to go find him. Ah — do you need him back down here?"

"No, we've replenished his fluids and I'm waiting for a couple more test results. I'll let you guys know if he needs to see me again."

"Thanks, Gus."

"Always."

When she opened the door, he said, "Remember, he's still the man you fell in love with. Inside his body, his soul is what it always has been. That hasn't changed — and neither have you."

"I need to believe that, Gus."

"So be like Nike."

"You mean, Mikey? From the Life cereal ads?" she asked, confused.

The best doctor she'd ever met lifted one of his feet and pointed at his sneaker. "No, Nike. Just do it."

FOURTEEN

"Xhex! Xhex — wake up!"

At the sound of her name, Xhex whipped up her head so fast, she nearly spiked her skull like a volleyball. Blinking furiously, she ground her fists into her eyes.

"Wha-what — what?" She started talking before she realized what she was saying. Then again, there was only one thing that mattered. "Where's Doc Jane — we need —"

"He's awake."

Focusing on her *mahmen,* Xhex couldn't understand the words at first. But when they sank in, she jumped up and looked around Autumn's robed figure. There . . . on the hospital bed . . . John was in the exact same position he'd been in, slightly elevated, a cannula under his nose and looped around his ears, his arms out straight by his sides, his lower body covered by a precisely folded blanket that she had tucked

201

around him herself. Down the center of his bare chest, the incision that had been sutured closed was a good twelve inches long, no bandages covering it so that the superfast healing of the species could be monitored for evidence of infection.

So yeah, everything was exactly how she'd left it when she'd put her head down on the rolling table for just a moment — except for one small and extraordinary thing.

His eyes were open.

"John," she choked out as she launched herself up to the head of the bed. *"John."*

That blue stare was the kind of thing that she hadn't realized she'd resigned to never see again. But now it was locked on her, the pupils evenly dilated, the whites only slightly bloodshot.

What about the stroke risk, she thought. That had been a concern, hadn't it?

Down at his hips, one of his hands flexed, and she clasped his palm. "Hi — hello. Oh, God, I'm so —" As his lips moved, she shook her head. "Don't force yourself to —"

The squeeze was stronger than she would have thought possible. And then he lifted up his other hand. In slow, halting positions, he spelled out in American Sign Language:

I. L. O. V. E. U.

Maybe she was just dreaming. Maybe this was one of those moments in the middle of a tragedy when you fell asleep and your subconscious performed miracles to make you feel better.

"I love you, too." She leaned over him and brushed his hair back. "You're going to be okay."

She didn't know if that was true — but assuming this was not a figment of a sleep cycle, an "okay" outcome was a helluva lot more likely now than it had been before she'd passed out on her forearm. Glancing over her shoulder, she met her *mahmen's* tear-filled eyes and mouthed, *Get Jane.* Autumn nodded and left as quickly as she could, the door easing shut as she limped off.

"One squeeze for yes, two squeezes for no," she said. "Are you in pain?"

Squeeze. Squeeze.

"Are you ready to feed if Doc Jane says it's okay?"

Squeeeeeeeeeeze —

The door was thrown open, and yeah, wow, it was like they'd won the doctor lottery: Doc Jane, Vishous, Manny, and Ehlena streamed in like they had been pacing just outside the recovery room. Instantly, activity bloomed around John, the staff checking his monitors, his vitals, his pupils, his lungs, like the pit crew at an Indy 500 race — and Xhex stayed right in the middle of it all, even though she was in the way. No one asked her to step back, though.

Not that she would have under any circumstance.

Doc Jane was the one who drew her aside toward the end of the assessment. "He really wants to be here," V's mate said with a smile. "He's doing so well, it's flat-out miraculous."

Xhex focused over the female's shoulder, noting the way John's eyes followed the activity like he was tracking it all: who was in the room, what they were doing, why it was necessary. Where she was.

"Can you tell me which foot I'm touching?" Manny was asking. "Raise the corresponding hand."

Left palm went up. Right one went up. Then Manny asked John to point his toes. Lift his legs. Lift his arms.

"Holy shit," the doctor muttered under his breath. "Amazing."

"Did he have a stroke?" Xhex whispered. "Or not?"

Doc Jane likewise kept her voice low. "I'd like to put him into the MRI with some contrast to see if there was any infarction in his head. We thought that was what was going on a couple of hours ago, but his pupils are reactive and equal, and he obviously has control over limbs. He's also very aware."

"When are we out of the woods?"

"Well, we've made the turn, for sure." Doc Jane shook her head, her forest green eyes narrowing. "And with the way that Brother is looking at you? I'd say the Grim Reaper is going to have to work a lot harder to pull this fighter into a premature grave."

Xhex wiped her eyes of tears. "Can I feed him?"

"Yes, that would be great." More loudly, Jane said, "I have a vein ready and waiting over here."

"Two secs." Manny put a forefinger up to John's face. "Follow this without moving your head, okay? Great . . . yup . . . that's right. Excellent."

Manny sat on the edge of the mattress and stared at his patient. "I don't suppose you can touch your nose for me — oh, you're just knocking it out of the park, aren't you."

With a clap on John's leg, the physician got to his feet and jacked up his blue scrubs. "A vein would be awesome."

As Xhex went to get up close with her mate again, Manny gave her shoulder a squeeze. "Never underestimate a bonded male's ability to recover."

Locking eyes with John, Xhex bit into her own wrist and then placed her open vein at his mouth. He latched on immediately, taking great draws, lifting a hand to secure her forearm to his lips — but again, like she was going anywhere?

Xhex looked down her mate's body and addressed her *mahmen.* "Tell Tohr to come in? And the Brothers — you have to go report in to the Brotherhood."

Autumn blew a kiss and exited. A moment later . . .

Out in the corridor, the cheer of John's nearest and dearest was so loud, so happy, it rattled the door in its jamb and echoed throughout the training center. But that was family for you, wasn't it. When tragedy struck, they were the first to be by your side.

And when a miracle came in for a landing?

Your relief and joy were their own.

"Thank you," she said to the medical staff as the ancient chanting of the warriors started up, the male voices strident and powerful, like they were vanquishing death from the training center. "You saved his life."

Manny looked at his patient. Then the human smiled in a lopsided way and spoke up over the victory din. "We played a part. But he stayed alive . . . for you."

After Daniel left the underground lab, he ended up outside at the mansion's garages. Opening the pedestrian door, he entered the interior and immediately noticed the warmth in the air. But of course C.P. Phalen wouldn't want her cars to get a chill.

Not that he was here for her rides.

Walking down the front grilles of her matched set of Mercedes sedans and then her baker's dozen of SUVs, he passed by her Aventador and stopped in front of his only possession that was worth anything. The Harley was a custom Street Glide, not that he'd been the one with the bright ideas about modifying the bike. He'd bought the motorcycle off a buddy of his.

Just before the guy had taken a bullet to the head and died on a job.

Trolling his fingertips across the handlebars, down the gas tank, and over the quilted black seat, he could hear the sound of the engine in his head. The growl was loud, sure, but not the kind of loud that Harleys were known for, not the kind that sucked your hearing out of your ear canals or rattled the windows of houses as you passed. That was the reason he'd liked the bike — because it had all the speed and handling, and none of the obnoxious, attention-getting stuff.

He'd never worn a helmet. Not a bad call, as it turned out.

Concussive trauma was not what killed him.

Going to kill him.

Whatever.

Returning to the handlebars, he locked a grip on both sides and took a deep breath. Swinging a leg over the seat went . . . as badly as he'd thought it might. He was uncoordinated, unbalanced, and weak. But when the seat hit his ass — or the other way around, as it were — he felt an unfamiliar feeling in the center of his chest.

And gee whiz, it wasn't heart failure.

He felt . . . like he'd accomplished something. There was just so much damned failure lately, even though the cancer was out of his control.

Moving his hands down to the tank, he felt the cool metal under his mostly numb palms, pointed both his toes so that the balls of his feet were on the concrete under the tires, took another deep breath . . . and swore to himself that he could smell the gas and the oil.

Where the hell was the key? he wondered.

Six months ago, he'd had it as he'd driven the bike in here and parked it facing out — as he'd fully expected to keep taking the Harley out for a spin now and then. Now it was November, and all he had was the memory of turning off the engine, dismounting, and walking over to close the door. At the time, he'd had no clue that it was his last ride, but life was like that, wasn't it.

You didn't always know something was over at the time.

Where the hell had he put the key?

In the pocket of his baggy pants, he felt his phone vibrate as someone called him. He let the rhythmic pulses go, leaving the thing where it was. No doubt it was Lydia wondering where he was. He should go back to the clinic —

"Will you take me for a ride?"

At the sound of her voice, he was momentarily confused and looked down at his hips, like the cell had spontaneously answered and put her on speaker. But then he looked up to the door he'd just come through. She was standing there in between the jambs, her feet planted like she was prepared to argue with him.

Her tone was gentle, however. So was her expression.

"I'm sorry I was a shithead," he murmured as he glanced back down at the bike.
"Walking off like that. And if I could, I
would like to take you for a ride."

"You will. Maybe not today, but soon."

"I don't know where the key is."

"We'll find it." As she came over, her trail
shoes made no sound on the concrete. "It's
probably in the closet. Or somewhere."

He made some kind of noise in the back
of his throat because he didn't know what
to say — and then he wasn't thinking about
words as she faced him and lifted a leg over
the tank.

"What are you doing?" he blurted.

"I'm getting on with you." She paused in
an awkward tilt. "Unless . . . you'd rather I
didn't?"

He assessed her grip on the handlebars,
the way her weight was off-balance, the
casual strength that was required to keep
herself upright.

"Usually the passenger gets on the back,"
he said. "But I'm not complaining."

"Good. Because . . . here is where I want
to be."

And suddenly she was on the bike just like
he was, her thighs split around the tank, her
face in front of his, their knees touching. As
he met her eyes, he became flustered, as if

she were a stranger — and it gave him insight as to why she'd covered her breasts. Intimacy was like a muscle. If it was unused, it evaporated and left you vulnerable in ways you weren't when you were with someone you felt close to.

"Hi," Lydia whispered.

"Hi." He cleared his throat. "Does Gus need me back in the lab?"

God, her eyes were beautiful, although he hated the sheen of tears that made them glow like sunlight through whiskey.

"Not right now," she said softly.

Daniel took a deep breath. And another. "Sorry this is awkward."

"It doesn't have to be. It shouldn't be."

For a brief second, an old familiar flame lit up in his chest, and he focused on her lips. Talk about last time you did something. When had he kissed her last? Really kissed her —

"Kiss me, Daniel."

Well, wasn't she a mind reader. And as a stupid fear curled in his gut, he recognized the moment for what it was: If he didn't bridge this gap right now, he knew there would be no going back.

"I don't have much to offer you." He cleared his throat as he remembered what his body had once looked like. "In terms of . . ."

He couldn't recall when he'd had an erection last, and he wasn't sure whether that was a permanent thing or not — or more accurately, he feared it was permanent.

Lydia brushed her fingertips over his cap, as if it were his hair. Then she blinked to keep her tears from falling. "Can I be honest about something?"

"I think you better be." As he took another deep breath, he ignored the rattle in his lungs. "Now's the time."

She dropped her arms. Covered her mouth with her hand. Squeezed her eyes shut. "Oh, Daniel . . . I'm going to miss you. I'm going to miss you so much."

As she started to weep, he put his hands on her shoulders. Considering he'd been braced for her to say she was leaving him?

"Come here," he choked out.

Lydia caved into his chest, and as he wrapped his arms around her, he felt stronger somehow.

"I haven't wanted . . ." She hiccupped. "I want to be strong for you. You need to concentrate on getting through everything, and I don't want you to think I'm not strong. That I'm not . . ."

She was babbling as she cried, the flood

released, all the tension in her let go — everything he had sensed was kindling beneath her surface out in the open.

Closing his eyes, he stroked her back. "It's all right. You can say all of this."

"I can't. I have to keep it —"

"Lydia." When she straightened, he brushed her tears away. "Just because I'm not physically strong, doesn't mean I can't lift you up. I can handle your emotions —"

"But —"

"No. No buts. If you can't be real with me? We're going to drift apart before I'm gone — and how fucking stupid is that?"

She sniffled. "I feel so out of control."

"That's because you are." He wiped his thumb under her eye. "Neither of us is in control. And it sucks — and I'm glad you'll miss me. I want to hear that. I . . . need to. Otherwise, I don't know where you are, and my mind spins into places that are even darker, you know."

As Lydia nodded, she looked down. Then she pulled the hem of her turtleneck out and wiped off the gas tank. "I've cried all over your bike."

"It's a Harley. It runs on the mournful tears of unforgettable women."

She laughed. "That makes no sense."

"Okay, fine. Plain old unleaded does the

213

trick, but I was trying to be romantic. I'm not very good at that, though."

Her smile was lopsided. "You do okay."

"Not lately." He ran his hand up her arm. "I miss that."

"Me, too." As his eyes went to her lips, she touched them with her fingertips. "I miss . . . that part of us."

"Me, too."

As she reached out to him, her hands were gentle as they caressed his face and drifted onto his shoulders. For a split second, all he could think of was how withered he'd become, and the pain in his chest about how he couldn't be a man with her anymore was nearly crippling. But then she was clasping his palm, bringing it forward . . . and cupping her own breast with his hand.

Daniel closed his eyes again, this time with reverence.

"Kiss me," she said. "We don't need to go any further than that. But just . . . let me feel your mouth on mine. Please."

As he hesitated, the barrier of her robust health seemed just as much of an obstacle as his illness, the distance between them nearly impossible to cross. Except just as he had left the examination room down in the lab and ended up here without conscious thought . . . he leaned in to her with no clue that that was what he was going to do.

Daniel was suddenly just . . . there. Tilting his head. Closing the final inch. Putting his mouth . . .

. . . on hers.

Lydia's lips were so soft, softer than he remembered, and as the sensation registered, he realized it was the first comforting feeling he had experienced in — God, he had no idea how long it had been. And it was *good*. Caressing her mouth with his own, everything faded away, from the stiffness in his lower back, to the pain in his ribs and shoulder from the tumors, to the cold that he felt in his feet and hands. He stopped thinking about the blood tests. The results. The future.

The instant became all that he knew.

Oh, to put the burden down.

This was what he'd been searching for when he'd poured that Jack or tried to inhale that fucking smoke. This return to what he had once been —

All at once, he kissed her properly, licking his way into her mouth, spearing a hand through her hair, caressing her breast through her turtleneck and her bra.

And she moaned, as if she liked it as much as he did.

Moving his hands down to her waist, he

215

wanted to pick her up and put her on his hips, but he didn't have the strength. She knew what he was going for, however. With careful moves, she shifted herself into place as he inched farther back on the seat to give her some room. She had lost weight, too, her ribs more pronounced, the curves of her hips sharper — except he couldn't think about the why of it all. Not right now. He wasn't wasting this moment.

Continuing down her thighs, he remembered the feel of them naked around him and the images that flooded into his mind consumed him. He saw her arching back as she orgasmed, her breasts rising up, her nipples —

Brrrrrrrrrr. Pause. *Brrrrrrrr.* Pause. *Brrrrrrrr.*

They separated and he leaned to the side. His phone was going off in his pocket, and thanks to his loose pants, it was vibrating on the seat.

Meanwhile, Lydia's breath was pumping in and out of her, and he made sure to catch a mental snapshot of her with her face flushed and her lips parted.

"You better answer it," she said. "In case it's Gus."

Fucking hell. They couldn't have ten minutes alone without cancer barging in?

"I'm not finished with you," he vowed as

he reached back and took the phone out.

"Who is it?"

Daniel frowned at the number. "It's not Gus. I'll tell you that much."

FIFTEEN

As Daniel answered the call, he watched Lydia ease back onto the Harley's gas tank and handlebars. He had to imagine that the contours were at odds with her spine, and it was clear the gauges prevented her from having a head rest, but she didn't seem to care. Not with the way she was looking up at him from behind hooded lids — and man, that stare was the medicine he needed. In this moment, right here, right now, she didn't appear to see the knit cap on his head, or his sunken eyes and cheeks, or his narrow shoulders —

"Hello?" came the female voice over the connection. "You there?"

"Yeah," he murmured. "I'm here."

Lydia reached up and ran a hand down the side of her throat . . . and over her breast. As his brain scrambled, he tried to concentrate on the voice in his ear, but it was hard as she toyed with her taut nipple.

218

"I'm sorry if I was a bitch earlier," Alex Hess announced.

"You're welcome —" He cursed. How the fuck did people talk to each other? "I mean, no problem."

Lydia brought her free hand up to her mouth, and caressed her lower lip, as on her breast, she circled, circled . . . circled what he desperately needed to suck on.

"Listen . . . I'll meet you tonight, if you still want," the woman who called said.

Daniel swallowed. Licked his lips. Tried to remember how his woman tasted.

Decided to find out.

Except then the phone call sank in. "Yes, we'd like that."

Lydia's hand stilled and then dropped down to her waist. As she cocked an eyebrow, he held up a finger for her to hang on a sec.

"What changed your mind?" he asked.

Alex Hess? Lydia mouthed.

When he nodded, she sat up and shuffled back a little. Then she lifted her palms, as if to say, *Now, what?*

"Hello?" he repeated.

That deep, intense voice on the other side dropped even lower. "I'll explain when I see you."

This is for Lydia, he reminded himself, as

the hassle suddenly seemed like a waste of time.

"Fine. Where?"

"Deer Mountain. Up on the summit. That's where we need to go."

"What time?"

"I'm off work. So midnight."

"Okay. We'll see you then."

As the call was cut, Daniel tried to put his phone back where it'd been, but between the shaking in his hand and the thin slot of the pocket, repeated attempts failed and he didn't want to drop the thing.

"So is that cool?" he asked. "We go meet her at twelve tonight?"

Lydia sat up. Backed up farther. Put her hands on his legs. As she rubbed up and down his thighs, he could tell that she was keeping her touch light, and he wished he didn't appreciate the awareness. He wished he didn't need it.

"What," he said as she didn't reply.

"I'll absolutely meet her. I know it's important to you. But why the mountain?"

Daniel swallowed a curse, though he wasn't frustrated with her. He just knew what she was thinking. "I can make it up there. The Wolf Study Project has an ATV, right — and I know the gas pan was fixed because I was the one who repaired it. We'll just park at your work and take it up the trail."

"Did she say where on the summit?"

"Where the overlook is, I'm assuming." He shook his head. "I know you hate that hotel across the valley. I do, too, but we can suck it up for an hour."

He was pretending that the sight of that enormous monstrosity of a resort was the problem. And the fact that he didn't have the energy to argue about whether he had enough energy to make it up the elevation on a four-wheeler, much less meet with some stranger over something as stressful as Lydia being left alone in the world, was probably the best commentary on his fitness for the plan there was.

But it was amazing what you could do when you had to.

"I'll be fine," he said. "Honest. We'll just get the ATV and —"

"That fuel pan didn't stay fixed, but you know what we can do? Take one of C.P.'s SUVs up the back side. I'll just run over to the lookout and bring her to you and the car. The view is not the point."

"No, it's not. But . . ."

The urge to argue was so strong, he opened his mouth, except then he realized something. How often had he fought against her just because he hated his own limitations? A lot. And she, just like everyone, gave him leeway because he was sick and he was a for-now-still-living tragedy. How many lines had he pushed through simply because he was frustrated . . . and what had it cost Lydia on the other side?

His illness made him a suffering saint of sorts, giving him a Teflon coating when it came to being reasonable.

"You know what," he said softly. "I think that's a really good plan."

The easing in Lydia's body was immediate, the tension flowing out of her shoulders, her breasts rising and falling as she exhaled.

"It'll be great," she said. "I promise —"

Crack!

The sharp impact shocked him out of his thoughts.

"Oh, no! Your phone."

With a lurch, Lydia leaned to the side — and then she slipped off the bike, her synthetic hiking pants offering no resistance to the black paint job on the tank. He tried to catch her, but with his useless hands, she slipped right through his grasp —

The lithe way she threw out her palm and stopped a face-first crash was something he envied. But it was too late for his phone. The screen was splintered in the corner that had taken the brunt of the hit.

"I think it still works." She curled over on her side and tilted the unit up. "Oh, it lights up. Good."

Extending her arm, she held the iPhone out to him.

That was when they heard the helicopter.

As he took the cell back, they both looked in the direction of the thumping noise even though they couldn't see anything as there were no windows around. The sound was unmistakable, however.

"Guess the boss is back," he said.

"Guess so."

He looked back down at his woman. "Can I be honest, too?"

Lydia nodded, even though fear crossed her face. "Yes. Of course."

"I want to keep kissing you. I want to lift up that shirt of yours . . . and I want to suck on you while I strip those fucking pants off you and rip your panties off. I want . . . to trade places with you, and have you sit on my bike with one foot on the muffler and the other on the turned tire . . . and I want to eat you out until you come against my face."

Her expression shifted as he talked, her mouth parting once again, her lids lowering, her head falling back as if she were already up there, already on the bike with her thighs spread for him, already holding him in place.

"That's what I want," he concluded. "And that's just a start."

She nodded. "I want that, too."

"But if I'm really honest . . ." He glanced around again, as if the cars could help or change things. "I'm worried you won't be satisfied because I can't . . . you know . . ."

He indicated the front of his hips with a gesture. "I mean, I'm not capable of —"

"Daniel."

As she said his name, he stopped with the rambling. He'd never had a problem talking about sex, about his body, about what he wanted or needed — but it was a whole different ball game when the syllables came out with so much shame and embarrassment.

"No matter how far it goes, it's you," she said. "And that's what matters."

Her smile was so beautiful to him.

Then again, acceptance was better than any kind of makeup, wasn't it. Especially on the face of the woman you loved.

As Gus St. Claire rode up in the lab's main elevator, he was in a ripe mood, as his grandmother would have called it. In a

224

perfect world, he would have been alone so he could talk to himself. No such luck. He was ascending with several colleagues, one of whom he'd hired a mere month before, all of whom were leaving after a very, very long night's work. Fortunately, none of them were talking because they were exhausted and all of them got off at the level that would take them out to the parking area. He continued onward.

But stayed quiet.

Glancing up to the camera's eye in the corner, he knew it was the better move, and besides, he didn't have to bother with the composure for much longer.

When the elevator bumped to a stop, he leaned into a sensor and got an eye scan, after which there was a pause, because for all of the state-of-the-art everything in C.P. Phalen's world, entrance into her house was still manually reviewed — and given who she was and what she was doing, he didn't blame her.

Nope, he blamed her for other shit now.

After the doors opened, he took a right and started walking. The corridor to the mansion's entry point was good and long, and he used the distance to get his face arranged while people on the other side of mirrored glass watched him — at least, he was assuming fully armed guards were what were behind the panels.

His Zen session worked. By the time he finally passed through the last of the security checks and entered by the back door next to the servants' quarters, he was good and balanced, everything where it should be, where it needed to be: nothing but perfectly-fine, showing the world — and his boss — that he was just as he'd been when he'd started at her company.

Before he'd fallen in love with her.

Emotions. Biggest pain in the ass there was — and considering who he worked for, that was really saying something. C.P. Phalen was like a nightmare he couldn't wake up from, the damn woman haunting him during his waking hours and in the dark as well.

"Hey," he said as he nodded to one of the security guards in whatever corridor he entered. He wasn't tracking the trip.

There was no response. They never re-sponded. Which was why he greeted them.

As he came to the next armed uniform, he hit the guy with a "H'w-r-ya."

He passed by three more sentries on the way to his boss's office. Jesus, it must be like living with a football team, just with semiautomatics. The food bill for on-duty, on-site snacking must be goddamn enormous.

As he made another turn and found himself in the kitchen, he halted. Across a field of stainless steel counters, a chef in whites looked up, and that was when Gus realized he was taking the long route on purpose: He was looking for the guard who had been fucking her.

Wow. That was insane. Because what the hell was he going to do if he found the bastard?

Nothing that made any sense, that was sure.

Fast-tracking the way to her study's door, he reached for the stainless steel — or was it sterling? — handle. Except then he stopped himself, remembering what he'd walked in on before. And noting that he hadn't found her piece of gym equipment.

Maybe another Orgasm Theory workout was going on.

He knocked loudly and made sure his voice was good and clear. "I'm here. And I'm not interested in waiting for —"

There was almost no delay in the entry opening — but what the hell was on the other side? He wasn't sure what he was looking at.

"What the fuck did you do to your hair?"

he blurted.

When the great C.P. Phalen didn't answer him, he glanced over his shoulder and then backed the woman up. Closing them in together, he took her forearms in gentle hands and eased her over to the sofa in the sitting area. When they got within range of those black cushions, he released his hold — but she just stood there, staring at him like she wasn't seeing him.

"Hello?" He waved a hand in front of her face. "Okay, so aliens are real and you've just come back from an abduction."

In the past three years, since he'd come on board and started developing Vita, the woman had been all about her buttoned-up, ultra-professional, ice-madam bullshit: Hair in place, black-suit-wearin', high-heeled, whatever. But here she was with her hair hanging in her face like she'd been trying to pull it out of her skull, her shoes off, her jacket opened like she'd needed more air than there was around her.

"Sit down," he said gently.

Second time today he'd told a woman he respected to do that. Maybe he needed to add the skill to his résumé.

As C.P. did what he told her to, she nodded, like she was a child following the orders of a teacher in school.

"What's going on?" he said as he sat down as well and brushed the blond out of her eyes. "Talk to me."

Her stare took its time focusing on him, and for a moment, she didn't seem to recognize him — to the point where he almost took out his badge and flashed his ID at her.

"Gus?" Then she shook herself. "Gus, I mean."

Right about the time he started thinking he needed to do a medical assessment, he caught sight of the closed bathroom door over her shoulder.

What a fucking idiot he was. He knew damn well who was in there, and that she wasn't in crisis. Her polish had been fucked out of her.

Gus got to his feet in a rush, jacking up his jeans, slapping the simp out of himself.

"You asked me to come up?" he demanded.

There was another pause and then she snapped back into place — or seemed to try to — her manicured hands going to her mop of hair like if she could just get the shit back into order, magically she wouldn't look like she'd just been fucked twelve ways to Sunday.

Losing patience with the bullshit, he

marched over to the bathroom, ripped the door open, and got ready to take the fucking guard to church. They had better things to be doing than —

No one was in the bathroom.

He looked back across the room. C.P. was eighty percent put-together, that hair in a better semblance of order, her jacket rebuttoned, but the undone was still graffiti all over her aura.

"Did you get my email?" she asked in a low voice.

"Yeah, I did. That's why I'm here. So you've found our patient one?"

When she didn't continue, he returned to the sofa. Sat next to her again. Frowned. "What's the problem."

"Did you review the medical record I sent you?" C.P. cleared her throat. "Actually, before you answer that, would — I'm sorry, could you get me a little seltzer?"

With a shrug, he got back up and headed for the bar. When he pulled up to the display, she said, "Actually, I think I'd like a gin and tonic if you don't mind."

He lifted an eyebrow. Then shrugged again. "Ordinarily, I wouldn't recommend drinking on the job or starting this early in the day. Somehow, this seems like an exception."

Making fast with the bottles and the glasses, he got a Coke for himself and brought the tumbler over to the woman. With a wobbly hand, C.P. took the libation and downed half of the Beefeater in a swallow.

"Thirsty, huh," he said as he sat back and braced himself for whatever was coming.

"My real name is Catherine."

"I know." When she glanced over at him, he shrugged. "What, you think I haven't read your Wikipedia page? Come on."

"I was Cathy when I was growing up." As she circled the ice in her tall glass, he wondered what she was really looking at — what part of her past, that was. "I, ah, I used to be her."

The silence in the study was resonant, which was what happened when the walls were insulated against fire and explosions — and so was the glass. It was so quiet that the cubes he'd made the drink with sounded loud as she took another sip.

"So," she said with greater command. "About patient one. You reviewed the medical records, including the most recent physical?"

"You need to tell me what the fuck is going on."

Now her blue eyes shot over to him, and

they were crystal fucking clear. "Do we have a good candidate."

As his stare roamed her face, it was hard to switch tracks to the subject that they always wanted to talk about — proof, not that he needed it, of how distracting Catherine Phillips Phalen could be.

"I didn't take a long time with the records." He cracked open the Coke. "But the AML is right, and the patient is healthy enough. The return of the disease hasn't been addressed yet, so the data will be clean. How're we going to get consent? When can they get here?"

The patient's history was significant for acute myeloid leukemia, but the real bitch? They'd had a bout with a Wilms' tumor when they were four years old, and carboplatin had been given for a recurrence about a year thereafter, following surgery. Anyone who received one of the platinum-based drugs was at an increased risk for AML, although typically the risk of the secondary cancer decreased over time. In this case, that truism was either false, or the patient would have gotten the leukemia as an adult anyway. What was clear was that the AML was back, following successful treatment about three years ago.

"Do you think . . . Vita is going to work?"

C.P. asked. "In this case."

"Isn't that the million-dollar question. Or billion-dollar, as the case is, right?"

He sat forward and focused on the bubbles on the inside of the glass he'd made for her. Then he checked out the freshly manicured red nails, so perfectly done.

"What do you think the response will be?" she prompted him.

"I think . . . I think it better work in this patient. Based on those records, there aren't many options available to them considering the amount of drugs given over their life-span. They're already at threshold doses between the treatment for the Wilms' tumor and what's going on now."

C.P. made a noncommittal noise as she finished the G&T.

"Guess this is good timing for you," he murmured. And mostly kept the bitch out of his voice. "What with the negotiations and all. Or will you sell, anyway?"

She put the glass on the coffee table and rubbed her hands together as if she were cold. Or ready for a big, greedy payday.

"So, who handles the contact for this patient?" he asked. "Have they even been approached?"

"Yes. They have."

"And they're up for it?" He frowned as

233

she nodded. "How the fuck did you manage this without me — never mind. I don't give a shit about that. When can they get here?"

C.P. put her palms on her knees and braced her shoulders. Then she faced him. "They're already here. It's me. I'm the patient."

SIXTEEN

Surfacing from a strange dream, Lydia came awake in a dim room, in a bed she didn't immediately recognize, in a house that she drew a lot of blanks on. But she knew who was with her. She knew the arms that were wrapped around her, and the body pressed against her back, and the leg that had wheedled its way in between hers.

Daniel.

In the gentle juncture between the amnesia of rest and the painful reality of consciousness, in the buffered, semi-dreamscape of rousing . . . she drifted into a fantasy where what she knew was real was the nightmare and what she was about to wake up to was a normalcy that made her eyes tear up —

"Hi," came a gravel voice in her ear.

She smiled and stroked Daniel's arm. They had fallen asleep together after she'd helped him back from the garages. Then they'd woken up and ordered a meal from the kitchen like they were in a hotel. Then . . . back to sleep on top of the covers, still in the clothes they'd been wearing down in the clinic.

"How did you know?" she murmured. "That I wasn't asleep?"

"Right there."

The arm she'd been stroking extended out over the duvet, and she followed the forefinger's direction across to the full-length mirror mounted next to the door out of the room. And sure enough, there she was with her eyes open — and right behind her, spooning in, was Daniel. With him mostly hidden by her body, she could almost pretend things were the way they should have stayed.

"What time is it?" she asked.

"Ten-thirty."

Frowning, she glanced over her shoulder. "That can't be right. We ate lunch at —"

"At night. Ten-thirty at night."

"Okaaaaaaaaaay." She rolled over and faced him. "And you? Did you sleep, too?"

"Out like a light. I don't know what was in that IV. Knockout drops, I guess."

As they stared at each other, she had the strangest sense of returning from a trip, sure as if she'd been traveling. Or perhaps it was he who had left and returned. Maybe it was both of them, separately departing.

In the back of her mind, she thought of what she'd talked to Gus about.

"Kiss me again, Daniel," she whispered. "I don't care where it goes. I just want to be with you."

He brushed her hair back. "I want that, too."

They leaned in together, and as he pressed his lips to hers, he tasted of mint, which was a surprise. Except then she remembered the Burt's Bees he always used to keep his lips moist when he was dehydrated from the drugs —

For a split second, her mind got sucked into dark thoughts, but she reined the chaos in with a hard jolt of gratitude. How stupid would she feel, a month from now, two months from now, that she'd had this moment when he was with her, when he was alive, and she'd wasted it dwelling on everything she couldn't change.

Closing her eyes, she concentrated on the caress, the warmth, the softness. And as she kissed him back, it got easier to feel him — and she realized that somewhere along the way, she'd decided that this part of their relationship was gone forever.

It was the kind of conclusion that she

hadn't been aware of making.

It was the kind of conclusion that was wrong.

Daniel had always been a dominating lover, and he took control of things now, rolling her onto her back and shifting over onto her. Deeper now with the kissing, his tongue entering her, his hand stroking down the side of her rib cage as his leg moved up on top of both of her thighs.

"Daniel . . ." she sighed.

"Is this okay?"

"God, yes."

Her body came alive again, just as it had back in the garage, her heart beating faster, her lungs burning, her core anticipating his touch, his penetration. That old familiar melting overtook her from the inside out, until her bones were flowing with the pulsing heat. When he slipped under her turtleneck and his hand rode up to her breast, she arched into him —

The top really had to go.

"Here, let me just —" With a wriggle, she disappeared the barrier on an up-and-over and threw it on the carpet. "Better."

"Much," he murmured.

Her bra was simple, white and cotton, and with her nipples peaked as they were, things were almost as visible as they would have been without the thing — and Daniel seemed captivated. Backing off a little, he teased her with his fingertips, the shaking in his hands much improved — and hey, if he needed occupational therapy like this? She'd be his PT any day.

The bra was a front clasp, and he paused as he went to the juncture between the cups. "Take this off for me?"

She knew why he asked, and instead of dwelling on the struggle he would have had, she turned it into a show. As he eased away, she freed the clasp, but left the cups in place. The reveal came as she arched her back, and the twin strokes as the bra's halves slowly parted off to the sides made her bite her lip.

Daniel's eyes burned as he looked at her, as if he were seeing her for the first time — and that expression of hunger in his face fed her on some level that had been starved for so long.

"You're just beautiful."

With that, he brushed a hand down her sternum and up one side. As he got to her nipple, he drew a circle around where she wanted his mouth, lingering, taking his time. Then he leaned in and kissed the underside of the breast he was stroking, nuzzling his way up to the tip that was aching for him. Everything he did was without hurry, as if they had all the time in the world — and she wondered whether he was giving her a chance to say no.

She wasn't going to, even though she was nervous in ways she'd never been before. How could he be satisfied if he couldn't orgasm himself? Wasn't this selfish of her to —

"Hey," he whispered as he stilled. "Where did you go?"

"I'm sorry." As she heard the sadness in her voice, she tried to snap out of it. "I mean, I'm back now."

His fingertips toyed with her nipple, giving it a tug. As a lance of pleasure shot through her core, she jacked back into the pillow with a hiss. When she recovered from the shock of the heat, she wanted to tell him it wasn't fair.

"Talk to me," he said.

"I just . . . I mean, what about you?"

"What about me." Before she could formulate some kind of response, he shook his head. "I still feel everything. The softness of your skin." He cupped her breast. "And where you're tight for me." He ran his thumb up and over her nipple. "And I get to watch you move under my touch."

As he swept his hand down her body and

around to the inside of her thigh, she opened her legs for him, her spine curling, her head moving back into the pillow again.

"Watching you feel pleasure," he said as he lowered his mouth to her nipple, "is doing more for me than whatever Gus pumped into me down in the lab. Trust me. Just be with me here, Lydia, let me make you feel good — for the both of us."

As his palm went higher, she gave herself into what he was doing to her, rolling her hips in anticipation. He refused to rush, though. He took his sweet time getting to her sex, and with every inch higher, her arousal intensified — when he finally made contact, she gasped, and that was when he kissed her mouth again. Sealing her lips with his own, he rubbed her back and forth, the heel of his palm taking the seam of her hiking pants and turning it into a torment she couldn't get enough of.

"Please . . ."

"Please, what?" he said in a low voice, a voice she remembered.

I need you.

Daniel needed his woman, too. His limitations were real, but so was what he could still do. He could use his mouth. He could use his hands — and he did.

241

"Lift your hips." When she did as he asked, he sat up. "Help me with the button, would you?"

There was no pause at all, and she attacked the fastening of her pants. And it was funny — or maybe liberating was more like it. He didn't even give a shit that he needed help. Who the fuck cared. All he wanted was to keep the vibe going, and give her as many orgasms as she could take —

"Oh, yes," he told her. "That's it."

He watched from above as she squirmed out of those hiking pants — as well as her underwear. The fact that she was impatient made him feel a male kind of satisfaction that had once been a familiar sensation, but nothing he'd sported since the spring. And then there was the way her breasts bobbed and swung, those nipples bouncing as she moved with none of her usual grace.

Which is not a bad thing at all, he thought as he licked his lips.

When she lay back down, he smiled and put his hands on her, stroking her from her tight breasts down her stomach to the bare cleft that was between her thighs. But he didn't want to give her what they both needed — no, he wanted them to wait. Anticipation was a sweet bitch, wasn't it.

242

Except he didn't last as long as he'd hoped.

The sex was different without his cock being involved, but he was juiced and hungry for her release, sure as if it were his own. And it was the strangest fucking thing. As he pleasured her, slipping his fingers up and down her slick, hot core, he lived through her response, every moan and twist something that was transmitted into his own body —

She cried out his name when he penetrated her, and his eyes closed as his own head fell back. She was so tight, and God, he was panting, too.

He could remember what it was like to have his cock in her, the way the constriction had been so electric, how his whole body felt the fiery hold. Riding those memories, he found a rhythm to his stroking, and he wanted to kiss her, but he needed to see her more — and what a picture she was, naked on top of the bed, one knee out to the side, her breasts pumping up and down, her hands fisting the duvet that was wrinkled underneath her.

"Come for me," he commanded. "Let me watch you come."

Three fingers now, going in and out of her, every penetration bringing the heel of his palm against the top of her core, her hips working her against him —

Oops, annnnnd there went a pillow. And another.

Her body was contorting now, jacking to the side, her knees coming up, her legs locking in against him, her hands punching down and holding him in place —

Lydia came hard, the contractions so tight he could feel them, and oh, shit, it was *good,* the tension releasing in his own body, a shimmering going through him as if he'd somehow absorbed part of the orgasm.

When she eased up and flopped onto her back, he kept his hand right where it was and smiled a big ol' yeah-I-did-that-to-my-woman grin.

Sure as if he'd never pleasured her so well before.

Lifting her heavy lids, Lydia looked up at him . . . and there it was. That love shining in her eyes, the thing he hadn't seen for so long.

"You're the best medicine I have," he said as he leaned forward and tilted her chin up.

Putting his mouth against hers, he stroked her hair back: Thanks to the writhing, the ponytail she'd put it in was no longer up to its job, all kinds of frizz surrounding her.

"Also, just so you know," he informed her,

"I could do this for hours."

"Really?"

"Oh, yeah." He caressed her sex some more and was really into the sound she made. *"Really."*

"Daniel —" she gasped.

Leaning back down to her breasts, he murmured, "Once more with feeling . . ."

Seventeen

A good fifty miles to the west, in the *symphath* Colony, Blade was fifty feet beneath the ground and fully armed under his blood-red robe. His private quarters were in the least desirable part of the rabbit warren of subterranean chambers, and he did that on purpose. No one bothered him here.

Secrecy was necessary — and not just the kind that came with people not entering your private space. Mental secrecy was critical to him. His kind had no hesitation to violate a person's mind, either because you had information or emotions up there they wanted or needed — or because they were bored and inclined to fuck with you.

If he was anywhere else in the Colony, his thoughts were locked down, his grid protected — and even here, he was careful not to become complacent.

Throwing part of the draping over his

shoulder, he rechecked his hip holster. Two guns, backup ammo, everything cleaned with an herb wash that hid any scents of metal, lead, blue oil. Not that this was all of his armaments. He had hidden a pack of explosives just off the Colony's territory, and he would pick that up on his way.

He knew better than to bring C-4 anywhere near here.

Resettling the robing, he glanced around. His pallet was across the way on the tiled floor. Then he had his locked wardrobe, two trunks that were secured with screws that penetrated into the bedrock five feet down, and a bank of cabinets.

None of that really mattered, though.

Not like his young.

Pivoting around, he stared at the wall of glass cages. The reptile enclosures were stacked together, eight across the bottom, six running up vertically. Each one had several heat lamps, at least four inches of soil or sand for burrowing, a hiding spot or two, foliage, and a water dish.

Fifty-seven white scorpions, collected over his lifetime, interbred as appropriate, with their venom collected and stored.

They were the only young he would ever have, and he cherished them as a parent would, tending to not just their basic needs, but nurturing their growth and development — and mourning their passings as they came.

Narrowing his eyes, he felt a creeping paranoia latch on to the nape of his neck. Though he was not a male who was at a loss very often, his throat grew tight. If he died tonight, he did not know who would feed them, and he imagined, under the lamps, with no fresh water or food supply, they would die fast. Unlike scorpions in the wild, his all contained recessive genes that made them more potent, but also more vulnerable.

Trying to collect himself, he went over to the left. His favorite was the smallest of the collection, but then, in their kind, size was the inverse to deadly danger. The big ones had the weaker stings.

"You are the queen, aren't you," he whispered as he tapped the glass.

The predator on the other side of the pane shifted her body around and stared at him. She was beautiful, white as driven snow, and he'd always found her elegant, her segmented stinger curling up over her back, a fascinator that packed a punch, her pincers curving like a rococo sculpture.

"I'll need you later. But not right now."

As a *symphath,* he had to regulate himself

if he went out into the world. Yes, he was part vampire, but unlike his sister, the evil side in him was more dispositive, and given the purpose that had animated him all these years, he'd had to have control as he worked with humans to accomplish his goals. The venom was the key for him. Back when the Princess had been alive, he had been in charge of her stable of scorpions, feeding them, caring for them — and of course he'd been stung. That was how he'd learned that the poison had its benefits.

And he had used them.

Not tonight, however. He needed to be at his full potency as he went out on this mission that could well be his last — either because he was killed in action . . . or because the final lab was taken out.

"Be well, *leelan* —"

"You expecting a response from that thing?"

At the male voice, Blade smiled in a nasty fashion, and turned back around. "The King has arrived. To what do I owe this honor?"

Rehvenge stood in the doorway of the quarters, all amethyst eyes and majestic menace. The male, who was also a half-breed, had his own way of controlling his urges in mixed company, but he never, ever came down here medicated. And instead of the long mink coat and nice silk suit he sported in Caldwell, the male was wearing a white sheath that fell from a short collar down to his loafers. Mounted on the satin, in a pattern of swirls and straightaways, were countless rubies, their facets and pigeon-blood color catching the subtle light and magnifying it back in such a way that he appeared to gleam.

"People who talk to pets," Rehvenge said as he entered without invitation, "have anthropomorphized animals — or in your case, arachnids, to be specific."

"These are not my pets."

"The Princess has been dead for how long?" The King made a show of looking at the cages. "With her gone, the only explanation for this continued husbandry is that you've formed an attachment of some sort. There is no longer any duty for you to uphold."

Blade continued to smile, though in his heart, a dark hatred kindled. But then that emotion was exactly what the King was hoping to elicit, and therefore, it was easily corralled.

"Habits die hard," he murmured.

"Perhaps I need to give you a job."

"I am ready for my orders." Blade bowed

slightly. "Whatever shall you have me do, my Lord —"

The King moved so fast, he was untrackable. One moment Rehvenge was over by the door; the next, he was right up in Blade's face, looking like he was prepared to bite something until he got to bone — after which, he would keep going.

Blade purred in the back of his throat. "I had heard you were happily mated, but mayhap the gossip is wrong. Would you like me on my knees? Or were you planning on forcing me to accept you in another fashion? I am a top, but as you are my King, I believe no is not an option."

Rehvenge's lips peeled off his fangs, the daggers in the roof of his mouth flashing. "I want you to stop fucking with your sister."

For a split second, Blade gave an honest reaction: "What are you talking about?"

"You're going to stop fucking with Xhex, or I'm going to take out my frustration with you on your little collection here — among other things."

Besotted with his ruler, Blade leaned in so they were chest to chest, nearly mouth to mouth. Tilting his head to the side, in case his King wanted to sample his lips, he murmured, "I am doing nothing to her. You can ask her yourself — you all but live with

251

her, don't you."

"In the last three weeks, at least two vampires have been found in Caldwell with their eyes taken out by a *lys.*"

"Mmm. Sounds like you have a collector on your hands — or someone who is making a hearty stew."

"And last night, somebody shot at John Matthew."

"Remind me who that is again —"

The grip on the front of Blade's throat prevented him from going any further with the line of bullshit he was spouting with such enjoyment.

"Don't stop," Blade squeezed out as he rolled his hips. "You're turning me on."

The pressure was released not in the slightest.

"Quit framing her for trouble," Rehvenge ground out, "and leave her mate alone. If there are any more bodies in the alleys down there, or another oopsie with a lead slug and John's chest cavity, you're going to wish for your grave."

With a quick shift, Rehvenge stepped back and took his death grip with him.

Blade coughed as he dragged oxygen down deep. "What . . . motive. Do. I have. For that."

"Your family has never needed a motive

when it comes to her. Or do you think I've forgotten who put her in that fucking lab in the first place." The King jabbed a finger across the tense air between their faces. "You people eat your own. You always have. You want me to spell out your motive? It's what's in your veins."

"As if you are not one of us yourself. Or has the Brotherhood worn off on you? If that is the case, I would beware down here."

The King leaned in, his jeweled robes shimmering as if he were covered with blood. "Try me. *Please.*"

That amethyst stare glowed with menace, and in the back of Blade's mind, he thought . . . ah, yes. This was why the male was King — and kept that mantle. With every fiber of his being, Rehvenge relished conflict, his favorite meal, always consumed with hunger.

Evidently finished with delivering his message, the King walked for the door, that robing flaring behind him.

"My sister is nothing to me," Blade said in a low voice. "I would no sooner waste energy upon her as I would beat a stray. Not because I am moral, but because I am logical."

Rehvenge looked back across the quarters. "Then you better hope whoever's setting

Xhex up loses interest in their pet project. Because the shit is going to come down on you if it keeps up, and I will enjoy what I do to you."

"I won't be gone long."

As Xhex made the pronouncement, John Matthew gave her two thumbs-up and a smile from his hospital bed. Then, like he could read her mind, he signed, *You're doing the right thing.*

"I don't know what I'm doing."

Go, I'm okay. Promise.

She kissed him on the mouth, brushed his hair back — and then pressed her lips to his forehead. After a lingering look into his blue eyes, she beat feet out of his recovery room before she changed her mind. She wasn't sure leaving John was the right thing. She wasn't sure what she was doing meeting that guy up on the mountain. She wasn't sure she wanted to go on that trail again —

No, she was sure she didn't want that ascent. She hadn't liked what she'd found up there the last time, and she had no expectation that the passage of months had improved what she was likely to cross paths with.

But if you do not start . . . you will never, ever finish.

Whatever.

Heading down the training center's corridor to the left, she proceeded past the unused classrooms and punched out of the steel door into the parking area. A couple of blacked-out box vans were parked facing toward the exit, and then there was Fritz's high-class version of a school bus — that had absolutely nothing in common with the orange-painted bread loaves that took human children back and forth to their places of learning.

She was halfway down the lane leading out of the parking area, on track to meet the first of the defensive barrier systems, when she realized she couldn't have taken a more inefficient route. Everything was wrapped with steel as a safety precaution. No dematerializing into, or out of, the facility.

She was going to have to hoof it for a while.

Then again, she needed to get her shit together, so maybe the delay was good.

The ascension to ground level went fairly quick, V clearing her at every security point just as she arrived. Man, if she'd intended to get off the Brotherhood property without anyone noticing, she'd picked the worst way. And the fact that Vishous never once asked her what she was doing or why she was leaving by foot along the vehicle tunnel? Probably meant she was going to be followed.

Take out the "probably." And dematerializing wasn't going to free her. No doubt the recovery room was bugged, so he had heard her talking to John about her plan. Hell, given that V was responsible for the cell phones everyone used? He no doubt had a record of her conversation.

At least Rehv would get off her back because she was finally following through with his fucking bright idea.

As she approached a triple lineup of twenty-five-foot-high bars that were thick as her thighs and wrapped with steel mesh, she glanced at the monitoring pods that were mounted around the concrete ceiling along with the fluorescent lights. The locking system released with a *clink!* and then the segments retracted one by one with a *whoosh.*

The fresh air was tantalizing and cool, marked with the fragrance of pine and dirt.

She wished John were with her, she thought as she started walking again.

Finally, she was aboveground, and as the gates relocked behind her with a series of clangs, she looked up at the stars. Seconds later, she was flying free, traveling through the downright cold night in a scatter of molecules, moving north and to the west. When she re-formed, it was at the foot of Deer Mountain, on the shoulder of a county road that wrapped itself around the contours of a riverbed. Glancing into the tree line, she heard a couple of nocturnal animals scamper away from her presence — raccoons, she guessed, given that they went faster than a porcupine could, yet were not so large as a doe or a buck would be.

Good survival instinct —

The sense that something was behind her made her turn around. And then she refocused on what was in front of her. Thanks to her vampire eyes, she could penetrate quite far into the trunks and stumps, but whatever it was did not want to be seen. All she caught was a fast shadow that darted off.

If it had been a Brother, they would have sheepishly identified themselves.

Putting her hand to her hip, she drew her autoloader and flipped the safety off with her thumb. Then she closed her eyes again and went for another travel through the November air.

This time, when she came back into her corporeal form, it was up on the summit of the mountain, in front of the broad view of a valley down below. From this lofty vantage point, the carpet of pines was solid as a train model's, looking almost fake in its perfection — except for the gouge across the way: At about the same altitude, on the other side of the evergreen'd topography, there was a manmade extravagance, the construction long as God's arm and set deep into Mother Nature's dominion. Work on the resort was ongoing, all kinds of earthmovers, bucket loaders, and cranes sitting dormant, like Transformers waiting to come to life the second there was enough daylight again.

"What a fucking eyesore," she muttered to herself.

Then she rolled her eyes —

— and swung her gun around. Pointing the muzzle into a stand of pines, she said, "I don't know what you're doing back there, but after the last twelve hours, I've got an itchy trigger finger and this gun is ready to go to work."

There was a pause, and then she saw the glowing hazel eyes. A moment later, a gray wolf padded out into the clearing.

Except it wasn't a wolf in the conventional sense, was it.

Drawing in some air through her nose, Xhex frowned and slowly lowered her weapon. "So you're the wolven V was talking about when he saw my future."

EIGHTEEN

As fate would have it.

What a saying, right? Blade thought as he stayed behind an outcropping of boulders and watched the two females on the summit: On the right, a four-footed wolf who was not a wolf in the conventional sense of the word. On the left, a biped who looked human enough, but had the blood of two different paranormal species running through her veins.

When he had come here to find the entrance to that final lab, the last person he had expected to see anywhere on the mountain was the very one his King had ordered him to stay away from. And then his sister had pointed her gun into the trees and addressed a presence she had clearly sensed — and he had obviously missed.

He'd been so shocked, both at the wolven's appearance and his own lapse of survival, that he had been rendered momentarily dumbfounded.

He remained as such.

Although that wasn't just because of the shifter.

Now he knew why Rehv was worried about Xhex. Her grid was collapsing, that which should have been three-dimensional now only two-. And he also knew why the superstructure of her emotions was folding in on itself.

With her, there was one and only one why —

No, that wasn't right. Something equally bad had happened to her after she'd gotten out of that lab. Another trauma . . . he could see the echo of it on her grid. But at least there were other, happier events that had affected her soul, as well. Profoundly good things. Her mate, the Black Dagger Brother John Matthew, for example.

Out at the clearing, Xhex lowered her gun and said something to the wolven that he wasn't able to track.

There was a pause — and then he saw for the first time a kind of magic that took his breath away.

The wolf transformed herself, her entire body reconstituting, limbs that were lupine shifting into human-like arms, human-like legs, the muzzle retracting, the jaw reworking, a face emerging as the fur pelt, which was luxurious and gray and white and brown, retracted into the skin.

When the change was complete, what stood in front of his sister . . . was naked in the night, with blond-streaked long hair and eyes that were unapologetic and unashamed by her nudity. As any animal would be.

His eyes locked on her high, proud breasts and traveled down her stomach to the cleft between her thighs.

The stirring deep within his gut was such a surprise, he looked at the front of his hips and frowned. Then he put a hand upon his own crotch.

He couldn't possibly be getting erect.

No offense to the female sex, but entities of the so-called "fairer" side of things generally did not interest him.

Blade refocused on the resplendent form before him — and what was going on between his thighs thickened even more.

Letting his head fall back, he stared at the overcast night sky. No stars to see, and he could have used the perspective of all those galaxies, all that space, all that epic scale.

Clearly, this was a confusion of some sort, he thought to himself. What sex he'd engaged in had always been with males; he liked submissives with big cocks. Therefore, there had to be another explanation for the fact that he was suddenly partially erect.

Maybe it had been the King's grip on his throat.

That had to be it. He'd come here directly after being vampire-handled. This arousal was obviously a delayed reaction to a male who had arresting amethyst eyes, and a mohawk that begged to be stroked, and a hand strong enough to powder a concrete block in its grip.

Following this very rational pep talk, Blade righted his head and refocused on the female —

Blink. Those beautiful bare breasts. *Blink.* Those tight, little hungry nipples. *Blink.* That bare cleft that was just begging for him to . . .

"Fuck," he growled into the darkness.

NINETEEN

About five hundred yards back from the summit, Daniel waited in the passenger seat of one of C.P. Phalen's SUVs — while the woman he loved went off into the darkness to meet a stranger. Under any other set of circumstances, he wouldn't have allowed it. He'd have gone first, all tip-of-the-spear macho.

And as recently as this morning, he would have been furious at being left behind like a child, all locked-in-safe against the big, bad wilderness.

Except here was the thing.

True, he was never going to be comfortable with Lydia going off into the dark, even with her other side being so incredibly powerful. But outside of that, even as his catalogue of you-can'ts glared at him, he remembered the way she had looked all undone and coming in their bed, her head back, her breasts tight and straining for his

264

mouth, her core hot and wet for him — for *him*.

She had cried out his name.

Three times. Because he had kept going after her first orgasm.

And when she had taken a shower, he had watched her, propped up against the head-board. Through the glass door, she had put a show on for him, soaping her body, leaning back against the marble wall, putting one hand between her legs and the other in her mouth as the water had gleamed over the contours of her curves.

So he wasn't bitter about not being able to walk all the way to the clearing. And he didn't care she'd locked him in for safety. And this female they were meeting? Maybe she helped them, maybe she didn't . . .

But he had been a man with his fucking *wife* —

Daniel frowned. "Oh, shit."

They weren't married.

As the thought occurred to him, he wondered how he'd missed that little detail somehow. Then again, he'd been pretty busy puking his guts out, having the cold sweats, and wondering whether, at any moment, the cocktail of poisons that were trying to cure him were going to overdo it and knock him off.

Well. Didn't he have something at the top of his list of things to do.

The smile that hit his face was nothing that he bothered to hide, and not just because there was no one around — and as his cheeks burned, he decided healing came in many different forms, didn't it: His medical landscape hadn't changed, but his mindset was improving big-time.

"No more cigarettes," he murmured as he ran his hand up and down the padded top of the center console.

No more Jack, either. It turned out what he needed to feel like himself was to make his woman feel like herself — and the rest fell into place.

As if the universe wanted to emphasize his new direction, Lydia walked out of the trees and into the trailhead's open area. She was gloriously naked and utterly unselfconscious about it, as if, to her, nudity on the mountain was second nature.

"My wolf," he purred.

But then the other woman came out, and not only was she clothed . . . she was fucking armed. Before he could think about it, he unlocked and opened his door and slid out with his own gun, his numb feet catching his weight.

The woman stopped where she was. She

was tall, at least five nine, with short hair, a lean face, and a body that was taut with muscle. In spite of the cold, which immediately started clawing into him in spite of his loose jacket, she was dressed only in a black muscle shirt — and she seemed wholly unaware it was fucking freezing out tonight.

"We going to play with metal?" she said in that low voice he recognized from the phone. "Or do this in a civilized manner."

Her weapons stayed strapped around her waist, but she put her hands right on her belt so they were within easy reach.

"I didn't know we were packing at this meeting," he tossed back.

"Then why did you bring your gun."

"I'm too weak to defend my woman otherwise. Can you really blame me?"

As his reply hit the airwaves, Lydia's head snapped around to him, and he was surprised at the admission himself. For however self-aware he had been, he had avoided acknowledging a lot, too.

That shit was done now.

In response, Alex Hess briefly looked down at the hardscrabble ground. "So when you said you were dying over the phone, it wasn't hyperbole. Or a metaphor for having a bad day."

267

"No, it wasn't." He lifted his chin and held out his hand to his woman. "I have cancer and not a lot of time left."

Lydia came over to him, and he sensed her tears sure as if he were looking at her. He kept his eyes on the soldier in front of them, however — because that was what this woman was. He'd spent enough time in special forces that like recognized like.

Plus she was as sure of herself as any other fighter he had ever seen.

"I'm going to throw some clothes on," Lydia murmured. Then, in a louder voice, she said, "As long as you two aren't going to make introductions in a target-practice kind of way?"

She clearly wasn't worried about the woman — and not only did Lydia have that thing where she made instant, valid assessments about people, but the two had walked back from the summit together. Side by side. Without tension.

And Miss Hess didn't seem bothered by the nudity. She was just staring at Daniel like she was trying to diagnose him.

"Are you a doctor?" he asked.

"No, I'm not." Her dark eyes narrowed on him. "I'm sorry I kept you waiting."

"We just got here, really."

"Not tonight. For all these months."

Over on the driver's side, a car door opened and there was some flapping and shuffling as Lydia covered her body. He supposed he should have been uncomfortable that she'd been naked in front of a total stranger, but if she wasn't bothered, why should he be?

"So what changed your mind, Alex?" He hobbled to the rear door of the Suburban and opened the back. "I'm going to have to sit down. 'Scuse me."

When he pivoted and tried to pop himself up onto the lip of the cargo hold, he fumbled — and was caught by the stranger with the weapons. But the woman didn't give him a lot of fussy sympathy or simpering compassion. She just hitched him up by the armpits, set him on the edge as he'd wanted to be, and stepped away. No muss, no fuss.

"So how long have you been in the military," he asked her.

Her eyes were gray, dark gray. Like her guns.

"I'm not. Well, not in the sense you mean."

"Me, either." When she cocked a brow, he figured as a dead man walking, he could afford to be more honest than he usually was. Ever was. "I'm also not in a formally recognized arm of the government."

"So how long do you have," she asked quietly.

When Daniel just cocked a brow back at her, she shrugged. "Running out of time means different things to different people."

"Two months," he answered. "Maybe. So why did you change your mind about meeting us."

Not a question, a demand. Because if she could walk around in his mental garden of delights, he expected some quid pro quo on her end.

"My husband, as you'd call him, almost died last night." As he recoiled, she nodded. "It was a reminder."

Lydia came around. "Of what, exactly?"

The woman, soldier — whatever she was — looked back and forth between the two of them. "That things can be taken away in the blink of an eye."

Lydia took Daniel's hand and squeezed it.

"Does she know what you are?" he asked in a quiet voice.

"Yeah," Alex Hess said. "I know she's wolven."

"But you're not one of them."

"No." Before he could ask her how she could help or what her connections were with Lydia's other side, the woman cut him off. "Exactly how did you get my number?"

■ ■ ■

She's a vampire, Lydia thought. *And something else.*

As she stood by Daniel and held his hand, she tested the air with her nose, teasing out and disregarding the scents of shampoo, deodorant, and fabric softener . . . so she could focus on what was under all that artificial surface stuff.

Vampire. Yes.

Since the spring, Lydia had run into them on the mountain from time to time — although rarely, because like wolven, they preferred to keep to their own. They always recognized her, however, just as she noted their presence, and invariably, there was eye contact over the heads of *Homo sapiens.*

But there was something else to the female. Something she had never sensed before.

"I got your number from a source," Daniel said in response to the question that was floating around them.

"What kind of source."

As the terse demand hit the cold air, Lydia appreciated the female's no-nonsense approach to conversation.

And she did bring up a question that was

271

worth asking.

"Just someone I know," Daniel hedged.

"Who is . . . ?"

"A person I once used as a source in a brokered deal for information — and no, I'm not going any further than that."

In a rush of memory, Lydia remembered the details of Daniel's previous life, before he'd met her, before the cancer had come for him: She recalled the terrible story of how his mom had thrown herself off a bridge when he'd been a teenager — and how he'd tried in vain to save her. After that, he had floated around under the radar of the system, a homeless kid who had stayed on the streets and learned to survive. Somewhere along the line, he'd joined the military . . . and after that, he'd worked for a clandestine agency, a shadow arm of the U.S. government tasked with protecting the human genome from bioengineering.

Which was how he'd come to the Wolf Study Project, and why he had lied to her in the beginning about who he really was and what his purpose in Walters had to be.

She could only guess what the information he'd brokered with the "source" for had been and why it had been required.

And no, she didn't want to know the contact he had used.

"Can you give me a name?" The female known as Alex Hess looked over at Lydia. "Or you?"

"He never told me," she replied. "And I never asked."

Daniel squeezed her hand. Then brought it up and kissed it. "I'll say this. I believe he, too, was . . . different. In some way."

"But how did you know he'd be a help?"

"After I met her" — he nodded at Lydia — "and learned what she was, I got sick. Or was diagnosed, whatever. I didn't know anyone like her, but then I thought of him . . . and figured he might have some contacts. That's how I got your number."

There was a pause. And then the female said in a dry voice, "Any chance he had a mohawk?"

"As a matter of fact . . . yes."

Alex Hess rolled her eyes. "He's a god-damn busybody. But what I can't figure out . . ."

"Is what?" Lydia asked roughly.

"I don't know any wolven, either. Yeah, sure, I'm sorry about . . . what's going to happen to you both in a couple of months. I just don't understand why I'm some kind of connector for you? I'm just being honest. A dying human, a wolven, and me? There just aren't any intersections here."

273

As Lydia lowered her head, Daniel stroked her arm. "Looks like all three of us are confused."

Lydia was trying to think of something to say when from out of the corner of her eye, movement registered in the trees. Flaring her nostrils, she got nothing in terms of scent. Then again, the wind was blowing from the opposite direction, so there was no way to sniff out who or what it was.

But someone — or something — was watching them.

"We've got company," she said quietly. "Right *there.*"

TWENTY

Down in C.P.'s laboratory, things had gotten quite quiet, the hustle and bustle of researchers dimmed down, only a few stragglers passing by outside of her patient room. Although what time was it, midnight? She checked her watch. Then slipped off the exam table and went over to the computer at the desk. After she signed in, she glanced at the clock at the bottom right-hand corner of the monitor. 12:17 a.m.

But who was counting.

Turning away from the blue glow, she tucked the two halves of the loose fleece she was wearing around her bare upper body and paced back over to the exam table. Then she returned to the desk. Went back to the table.

Glancing down at her bare feet, she noted the pressure marks from her high heels, the bunions, the callouses. Wearing stilettos was hard on the toes and heels, but mostly where it didn't show . . . on the balls of one's footsies.

When she'd arrived down at the facility, she'd had no intentions of getting into a hospital johnny. No, thank you. She'd come in fully clothed as she always was, ripping the door open with her chin held high and her professional facade firmly in place. It had only been after Gus had shut them together in this exam room that things had gotten undone. And not just her jacket and blouse.

Goddamn, you were never more naked than fully clothed in front of a doctor — when you knew something was wrong with you.

On his side, Gus had been amazing. To keep down the chatter among his fellow researchers, he had been the one who'd drawn her blood, taken her vitals, and run the tests. He had also asked her more questions than she could count about her medical history — and when she'd gotten cold and started to pull her jacket back on over her blood-draw sites and the electrodes he'd stuck all over her, he'd taken off the fleece he had on and draped it around her.

She hadn't zipped it up. But like that made it any less intimate? At least she had kept her bra on the whole time.

C.P. checked the door. Still closed. No footsteps coming down the hall to it, either.

Tilting her head to the side, she brought up the fleece's sleeve, closed her eyes, and drew in a deep breath.

What cologne did he use? It was incredible —

"Did I spill something?"

C.P. gasped and dropped her arm. "I'm sorry?"

"On the sleeve?"

She blinked at him stupidly and tried to translate the words he'd spoken —

"Ah, no." She straightened her shoulders. "You didn't."

"I just washed it, actually." He went over to the rolling chair and sat down. "Good thing I don't like the cold, right? Otherwise, we would have had to wrap you up in layers of lab coats."

"What kind of car do you drive?" she blurted as she sat down in the chair next to the desk.

Annnd where had that come from, she wondered.

Gus paused as he logged out of her sign-in and put in his own. "I — ah. I drive a Tesla?"

"Oh."

He sat back. "Is that a problem?"

"Oh, no. It's great." She refolded his fleece over her torso, wrapping it all around herself. "Really."

"Don't tell me . . ."

As he refocused on the screen, she frowned. "What."

His fingers hit the keys in a hard pattern. "You're a car guy, aren't you."

"I'm a woman who likes cars, yes."

"You're a motor head, I mean. Who doesn't approve of electric cars because you're a dinosaur who refuses to give a shit about the environment."

C.P. thinned her lips. "Guess you've got me dead to rights. Tell me, all that electricity you're using, are you going to ignore the amount of fossil fuel that's used to produce it?"

"You're really playin' like that. After gas-guzzlers have ruined the —"

"And anything that needs engine sounds piped through the speakers to —"

Both of them shut up at the same time. And she wasn't sure who started laughing first. Maybe it was him, probably it was her, but either way, all of a sudden, she was wheezing and wiping her eyes while he was holding his belly, the release of tension like a sea change in her, in him.

When things had run their course and

they were both sitting back in their seats and smiling, she was the one who refocused them.

"So," she said on a sigh, "what do you think, Doc."

Gus cleared his throat and brought up a couple of different reports, minimizing the windows so he could look at all of them at once. As his dark eyes went back and forth, it was like he was trying to read tea leaves in the numerical values in those columns, and though she was sure to know what some of the results meant, she wasn't going to look.

Instead, she focused on his face, noting everything from the way his lashes curled up and his brows arched . . . to the cut of his jaw . . . and the curve of his lower lip. He'd had his ears pierced on both sides, but he never wore earrings so the holes were just pinpricks that were slightly darker. And he had a chicken pox scar on his cheek.

She found herself wondering what he'd been like as a teenager, all lanky limbs and dreams of basketball. He'd told her once, in an offhand way, that he'd wanted to be Kareem Abdul-Jabbar when he was younger.

No wait . . . he hadn't told that to her. He'd made the comment to someone else, when they'd been riding the elevator in a group.

Gus turned his whole body toward her, swiveling his chair around. And even though they had known each other professionally for a couple of years, and she trusted him as much as she trusted anybody, she was suddenly scared of him. But that was more what he might say, wasn't it.

His face was a mask, no emotion showing.

"Tell me," she said in her best C.P. Phalen voice.

"I think you're a good candidate for Vita."

As C.P. released the breath she had been unaware of holding, she couldn't tell what exactly she was relieved by: That she was the guinea pig they'd been looking for . . . or that, as a patient, she might have a last-ditch option that could, possibly, give her a little more time — because she knew better than to think in terms of a cure. Not after childhood cancer, then the two bouts of the AML before this moment.

Time. That was all she wanted.

"Yeah," Gus said. "That's what we all want."

"I didn't know I'd spoken that out loud." She gave an awkward laugh. "Anyway. Good. This is what we want, right? This is . . . a good outcome."

As he blew out a breath, he put his elbows on his knees and leaned in to her. The triangulated pose emphasized the size of his shoulders and his biceps, and for a self-defined geek — she'd heard him in the break room calling himself that — he was in better shape than most college guys. Then again, with the amount of Coke he sucked down on a regular basis? He had to burn all that energy off somehow, and evidently that would still be on the basketball court. Or at some gym.

When he stayed quiet, she frowned. "Okay, spill it. What isn't going to work."

"You know what my concerns are. All along, I've worried about what it's going to do to the liver. If we get the leukemia under control, but leave you on dialysis? That's not what we're after."

Her eyes went to his hands. They were blunt-tipped, his fingers squared off, his nails precisely trimmed and totally clean. He was lean enough that the veins that ran down into his hands were evident, and for some reason, that was sexy as hell.

Maybe because it made her wonder how tight his abs were.

"Anything else you're concerned about?" she prompted.

"Where are you with all the negotiations?

I know you went somewhere this morning? Can you tell me anything?"

"No, I can't."

His mouth thinned. "Well, what do we do if you crash? What if you can't be . . . C.P. Phalen anymore?"

She opened her mouth. Closed it. "I don't know. We'll have to cross that bridge if we get to it."

"Do you have a second-in-command?"

"On the business side? No. I'm a solo operator — it cuts down on the conversation."

He laughed in a short rush. "Why am I not surprised." Then he got serious again. "Okay, so as your oncologist, I'm going to go into my spiel here. You need to be prepared for side effects, some of which may be debilitating. I'm going to ask that you stay down here when we administer the protocol —"

"Why can't I just be upstairs in my home."

"Your bedroom is not a clinical space."

"Yes, it is —"

"Look, I'm not going to argue with you, or remind you that we will be introducing a novel agent into your body that has never been in a human before."

She pointed to the screen. "Is there anything else we need to discuss with the tests?"

"No, MD Anderson did an extensive workup when you were there two weeks ago. Is that where you went today?"

"I did go to Houston. But I didn't follow through on my appointment."

"Ah, yes, the email I received from you this morning. Was that when you decided you were done with the conventional treatment? Or did your team at Anderson pull the plug earlier?"

C.P. got to her feet and thought about the way she'd pulled out of Gunnar Rhobes's penthouse conference room.

"My doctors told me I couldn't have any more treatment a day or so ago."

Actually, Gus had walked in just after she'd hung up the phone with her team there. He'd assumed her distraction was from her having seen Daniel's results, but it had been her own medical data that had rattled her — although of course, she'd felt awful for Lydia and Daniel given their own situation.

So much bad news lately.

"My oncologist in Houston had suggested a couple different clinical trials." She shrugged. "But after Daniel gave his final no, I figured, why not do my own for Vita? And now I'm going to suggest we go up to the house so you can see exactly how my

283

bedroom is decorated — and I'm not talking about the drapes."

She reached for the door.

"Who else knows you're doing this?" he asked as he looked up at her.

"No one. And no one can know. I need to be anonymous, or the corporations I'm negotiating with will see this as the biggest conflict of interest since Pharma Bro."

Gus stared at the screen for a little longer. Then he logged off and stood up, too.

"You need to have someone in charge of your business affairs. If something goes wrong with you, I'm going to lose everything I've worked for — and hell, that may happen anyway with whatever terms you're negotiating."

She thought of all those stock options that were part of his employment contract. And then there was Vita, herself, the culmination of his life's work.

For all she didn't want to die, she hadn't really considered the practical implications of having no will. No clear heirs. No successor for her business.

C.P. focused on Gus. "I'll take care of it."

Back up at the trailhead on the mountain's summit, Xhex palmed her gun and trained it just past the front fender of the blacked-

284

out SUV. Narrowing her eyes, she searched the dark contours of the pine trees and the boulders — but she saw nothing.

Just as she was thinking about making some kind of threatening announcement, Lydia, the wolven, had the brass balls to simply walk forward.

As Daniel went to get up from the tailgate, Xhex shook her head. "I've got her."

She expected an argument. And respected the fuck out of the guy that he didn't waste his time or hers. He just nodded and stayed where he was.

Xhex jogged a little to catch up to the female, but then she remained in the rear. There was something about the way the wolven scanned the landscape — it was different, like there were other senses being called into service, other instincts being relied upon. Meanwhile, on Xhex's side, she was scenting everything she could and getting a big fat zero. Nothing moving, nothing that tipped her off —

"Stop," Xhex said.

The wolven instantly froze.

Xhex looked down to the ground and pointed. "Here. They were standing right here."

She dropped to her haunches and took out her cell phone, triggering the beam. The

285

footprints were obvious but not distinctive, big enough to be a male's yet nothing of particular note when it came to treads or a heel. Running the little light up the closest trunk, she saw no disturbance in the pine tree's bark pattern or its branches.

Just as she was about to suggest they go back, Lydia lowered her whole body to the ground. Planting her arms on either side of the prints, she leaned down and put her nose close to the markings.

"What is it," Xhex said as the female straightened and sat back on her heels.

The wolven looked over. "It smells . . . like you."

"I'm sorry?"

"The scent. It's like yours."

Xhex glanced around. The Brotherhood, she thought. Of course they'd followed her here — after what had happened to John Matthew last night, everyone was still jumpy. But they were clearly going to be discreet about it.

"I know who it is," she said as she stood back up. "Who followed me, who's checking up on me, I mean."

"Is there a problem?"

"No, just backup I didn't ask for." Xhex wondered where they were hiding out. "But I appreciate them looking after me."

"It's good to have friends." The wolven got to her feet as well. "You're lucky."

Xhex focused on the female. "What's your name?"

"Lydia." A hand was extended. "Lydia Susi. It's nice to meet you, Alex."

"That's not my real name." She shook what was offered. "Xhex. That's who I am."

A true smile came back at her, the kind that lit up those eyes. "Nice to meet you."

Don't do it, Xhex told herself.

Except . . . of course she read the female's grid.

"Oh, shit," she murmured.

"What? Are you all right?"

How do I explain, Xhex wondered.

"Ah, sorry. Nothing — I just . . . I know your man's sick. And that's got to be fucking awful."

"It is . . . a living nightmare. I'm just muddling through, really — I worry about him, he worries about me. It's a circle of madness that spins faster and faster as time gets tighter and tighter. I get these flares of hope and then we grate against each other and then . . . we find a connection. There's no consistency to anything other than the terminal diagnosis."

If only it were Rehv stalking around in the shadows, Xhex thought. He could tell them

287

all why in the hell he —

All at once, an image of the entity Xhex had run into on the trail from before crossed her mind . . . sure as if it had been implanted into her skull.

"I think I know why we're all here," she said with a kind of defeat.

Blade, that bastard, had told her to come here, not Rehv. Rehv might have been the conduit . . . but what her brother had set her up for was the destiny. Was this her journey? Just to pass along what she had seen of that glowing entity? If so, being a messenger wasn't a tough job — except what the fuck did it have to do with the nightmares from the past that had haunted her for so long?

Although not anymore. She hadn't woken up screaming during the day for months.

"Your Daniel told me he was worried about leaving you all alone," she heard herself say to the wolven. "So there really is no medical hope for him, is there."

Lydia took a deep breath. "No, there isn't."

Xhex narrowed her eyes as the female's grid shifted: She was lying. "None?"

When a quick shake of the head came back at her, Xhex left that alone. "Well, he's concerned that he's going to die, and there's going to be no one who will help you through your grief."

As she spoke, it was strange. The voice was hers . . . but the words felt like someone else's, like an energy was flowing through her to the female.

"You need to come to the mountain," Xhex said. "This is the place where you will find your support."

Or more like, it will find you.

Lydia put her hand on the base of her throat. Then she began to blink quicker.

Xhex reached out and touched the female's shoulder. "You're supposed to be here. I think that's why you and I were put together through your man. You need to go and find the light. You need to hear the message that there is something here for you, and it will be your solace when you feel like there is no peace to be found anywhere. The mountain has something to tell you — just like it had something to tell me. The light . . . is the key."

Lydia sniffled and wiped her eyes. Then wrapped her arms around herself. "How . . . did it speak to you?"

"Look, I realize that you don't know me, so there's no frame of reference. But when I tell you I'm not into the whole divine-message thing, you've got to believe me."

Xhex rubbed her short hair, running her palm back and forth over her skull. "I came here one night, not knowing what to expect. I walked up the trail and this . . . I don't know what the hell it was . . . appeared in front of me. I didn't understand it then, but the only way this moment here, between you and me, makes any fucking sense, is that I'm supposed to tell you to come up and find it, too."

Jesus, she sounded nuts. Flat-out insane.

"You have to believe me," she said with some urgency.

"Oh, I already know what the mountain has to offer." The female glanced out toward where they had come from, where the summit was. "I know where my home is. That's not the problem. It's imagining being up here, being anywhere, without Daniel . . . that's what is killing me."

Xhex thought back to the night before, all those hours when she'd been sure that she was going to lose John, that maybe he'd already left her in all the ways that counted.

She was not a hugger, not by a long shot — and certainly not with people she didn't know. But there was no way she wasn't going to reach out.

With a heavy soul, she embraced the stranger in front of her.

"I'm so sorry," Xhex said as she closed her eyes.

"Thank you," the female — Lydia — said.

They were standing together, in commiseration, when something moved in the shadows once again. But Xhex just ignored it as the scent of a deer came over on the breeze.

Funny how helping someone else made you feel like things were going to be okay in your own life. Not that there was anything wrong in her own, at the moment. She really was fine — her mate had survived his injuries, and at the end of the night, what mattered outside of that?

Nothing. Nothing else fucking counted.

And maybe she had given this female and her tragedy a little direction.

It still didn't feel like enough to justify all the carrying on, but as a mortal, who the hell was she to judge.

Twenty-One

Back at the Phalen estate, Gus walked into his boss's bedroom — and was not surprised. Well, he was surprised he was in her private, sleepy-time space, sure. But the decor? He might as well have been in her cavernous front lobby or that dining room or any of the other halls or staircases in the place: Everything was black and white as a chessboard, and the furniture arranged with a decorator's eye, no mistakes in scale or arrangement.

Nothing personal to any of it, either.

His eyes went to the bed. It was a king, with draping on the wall framing a huge headboard so that it looked like the ceiling was melting and pooling onto the floor.

Did she bring that blond guard here, he thought idly. *Did she —*

"So here's where the magic happens," C.P. said dryly.

As she went over to the bedside table and

triggered something, he wondered if she realized she still had his fleece on. Probably. She'd zipped it up.

And since when did he go back to being a fifteen-year-old and liking the look of a piece of his clothing on a girl?

He needed to get a grip —

"What the fuck," he breathed.

The entire headboard dropped down to reveal a critical care setup, all of the monitoring equipment on swivel arms that could be extended out.

"And the supplies are here." She went over to what he'd assumed was a bathroom door and opened things. "There's room for more, too."

Gus walked toward her and — "Fucking hell, Phalen. Why don't you just move the whole lab up here?"

Squeezing by her, he entered a room that was big as the row house he'd been raised in. Not only were there portable X-rays and ultrasound machines, there was —

"Even an autoclave?" he muttered as he went deeper through the ER-worthy equipment.

"Anything you want. Anything I need. And there's a surgical light that drops down from the ceiling out there."

All of the machines and computers were

first-rate and ready to go, and the nursing supplies were worthy of a teaching hospital's larder, from the bandages to the IV bags.

"Who set all this up?" he asked as he put his hand on an EKG machine.

"I did."

He pivoted and looked at her. She was half Phalen-ized, the bottom of her professional with those heels and slacks, but the top part was work-from-home casual in his baggy-ass fleece. But hey, the hair was back in order.

So maybe the look was three-fifths a Phalen.

And hey, she'd be perfect for a waist-down Zoom call.

"This is not going to work," he said. As she opened her mouth to argue, he put his palm up. "It's not that there isn't a lot here, it's the staffing. If something goes down, I'm going to need help. Unless you think I have an extra set of hands hidden on me? What if you go into cardiac arrest, for example?"

"We'll get private nurses. There's a suite right next door that sleeps three in a very comfortable arrangement."

"With critical care training?" He noped the shit out of that. "I want my people and they're downstairs. It's in your best interest, and if you can't recognize that, it's my job as your doctor to insist on your standard of care."

"So bring them up here."

"That's not feasible and you know it. I've got doctors I want on this, too."

He could tell by the way she crossed her arms over her chest she was spoiling to give him a fight. So he went back out into her bowling alley of a bedroom. While she formulated some kind of defense against being reasonable, he wandered around. No pictures. No paintings. Another modern sculpture that looked like a high schooler with a power drill had hit a block of marble with everything they were worth.

The bathroom was across the way and he leaned into it. Nothing on the counter. No makeup. No brushes. No hair spray. Not even a towel. And the pair of sinks with their black metal faucets gleamed.

He couldn't resist. He went over to the shower and opened the smoky glass door. One bar of soap, and a twinsie set of shampoo and conditioner with some fancy French name on it.

"So you actually do live here," he muttered as he turned around.

"Fine," she said over at the bathroom's door. "I'll do this down in the lab for as

295

long as it's medically necessary. After that? I come here — but there has to be some way to manage the talk. I don't want any distractions in the lab or talk outside of it. The work has to continue and there can be no leaks."

"Those people have been working on a secret drug for how long?" he said dryly. "You think they're going to break their confidentiality agreements now?"

As she looked away with annoyance, he shook his head. She'd known all along that she was going to get to this critical juncture, when her disease tipped the scales and started to get away from her. She had planned everything, that bedroom out there a magnum opus of medical support no doubt set up as soon as she'd landed with all her one-note tables and chairs and her stupid-looking, pretentious sculptures.

Gus went over to her and put out his palm. "My rules. I'm just trying to make sure you survive this."

In a sick way, he enjoyed how hard it was for her to submit. But that was the asshole in him who liked to fuck with people — and also maybe the romantic who felt like she was cheating on him with that guard. Which was nuts.

Somehow, though, if she'd been banging a

guy from outside of the operation, it wouldn't have bothered him so much.

Or maybe it would have.

Just before she shook what he was putting to her, he retracted his forearm. "One more thing."

"What."

"When it's just you and me? I'm calling you Cathy."

Well, wasn't Gus St. Claire full of demands tonight, C.P. thought.

And she was beyond done with it.

"That hasn't been my name for a decade. Maybe two. So I'm not answering to it."

"Okay, Cathy."

His dark stare seemed to bore through her, and although she was the last person to drop out of a game of eye chicken, she did look away first.

"And of course you're going to do what you want," she muttered.

"You got that right." In her peripheral vision, that hand of his extended forward again. "Always."

"Really?" She cocked a brow at him. "Like this is a deal?"

"Don't kid yourself. We were in a partnership before, but this is all new territory for you and me." He tilted in over his lean hips.

"Unless you need a reminder, we rushed Vita's development and the testing we did on those wolves was limited in scope. This is the Wild fucking West and your body is the battleground."

Her gaze lowered to his chest. The t-shirt of the day was Schoolhouse Rock!, the bill who was going to Capitol Hill chugging up the steps, looking over his shoulder.

"Try not to let me die, Gus," she said in a weak voice.

"That's the plan."

As they shook, she was aware that she didn't want to let go of the man's hand. And then he didn't drop the hold, either.

"You going to tell your fuckboy about all this," he said in a low voice.

"Who?" she blurted. When she realized who he was talking about, she broke the connection and stepped back. "No, I'm not telling anyone."

"Not even your parents?"

"They're dead, so they're not answering their phones." She crossed her arms again. "And no, I have no brothers or sisters. It's just me."

Gus mirrored her pose and shook his head. "Not anymore. You're not alone as long as I'm around."

C.P.'s breath caught. Funny how someone

could say something and rip your defenses clean away. Then again, did she have any left when it came to her new oncologist? After the last however many hours when he did everything but give her a Pap smear?

"Thank you," she said roughly.

"No problem, Cathy. I got you."

"*Please* don't call me that."

"Why? Too close to home?" He took a step toward her. "You need to get ready for what's ahead, and wasting time with me putting on some bullshit act is energy you and I are not going to have to spare."

Glancing down, she focused on her stilettos. "My feet are killing me."

"So take off those fucking shoes, woman."

She kicked one and then the other across the marble floor, and when she was flat on her soles, she looked back up at Gus. He was taller than she remembered — no, that wasn't right. He'd always been that height. She was the one who was different.

As they stared into each other's eyes, she was struck by a need she was unfamiliar with. Yes, it was about sex, but there was a lot under the lust. Her mind was in a tortured twist and her emotions were right along with it . . . but Gus had always gotten her attention, ever since the moment she had first seen him presenting a paper on immunotherapy at a Stanford symposium almost a decade ago.

Back then, he had been a youngster new on the scene with all kinds of iconoclastic ideas. This had made him a target for some . . . a goal for others. She'd been the latter.

"Can I ask you something," he said in a deep voice.

"Yes." And wasn't that an answer to more than just the question he'd asked.

Gus glanced around, which gave her a good chance to look at his profile again. He was handsome in the conventional sense, but with his hair and his clothes, he was also attractive in an unconventional way. Add to that all his intelligence? He was epic, and she had ignored that fact for so long.

"What are you going to ask me?" she breathed.

"Where do you really live?" When she blinked in confusion, he motioned around. "You haven't moved into this house."

"What are you talking about? Or have you somehow failed to notice all the furniture?"

"Furniture doesn't count. I could have only a folding chair and a futon at my place, and it would still be clear who lives there. This shit?" He pointed out into the bedroom. "It's a stage set."

That she had braced herself for a sex question she'd really wanted to answer, only to have him throw something else out there, something that didn't matter, made her a little pissy. But he kept going before she could cold lab some reply to his residential-address probe.

"I just want you to tell me the truth," he said. "You created Vita for yourself, didn't you. You went through your last round of chemo three years ago — right about the time you hired me and this all started at the smaller lab. When we relocated here after the first of this year, I'm guessing that you didn't bother getting personal about this house because you didn't know how much time you had. Had you started to feel symptomatic with the AML then?"

C.P. wasn't about to go into her frailties, not when he was imminently going to see so many of them. "Are you really going to get judgmental about my trying to engineer my last chance? Fine, the next time you're drowning, by all means, tell that lifeguard to fuck off when they jump in to save you —"

"I don't blame you." He put his palms up. "Not at all. I just wish you had a home to go to, not a hotel. And maybe . . . maybe I'm trying to make sense of everything up front so if things don't go the way we plan, I can find some peace in the failure."

As C.P.'s brows popped, she reached out and squeezed his forearm. "If I die . . . if I don't make it, Gus, it's not your fault. Do you understand —"

"Oh, yeah." He shook his head. "I mean, I know that. Come on, I've been in this research and development racket for —"

"*Gus.* Listen to me." She waited until his eyes swung back to her. "If I die because of our Vita, it is not on you. You just keep going with the research. I'll be a stepping stone, and you put your foot right on my grave and get to the next level up. Do you hear me? And I promise, you will know where Vita ends up — and I will make sure it's the right place. As good an oncologist as you are? I'm just as good at the negotiating table. You can trust me to take care of your work on the business side — and your career. I'm not going to fuck you like that."

He glanced away again. "I'm not worried about that."

Bullshit, she thought. But she let him lie out loud.

"And the next thing I don't want you to worry about is me." She stepped closer to him. "I'm a big girl and I've had a lot of experience with cancer treatments. This is going to go where it does — and look at it this way. I'm not just putting my money where my mouth is — I'm putting my life on it. At least if I die on my own protocol, I've got some integrity, right?"

Gus exhaled as if he were letting a burden go. Or trying to.

Then he looked at her . . . and brushed the fall of blond hair back from her face.

When they stayed where they were, she knew he was going to kiss her. And she wasn't going to stop him.

Leaning into his body, she curled her hands around the backs of his upper arms and parted her mouth. As her lungs got tight, an anticipation that was about so much more than mouth-to-mouth contact took hold in her gut.

Gus stroked her hair again and searched her face as if he were measuring her features, memorizing them.

Then he tilted forward. And placed a chaste kiss on her forehead.

Stepping back, he said in a sharp voice, "I'm going to repeat two scans tomorrow morning before I'm prepared to administer. MD Anderson did them, but I want them on my equipment. We'll do the infusion tomorrow night after the majority of people sign out."

As he went to leave, and not just the bathroom, she spoke up. "Gus —"

Without turning around, he held his hand up and said over his shoulder, "You have men for fucking. I'm not going to be one of them."

But then he paused in the doorway and glanced at her. "But what I will do for you is be the best goddamn doctor on the planet. That you can count on."

He left in a hurry, striding out and not looking back. The close of her bedroom door was loud, even though it was just a click of the fixture.

When the tears came, they were hot and burned her cheeks. She didn't bother wiping them off. Who was going to see, anyway?

And the fact that there was no one around her in this house filled with people was the one commentary on her life that she worked so hard to avoid dwelling on. But at the end of the day, everyone died alone, didn't they. Even if there was a crowd surrounding your bedside, no one ultimately could reach you as you took your last breath.

At least . . . that was what she told herself as she put her stilettos back on.

TWENTY-TWO

Back up on Deer Mountain, Blade knew he had to get the fuck away from his sister and that shifter. The former was going to sense his grid at some point — she was just too distracted at the moment — and the latter was so observant that even a subtle tilt in his balance had tipped her off to his new location by the SUV.

He should move very far away. He should resume his search for the steel-capped tunnels that led to the underground lab, the one that should have been destroyed back in April.

He should set his charges and leave to watch the light show from a peak across the valley.

And then he should rest his weary head.

Instead, he dematerialized farther away from Xhex and the wolven, to a point back by the rear of the blocky vehicle, and as he resumed his corporeal form, he narrowed his eyes to improve their focus — even though he could see just fine. The issue was that he was having a problem understanding *what* he was seeing: Daniel Joseph, Blade's former soldier, was supposedly dead.

And from the looks of the guy, he might as well be.

The previously fit pain in the ass was sitting on the back of the SUV, looking like he was still recovering from some serious wounds, six months after the skirmishes on this very mountain. Except that wasn't it, was it. As the wind shifted, the scent of the human man drifted over to him, and Blade flared his nostrils. When he caught what was on the air, he refused the conclusion outright. Except there was no denying it.

Daniel Joseph was in fact dying. The scent of the tumors inside of him was obvious — and it explained the withered state of his body.

Blade took a step forward. And another. And sure enough, as he intended, one of his boots landed on a dry stick and snapped it. In spite of his frailties, Daniel was on the sound, swinging that gun around as he carefully shifted off the back of the vehicle and onto legs that were clearly unreliable.

"I thought you were dead," Blade said in

a low voice.

Daniel's facial expression didn't change and he did not lower his weapon. He did weave a little in his boots, however, proof that he was affected by his surprise visitor.

"And it looks as if you've gotten yourself sick," Blade tacked on.

Knowing that there was little time, that the females would be returning soon, Blade burrowed into the man's mind and sifted through Daniel's memories. One thing hadn't changed. Of all the humans whose thoughts he'd intruded into, the soldier gave him the most resistance —

"You're a patient then." Blade laughed in a low purr. "I send you in to destroy the lab, and instead, you use it. Why did I not see this coming?"

The obvious answer was because he'd never caught the scent of the cancer before, but then he hadn't been looking for it. Amazing how you could miss things when they didn't fit into your confirmation bias: He'd been primarily concerned with Daniel betraying the mission. He hadn't been aware there were any other fate vectors to manipulate.

And there was another now.

This human with the bad prognosis . . . was with the wolven. The love and the struggle with her were all over his grid, consuming him as much as the illness was, a different kind of cancer to eat him alive.

Plus her scent was on him.

Well, wasn't this a night for surprises. And the simplest solution was to implant into Daniel Joseph's mental chaos a clear and present imperative to blow the lab up, turning the patient into a Trojan horse. The man was the perfect ticking time bomb, accepted by the doctors and staff in the lab, and fully knowledgeable about the layout. Work of a moment.

Except . . . a mind under the kind of stress his was? Bad platform for instruction. When influencing a human, when getting them to do your bidding, stability in the receptacle was required. Daniel had been extraordinarily stable previously, tied to no one, with nothing but an amorphous need to destroy things and a fine shooting arm defining him. He'd been a weapon Blade had pointed at his will, and Daniel had never known the extent of the influence poured into his brain. Even when it became clear the weapon had fallen in love with a woman, Blade had thought nothing of it — other than using the emotional attachment to his own benefit.

As any *symphath* would do.

Except he had not known . . . exactly what it was that the man had fallen for.

A wolven. Who was utterly captivating.

"I have to go," Blade lied. "I think you'll agree it's best for everybody that our reintroduction is something kept between ourselves."

"Wha—"

Daniel Joseph, former operative, winced and put his hand to his head. As he did so, Blade cursed himself. Xhex had the ability to read those *Homo sapiens* minds, too. And if the patient was looking like he had a sharp stinger in his frontal lobe, there was a fair chance she'd probe the reason why.

And then Blade's cover would be blown.

She had her own issues, however, so perhaps he would get lucky.

"Bye for now, Daniel Joseph," he murmured as he stepped back into the darkness. "Rest assured, I won't be far."

Lydia returned to the SUV alone, the vampire having dematerialized off into the night — which was a little freaky to be around. Although given what Lydia was capable of? The fact that a person could just be somewhere one minute and gone the next shouldn't have been that alarming.

Yet it was.

309

As she hotfooted it back to Daniel, snippets of the conversation played ticker tape in her mind, the memory flares precise because the interaction had just happened, and yet resonant because of her situation —

"Daniel!" she called out as she came around the rear of the vehicle.

He was right where she'd left him, but he'd slumped to the side and had his hand up to his head.

"What's going on?" She rushed over and straightened him. "Talk to me —"

"I'm fine." He batted at her hands. "I'm just — I've got a headache all of a sudden."

"Can you stand?"

"Yeah, of course."

The bravado was lost quick as he shifted off the back bumper and lurched into her. Gathering him up, she helped him over to the front passenger side, belted him in, and raced to get behind the wheel.

She should have known, she thought as she started the engine and put them in drive. Things never stayed on the level for very long with them.

Hitting the gas, she had a thought that she should stay up here and just find one of the access hatches into the lab. She could take him directly to the doctors that way — except no. After the showdown back in the spring, C.P.'s security team had sealed all the tunnels that ran from the mountain's flanks into the lab. The only way to enter now was through her house, which was like Fort Knox.

She had no choice but to take the long way home.

The trail they'd used to go up to the summit was the road-like one specifically cut and maintained to ensure access of heavy machinery to the highest elevation. She'd been the one to insist that the Wolf Study Project, which was responsible for the acreage, create the emergency access for use in the event any hikers were injured.

And now she was using it for just that purpose. Not that Daniel was a hiker.

"The headache's getting better," he said as he sat up a little higher in the bucket seat. "I don't know what it was."

"Okay, but we'll still hustle on down."

He turned his head on the rest and looked at her. "Well, there's one piece of good news."

"What's that?"

In his best Arnold Schwarzenegger voice, he said, "It's nought a toomah."

Lydia blurted out a laugh. "That's not funny."

"Sure enough is, and we have the scans to

311

prove it." He smiled at her. "Hey, maybe one of the undisclosed side effects of carboplatin is a sense of humor. I'm going to try some more jokes out. Knock, knock."

Lydia pumped the brakes to keep them from gaining too much momentum. Then she jerked the steering wheel to the left to avoid a rock in the middle of the lane.

"Who's there."

After a pause, he said, "Guess not."

"Guess not who?"

"No, I mean, I guess not on the jokes. I got nothing."

She glanced over at him and smiled. "We'll work on it together. Take a master class in jokology."

"Sounds good."

When she looked back again, he had closed his eyes and parted his lips. And for a split second, she pictured him in a bed somewhere, maybe in their room at C.P.'s, maybe in the clinic, his lids shut, his breathing slow, too slow.

Until it stopped altogether.

As her mind spun out over old familiar terrors, she distracted herself by thinking of the way her life had been before, her days spent counting and monitoring the wolf population on the mountain, dealing with the WSP board — which C.P. Phalen had been head of — filing for grants for money. Dealing with her boss. Working with Candy, the receptionist. There had been stress, of course, but nothing like what Daniel was going through. Things had been so much simpler then, back before her boss, Peter Wynne, had been killed . . . by their veterinarian. Who had been working with C.P. to test the Vita prototype on the wolf population — and prepared to betray them all.

At least until he had gone to the resort site across the valley to set an IED, so he could pretend to blow himself up and take off for parts unknown.

She and Daniel had come up on him and stopped him.

After which he had gone home and blown his own head off with a shotgun.

Between one blink and the next, Lydia remembered walking in on him.

"It's going to be fine," she blurted, unsure exactly what she was talking about.

"What is," Daniel murmured.

"Everything."

Fifteen minutes later, just as they bottomed out at the trailhead's parking area, Daniel announced, "You know, I really am feeling better."

"Good." Crossing the vacant gravel square, she hit the brakes and looked both ways at the county road. "But maybe we check in with Gus anyway?"

"It's after midnight."

"He told us to call anytime."

"Let's wait a little?" He put his hand on her arm. "I swear, if I feel weird at all again, I'll tell you. No bullshit."

"Okay." She forced a smile. "It's a deal."

As she hit the gas and got them on the rural route, he said, "What did you talk to her about? Xhex, that is. You guys were gone for a while."

"Ah, nothing much?" She slowed down as they came into a turn, her eyes searching the shoulders for deer. "I mean, she was kind enough. I liked her. She told me to go to the mountain and I know part of my heart is always going to be there. I'm just not sure why she's so significant."

He cursed. "I don't think it helped as much as I hoped."

"You never know what comes of anything, though." She covered his hand with her own. "I mean, I thought I was hiring a handyman and look where it led me."

For a split second, there was a pause, but then, like he'd resolved to focus on what positives there were, Daniel smiled — and in the glow from the dashboard lights, he looked more as he had before.

"I love you," she said.

He stretched over the console. "I love you, too."

They kissed briefly and resettled in their separate seats, and as she refocused on the road ahead, she wrapped the normalcy of the quick contact around her like a shield.

Hold it close. Keep it close.

Beat the demons away with it.

By the time she piloted them through the gates of the Phalen estate, she was a little less worried about Daniel — although it was still a relief to pull up to the mansion's porte cochere, walk him directly back to their bedroom, and lay him out on their bed. The way his eyes closed so quickly caused a ripple of worry, but it was nothing compared to how she'd felt as she'd come around the back of the SUV to find him slumped and holding his head.

"I'm going to go park the SUV in the garage."

"Okay," he murmured as he curled on his side and tucked his arm under his head. "Take your time."

As he repositioned his cap, she leaned down and tugged it a little more into place. "I won't be long."

Lydia left their bedroom and had her phone in her hand even before she closed their door behind herself. But she waited to make the call until she was out in the grand foyer —

A soft chiming sound stopped her, and as it came again, in a precise rhythm to what was being piped into her ear, she pivoted around and looked up the stairs.

"Speak of the doctor," she said as she lowered her iPhone.

Gus didn't seem to hear her, but just as she was going to say his name, he paused in his descent and glanced down. "Oh. Hey."

He seemed to have no clue his phone was ringing, so she held up her own. "I was just calling you."

"You were?" He took out his cell and frowned at the screen. "Oh, so you are. Sorry."

What was he doing upstairs, she wondered.

"Everything okay?" he asked as he continued down and stepped off the last step. "How are we doing?"

Lydia breathed in through her nose, and the subtle scent rolling off the man was a shock. If she'd been a human, she wouldn't have caught it. But as a wolven, even in her biped form, she sure as hell did.

Gus had spent some time in very close proximity to C.P. Phalen.

"Lydia?"

"Oh, ah, sorry. Daniel has a headache. Is there any way you could —"

"Pay him a little visit without it looking like I'm doing anything?" Gus put a friendly arm around her shoulders and started walking in the direction of her bedroom. "There's nothing I'd like to do more. Good thing I'm on call tonight, huh."

He was so casual and relaxed . . . that she wondered if maybe there was a professional reason he'd been up on the second floor and smelled like the perfume C.P. always wore.

Either way, it was none of her business — and God knew she had enough on her plate.

"Yes," she murmured. "It's a very good thing."

TWENTY-THREE

There were too many reasons to count, really.

Why Blade shouldn't be here, that was.

This was what he told himself as he stood draped in darkness outside of a home that was a modern castle. The sprawling structure was stone and quite horizontal, only two, or perhaps in places three, stories high. Interestingly, there was no seeing into the interior. Between the security lights that glowed and some kind of covering on the windows, it was clear that both privacy and fortification efforts had been taken quite seriously.

An SUV was parked under an extensive overhang by the front entrance, and the passenger's side door had been left open — as one would do if one were helping an infirmed into the house. Further, the vehicle was at a cockeyed angle, as if ensuring a proper angle had been the last thing on the operator's mind.

So the wolven was going to come back, either to shut the heavy panel or to move the SUV somewhere else.

He imagined the wolven helping Daniel Joseph up the modest number of steps to the grand portal — would she have to wait for the door to be opened by a security detail, or would they have greeted her upon arrival? And once inside, where did she go?

Exhaling, Blade looked up to the sky and then he glanced around the estate. There was a detached garage set to the right, and he was willing to bet there was an underground tunnel connecting the chick to the hen beneath the parking square. Behind the mansion, a field. Behind the field, a forest.

He knew the setting by heart, even though he had never been here before. Then again, he had done his research about eighteen months ago. Aerial photographs of Deer Mountain, as well as the valley to the west of it and this flat acreage to the east, had been his first order of surveillance when he'd learned through various sources that an antiquated, subterranean laboratory had been resurrected into service. A drone had done the surveying duty, and Daniel Joseph had been the one to fly it over the area about two months before he'd been assigned the case and started his infiltration.

By applying for that handyman's job at the Wolf Study Project.

Funny, how things came full circle. Now Blade was here, waiting for —

The door to the mansion opened and his wolven appeared in the entryway, a slip of a female compared to the scale of the place. As she exited, she was quick and light on her feet, descending the steps with alacrity — and he was so consumed by her presence that he didn't bother to try to get a glimpse into the interior of the structure.

Whilst she shut the passenger door and then rounded the rear of the vehicle, her head was down and he was disappointed. He wanted to see her face. He settled for watching how her body moved in her casual, simple clothing.

How did her corporeal entity shift like that? How did it work on a molecular level, two forms sharing the same space?

It was as his mind chewed over the implications that he realized why he was captivated by her. He was also two things in one, part vampire, part *symphath,* and he had always struggled with the incompatibility of his biological makeup. As the latter, he cared about no one; as the former, he had a loyalty that was dispositive.

Thus he had to hide while he was in the Colony. And he was not accepted when he visited Caldwell. Both made sense. He had to protect himself to survive, and he didn't trust his impulses any more than anybody else did —

As the wolven arrived at the driver's side door, she opened it — and then paused with one foot lifted up on the runner. After a moment, she twisted around . . .

. . . and looked straight at him.

Blade's heart stopped, and he felt that stirring go through him again. Her regard was so frank, so pointed, that he glanced down, wondering how in the fuck she saw him. He was dressed in black and even wearing a mask —

The tackle came from behind him, a body taking him down into the dry, pre-winter grass — and as he was roughly rolled over and a gun was pressed under his chin, he thought, Ah, she hadn't seen him. She had tracked the movement of this human man.

Who had seen Blade.

As a broad hand pressed into the center of his chest, he assessed the intrusion into his personal space. It was a stunning blond specimen of a guard with a military haircut and military clothing, precisely the kind of man who, under very different circumstances, he might properly have enjoyed making the visceral acquaintance of — provided their roles were reversed and he was the one doing the mounting.

"Bad decision, my guy," the human said.

On the contrary, Blade thought.

There was a communicator mounted on the guard's shoulder, and it required a patience Blade had in abundance to wait until the hand on his sternum went for the Velcro-mounted unit —

Just as a shout traveled over from the porte cochere, Blade slapped both his palms on either side of the gun's muzzle and rerouted its business end off to the side. Then he pulled a trade-place, overpowering the human and pinning him facedown to the browned lawn.

Blade didn't hesitate. He jerked the man's head back and twisted.

The crack was loud enough to carry, and the Adonis instantly went limp.

A quick glance back to the porte cochere, and Blade became infuriated. The wolven was starting to run — and not for reentry into the safety of that house. No, the female was coming at him, even though she didn't know how many of whatever it was were out in the darkness.

He allowed himself a brief moment for a

mental snapshot: She was beautiful in motion, her arms and legs pumping, her mouth open as she yelled in anger, her body a powerful, athletic coordination kicked into gear by a keen, assertive mind.

Alas, he would have to depart.

And dematerialize he did.

But not before, in the darkness . . . he blew her a kiss.

When Lydia reached the guard, she stopped so short that she tripped over her feet and landed on her hands and knees — which gave her an up-close-and-personal that was horrifying: The man was facedown and limp in the scratchy grass, his head turned away at a bad angle.

Very bad.

"Help!" she called out again.

Where was security when you needed them?

"Sir," she said as she gently patted his shoulder, "it's okay. You're going to be okay?"

As if that was a question she expected him to answer or something.

Crab-walking around him, she — "Oh . . . God."

Lydia let herself fall back onto her seat. The man's eyes were open and unfocused, staring straight out of the sockets, as if he were transfixed by a view. Likewise, his lips were parted, but he wasn't breathing —

Suddenly, two guard dogs flashed by her, silent canine missiles, and then a pair of guards arrived, their heavy footfalls seeming to crash into her. Without preamble, she was picked up by two heavy hands and moved over as if she were as inanimate as the dead man.

"I saw something out here," she babbled to no one in particular. "It was him, moving fast. The blond hair caught my eye. All of a sudden, he seemed to capture something — but then there was some kind of tussle and I heard this crack and I came running and —"

"Get her inside —"

"I'll take her in — give me a sec."

At the familiar voice, Lydia looked up. Gus had run out of the house, and as he dropped down and took hold of the guard's wrist, he seemed tense and professional.

Glancing up, he shook his head; then he focused on her. "Come on, Lydia. Come with me."

Things became a blur at that point. Then again, every time she blinked, she saw the guard's face, so handsome, so static. When her awareness properly checked in again, she was sitting at the breakfast table, in the alcove off C.P.'s industrial kitchen, the light fixture that hung from the ceiling glowing softly. The scent of coffee drifted over to her, and so did a volley of conversation that was hushed and urgent.

Clearing her throat, she said, "Where is Daniel —"

"I'm right here." There was the scrape of a chair, and then he was by her side, his hand on her back. "Are you okay?"

She didn't know what she said to him. She hoped it was reassuring.

Gus was the one who brought the coffee. Two mugs — one for her, one for Daniel. Then the doctor disappeared and came back with a Coke for himself.

"What happened out there?" he asked.

Lydia shook her head and glanced across at the man. "I don't know. You were with Daniel in the bedroom, and I figured I'd give you both a little privacy. I went out to move the car around to the garage . . . and I saw something out on the lawn . . ."

She had a feeling this was a story she was going to have to repeat to many people. Just like Daniel did with his list of symptoms.

Abruptly, she closed her mouth and looked through into the kitchen. A pair of men were standing off to the side, their guns drawn, their mouths pressed to communicators mounted on their shoulders.

"You — you know," she stammered, "I sometimes thought that all this security of hers is overdone —"

"It's not."

Lydia glanced over her shoulder. C.P. had come into the alcove from the other side, and it was weird. She was only half dressed, a loose fleece on top — wait, wasn't that something Gus wore around the lab sometimes? And why was she barefoot?

"Are you going to let Sheriff Eastwind know?" Lydia blurted at the woman who was in charge.

Not that she particularly cared about the answer — it was more something she felt like she should ask, just to show she was comprehending the common reality. One thing that was nice about being on the fringes of humanity because of her mixed blood? She didn't feel the need to worry about the particulars — and something told her that C.P. might very well handle this in her own way.

"We'll take care of everything," the woman replied in a level tone.

Bingo —

All at once, C.P. came into sharp view, as if Lydia's attention were a camera lens that was finally being operated properly after a period of incompetence. The other woman seemed pale and frazzled, but then again, there was a dead guy on her lawn. Except . . . there was something else that was off about her, something that was so much more than her wearing a total mismatch for her fine, formal slacks.

Flaring her nostrils, Lydia breathed in deep. Then she repeated the inhale.

C.P. frowned. "Are you okay? Are you hurt?"

I'm fine, Lydia thought to herself. *But you're . . . pregnant.*

TWENTY-FOUR

The following morning, Daniel was staring at the ceiling over their bed as the sun rose.

He figured he wasn't the only one in the household who hadn't slept well. Even after he and Lydia had gone to their bedroom and lay down, it was a long time before there was any shut-eye going on. He was very sure she was shocked that she'd seen a dead body, but maybe, like him, she was also worried about the what-ifs: What if the killer had been out there with her? What if she had been taken down, too?

Assuming that guard didn't trip in a groundhog hole and fall in such a way so as to snap his own frickin' neck, someone must have done the job for him — which meant somebody with serious skills had managed to slip past C.P. Phalen's security.

And there was only one group of individuals he could think of with that kind of know-how —

As a sharpshooter went through his frontal lobe, he hissed and rubbed over his eyebrows — then again, his brain felt like a muscle that had been unused until very recently. Fortunately, the pain faded quickly, especially as he replayed, for the hundredth time, the fact pattern of Lydia walking out of the house, and seeing something on the lawn, and going over to find a man whose neck had been snapped.

He looked over at Lydia. She had tossed and turned beside him throughout the night hours, settling only when he'd wrapped his arms around her and held her close. And wasn't that another moment when he'd felt like a man instead of a cancer patient.

Not that the two couldn't exist at the same time, as he was beginning to learn.

As if she sensed his regard, her lids opened. "Are you okay?" she asked in a gravelly voice.

"Yeah, I'm fine." He brushed her cheek. "I'm just going to go down to the lab for another round of fluids and perk-me-up. If you can, stay here and get some rest, even if you're not sleeping?"

The murmur that came back at him was encouraging. It was the sound of drowsiness, and sure enough, her even breathing pattern resumed.

Being careful not to disturb her, he sat up, then stood up. She was so vulnerable, all tucked into herself, her legs drawn up, her arms, too, her hands cupped beneath her chin. They'd fallen asleep once again in their clothes on top of the duvet, and he reached down and pulled the extra comforter all the way over her so she would be warm.

"Love you," he whispered in her ear.

"Love you," she mumbled as she puckered for his kiss.

After he obliged, she sighed — and he put his feet into his running shoes and headed for the exit. Outside of their room, he took a quick listen. When he heard no voices echoing through the polished stone halls, he went down to the kitchen. He was surprised no one was at the counters or the stoves, not even the chef, who, ordinarily, would be slinging gourmet hash for a dozen or more breakfast plates.

Had C.P. ordered an evac of nonessentials? he wondered.

The guards were all at their usual posts in the house, and they did look on duty — but when did they not?

Heading out to the front, he passed through the foyer — where you could have played two or three games of professional volleyball simultaneously — and approached a closed set of double doors. Back when he'd been in better shape, during the early days of his diagnosis, he'd memorized the layout of the mansion, the intel garnered thanks to all those nights when he hadn't been able to sleep.

So, yeah, he knew where C.P. Phalen's war room was.

Arriving at the closed door, he knocked, and then looked up to the discreetly mounted fish-eyed camera that was at the ceiling. Giving a little wave, he waited.

If she wasn't inside, she'd probably be down in the security center that was one floor below —

Things opened, and what do you know, not only was the woman herself the one doing the duty with the knob, she was also still in that fucked-up outfit of navy blue fleece and formal slacks. Still no shoes, either.

"Daniel," she said with exhaustion. "If you're looking for Gus, he's in the lab —"

"No, I'm here for you."

"I appreciate your concern —"

"You know what I am." As the woman went silent and narrowed her tired eyes, he nodded. "There's no way you let me stay in this house without doing a background check, and when you found my created identity, you probably tried to probe further. When that came out with nothing, you drew the right conclusions — and kudos for never asking me what I wouldn't tell you, by the way."

She glanced over his shoulder. Then she stepped back without a word and indicated the way in.

He'd never been inside her sanctum sanctorum before, and he was not surprised that the stark, glossy decor of the rest of the house was front and center. Had the woman never heard of knickknacks? A pop of color?

She really needed to watch some *Scott Living by Drew & Jonathan.*

Did she even know what QVC was?

C.P. went across and sat behind her slab of a desk. As she leaned back in her black leather chair, her eyes were steady and he admired her composure given all the shit that was going on: him flaking out on trying that compound of hers, dead body on her front lawn, possible law enforcement issues — although if she could hide from the FDA as effectively as she did, disappearing a corpse was probably not a problem that was new to her.

"I'm not unaware of the nature of your work," she said remotely. "Or that my lab was likely your target. You were on my acreage with a bomb and detonator. I am not confused as to your intent."

"And yet you let me stay on." He went over and sat down in the chair opposite her. "But by then, you knew what was wrong with me — did you hope I was a candidate for your trial right away?"

"No offense, I'm not really in a chitchat mood right now."

"Yeah, I'm pretty sure you aren't. Then again, neither am I." He sat forward. "I know who killed your guard — and no, it wasn't me. You can check your security feeds. Gus and I were in your guest bedroom."

"I know where you were."

"I think my old boss is back in action and still wants to take you down." A return of that sudden tightening across his frontal lobe made him rub over his eyebrows again. "Back in the spring, my commander attempted to leverage my relationship with Lydia after I tried to pull out of my mission — and I had hoped, when things stayed quiet through the spring and summer, that he'd moved on to another target. But your dead guard last night? I think you're in play once more."

"So who did you work for?"

"The Federal Bureau of Genetics."

C.P. shook her head. "I've never heard of such a thing."

"That's the point." As his headache seemed to be sticking around, Daniel shifted his position to relieve the pressure on his spine. Not that it helped. "No one has. We were tasked with protecting the integrity of the human genome against unlawful manipulation — by clandestine labs just like yours. I was part of an expert team of mercenary soldiers who, shall we say, were deployed to dismantle such operations."

"And to think I assumed I only had to watch out for my competitors," she said dryly. "I'm impressed the government managed to keep you such a secret. So who is your boss, if you don't mind me asking?"

"He goes by the name of —" A real spear of agony rocketed through Daniel's skull, but he refused to be derailed. "Blade. It's code for fuck only knows what. He had resources that were very deep, and he coordinated our squads of two to three soldiers, doling out the assignments and priorities. He's efficient, highly rational, very deadly. I can only assume from the way he operated with such autonomy, and stayed so far outside the reach of conventional law enforcement, that his orders come from the highest levels."

"Well." C.P. laughed a little. "If I can do it, why can't the president of the United States? Function under the radar, that is."

"Listen, I've been really grateful for you." He shrugged and was relieved as his headache began to ease up. "For taking Lydia and me in. Even if your intention was for me to be your first test subject, when I changed my mind and stuck to it, you haven't kicked us out."

"Don't make a hero out of me, Daniel."

"I'm not, don't worry. But I'm surprised that you let me stay at all. Given what you know about me. What if I were a fox in your henhouse?"

"You aren't. I monitor everything that happens around here. I know what everyone is doing — all their conversations, their calls, their movements. I have quite a comprehensive system — although there are certain provisions that are made for . . . privacy purposes."

With a smile, he thought about what he'd done with Lydia the night before in their bed — when they hadn't been able to sleep. "I appreciate the discretion."

Her mouth lifted briefly at the corners. "You're welcome."

"Anyway, I'm a quid pro quo kind of guy.

So in return for what you've done for me and my woman, I'd like to offer you a little help."

A finely tended-to eyebrow lifted. "How so."

"I have some ins with the organization I worked for. I'm prepared to exploit them to find out what's going on with respect to your lab — and before you ask, you can have one of your security guys sitting at my shoulder when I do it. At least if you know what you're dealing with, you can drive your strategy of retaliation better."

There was a long pause. "Will your former boss be shocked at your disloyalty, I wonder."

"I'm not being disloyal. I don't work for people who threaten my woman's life."

"Fair enough." C.P. inclined her head. "But I'm not sure I require anything. I am curious why this is all coming up now."

"Apart from the dead guard, you mean?" As C.P. tightened her lips, like she was going *well-duh* in her head, he continued, "I want Lydia to be able to pick when she leaves this house. If you feel like you owe me something, that gives her some time. Even if I'm dead."

"You don't have to worry about her. She's welcome here for however long she wishes

to stay. I am . . . aware of her differences."
C.P. cleared her throat. "Security cameras
have shown me . . . incredible things. She is
a miracle."

"I couldn't agree with you more."

And he respected that C.P. hadn't tried to
exploit any of that — or brought it up with
Lydia as far as he knew. Stress was stress,
after all, and he wasn't sure how much of
that dual nature she wanted out in conversation.

"You know what," C.P. said, "I think I will
take you up on your offer."

"Good." He laughed a little. "I figured I'd
have to argue with you — or wait until a
couple of others died on your property
before you came to your senses."

"I'm far more logical than you give me
credit for. And at any rate, you are an
unusual situation."

He waited for the expound on her reasons
for taking someone she hadn't hired, and
perhaps shouldn't trust, into her confidence.
But when she didn't go any further, he ap-
proved of her closed-lip routine. He would
have been the same in her situation: She
had a big operation to protect and the
resources to do just that — but an unknown
threat was on her horizon. If she could
somehow extract intel from him? She bet-

tered her position without a lot of exposure, given he had already been on the inside of her lab and had done nothing to violate her privacy.

"What do you need from me?" she asked.

"A computer with internet access. That's it." He held up a forefinger. "And I don't want to stress Lydia out about this. I worry her too much already — and besides, it's not like I'm going to go out into the field or anything."

At least . . . he didn't think he was headed in that direction.

Nah, he thought as he got to his feet. That wasn't what was going to happen.

After C.P. told him she'd deliver a laptop to his room, he turned and started crossing the distance to the door. Halfway there, he paused and looked down at himself.

Well. What do you know.

He'd forgotten his cane, and didn't even miss it.

TWENTY-FIVE

Down at the lab, Gus was pacing around his office, dribbling his basketball. In the entire facility, his work crib was one of the few that had four walls and a door; everything else was those open-air workstations. Of course, in typical C.P. Phalen style, he was monitored like everything else on the premises, but he certainly had more privacy than most.

And good goddamn thing, too.

He was supposed to be getting things ready for the first transfusion at midnight. Instead, he was fucking around, playing ghost jump shot with the door, working offense against absolutely nothing coming at him: He'd lied to good ol' Cathy. There were no more tests to run. The shit that had been done at MD Anderson recently had been more than sufficient for relevant baselines and an assessment of her general health, and he'd done his own snapshot last night.

No, he was giving her a chance to back out.

He disagreed with the Houston people. She could get more chemo if she wanted; they could push it a little farther with the conventional drugs. Sure, sooner or later her body was going to fail by inches and then feet with as much chemo exposure as she'd had — but when you were staring down the barrel of a funeral anyway, what did you care?

And maybe he was getting cold feet.

Glancing at his watch, he noted the time. Maybe *she* was getting cold feet.

With a grim curse, he thought about the guard who had been killed. How was she feeling about the fact that her lover had lost his life in the line of duty on her front lawn —

As his phone rang, he took it out of his lab coat and answered like he was back in residency — no checking the screen, no preamble.

"St. Claire."

There was a pause, and then a clicking sound. "Hello?" he demanded.

Just as he took the thing away from his ear to hang up, a tinny voice emanated from the unit. "Augustus Reginald St. Claire Jr., resident of Plattsburgh, New York. Aged thirty-two years, nine months, five days, four hours, and —"

"Who the fuck is this?"

The male voice was ever so slightly distorted, like it was being run through an electronic synthesizer. "— some change. Stanford University undergrad at the age of twenty. Stanford Medical graduate four years later. Residency at Massachusetts General Hospital, Boston. Fellowship in oncology completed there five years later. Hired by Merck to focus on research in immunotherapy —"

"Where did you get this number?" He switched ears. "Who the —"

"But dropped off the public radar a mere two months later, never to be heard from on the national stage again. Parents, deceased. No living siblings. Estranged from other family, due to the embezzlement of Augustus Reginald St. Claire Sr. —"

"Fuck you." Gus sank down into his thighs like he was about to fight the fucker. "You get my father's name out your mouth —"

"Allergic to sesame seeds. Lactose intolerant. Favorite color . . . LA Lakers gold."

As his eyes shot to the framed Kobe shirt over his desk, Gus tightened his hold on the

341

phone. "You finished showing off? Or do you want to tell me my favorite movie."

" 'Today we don't fight for one life. We fight for all of them.' "

As a feeling of foreboding came over him, Gus heard himself say, "You're going to have to do more than quote T'Challa to me if you want to —"

"You saw the movie when it came out. In the Framingham AMC theaters. Across from Target. You were alone."

When Gus's knees gave out and he smacked down into his chair, he half expected the sonofabitch on the phone to ask him if his ass hurt.

"I recite your rather impressive résumé back to you," the voice said, "as well as give you a sense of the depth of our research, to provide you with context for our sincerity and our thoroughness."

"Tell me who you are and what you want. So I can tell you to go to hell and we can end this bullshit —"

"I am very familiar with your research under Phalen. I'll leave you to guess why. I want you to be aware that your drug compound, while innovative and certainly promising, is still speculative. No clinical trials." There was a pause, like whoever it was expected him to give an update to the contrary if things had changed. "I have five patients prescreened and ready to go. I have monitoring facilities that make Phalen's lab look like a high school chemistry room."

"So this is a job offer?"

"Yes, it is. Come work for me, and I'll give you the time and space you need to create whatever you want. And before you tell me you're happy where you are, you know things are changing. You know she's going to sell Vita-12b, and no matter what she told you, the money is the most important thing to her. Not you, not the principles. It's the money."

Gus rolled his eyes. "And let me guess. You're a paragon of morality, who's just doing background checks as a hobby?"

Besides, this fucker on the phone had no idea that C.P. Phalen had a biological imperative that made profit totally irrelevant. You couldn't spend money from the grave. For all the facts the caller spouted, he'd missed the big reality —

"Phalen's going bankrupt." The chuckle of satisfaction coming over the connection was downright nasty. "I'm assuming she hasn't told you or anyone else that? I wouldn't, if I were her. But ask yourself, why, if Vita-12b is such a promising innovation, is she selling it right from under herself. I'll tell you why. She cashed out of all her positions, sank everything into that lab you're working in, and has been burning through her equity at twice the rate that is sustainable. You're not in finance, but you've balanced a checkbook. At the end of the day, in spite of all the creative accounting, it's simple math."

Gus put his head in his hand, but kept his voice level. "You don't know what you're talking about."

"Yes, I do. She's selling your work, your research, your vision, right out from under you. I have a copy of your employment contract with her." There was a pause, like the man was waiting for that to sink in. "You think you have equity, but there's an out clause I'll bet you didn't pay any attention to. If she sells the company, there's no assumption clause. You're at the mercy of the acquirer. They don't have to give you anything or honor her terms. They don't have to even hire you."

In the back of his mind, he heard C.P. promising she'd take care of him.

"Assuming that is true" — and Gus had no idea; he wasn't a lawyer and all he'd cared about was the work, not the benefits — "why wouldn't whoever buys Vita want me."

"Because they'll already have what you made. They won't need you. They'll have purchased the data, the research, and the formulation. Me? I want you. I'll give you whatever runway you need to keep innovating, not just on this project, but anything else you want to do."

Gus rubbed his face. "I don't even know who you are."

"In good time, my friend. That will come in good time. Think it over. You're in business with someone who's already cheated you. She knew her financial exposure when she hired you, and you signed a contract that cuts you out of any sale. Your deal with her is null and void if she takes the third-party route and there isn't a damned thing you can do about it — hell, you can't even list this research on your résumé because then you're going to have to explain under what circumstances you conducted your experiments. And even if you tell me you're a Good Samaritan and are just in it for the science, then I'm going to remind you you're doing the business of your convictions with a double-crossing swindler who has no principles. Not even when it comes to her key man."

"You don't know what you're talking about." How many times had he said that?

345

"You have no fucking clue."

"Well, what a relief for you then, right?" That chuckle came back over the connection. "I'll be calling you back in a matter of hours, Augustus. You've got a lot to think about."

Before Gus could say another thing, the connection was cut.

As he took the phone from his ear, he went into his call log. "Blocked Caller" was all that appeared on the first line of the list.

"Shit," he breathed as he stared at his monitor. "Fuck . . . *shit.*"

Oddly enough, given the conversation, he didn't think about his employment contract.

He thought about going into that bathroom in C.P. Phalen's study and seeing a man who only had twenty-four hours left to live zip up his pants. Which was stupid. Of all the things that could have been on his mind, that woman's love life should not have been any kind of preoccupation.

Then again, she had always fucked him up.

What the hell did he do now?

Twenty-Six

Lydia woke up with a start and the first thing she did was throw her arm out and pat around the bed next to her. When it became clear that Daniel wasn't with her, she sat up and pushed her hair away from her face. Just as she was about to jump to her feet and bolt off to find him, she heard the shower running.

"Thank God," she muttered as she shifted her legs over and stood up.

Putting her hands on the small of her back, she stretched and heard her spine crack. Then she padded into the bathroom.

Daniel was faceup to the spray, his head tilted back as he rinsed the shampoo out of the fuzz that was on his scalp, the suds running down his shoulders, his spine, the backs of his legs.

As if he sensed her, he twisted his torso around. "Oh, hi. I didn't want to walk you — wake you, I mean."

"Hi." She glanced back at the bed. "I don't know what time it is —"

"We're creeping up on dinner."

"What?" She shook her head. "You mean, I slept all day long?"

"Good thing it's Saturday and you didn't have to go to work, huh."

"Ah, yeah. Wow."

The fact that he didn't turn all the way toward her made her wonder if he was hiding his body from her. She could understand why. The overhead light in the stall was on, and its harsh illumination was unforgiving.

But as she stared at him, she didn't care what he looked like.

"Mind if I join you?" she asked softly.

"Oh, God, yes —" He shook himself. "I mean, *no.* I mean, come in. Please. Fuck."

Her clothes came off so fast, it was as if they were as sick of her as she was of them — or maybe it was just that her hands, when properly motivated like this, could be really damned efficient with the buttons and the zippers and the over-the-head, down-the-legs stuff. The second she was naked, Daniel opened the glass door, and her eyes clung to his as she stepped into the warmth and humidity.

And then her body was against him.

It all felt so good, so right, this need to be

touched by him, to feel his hands on her body, to taste his mouth and —

Their kissing started slowly, the caressing of mouths lazy and slick from the water, but the heat came quick, and that was good. That was so good. Even if he looked different and his shoulders were not the same, the way he handled her was exactly as it had always been, his palms sliding down her ribs, grabbing her ass, pulling her in tight to his hips.

When he started kissing down the side of her throat, she eased back into the corner of the shower, and then she was sitting on the shelf and he was kneeling before her. Between his palms, he worked a bar of soap, the fragrance rising up between them. With hands that barely shook at all, he cupped her breasts, covering them with suds, slipping his fingers over her nipples, cupping water and rinsing her off. To give him every access he could want or need, she stretched her arms over her head and held on to a chrome hook that was mounted on the marble wall.

Arching her back, she offered her aching, taut nipples to him.

And he didn't disappoint. Planting his palms on the tile, he leaned in and latched on, his mouth suckling at her, the wet, warm draw of his lips, the lick of his tongue, the way he straightened a little, spread her legs, and stroked her inner thighs, every bit as good as it had ever been.

As she looked down at herself, he was utterly focused on the job he was doing, ravishing her, pulling away as he sucked so that her breast snapped back as the seal was broken, the tugging and releasing going right into her core.

Which was where this was all headed.

As the rain from above traveled over her body, sweeping the suds away, everything flowed down her torso — and seemed to give him direction. With his hands on her knees, he kissed his way to the heart of her, taking his time, lingering on her hip, nipping the inside of her legs, licking around her belly button.

When she called out his name in frustration, he still didn't give her what she wanted. And then she was whimpering, trying to rub her thighs together, but unable to because he was between them. Shifting around on the ledge, she got to the edge of it —

The slip-off was quick.

And Daniel caught her. Proving that he still had good reflexes, he made sure she didn't wreck her back on the marble seat, cupping her butt and easing her to the tile floor of the shower.

Stretching out, she kept her arms overhead still, and she was shameless. She brought up her heels and let her knees fall all the way to the sides until the hot water from the fixture rained down on her hot, slick sex.

"Oh, Lydia . . ."

For the first time since she'd moved in, she thanked C.P. Phalen's love for enormous scale — because the shower had room enough for Daniel to stretch out, too, if he folded his legs up at the knees — and he did.

His eyes glowed as he settled in between her thighs, and keeping his stare locked on her, he extended his tongue and licked her once, nice and slow.

When she moaned, he did it again. And then he was kissing her sex, all the while playing with her breasts, his face moving against her as he tweaked her nipples and cupped her weight and caressed her. The sensations were so intense, she lost any sense of how hard the marble floor was under her or the fact that there were security cameras everywhere.

What the hell did she care if someone wanted to watch?

She was about to come, and that was the

only thing that —

As Lydia orgasmed, Daniel rolled her hips to the side and used the inside of her thigh as a cushion for his head. With her leg cocked over his shoulder, he nuzzled her sex and took long licks as the warm, gentle rain fell upon them both.

When she came again, he couldn't resist.

He reached down between his own legs to see if — no, he wasn't hard. There was still little to no sensation in his cock, and he had a thought . . . there had to be clinical options for this. Weren't there shots?

Maybe he needed a bicycle pump.

Whatever, he'd worry about that later. Flicking with his tongue, he slipped his fingers inside her and started working her with penetration while he took care of the top of her cleft.

"Daniel . . ."

It was amazing how empowering this was, proof that sex could be transformative in so many ways — and in his case? The pleasure he was giving her was making him feel like a total man, even though he was flaccid.

So, yeah, he continued to drive her harder and harder, until she was writhing and jerking in the midst of the falling rain, a gleaming, glistening display of a woman in ecstasy

— and he had fucking put her in that state. Why did he keep going? Because he could. Because he wanted her to feel him in any way he was able. Because he was breathing her in and swallowing her and making a mark on her that she would not forget after he was gone.

Every time she came into this bathroom? For however long she stayed here?

She would think of what he had done to her right here, and hopefully, after the sting of losing him faded, she'd remember the way he'd been able to do her. And when she took another lover? He could guarantee that the man wouldn't treat her like this.

Whoever the fuck he was.

Lucky fucking bastard.

As a wave of sadness busted through Daniel's focus, he pushed it away, but he did slow down. And then he was crawling up her body. With heavy-lidded eyes, she looked at him and smiled in a dreamy way.

The grief lingered as he kissed her mouth and felt her hands run down his ribs. As he lay down next to her, one of her legs kneed between his own, and when she moved her hips into his, he had a feeling she was trying to see if he was hard without being obvious about it.

"Hey," he said against her mouth.

Her eyes ducked his, and her face grew tighter — and not in a good way.

"Hey," he repeated as he stroked her wet hair back. "You turn me on, you know that?"

Lydia's honey-colored stare came back to his own.

"It's true." He eased back a little and trolled his fingertips up the curve of her breast. "You make me hot. You make me glad to be a man. When I tell you I could do that to you forever, I mean it. Don't let my body cause you to question a goddamn thing."

She ran her hands up his shoulders. "I just wish we could . . . I mean, not for me. For you —"

He cut her off. "I know you do —"

"I wish I could do something. For you."

After a moment, he said softly, "Actually, you can."

Don't say it, he warned himself. *Don't you fucking ruin this.*

But if not now, when was he going to say this, he wondered. What if something went wrong with him?

Pillowing his head with his arm, he touched her face, and for some reason, the sound of the water hitting the marble shower grew loud, very loud.

As his chest got tight, she clearly became

concerned.

"It's nothing bad," he whispered as he ran his thumb over her lower lip. "I just want you to remember me, after I'm gone."

Her recoil was instantaneous and the sputtering immediate.

"No, wait, let me just say this. And then I won't bring it up again." He waited until she'd calmed a little. "I'm a selfish bastard, and I want you to remember me when the spring comes because we met in the spring. And when you go up on the mountain for work and you look at that bridge I built, think of me then, too, 'kay? The wolves you track? When you cross paths with the one whose life you saved with my help, who we released back into the wild together? Remember me when you look into his face." Daniel exhaled slowly. "I don't need to be all around you or in your mind all the time. I don't want that — I want you to move on and find your way and live a new life that is different, but eventually happy. Just . . . don't forget me, okay? That's death to me. You not remembering me is death. You thinking of me from time to time? That's . . . my forever."

Ah, shit, he was making her cry. But he had to speak this, he needed to get this out.

"I want forever with you." He touched her

temple. "And it's right up here. This is not meant to be a burden, I swear, and I don't want to upset you. I just . . . oh, fucking hell, come here."

Leave it to him to ruin everything, he thought as he pulled her into his scrawny chest with its new map of scars from operations, biopsies, and his PICC line.

"I'm sorry, just forget it," he said against her ear. "I'm an asshole —"

She pulled back sharply. "No, don't say that." Her eyes bounced around his face. "Daniel, I promise you. I'm going to give you your forever. For as long as I live, you'll be with me and it's no burden. How could an amazing man like you be a burden? And yes, when the spring comes, on the first sunny day, I'll go up to the mountain, and I'll walk over the bridge you built. When the rays hit my face, I'll remember your kisses, and when it falls on my shoulders, I'll remember you holding me. Just send me a sign if you can, okay? I don't know what I believe about the afterlife, but if I can give you forever in my mind, how about you give me a hint about heaven, or whatever you call it?"

Tears entered his eyes, hotter than the water falling on them both.

"It's a deal." He brought his arm back

around and offered her his hand. "Let's shake on it, my wolf. Isn't that what people do?"

"Deal," she said hoarsely.

As they shook and then melded their bodies, he realized that some goodbyes were over in an instant, and some were a gradual drift apart. Others . . . were lived and breathed through, a deliberate process of parting that was as much a part of the relationship as the beginning and the middle.

He and his woman were going to make theirs count.

They had no other choice.

TWENTY-SEVEN

That evening, C.P. went downstairs to dinner in sweatpants. No tight-fitting skirt or slacks. No fucking stilettos that were giving her a bunion. No curled and sprayed hair, or tasteful makeup, or diamond studs. She had thick socks in lieu of shoes, and she told herself she'd kept Gus's fleece on just because she didn't really have anything else to wear.

That was a lie.

She wanted him around her.

It was precisely the kind of sentimentality she'd sneered at over the course of her life — but who knew there was a place for that kind of sap? Then again, she was dying, and that sure as shit made you toss rules that didn't work for you.

Gus's fleece worked for her.

She got the first of the surprised looks as she hit the foyer and passed the pair of guards who were stationed by the front entrance. She ignored them. The next set of double takes came as she entered the kitchen, but Chef recovered quickly and barked an order to his second-in-command to get back to work.

"How many tonight, boss?" Chef asked.

"I don't know. Could be five. Could be a dozen."

"Good thing I planned for a buffet. Time?"

"Thirty minutes from now."

"Roger."

And that was that. The fact that he didn't need anything else from her was usually a good thing, but tonight, she wanted to talk to him. Make some decisions about simple stuff like chicken or fish, rice or potatoes, ice cream with the pie for dessert?

Instead, she turned away. God, how much longer did she have to wait? Gus had texted and canceled the tests he'd scheduled for the morning, saying that he had the data he needed after all and that he'd reconvene with her at midnight to move forward. When she'd sent back a response suggesting they just move forward, he'd replied that he was leaving the lab for the day to get some clothes from his house.

And that was that. No more communication —

Daniel Joseph stepped into her path and she jumped back.

"Sorry," he said as he put out his hands. "Didn't mean to startle you."

"It's fine." It wasn't fine. "I'm okay."

She wasn't okay. Daniel, on the other hand, was looking much better. He was freshly showered, and smelling of the shampoo, conditioner, and soap she stocked the house with. He hadn't put his knit hat on, for once, and she could see how his hair was growing back in evenly, the dark shadow tinting his scalp. He was also bundled up, the sweater and cardigan on top of his thick pants adding some weight to his narrow frame.

His eyes were particularly bright, she thought. And though he wasn't using words, he was communicating with them, loud and clear.

She nodded over his shoulder.

Together, they went wordlessly down the front of the house, passing by those guards, entering her study. As she closed them in together, she hit a button on the wall, her fingerprint the code to activate the lockdown: All at once, panels descended over the bulletproof windows and a locking mechanism dead-bolted the steel-reinforced door.

"Fancy," he murmured as he went over to the chair on the other side of her desk. As she sat down across from him, he nodded at her fleece. "Nice clothes."

"Don't be absurd."

Daniel tilted his head. "I'm serious. You look younger. You know, less like a battle-ax."

C.P. opened her mouth. Closed it. Then laughed a little. "I wasn't aware that was the impression I made."

"Bullshit." The guy smiled back. "And it's a successful set of armor. You could totally be on the *Game of Thrones* prequel."

"I'll take that as a compliment."

"So you know a guy named Gunnar Rhobes."

Ah, yes, C.P. thought. *Here we are.*

"I've heard of him," she said smoothly.

"Yeah, I was thinking that you people" — he moved his hand around — "who play at this undercover-lab game know each other. No one starts out running medical research under the radar. You all had to begin some-where legit."

"This is true."

"Gunnar Rhobes was on our agency's list as a target."

She didn't bother to hide her surprise. "Was he."

"Yeah, and his lab in Tuttle, Pennsylvania, had a little accident the day before yesterday."

C.P. thought back to being in Houston, in that skyscraper of Gunnar's . . . all those suits running down to the conference room.

"What kind of accident," she asked.

"It was bombed out of existence." Daniel made a starburst with one of his hands. "Boom! Someone blew it up."

C.P. sat forward. "Did your organization do it?"

"I don't know. I back-ended the F.B.G. database using a sign-in that was still live — and don't worry, I covered my tracks even with your virtual server. Anyway, there were ops notes on the site from the spring. Another squad, other than mine, was working on the project. Maybe it took them six months to get it done, although usually things moved faster than that."

"It could have been terrorism. Or someone from the inside."

"Whatever the case, it's gone and that's irrefutable. Local sources are saying there was an earthquake radiating out from the area and a sinkhole opened up. It was all over the morning news. Law enforcement aren't doing shit at the site, which leads me to believe they were bought off pretty quick."

C.P. thought about Gunnar Rhobes. And everything she knew he was capable of.

Would he blame her somehow?

"So," Daniel murmured. "You want to clue me in on exactly how well you know that guy and his company?"

She frowned and shook her head. "No, I don't."

"Listen, if it's a case of you'll-have-to-kill-me-if-you-tell-me?" The guy pointed to his lungs. "Nailed it on the dead part already — so you might as well get talking."

C.P. smiled again. "You're not supposed to be making me laugh."

"Oh, I don't have any sense of humor. I told Lydia that right when I met her — even gave her my uncle's suck-ass knock-knock joke to prove it. I did do one good joke tonight, though. Thought it was a trend. It wasn't."

"You know," she murmured as she regarded him with a tilt of her head, "you really do look better all of a sudden."

"Gus is a miracle worker." There was a pause. "Hey, I'm sorry I flaked out on you, and your drug trial —"

"Oh, do not apologize." She put up a hand. "There is nothing more personal than health care decisions. You've got to do what's best for you. That's what really matters."

The man sat forward and put his elbows on her desk. "Talk to me about Gunnar. You might as well. Something tells me you don't talk to anybody."

Later, she would wonder why she opened up. But then again, they shared a big commonality, even if she was the only one who knew it.

"I'm selling Vita-12b."

Daniel got very still. "And Gunnar is one of your potential buyers."

"You're quick. And he hasn't made an offer — just a bunch of posturing."

"You've got a very narrow market, haven't you. Few will know what to do with it — or have what is required to continue your work." Daniel's eyes narrowed. "Why are you dumping the compound? Does Gus know?"

"He does. As for the sale? That's complicated."

"And . . . ?"

"It's the right thing to do." She frowned and opened her middle desk drawer. "Hey, would you mind if I have you witness something? You're just attesting that you've seen me sign it."

"Sure. Happy to."

She took out a sheath of documents that represented a good ten or fifteen hours' worth of legal work. Flipping through to the last couple of pages, she gripped a blue pen.

"Smile at the camera," she murmured.

As Daniel gave a wave up to the corner behind her, she drew her name, slowly and carefully, on her signature line. Then she dated her John Hancock, gave Daniel the pen, and shifted the document around.

Daniel flexed his hand. "The shaking is better. Gus told me the side effects would leave quick, but I didn't believe him."

"He knows what he's talking about." Abruptly, she nodded down at the desktop. "You're not asking what the document is about."

"Not my business." He pointed to the text below where he was signing. "I'm just a witness. The only thing I gotta worry about is that I saw you sign whatever the hell this is, and I did." He passed the papers back to her. "No notary."

"I'm going to take care of that." She pointed over her shoulder. "We have both our parts on video."

"Sure enough do." Daniel sat back. "Any chance I just witnessed you selling Gus's drug out from under him?"

"I thought you didn't care what the papers

were for."

"Just kidding."

C.P. smiled for the third time — and wondered what the hell was wrong with her. "You do not kid, Daniel Joseph."

"Ah, but I'm trying to turn over a new leaf. I'm running out of time for self-improvement, you know. Winter is coming, so if I'm going to do any kind of evolving, I better get to it."

C.P. tapped the documents and lied. "It's a DNR, actually."

Daniel's brows went up. "I'm sorry, what?"

"Do. Not. Resuscitate."

"Yeah, I know what the initials stand for. You planning on dying sometime soon there, C.P.?"

The words were spoken lightly, but his eyes were intense.

"No," she said. "I'm not. But you never know. Back to Gunnar. It's possible . . . just possible . . . that he somehow thinks I was involved in the bombing."

Daniel sat forward again. "Really. Why?"

"And he might have come onto this property last night to retaliate. If I'm right? We're all in danger, and it might make sense for you and Lydia to relocate. Gunnar is a follow-through kind of man, and he's ruthless — even when he's wrong. I've done a lot of things in my life, but bombing his little toy box was not one of them."

Daniel glanced around, his eyes lingering on the panels that had come down over the windows. "No offense, but I went through this house and grounds, back in the beginning when Lydia and I first moved in. Old habits dying hard, you know the drill. This property is a fucking bank vault."

"Going with your FDIC-inspired metaphor, there are thieves out in the world, Daniel. If what you've led me to believe about you is true, you know that better than anyone else."

"I'm not the running kind, Catherine." He nodded at the documents. "Always wondered what your first name really was. Finally found out."

She shook her head, and felt a stab of sadness. "No, you knew before now. You came here to the mountain for the same reason that whoever blew Gunnar's site up went to Pennsylvania, and that means you've read up on me. I don't blame you. I don't judge you. But let's not pretend that we don't know how all this started."

The man who was dying stared at her for a moment. Then he smiled. "Roger that, boss."

C.P. folded the document back into proper order. "Thank you for this."

"My signature ain't worth much."

Now she had to laugh as she got to her feet. "Actually, you'd be surprised exactly how much value it has. You really would."

Daniel stood up as well. "So Gunnar is going to think you launched an offensive at him and that's why his lab went boom. And he sent you a message last night. Is that our conclusion?"

"One possible conclusion."

"Fair enough. By the way, what did you do with the body of that guard? And before you tell me it's none of my business, I'll agree with you, but I'm a member of this household, at least for the time being, so I'd like to know in case the cops come a-knockin'."

C.P. looked over at the bathroom door. It was a moment before she could find her voice. "He was a ghost, just like you are. According to what his family knows, he died a long, long time ago, and there was no legal next of kin."

"You cremated him on the premises, then, didn't you."

For a split second, she remembered the last time she and the guard had been together, when Gus had walked in. His name . . . had been Robert. He had gone by Rob. And she was sorry that he had been killed — and also shocked. He'd had lightning reflexes and the kind of training where bare-knuckle fighting was nothing more than a fun way to blow off steam.

Whoever had taken him out had been highly trained and very deadly.

She had to clear her throat. "I made sure that his remains were handled with respect. He is not my first loss."

"That I believe. On both accounts."

As Daniel headed for the door, C.P. said, "You're walking better, too. No more cane."

He paused and glanced down at himself. "You know what Gus always says."

"What's that."

"It's remarkably hard to kill a human, especially one in their prime like me. In most cases, you have to work in order to die." Daniel shrugged. "Helluva Christmas card, right?"

"Hallmark should hire him."

At the door, the man looked back. "You ever hear of a guy named Kurtis Joel."

C.P. frowned. "No. Who's that?"

"You sure?"

"Yes. Who is it?"

Daniel shook his head. "I'll let you know. I'm going to keep poking around that

F.B.G. database. Talk to you soon."

As Daniel took off, her first impulse was to go after him and ask him about the name, but as a wave of dizziness swamped her, she sat back down. She'd given him a workspace in the lab just because it was easier and more secure. If he found anything, he'd just demonstrated he'd come to her, and anything he did on the computer? She could see just by pushing a button up here.

If only all her problems were so easy to solve.

TWENTY-EIGHT

As Lydia sat alone with Daniel at the table just off of C.P.'s kitchen, she pushed the food around on her plate. It was late for the whole dinner thing, and she couldn't remember the last time she'd eaten anything, and yes, of course, the chicken was perfect. But that conversation with Daniel had knocked her off her stride.

The future was . . . too awful to contemplate.

Reaching under the table, she put her hand on his thigh and squeezed. As she glanced over at him, he was looking at her and his face was glowing. Especially when his eyes drifted down to her mouth and he licked his lips.

As she blushed, she smiled back at him, and the moment lasted a split second and also an eternity. Then she nodded at his plate.

"Look at you. Your appetite is coming back."

"The metal taste in my mouth is fading so everything is a frickin' revelation, you know? And I'm still hungry."

"Don't fight that feeling. Go get more from the buffet."

He put his hand on his stomach. Then nodded and got to his feet. "You know, I think I will."

By the time he came back, she'd managed two baby new potatoes and the rest of her chicken. The asparagus was a hard pass. Putting her knife and fork down, she was more than content to sit and watch Daniel shove food into his face like he hadn't had anything to eat in years.

For a moment, she entertained her usual fantasy that he'd just had a really bad bout of pneumonia and was recovering.

"I love taking a shower with you," she murmured.

"You know, I couldn't agree more." He wiped his mouth with a fancy white napkin. "What do they say, cleanliness is next to godliness? Although I feel like we got pretty dirty."

"Yes, we did."

He continued to eat some more, and then, between bites, he said, "Listen, I'm going to head down to the lab for a while."

"Oh, okay. More of Gus's magic sauce? Or is he finally letting you exercise some."

"Yeah, something like that." He moved a potato around with his silver fork. "Actually, I'm doing a little research for C.P."

"About what?" When he didn't immediately answer, she murmured, "Oh, that."

"In a weird way, it feels good to do something productive." He motioned back and forth with his fork. "I'm not going out into the field or anything. I'm just trying to make sense of some old files in a database. Trying to figure out who was knocking on our door last night."

"Are we a target here?"

"Well, the dead man on the lawn suggests yes. The question is whether whoever it is will have the resources to get through all our defenses. The smartest thing C.P. ever did was move into this house. Blowing up something under a cornfield in a rural town is one thing. This estate? Sure, Walters has a population of a hundred, but the footprint of a mansion like this? It is as far from invisible as you can get."

"Yet that's what you were sent here to do." Lydia put her hands forward. "I'm not accusing you of —"

"Oh, you're right. That is what I came to

do — but my focus was the lab. And the difference now is that she plugged up the entrances and tunnels on the mountain. Even if somebody were to blast the hatches — which would create a light show and set off some really big boom-booms — they're just going to face concrete caps and an excavation job that will take days, if not weeks, to get through." He pointed to the floor. "She's centralized the access now, which means fewer entry points to defend. You need a lot of firepower and know-how to get into the lab now, and until I know otherwise, this house is still the safest place for us to be."

"Are we prisoners here, then?"

"It's safer that way. At least until we know what's going on."

Lydia thought about what Xhex had told her, about how she had to go to the mountain, and found herself standing up in a rush. "Well, I'm not going to live in fear. I'm still going to go out."

"Lydia, be reasonable —"

"I'm not the target and neither are you."

"Anybody associated with C.P. Phalen is a target."

Crossing her arms, she tried to imagine not being able to run free, and the panic choked her so badly she had to pace around the table. As she circled, she stared out into the darkness, picturing the meadow, the forest, remembering the smell of the clean air and the feel of the grass under her feet, her paws.

"I'm going to keep living my life."

Daniel put down his fork. "Be serious here. You don't know what this type of killer is capable of."

"I was out there last night by the car. They went after the guard, not me. I walked right out into the darkness. They don't want us —"

"That is not a reasonable conclusion. Maybe whoever it was knew they'd gotten spotted and backed off in case defensive reinforcements were called. Which in fact they were. You've got to trust me on this. I understand you're frustrated at the thought of —"

"I'm not like you, Daniel. I think you're forgetting that."

Daniel opened his mouth. Closed it.

Going around to her chair, she sat back down. "I have instincts and capabilities that humans don't, and I've never hesitated to use them. I'm already living in terror of your disease, I'm not making space for that kind of fear anywhere else."

"Lydia." Except then he stared at his

plate. As he pushed his half-eaten seconds away, he cursed. "I'm not going to tell you what to do."

"Good. Thank you."

After a moment, he put out a hand, palm up. When she covered it with her own, he cursed. A couple of times.

"I'll be fine," she said. "You can trust me."

Eight p.m. Showtime was early, and the fact that Gus had decided not to wait until midnight was just fine with C.P.

As she took the elevator down to what she thought of as the highway to the lab, she was in a trance. And when she started the long walk to the main access point, she was going against the grain — and causing a stir. Many staff were leaving for the night, and a lot of the lab techs and researchers tripped up as they passed her.

She thought of Daniel as she nodded at them regally, like she was dressed as her usual self.

Battle-ax, huh. At the moment, she was feeling more like a thumbtack.

When she got to the checkpoint, she watched from a vast distance as her hand reached out and put her forefinger on the reader. The steel panel retracted to reveal a bald hallway with one-way mirrors running down the long sides, the bulletproof glass obscuring the security detail that would hit the nerve gas if there was any kind of infiltration.

She thought of Rob again.

She was still thinking of him as the panel ahead of her slid back and she stepped through. Out in the lab proper, there were a whole lot of vacancies at the workstations, but a few stragglers remained hard at work in their white coats and their goggles and their computers. She was struck by an absurd desire to go over and hug them, one by one.

"No more battle-ax," she murmured.

The clinic area, where Gus was going to treat her, was way down the line, the patient rooms and nuclear medicine equipment set away from the open area as well as the negative pressure labs. Gus's office was also among this lineup, and she stopped at his door first. After her knock wasn't answered, she went farther along, rounded the corner, and came to the treatment space she was going to be in.

Looking down at her thick socks, she felt as though she were stepping over a barrier, and once she was on the other side, there would be no returning.

She had rolled so many dice over so many

years, and this was her final throw.

"Luck be a lady tonight," she murmured as she pushed the door wide.

Gus was there, sitting at the built-in desk across from the hospital bed, the glow from the computer monitor casting blue light over the face she had come to rely on when she was feeling at loose ends. As usual, there was a lab report up on the screen, and she dreaded more testing.

Maybe he'd changed his mind about the results from the other facility and reversed his decision about not doing any more scans.

At this point, she was prepared to just consent away any risks and move on with it.

"I'm ready," she said when he didn't look over at her. "Hello? Gus. Are we starting or what?"

When he just shook his head at his screen, and then rubbed his eyes, a pit bottomed out in her stomach. In a hollow voice, she demanded, "What's going on."

"I need you to take a seat."

"Okay."

She started in his direction, but he shook his head. "Over there. Please."

"Okaaaay." Rerouting, she went across and sidled up onto the hospital bed. "Now tell me what's going on."

As her heart started to pound, she put her hand at the base of her throat and reminded herself that as far as bad news went, she'd maxed out on dire straits. There were no more breaking stories that could be worse than what she had already heard.

"I swear to God, St. Claire," she snapped, "if you don't start talking *right* now, I'm going to put my head through the wall."

He turned around on his swivel chair and almost met her eyes. "You're pregnant."

C.P. blinked. Then shifted herself a little farther back on the mattress. "I'm sorry, what did you say."

"You are pregnant."

The words were spoken crisply, with enunciation worthy of an English professor. And yet she still didn't understand them.

"You're mistaken." She shrugged. "I'm infertile."

"Clearly not." Gus's eyes lowered to his hands and he cracked his knuckles one by one. "Needless to say, this changes everything."

"No, it doesn't. I'm not pregnant."

"As part of your work-up at MD Anderson, they tested your urine for a variety of things."

"The test is wrong."

"It's not."

"It is."

As they went back and forth, the volley of their syllables rose in both speed and volume — and meanwhile, in the back of her head, a low-level scream started rising in pitch.

"Gus, someone messed up."

"I seriously doubt it." Now his eyes locked on hers. "And you have some very critical thinking to do."

She put both her palms straight out, like she was stopping a speeding car. "After all the chemo I have had, over the course of my life, there is absolutely *no* way I'm pregnant." When he just stared at her, she threw her hands up. "What. I'm not. So I don't know what to . . . tell you."

At that moment, she made a connection that chilled her to the bone. And as if Gus had been waiting for that one-plus-one to get to its equal sign, he once again looked away.

Her guard, Rob. Who had been killed last night.

"I'm not pregnant," she said firmly. "Let's run the test again."

There was a sizable pause before Gus got to his feet. "Fine. But while I'm dipping the stick, I suggest you start thinking about what you're going to do."

"What do you mean, what-I'm-going-to-do. The test is going to be negative and then we're going to finish whatever else you need to do so we can get moving."

"Just so you and I are perfectly clear, I am not administering Vita-12b to a pregnant woman." His dark eyes were grave. "I am also *not* advising you to get an abortion. That is none of my business."

"There's nothing to discuss. Because I'm —"

"Not pregnant." He went over to the door. "We'll see about that."

TWENTY-NINE

After Daniel headed down to the lab, Lydia went to their bedroom — and lasted about fifteen minutes before she got so antsy, she was ready to pull her own hair out. As she paced around, she kept looking into the bathroom, and every time she saw the shower and their two damp towels hanging together on the rods on the wall, she felt a fresh wave of sorrow come over her.

There was one, and only one, remedy for her agitation.

But she was going to be a little more careful if she was going out. In light of what happened the night before, she didn't feel right about just slipping out the sliding door. Instead, she went back through the house and then down into the basement, to the tunnel that ran under the parking area to the garage. At the far end, she ascended a short stack of steps and entered the heated interior thanks to a passcode — and promptly decided against taking one of the SUVs to some remote location before she shifted. She'd just get herself followed, right? After all, humans expected people to take vehicles places, and assuming the estate was being watched on its periphery, it would be more dangerous for her to try to leave that way.

Besides, she was going to go out with four-wheel drive of sorts, wasn't she.

Striding down the lineup of grilles and taillights, she went to the side pedestrian door, entered a code, and propped the weight open about an inch with a rock. After quickly shedding her clothing, she folded the pullover, the jeans, even the socks and underwear, into a neat pile, and set the lot on top of a bag of salt that had been brought in for the coming snowfalls.

Then she closed her eyes.

Her transformation was fast, like her body was a well-oiled machine, and in fewer than a dozen heartbeats, she was down on her paws and whispering out into the grass. As she stared out of different eyes, the landscape of the house and grounds was shaded in a new way, everything dimmer yet sharper, too, like an oil painting's depiction had been re-rendered with a fine-nibbed, black and white ink pen.

Staying in the lee of the garage, she sent her senses out into the darkness, and when she came up with nothing, she started off, her tail down, her head lowered as well. She wasn't worried about the guard dogs. The pair of Dobermans knew her in both her incarnations now.

They were no danger to her.

Tonight, the moon was early to rise, and the clouds that drifted over its crescent provided her with a little camouflage as she skulked for the tree line. Once she penetrated the pines and oaks, she started to move with greater alacrity, cantering now, making good time over the distance. As she went along, forest animals got out of her way, even though she presented no threat to the deer or raccoons. She hadn't been hungry in her human form; she wasn't hungry in this one, either.

And soon, she was really going at it with the speed.

As she leapt over fallen trunks, and dodged around boulders and stumps, while she tested her strength and endurance, a part of her soul started to sing — and the uncomplicated joy was like a drug to her, the feeling of freedom mixing with the cold night air to intoxicate her, especially as the ground began to rise and her ascent of the mountain's base steepened.

The harder the going, the faster she went.

She needed the exhaustion that she would find when she reached the summit. She needed the solitude, too.

An hour later, when she finally crested that last rise and trotted around to the clearing that faced the valley, she was panting so heavily that her ribs were like fists around her lungs, squeezing and releasing to pump air. And as she looked up at the heavens above, the clouds decided to part like stage curtains, the full glory of the moonlight piercing down from the sky.

Lifting her head, she began to howl.

And tried to take solace as her nocturnal call . . . was answered by others of her kind.

She had meant what she'd told Xhex. She already knew that the mountain was her home —

Crack.

At the sound of the stick off to the side, she wheeled around, bared her fangs, and began to growl.

And that was when a male voice spoke to her: "You don't have to be afraid. I'm not going to hurt you."

Blade had known that his wolf would have to come to the mountain. It had been in her grid the night before when she had been up here. And it had remained in her grid when she'd been down at that house. In fact, the intention was perpetual — although after she'd stood in the pines with Xhex, what had been impulse became obsessional to her.

He was going to have to thank his sister for encouraging this.

So yes, he had been certain Lydia Susi was going to be here, and all he'd had to do was wait for her — and he hadn't been worried that she'd bring Daniel Joseph.

Her memories told Blade that she preferred to come here alone.

This was her solace away from her dying mate, the place where she could breathe and shore up her strength for the sadness and grief she stewed in down below.

Thus, she was before him. And she was magnificent.

"You were told to come find something on the mountain," he said in a low voice — and he knew she understood him in her wolf form. He could tell by the way she tilted her head. "Therefore, I am here for you."

He'd deliberately kept his red robes on because he'd anticipated she would ascribe to him a religious connotation — and with the way those glowing lupine eyes stared up at him, he knew she had.

"Your mate is dying. There is nothing you can do. You are in the transition between what is your present and what will soon be your past. You worry what is next, but that is no longer a concern. I have found you. I am here . . . for you."

On a lot of levels, he couldn't believe what was coming out of his mouth, but then he reminded himself that he was just trying to get her to stay with him a little tonight and then come again tomorrow. He needed time to understand this reaction of his, time to figure out — and neutralize — the burning he felt in his veins when he saw her.

"I will never hurt you," he repeated. Like it was a vow.

And strangely, he meant it.

In response, her nostrils flared, and her twitching jowls relaxed a little, less of her very impressive set of fangs showing. Likewise, the muscles in her thighs stopped spasming. But she didn't trust him yet, not by a long shot — and he was under no illusions. If she didn't like something, anything, about him, she was going to be off into the night, possibly never to return.

Either that . . . or she was going to attack him.

And he would have welcomed that.

For a moment, he had an image from back in his private quarters: his beautiful scorpion, so small, so deadly.

Ah, so that's what this is, he thought with some relief.

Lydia could kill him. Not easily, because he would fight back to the death against her. But it was impossible for him to respect anyone or anything that was not a threat to him and likewise . . . he was compelled by anything that presented him with a mortal danger.

"You will come here," he told her, "and I will be waiting for you. That is all for now. I shall see you on the morrow at this time — and worry not. There is no threat down at the house, not against you. You are safe to come and go."

He knew she was itching to change form, and it would be entirely pleasing to see her naked — another surprise for him. Except he could not be here for very long. He had to condition her to want to meet him, and therefore, he needed to leave her curious and a little confused.

He would be on her mind.

She would come tomorrow.

And then, one way or another, he could get her out of his system so he could finish his work — and move along to destroy that lab.

After which . . .

Well, he was going to take a long fucking vacation, he thought just as he was about to dematerialize away — from his wolf and her mountain.

THIRTY

"So you have things to think about."

As Gus spoke, he held up the test in front of C.P. Phalen. Then he put the wand with its two windows and all its lines down on the rolling table next to the hospital bed. Turning away, he was at a loss — but that had to do with so much more than where his physical location was.

He went over and sat on his stool because he didn't know what else to do. The good news? He'd been a doctor for a very long time, so his role in this bombshell moment was fairly prescribed.

Har, har.

Over on the bed, C.P. took the test by the end you were supposed to hold, and tilted it so she could see those peepholes. When she just stared at the result, he cleared his throat.

"That's a strong response," he heard himself say. "But to be more precise, we'll need a blood test."

"This can't be happening."

"So you weren't using protection, I'm guessing. Or was there a malfunction?"

He had no clinical reason for going there, and he feared his personal one was making him behave like an ass. But he couldn't stop himself.

"Of course I didn't use anything," C.P. said in a numb way, like she was talking to herself. "I was told I couldn't have children — why did Anderson not catch this?"

"They did." He shrugged. "As for why it didn't come up in your patient assessment report? I can't answer that — maybe they were waiting to tell you at that appointment you skipped."

And yes, it would have been more likely she'd be infertile because of the amount of chemo she'd had over the course of her lifetime, but who didn't use protection for other reasons?

Someone who didn't think they had a long life ahead of them, that's who, he thought.

Across the way, C.P. came into sharp focus for him. She was dressed for treatment, nothing binding on her body, everything loose, cotton, and comfy — and goddamn, he wished he'd never lent her that fucking fleece. He certainly didn't want it back now.

Pregnant. As if he needed a more obvious confirmation of what he'd walked into with that bathroom of hers — and the father was dead.

Sitting there all alone, she looked so tired, so vulnerable, the dark circles she usually concealed with expensive makeup smudging under her eyes, her lips pale without their applied tinting, her hair limp as it fell forward into her face, no spray on it to keep it curled and in check.

She didn't even have shoes on, just thick, fluffy socks.

Then again, she'd come here expecting to receive therapy.

He glanced to the door. He'd told the three nurses and the other oncologist he'd asked to stay for the administration of the drugs to go home as soon as he'd noticed the test in her voluminous records. That had been back at five in the afternoon. And then he'd called C.P. down here — only after he'd gotten his own shit together.

"What's going to happen if I keep . . ." She cleared her throat. "If I keep the pregnancy going."

Clearly, she was having trouble saying "baby."

His eyes went back to the test. "It'll be a race between the pregnancy and the leukemia. And excuse me for being blunt, but that's assuming you don't miscarry along the way."

The way her hands went to her flat stomach told him everything he needed to know about what her decision was going to be — and maybe more than she realized: She was going to want to keep what was inside of her, no matter how the baby came out. No matter what had happened to the father.

A kindling respect crushed what little was left of his stupid-ass hopes. Which should never have existed in the first place because, really, what was he hoping for? Well, he wanted her, still, and maybe he had lived inside their professional relationship, creating a house of intimacy that he had been shacking up in without being cognizant of his new address.

This was a good thing, he told himself. This refocus he had going on.

"You're going to need to get a high-risk obstetrician," he said. "Your age isn't necessarily a problem, but your AML is going to be a challenge."

"You'll be my oncologist still."

She was speaking absently, like she was developing her plan and he was the top bullet point.

Sorry, C.P., he thought.

"No," he said. "I'm a researcher, not a clinician."

That was not entirely true, the lines between the two obviously being blurred given his work in the lab. But there was no way he could give her the treatment she needed and deserved. His objectivity was shot to shit.

Well, and then there was the other reason he couldn't be hers.

Her physician, that was.

Gus cleared his throat and tried like hell to pull himself back from the abyss. "You need to go to Houston and follow through with whatever Anderson tells you. You and this baby require a team, an integrated team. Get yourself a nice crash pad down there, and do what you need to." He waved his hand around. "Forget this shit with Vita."

He thought about what that mysterious caller had told him. And what had been offered.

What he had accepted when they had called back an hour ago.

"Sell the bitch and let it go," he said hoarsely. "Take your money and live your life because you may have an heir who'll need resources at the end of . . . it all."

As he rattled on, C.P. Phalen was just staring down at her stomach, and he doubted she heard what he was saying. Probably for the best. His pain had leaked out there at the end.

C.P.'s hearing was on a delay: She was processing so much that it was hard to internalize what Gus was saying to her — except then his words sank in.

Looking at him sharply, she said, "You can consult on my case, though."

"No, C.P." He shook his head. "I'm afraid I can't."

"But —"

"For one, how would you explain the relationship, how I was involved in your care? I dropped off the national stage like three years ago. Now I'm back and talking to a bunch of experts about your case? Be real."

"We can work around that —"

"I don't have admitting privileges any-more, anywhere, either." He put his hand up. "It's a hard no, C.P. So stop arguing. You've been too rich, for too long, and that makes you think you can have your way just because you want something. You can't with me. Not on this."

She opened her mouth. Closed it. As a feeling of buzzy paranoia vibrated through her chest, she said, "I'm still going to see you here at my lab, though. Even if I sell, it'll take half a year to close a deal. Minimum."

"Well, that's the other thing I need to talk to you about."

There was a long pause, and then he began to run his hands back and forth on the tops of his thighs.

"You're not leaving the lab," she said in a rush. "Gus, what the hell? You're *not* going."

"I, ah . . ." His eyes swung in her direction, but avoided a direct lock with her own stare. "I accepted a new job about an hour ago."

A cold rush hit her head and shot throughout her body. "What? What about Vita? What about —"

"I'm moving on. I've done what I can here and I'm —"

"You have a non-compete clause," she cut in. "In case you don't remember your contract."

"Oh, I remember. I reread everything this afternoon. Every last fucking word — so thanks for the refresher, but I don't need it." He got to his feet and jacked up his jeans. "And as for that non-compete? Try and enforce it in court. You'd have to out what you're doing here, and that isn't going to be a good look."

For a moment, she just stared over at him. His t-shirt was Pink Floyd's *The Dark Side of the Moon.* How perfect.

As for the contract, she had to laugh. "Okay. When's your last day."

"Today."

"No notice? You . . . bastard. I can't believe you're just leaving me — the lab, I mean. After everything you've done here. Are you even going to say goodbye to your staff?"

He reached into his pocket and took out his pass card to the garage. "I'm assuming you'll have the IT guys wipe my prints off the security checks. I'm leaving my laptop, obviously."

"Where are you going?"

When she didn't take his card, he put it on the rolling table, next to the pregnancy test. The image of the two side by side was instantly etched into her memory, and she thought of that moment, so recent and yet another lifetime ago, when he had nearly kissed her.

"That is none of your business. Goodbye, C.P. It's been a helluva ride." He glanced down her body for a split second. "And I wish you luck, I really do. If something happens, Leonardo can administer Vita. He knows the protocol backwards and forwards because he developed it with me."

Tell him not to go, she thought. *Just tell him —*

Gus shrugged and went over to the door. "Life sends us curveballs sometimes. All we can do is make the best of them, you know? You're a strong woman. If anyone can get through all this, and come out with a healthy baby? It's you."

And justlikethat, he was out of the room, the panel closing slowly behind him.

C.P. stayed where she was, and as the minutes ticked by on the clock that was over on the wall — the one with the digital readout on a twenty-four-hour cycle, the one that went to tenths of a second — she realized she was waiting for him to come back.

When he didn't, she hustled out into the hall and went to his office. The door that had been closed was now open, held wide with a kick foot.

He'd taken all his things: The framed and signed Kobe jersey. The Michael Jordan basketball in its Lucite cube. The corkboard with the ticket stubs on it. The stuffed Kermit the Frog that she had resisted asking him about —

Footfalls. Out in the hall, closing in.

Oh, thank God.

Pivoting around, she said, "Let's talk this through —"

Daniel Joseph stopped short. As he noticed what was going on inside the office, his mouth opened, like he was about to say something, but then he clamped his jaws shut.

Looking around at the blank walls, he said, "What happened to Gus?"

The urge to prevaricate was so strong that C.P. tried out a lie or two to herself: He's redecorating. Or how about: He's adopting a minimalist lifestyle. No, wait: He's moving his office up to the house.

"He's left," she blurted.

Daniel leaned forward and cupped his ear. "I'm sorry, what?"

"He's gone. Moved on to another position — and before you ask, no, he refused to tell me who he was going to work for."

But she had an idea who it was. Fucking Gunnar. It had to be Gunnar.

"Oh. Okay." Daniel swept his cap off and rubbed his skull. "All right."

"Is there something you need?" she asked, by way of getting him to change the subject.

She could understand, given how much Gus had had to do with his case, that the news must be a visceral shock and very destabilizing. But she couldn't help anybody else with their issues at the moment.

"Yeah, actually." Daniel thumbed over his shoulder in the direction of the vacant office she'd let him use. "I've been rattling some cages. You mind if I ask you a really fucking crazy question?"

Rubbing her eyes, she wondered when her brain was going to come back online. Probably never. "You know what, now's not a good time."

"I'm not sure we have a choice when it comes to timing."

Truer words had never been spoken. "Okay, what is it?"

Daniel took a deep breath and then started talking. Standing next to the man, C.P. watched his mouth move, and his hands lift up and shift back and forth in front of him, and his Adam's apple ride up and down in the front of his throat.

And then he stopped.

Oh, so he must be done. And as his words sank in, she had to say, she was not surprised. This was the way the night seemed to be going, and if there was one thing she had learned over the last decade, it was that choice had less of a role in destiny than she would have wanted.

"Come with me," she said with exhaustion.

Then again, anything was better than this empty office.

THIRTY-ONE

Well, what do you know, Daniel thought.

As C.P. led the way into a windowless, secured vault, lights came on across the ceiling, and he had to blink the glare away. After his retinas adjusted, he was able to focus on what was lying, in pieces, on the examination table in the center of the space. The android was so human-like, it was something out of the mind of James Cameron, the skin some kind of polyurethane that retained its peachy color, the face structure molded to perfection, the body dimensions exactly correct. And underneath the surface? So many stainless-steel parts, all connected and state of the art, a full set of artificial limbs that were coordinated by some kind of motherboard.

A warrior who needed no food, no water, no sleep, and no recovery or healing from injuries.

"Is this what you're talking about?" she

asked him as she went right up to the body.

"Yup." He joined her at the table and focused on the eye sockets, which were empty. "And it looks exactly like the ones I killed. I always took the eyes."

Leaning over, he took the head and angled it to him. The skull had been disconnected from the spinal cord, just like the arms and legs had been unplugged from the torso. As its vacant sockets seemed to seek his own stare, he thought, not for the first time, that this shit was straight-up Terminator, a bio-mechanical unit created to function among people while being controlled by directives that were programmed into its CPU.

"How long have you had these remains?" he asked.

"Since the spring. We found it out in the woods. Someone had hid it —"

"Yeah, this was my kill." He pointed to damage on the skull. "These bullet wounds are mine. This unit came after Lydia and me."

"We didn't know what it was. But we were tracking the pair of you. I was aware things at the Wolf Study Project were unraveling and that the setup I had there for testing compounds had gotten out of hand. When my guards found the android body, it was quickly apparent there was someone else in

Walters."

He tapped the eye sockets. "I always took the peepers because these machines can be regenerated. Reused? Is that the word? And I wanted to slow down their return into service."

"So whose are they?"

"We were trying to find out because they were getting inconvenient. More and more were interfering with our work — and I'll be honest. When one of them turned up here? Tracking Lydia and me? I thought maybe they were a creation of yours."

"No, I'm strictly research. Not . . . whatever this is. We took the thing apart because we wanted to understand it — but there are no clues as to who made it. The skin — is extraordinary. It's bioidentical nearly. The circulatory system? The brain? It's like no computerized anything — or mechanical, for that matter — that any of my men had ever seen. I keep it here because this is a lead-lined containment room. I figured that whatever tracker was on it would be neutralized, if not because it was functionally compromised then because of the insulation."

"Smart."

Daniel went down the table, inspecting the body. The skin had degraded a little, but nothing like a real human's would have once its oxygen source was cut. The muscles were the same, peeling back from the stainless-steel joints, yet still rosy in appearance.

"So I'm about halfway through the F.B.G.'s database of reports," he said. "And the thing that stands out is that there's nothing current filed after this past spring. I don't know where the staff went — or whether they switched their IT shit to a different platform. But something has changed in a big way."

C.P. made a noise that could have meant anything, and given the way she was staring into the middle distance in front of her face, he knew he'd lost her attention.

"If this is not yours," he said, "then I think there's someone else out there looking for immortality."

This got her to focus and her eyes shifted to his. "What do you mean?"

Daniel put his hand on the biomechanical soldier's shoulder. "Whoever is making these has serious resources, and they're not using them for medical research. This is about war — someone has developed and is testing a better-mousetrap soldier. So I'm curious, has Vita-12b or any of your compounds — do any of them have chemical weapon applications?"

C.P. recoiled. "No. I mean, we work with the immune system. Ten years ago, the original compound I was trying to develop was about reversing the aging process — or at least slowing it down. Through our results, we sidestepped into immunotherapy for cancer. That was when I hired Gus. I've been parallel processing the two strains of research ever since, but Vita was what took off. Mother Nature is stingy with her life cycle secrets, as it turns out. It's not just about the length of the telomere."

Daniel pursed his lips. "Okaaaay, I'm going to pretend I understood any of that. But my question stands. Are there any applications for warfare from your research?"

C.P. crossed her arms over her head physician and researcher's fleece.

Former head researcher, that was, he tacked on.

Then one side of her lips lifted in a smile that absolutely did not reach her eyes. "Not that we're aware of. But you know, just because you're not looking for something doesn't mean it doesn't exist."

As Gus hopped onto the pediway that progressed out to the remote parking lot, he had a hard time believing that it was the

406

last time he was making this smooth, gliding trip. And in the manner of a final passage, he found himself absorbing details he'd never noticed before: From the tube-like nature of the corridor to the all-white, George-Jetson-techno-futuristic design of everything, it all made him think of what an airport in 2050 was going to look like.

One thing wasn't new. At the end of the ride, as he stepped off and the double doors automatically opened for him, he once again felt as though he'd been shit out into the garage.

While the stainless-steel panels clicked shut behind him, he stopped and looked back, marveling at how you didn't always know when you were going to do something for the last time. When he'd come into work today? After he'd gone home to his rental house for just a shower, a change of clothes, and a bowl of cereal?

He hadn't known his work with C.P. Phalen was going to end.

Walking over to his Tesla, he remembered arguing with her about the damn thing. And then he thought about nothing in particular as he drove out of the garage, hooked up with the rural road, and eventually found his way to the Northway.

His commute back and forth to the lab

was a good twenty-five minutes in each direction, even if you assumed he went eighty, which he always did because his version of rush hour was either crack-of-ass early or red-eye late. And as for why the distance was necessary? Walters, New York, where C.P. had located her lab, was in the middle of nowhere. If you wanted to live in a town where you could order Thai food and get it Ubered to your door? You needed to put in the miles.

The next thing he knew, his headlights were washing over the front of the condo he'd been in for the last three years. Thanks to renting the modest, two-story crib, he'd banked plenty of scratch — in the back of his mind, he'd always known he wasn't staying permanently, so there was no reason to commit a bunch of cash to a real estate anchor. Good thing he only had two months left on his lease, not that it would have mattered.

His new boss had put his money where his mouth was —

I'm not just putting my money where my mouth is — I'm putting my life on it.

As C.P.'s voice barged into his head like a squatter pitching a pup tent in the front yard, he punched the garage opener as if his forefinger were a fire poker.

Great. If these sound bites were the way shit was going to go from now on? He was going to lose it.

As the horizontal panels took their sweet time ascending their track, he glanced around at the condo development. There were probably fifty units circling a central core, and most of them had an extra vehicle in their short driveways or parallel parked on the street in front because no one had a two-car garage. Landscaping was kept to a minimum, but maintained well, and the streetlights were glowing peach in the darkness, turning the cold night into something that made him think of an old-fashioned movie set.

North Dakota, huh, he thought as he drove forward and turned off the Tesla. *Guess it's as good a place as any — although talk about remote.*

Then again, that was the point, wasn't it.

Getting out, he went to the door into his kitchen and hit the button mounted by the jamb as he opened things up. Inside the condo, he tossed his keys on the counter and then stalled out. The fact that there was no one to call with his news — and he wouldn't have had the energy to go through it all anyway — was kind of depressing. But the former was the consequence of his focus, and the latter something that could be cured with a trip to his refrigerator and a fucking nap.

On that note, he went over, cracked his icebox, and reached in for a Coke. Two cardboard boxes with half-eaten takeout were molting in a field of single-serving condiments, and instead of throwing them out, he just let that door shut itself.

Bet Frigidaire would have been surprised to know that their product could be used as a calorie crypt.

He cracked the top on the Coke and looked out to the front of the condo. There was a mail slot in the door, and the pile of unopened mail that fanned out on the square of entry tile was another mess caused by his neglect.

For all his IQ, he'd never been any good at the nuances of adulting, and yeah, it was true, he hid behind the noble pillars of his Very Important Work to blow off things like registering his car, doing his taxes, getting annual physicals. Thank God for online banking or his credit score would have been in the double digits.

As he wandered across to the envelopes and flyers — because he didn't know what the hell else to do with himself — he frowned and got down on his haunches.

Putting the soda aside, he picked up a large manila envelope that was on top of the scatter. When he turned it right side up, he read the handwritten inscription that included his name and address, and then noted, at the bottom, the red letters: HAND DELIVER ONLY.

"What the fuck?"

Letting himself fall back onto his ass, he went to open the flap, only to find it taped shut to within an inch of its inanimate life.

He got up and went into the kitchen with whatever it was, and he needed a full minute to find a sharp knife because he never cooked and always ate with the plastic stuff that came with his takeout. Digging the tip of the blade into the layers of packing tape, he reflected on how he had no more interest in cleaning dirty cutlery than he did in dealing with his Visa bill —

What came out of the envelope . . . stopped the whole world.

It was a legal document that, after he scanned it . . . twice . . . seemed to suggest . . .

. . . that one Catherine Phillips Phalen, being of very sound mind, had given to him all of the rights to the ownership of Vita-12b, its precursors, and any forthcoming research associated with the compound.

"What the fuck did you do, Cathy," he breathed as he read things for a third time.

After which he looked up to find a shadowy figure standing about five feet away from him.

"Greetings, Dr. St. Claire," a mechanical voice announced.

When a gun was pointed at him, Gus shouted and thrust his arms forward. But that didn't do shit. As the contract fell off the counter in a flutter, he was shot, right in the chest.

THIRTY-TWO

The male figure was about to disappear, so she had to act fast.

Up on Deer Mountain, that was the thought that went through Lydia's mind as she stared through wolven eyes at the red-robed entity before her. Spurred on by a sense of urgency, she immediately went into her transformation, shifting her form — and sure enough, as she initiated the change, he became totally transfixed.

Whatever it took, she thought as she gave herself up to the magic, the energy flowing through her being, her body trading its identities as easily as a suit of clothing.

When she was once again of biped nature, she put out her hands. "Don't go."

The male in all the robing simply stared at her, his eyes wide, his stance steady and tilted forward on his hips as if he were utterly astonished with what he had just seen — and for some reason, she didn't think that boded well for him as some kind of savior. Weren't destiny's messengers supposed to be otherworldly and all-knowing?

Was this what Xhex had told her to come and find? If so, where was the light?

In the tense silence, Lydia thought of the number of times the ghost of her grandfather had visited her when she'd most needed his guidance — except he had only ever been a beacon warning her of a threat or dire consequence. He'd never actually told her anything about her situation.

Was this male here to give her direction about Daniel?

"Don't go," she repeated more softly.

As his eyes left hers and ran down her naked form, she had a thought he was just marveling about what she could do at will. Except then they returned and lingered on her breasts — and all at once, a scent carried over to her on the breeze . . . a scent of arousal.

Just as it registered, she was blinded by light, the illumination bright as a lightning strike, its origin unknown.

Yet she knew what it meant.

"Oh . . . God," she whispered as she covered her mouth with one hand and her breasts with the other arm.

"Are you unwell," the male blurted.

"Here, allow me."

As she heard a flapping of cloth and felt a swoosh of fabric around her body, she knew he had covered her with his robing. And she gripped the fine folds and held them to her trembling body as if they were a shield against arrows.

"What ails you," he demanded.

"Who are you?" she tossed back as she blinked blindly and tried to make sure her legs continued to accept her weight.

But then the illumination disappeared. As quickly as the light arrived, the glow was gone, and the mysterious man reappeared to her. Not that he'd gone anywhere.

When she just stared at him, he took a step back. No longer covered by the robes, she saw that he was dressed in a tight-fitting black uniform that made her think he was a soldier, especially given the gun belt around his hips.

Blinking quickly, she sagged in her own skin as tears welled.

"Why are you looking at me like that?" he said in a tense voice.

Lydia shook her head and it was a while before she could find her voice. "I was told to come to the mountain, that something would be waiting for me, something that I was going to need to go on . . ."

415

She started shaking her head. "Oh, God . . . no. I don't want this . . . I don't . . ."

Lydia stumbled back from the male, thinking about what her grandfather had told her, about where to go to see her future.

This was not dawn, though. This was still night —

"Watch out," the stranger said, "you're about to fall off the rocks — stop!"

"I don't want you!" she screamed at him. "I won't have you!"

Just as her foot twisted out from under her, the discharge of a gun, high-pitched and alarming, sounded right behind her.

The last thing she saw, before she stumbled to the ground and hit her head on something hard, was the male who had taken off his robes to protect her modesty getting shot in the shoulder.

Disorientated, she forced her eyes to focus.

The man who came up on them with the gun was also dressed in all black, but the uniform was different — and there was something about his face that didn't make sense. Then again, she'd been knocked in the head pretty badly —

As the soldier stepped over her, with his weapon still pointed at the male who had fallen to his knees, it dawned on her that she had seen him before. Back in the spring. When she and Daniel had been in the woods, up in the deer stand. He was the one who had been stalking them, who Daniel had taken down to the ground.

She couldn't forget that face.

With that connection going through her mind, her eyes narrowed on the attacker, who was clearly taking for granted that she had lost consciousness. Just as that gun took aim at the mysterious male again, she lunged up and threw herself onto the shooter. She had no idea what she was doing, but she had the sense that if she could just get that muzzle angled away —

Somehow, she nailed things exactly right, pile-driving into the soldier, knocking him off-balance just as he pulled that trigger. As the bullet sailed harmlessly into the view, he shoved her free of him with such force, she went flying, her body airborne and then some.

This was going to go very, very badly, she thought in mid-flight.

Sure enough, the soldier steadied himself in what seemed like slow motion, rerouted the gun back toward the other male . . .

. . . and pulled the trigger —

They knew who he was. And he knew about them.

That was what was going through Blade's mind at the moment the soldier came out of the pine trees right behind Lydia while she stumbled. He barely had time to turn away from the gunshot, and even as he did, he was caught in the shoulder, the bullet entering the meat of his upper arm. But he didn't give a shit about that.

The wolven. He had to save the wolven.

As he landed on his knees, the soldier with the gun stepped over Lydia and retargeted that weapon in Blade's direction.

Going for his own weapon, he fumbled and dropped it because of his injury —

From out of nowhere, Lydia threw herself at the soldier, hitting the uniformed fighter at precisely the right moment, not a second to lose, and in exactly the right place, not an inch to spare. She knocked that aim off, but not for long. The soldier swung his arm and sent her pinwheeling through the air, her body cast away as if it weighed next to nothing.

And then the gun was back, like Blade was its home.

Death, he thought. Finally. After all these years . . . it had come to find him.

"Not tonight, motherfucker," he said out loud.

Barging into the soldier's mind —

He got nothing; it was the strangest thing. There were no thoughts behind those eyes, no impulses, no emotions.

Oh, fucking hell, it was one of those —

A wolf attacked from over on the right, leaping from an outcropping of boulders, tackling the biomechanical nightmare off its feet — and then there were more of Lydia's kind, too many others to count, a swarm of the lupines covering the male form, biting, protecting their own.

Blade looked over at Lydia. She wasn't moving as she lay in the dirt.

Groaning, he crawled over uneven rocks to get to her, terrified about what he was going to find. His robes were heavy, he told himself; they would protect her.

Bullshit they would protect her.

Behind him, a series of yelping stopped him, and he looked back. The wolves were rearing away and shaking their heads as if they'd been stung. But of course . . . the electrical current. They'd breached the skin and gotten into the volts of the thing.

He kept going to Lydia. And as he came

up to her, her eyes fluttered.

"Are you okay?" she mumbled at him.

"Yes, but are you . . . all . . . right . . ."

Those were the last words he said before he lost consciousness from blood loss.

Guess he'd been hit somewhere more serious than just his shoulder.

But at least his wolf was with her kind.

THIRTY-THREE

As soon as Lydia had recovered a little, she got back up on her feet, and even though she had a head wound that was bleeding and her vision was blurry, she managed to get herself together and pull the male's body away from where the wolven attack had occurred. As she dragged him by the armpits, she met the eyes of the lupine predators who were standing around the soldier they'd taken down. The wolven had formed a circle around him, but they weren't savaging him, as if they were determined to keep him alive.

She nodded in thanks, recognizing each of their faces, all of their coat patterns, every tilt of their ears. They would hold the soldier where he lay while she assessed the male who had come to find her. And then she would call Daniel. He would know what to do —

"Ow."

421

She stopped and looked down. "You're alive?"

The male she did not want to know glanced up at her. "Stop. *Stop.* You're going to tear my arms off."

"Oh, sorry. I —"

As she dropped her hold, he landed like a side of beef. *"Ow!"*

"Shit!"

One of the wolves angled its head as if inquiring whether she needed help.

"Please," the male said as he sat up with a groan, "do resist the urge to help me. I'm already on the verge of passing out again."

"Sorry. You're bleeding."

"Thank you, I had *no* idea." Annoyed eyes struggled to focus on her as he put his hand up to the red rush at the top of his arm. "Now do us both a favor. Take my other gun out of my holster and flip the safety off. That thing over there is going to wake up again."

"What?"

"Gun — now! You're going to have to use it in —"

As he trailed off and listed to the side as if he were about to faint, she lunged down his body and grabbed the weapon from its holster. Releasing a howl into the air, she warned her brethren, even though surely that torn-apart soldier was well and truly dead —

Somehow, even though their attacker had been taken down and one of his legs had been ripped off, he sat up, turned his head toward her — and lifted his gun again.

"Fuck you," she growled.

Rage at everything, at Daniel's disease, at the death that was coming for him, at the male who had turned up in a blaze of light on this mountain — and at the goddamn soldier who had started shooting in the first place — came out in a shower of bullets. Lydia pulled the trigger over and over again until she was walking toward an enemy that she didn't need to define or to understand.

To utterly hate them.

In the back of her mind, the pinging noises of metal hitting metal didn't make a lot of sense, but she was too into her fury to care about anything. All of the built-up pressure from the previous six months came out until the magazine was empty — and when the clicking of the trigger was the only sound rising up from her spasming hand, she went still.

But not for long. With no more bullets at her disposal, she switched her grip and jumped forward. Landing with one knee on each side of the chest, she began pistol-whipping the soldier, beating his face and head, becoming even more unhinged.

Images of the most recent two weeks were fresh gasoline in her veins, especially those scans that had shown the tumor growth and new development. Her anger that it was all so unfair was the spark that started and kept her explosion going. She had endless reserves of strength and power, more than she'd ever had —

Someone was hauling her off the body. Someone was peeling her back.

She fought against them because she was outside of herself, beyond anything rational —

"Stop! Jesus Christ! It's fucking dead! Not that it was ever alive!"

Xhex just kept hauling the female back, no matter how much she got a fight in return. And finally, the wolven's energy started to fade, thank fuck. No one needed any more kicks to the shin.

"Lydia!" she barked. "Chill, just fucking chill!"

Saying the female's name helped get the wolven's attention, and all of a sudden, everything that had been engaged in the beatdown went limp: arms, legs, torso, the whole body turned into a noodle.

As Xhex held the female up off the ground, the wolven's panting was hoarse and the ocean-breeze scent of her tears replaced all the pine tree fragrance.

"You cool," Xhex muttered. "We fucking done with this?"

When a nod came back at her, she was careful as she lowered the female down to a soft patch of pine needles — and then it was a case of spoiled for choice when it came to focusing on something: She could pick either that apparent cyborg sonofabitch in a chewed-up uniform over there . . . the ring-around-the-dog-pound of wolves who were pacing the periphery . . . the female shapeshifter with the Rocky Balboa complex . . . or —

"Is he okay? Oh, God, is he dead?"

With a sudden surge, Lydia scrambled over to the gunshot victim, which was the last in the buffet of bullshit.

Blade, Xhex's brother, lay on his back with blood all over his chest. But the fucker was alive. Of course he was. Talk about your nine lives.

"Thank God you're here," Lydia said as she looked up at Xhex. "I didn't know who to call for help. Can we get a doctor — we need a doctor — or I can call Gus —"

Her brother's robes. The wolven was

425

draped . . . in Blade's red robes.

Jesus *Christ*.

"I'll handle everything," Xhex heard herself say with an edge.

Lydia leaned over the fallen male, patting at his chest. "He's still breathing. Quick, we need a —"

"I'll take care of him. You need to go."

"I can't leave now." Lydia shook her head. "I have to stay and make sure he's all right —"

"No, you don't."

"It's my fault he's hurt. It's too much to explain, but I think I was somehow being followed, and I came up here because you told me to. I brought that soldier with me. When this male here came out, and I spoke with him, I saw the blaze of light, just like you told me I would — and then — the shooting — and —"

"I'm going to take care of him —"

"I need to —"

"He's my fucking brother, okay?" Xhex snapped. When the female froze, it was a case of babble, babble, babble. "As much as I hate him, and in spite of the fact that I would move heaven and earth to avoid being anywhere near the asshole, I will, out of a misplaced loyalty — which, trust me, he doesn't deserve — make sure he is cared

426

for. Now get the fuck out of here because that" — she jabbed a forefinger at the metallic mess who was torn apart and full of bullet holes — "isn't a man, sweetheart. I don't know what the fuck it is, but I know we're both clear that you need to stay alive for that mate of yours."

"Your . . . brother?"

Xhex rubbed one of her eyes — and made the speck of dirt that was irritating it somehow worse. "Look, if you really are being followed, and there are no bullets flying around you right now? Take this goddamn opportunity and leave."

"But . . . he's your brother?"

"I don't like it any better than you do." Xhex took out her cell phone. "And I'm going to get him help, I promise. But that's because it would bother the shit out of you if he died up here and I already know how much you're carrying on your plate. Now please, do us both a favor and get the *fuck* out of here."

Lydia brushed at the red robe that covered her, and as she did, the bottom half fell open. She was naked, it seemed.

Oh . . . so it's like that, Xhex thought.

"What the fuck are you doing now, Blade," she muttered under her breath. Then more loudly, she said, "Go. He's in good hands."

At that point, there was a squeak — and the wolven froze as she stared over at the half-man, half-metal carcass.

"What is *that.*" She pointed at the remains. "What . . . the *hell* is *that*?"

"You were the one shooting at it — damned if I know. But I'm going to find out and I have the right people to help me."

Lydia glanced around. Then she refocused on Blade. "Will you let me know what happens to him?"

"Only if you leave."

The female took a deep breath. Then she unclasped the red robe and let it drop to the ground. A moment later, a wolf was in the place where she stood — and that lasted little longer than a blink. Finally, she was gone, disappearing into the pines on fleet paws that made absolutely no sound.

As wolf calls echoed in the distance, like the female's kind were howling out for her, Xhex refocused on her motherfucking brother: Blade's eyes were open and locked on her.

"I knew you were faking it," she muttered. "And what the *fuck* are you doing."

"Well," he said in that annoyingly superior voice of his, "currently, I am about halfway to bleeding out. Thank you for the inquiry —"

"You leave that female alone. I don't know what you're playing at, but her stakes are way too high, and she does not deserve to be fucked with."

Blade coughed weakly and closed his lids. "Are you calling for help, then, or is your cell phone some kind of fashion accessory."

"I'm not saving you unless you leave her alone."

"Why do you care so much about a stranger, sister mine."

Because I was in her shoes the night before last, with a mate who was dying and nothing on the other side of that death.

And Christ knew Blade was no kind of lifeboat — and if that wolven thought he was the one she was sent up here to find, because of something Xhex had said? Even if it was a big misunderstanding, Xhex wanted no part of that fucking karma.

"What's it going to be," she said. "Are you going to give me your word, or are you going to die? Either way, I'm fine with the outcome."

Blade looked at her again. Narrowed his eyes. "Are you . . . okay?"

"I'm not hemorrhaging. You?" She took out her phone and waved it around, the glow from the screen strobing over her brother's beautiful, cruel face. "What are

429

we doing? Are you getting medical help, or am I waiting another fifteen minutes before I call the Brotherhood to figure out what that thing is over there. Tick. Tock."

When he didn't reply, she glanced over her shoulder and took in the majestic view. "What are you doing out here, anyway."

"The same could be asked of you, sister mine." He coughed again. Then he lifted a weak hand and brushed the blood off his mouth. "You know, the irony of fate is something worthy of a *symphath.*"

"How so," she said with boredom.

"I cannot escape the conclusion, though you will no doubt not share it, that the two of us were meant to be here together, tonight . . . on this mountain."

"So turn me into a savior, why don't you. Don't go near that female again."

"Fine." He smiled a little. "You have my word."

For what it was worth, she thought to herself.

"Good answer," she muttered as she initiated the call to Doc Jane. "You just saved your life."

"You're the one with the phone, sister mine," he said between weak coughs. "Not me."

THIRTY-FOUR

The following morning, Daniel woke up after logging five hours of passed-the-fuck-out on the bed. The instant his eyes opened, he realized he was alone — so he sat up and put his feet on the rug. A quick glance over at the bedside table, and the note was right there.

Picking up the slip of paper, he unfolded it and smiled as he read the short missive. There was something quaint about Lydia leaving him a note before she left for work, something so wholesome and old-fashioned in the gesture — and the words were just as sweet: She hadn't wanted to wake him. She would be home early so they could talk. She was sorry to have missed him. She loved him.

He stroked his thumb over her signature. Twice.

"You're a sap. You're a fucking sap," he murmured.

431

In the bathroom, he took a shower and shaved. Then he brought the note with him into the closet and dressed in fresh clothes. It was clear she'd been in there earlier, a couple of her fleeces out on the center island, a pair of pants discarded like she hadn't liked the way they'd felt or looked.

Just as he was about to leave, he doubled back to the sets of built-in drawers that ran down the center of the space. Going to the left side and pulling open the top panel, he looked down. His wallet was an unfamiliar artifact from a distant era, and as he opened the flap, he frowned at the driver's license that was in the little clear plastic window.

It was like staring at an image of a son he'd never have: He felt like he'd aged an entire generation since the bureau had provided him with the fake ID.

Splitting the wallet's interior slot wide, he said, "Oh, I'm rich. Two twenties."

Going back into the drawer, he patted around the socks and underwear — until he was shoving what felt like half his arm into the space — and that was when he felt the key. The slip of metal was smooth and cool as he took it out, and as he put the motor-cycle's magic wand on his palm, he took a deep breath. Then he looked out toward the bedroom and thought about the guard who had been killed. And the fact that Lydia was refusing to stay inside.

He respected the confidence in herself, he really did.

It also made him nauseated with fear.

Two minutes later, he was pulling his leather jacket on, shoving his wallet into the ass of his too-baggy pants, and tucking a gun into an inside pocket by his chest wall. When he checked the rest of what he had in the coat —

He found a pack of Marlboros.

It was like getting pummeled from behind, and he even weaved on his numb feet.

Staring at the cigarettes' eye-catching red-and-white label, with its iconic lettering, he was filled with a piercing regret — and the emotion found expression as he crushed the pack in his fist.

He tossed the ruined mess in the waste-paper basket on the way to the door.

Down at the kitchen, he grabbed a bagel to go that was set out on the sideboard in the little dining room, and then went into the kitchen, following a fast chopping sound that made him wonder if Chef was having a seizure. Sure enough, the guy was bouncing a knife on a cutting board like the thing had cast aspersions on his manhood.

"Is C.P. around?" Daniel asked.

"Do I look like her secretary?" The man glared over the scallions he was slicing. "And no, she's gone. Said she would be back tonight or tomorrow."

"Okay. Thanks." The grunt he got in return was like a fuck-you left in the holster of the throat. "Listen, did Lydia have breakfast?"

As Chef looked up, Daniel held his palm out, all whoa-Nelly style. "Yeah, I know you're not her secretary, either."

"No, she didn't have breakfast. She took a traveler of coffee with her."

"Cool. Thanks."

Another grunt. And Daniel turned away because he was not ready to have that knife trained on him.

Back in the little dining room, he packed up a second bagel in a napkin and took a couple of the mini-tubs of cream cheese from the basket of jams and spreads. Then he stole a sterling silver knife.

"Borrowed it," he corrected under his breath as he left.

At the front door, he gave the security camera a little wave — and sure enough, the lock was sprung for him. As he stepped outside, he told himself he was glad the house was so tight — but then he looked over the lawn to where the body of that guard had lain.

And felt like they were all sitting ducks.

Down at the garage, he entered through the side door and then squared off at his Harley. He wished he could check in with Gus about what he was contemplating, but the guy hadn't returned the call he'd made late last night — and honestly, his motivation for such a touch-base, outside of an I'm-really-going-to-miss-you, was bullshit. No one, not even his (former) oncologist, could tell him whether he was going to have enough energy to drive into town on his bike — or whether he was going to wrap himself around a tree on the way there.

Or get shot by someone. Anyone.

Maybe his old boss.

After Daniel hit the door opener, he threw a leg over his bike — and kept thinking about that mechanized soldier. He wouldn't put it past Blade to have created subordinates that were automated. The control-freak fucker would appreciate the utter lack of insubordination — and it would explain why those hellish creations kept showing up wherever the operatives who worked for the guy were.

Then again, maybe they were a third party.

Either way, he'd never trusted his boss.

Putting the key in the ignition, he won-

435

dered whether the Harley was going to start. He wondered if he was going to remember how to shift. He wondered whether he was going to have the strength required to drive it at all. He wondered —

Started on a dime. With just one jam of his leg.

And then he was leveling the Harley on its tires, kicking free the stand, and revving the engine. The smell of gas and oil brought tears to his eyes, and so did the sound of the RPMs rising and falling.

Easing things into first gear, he was petrified, like he was an eleven-year-old taking something of his dad's.

But oh . . . you never forgot how to ride a bike.

As the garage door automatically shut behind him, he proceeded down C.P. Phalen's smooth driveway, passing into the chute that was created by the dual lineups of trees. When he got to the gates, they opened right away.

That was when he gunned it.

The powerful surge of speed took his breath away — or maybe that was the blast of wind in his face. With perfect coordination, he shifted, and with growing confidence, he added more gas. And that was when it came back. As the bright, cheerful fall sun fell unimpeded by humidity or clouds onto the winding gray asphalt strip in front of him, a wave of high-octane happiness — akin to what he'd experienced after he pleasured Lydia — flooded his interior.

Yes. Fuck *yes.*

This was what he needed: Out of the hospital. Away from the drugs. Not consumed with side effects.

When his eyes teared up, he told himself it was because of the rush of fresh air in his face.

But it might have been the gratitude.

Either way, what a gift.

The Wolf Study Project's quarter-mile-long driveway was right where Daniel had left it, and as he made the turn onto the organization's property, he was grinning and thinking of the bagel he was bringing his woman — but he was also on high alert. Yes, this was about delivering her some breakfast, and yes, he loved being back on the bike, and sure, it was terrific that he had made it this far on his own steam — yet he remained worried for her safety.

Maybe he needed to ask C.P. to send one of her guards over to the building while Lydia was on site working. They could be discreet about it — and if his woman thought it was overkill, maybe C.P. could help him talk some sense into . . .

As the WSP headquarters came into view, he eased off on the gas. And then hit the brakes with a sharp jab.

With the engine still purring between his legs, and his hand cranked on the brake, he stared in shock at the place where Lydia worked. Then he cut the Harley's engine, kicked out the stand, and dismounted.

The building had never been in pristine shape, but now it was totally run-down: The gravel parking area was choked with weeds, the single-story structure looked like it was growing a beard from all the vines, and there were branches down on its roof. One gutter had even been peeled off by some storm, and the exterior light sockets were empty of bulbs.

Walking over to the entrance, he cupped his hands to the glass and leaned in. The waiting room was picked clean of furniture. From Candy the receptionist's desk, to the chairs and sofa in the open area, to even the magazines that had sat, faded and unread, on the coffee table . . . it was all gone.

He tried the doorknob. Locked.

Heading down the long side of the building, he went to the rear clinic entrance. Also locked — and the part of the facility where the wolves were treated had no windows so there was no checking what had been cleared out of that part of the operation.

The last thing he did, before he got back on his bike, was go to the window in Lydia's office.

The venetian blinds were hanging all cockeyed, so he was able to get a look at the space. Inside . . . her desk was a dead zone, free of all computer equipment, paperwork, even her landline phone.

Back at his Harley, he jump-started the engine again and then looked over to the outbuilding where he'd briefly worked when he'd been fronting the role of a handyman. He didn't bother going over and trying to open the double doors. It was either going to still be the mess of hardware and seventies-era equipment it had always been, or it would be cleaned out.

Either way, his conclusion was unchanged.

The Wolf Study Project had been closed down. For a while.

And Lydia had been lying to him about where she went every day.

THIRTY-FIVE

Daniel had to go into the Walters town center to get gas before he could keep going. As he drove into the tiny constellation of businesses, the bank, grocery store/diner combination, and private-branded pump station were the same as before — which seemed like a miracle, although that made little sense. Only his world, not the larger, commonly held one, had been upended since the spring.

Since ten minutes ago.

And of course, as he went by the diner, he glanced at the lineup of customers having breakfast in the windows — and thought about how he and Lydia had met up there by chance after his interview with her.

He had lied to her at the beginning of their relationship.

She was lying to him at the end of it.

But why?

At the station, he pulled into a pump and

was distracted as he filled up, his mind whirling as he tried to keep his emotions in check. When he was finished, he twisted the cap back on his tank and knew where he was going to next — assuming he remembered the way.

Back on the county road, he followed the twists and turns, but the magic was gone. He was simply about getting himself from point A to B now.

When he came up to the house that Lydia had rented, he pulled off onto the shoulder, but didn't go down the driveway. No reason to. There were children's bikes in the front yard and a swing set off to the side. A minivan was parked by the back door, and a black Lab who was thick as a couch cushion got to his or her feet and started barking at him.

Well, guess she had given up her lease. He'd assumed she was still getting her mail there and that that was where she had gone when she'd brought her fall and winter clothes over.

Maybe she'd moved out then.

Hitting the gas, Daniel kept going, even though he wasn't sure where to head next. That issue was solved quick. Candy, the WSP receptionist, had a small house just out of town, and even though he couldn't remember her last name, he knew where her place was. Cutting the acceleration as he came up to her mailbox, he didn't bother with a turn signal as he piloted the way onto her drive —

Another short stop.

Lydia's car was in the driveway. Which might have been good news — the kind of thing that suggested the WSP had lost some funding but was still a going concern working out of Candy's home — except he'd been told the sedan had been totaled when his woman had hit a deer.

The vehicle looked very structurally sound, not a ding or a dent on it.

Footing the bike forward, he left the engine at an idle, got off, and walked around the front of the car. Nope, no catastrophic damage. No obvious repairs — and besides, given that she'd told him it had been totaled, there should have been no way that kind of shit could have been fixed in a week or ten days, especially out here in the sticks.

The town's mechanic only worked when he felt like it.

"Well, aren't you a sight for sore eyes."

At the Brooklyn accent, Daniel looked over to the front door of the cottage. Candy, last name chemo-brained and forgotten, was leaning out, and yeah, wow. Her hair was the color of a pumpkin, an orange that had absolutely no foundation in the natural chromatics of human follicles. The sixty-year-old was wearing a knitted sweater that had a Santa scene on it, the reindeer racing over her shoulder, the big guy in the red suit with the white beard perched on her hip. The yarn's knotting was such that there was a sculptural quality to the depiction.

In contrast to all that winter-ready, she was wearing flip-flops — and her toenails were a shiny red and green, like she was in the process of polishing them.

Clearly, she was all ready for Christmas. Like maybe she'd started her countdown on Labor Day.

"Hey," he said as he went over to the woman.

"You're looking . . . great."

"You never were a good liar, Candy."

"Ah, how would you know." She stepped aside. "Where's Lydia? You wanna come in?"

Well, that answered one of his questions. "I'm okay, and I don't want to take up much of your time."

"Time's all I got. Come in."

After he shut off the bike's engine, he was

all but sucked into the house, and the decor was like the dress code the woman always sported, full of knickknacks and homey stuff.

"Hey, I know that," he said.

"What?"

Going over to a diorama that was on a bookshelf full of figurines, he nodded. "Thomas Kinkade. They sold twelve hundred of these things in two minutes last month."

Candy's blue lids went wide. "How the hell would you know that?"

"I'm a fan of QVC, too."

"No shit. I guess all those drugs really did fuck you up." She laughed. "I'm kidding."

"No, you aren't." He didn't want to sit down. But where was he going? Not back to C.P. Phalen's right now. "Ah, so can I ask you a couple of things?"

"Is this a job interview? Because I'm technically enjoying unemployment and I have another six months to go. I'm treating it like a staycation. I'm making bread and knitting." She ran her hands down her sweater. "I made this. It's ugly as hell, but I'm proud of it. Then again, I live alone with cats who don't have an opinion about my clothes — what was the question?"

He debated about how honest to be. Then

decided to take a page out of Candy's vibe. And fuck it.

"How long has the WSP been shut down?"

Candy went over and sat down on her plaid couch. Moving a set of needles into her lap, she resumed some kind of knit-purling with bright pink yarn. "It's about three months now, but I'm doing good. I got a year of severance up front. I have to say . . . Lydia really took care of me when she closed shop."

"So she was . . ." He cleared his throat so he could lie. "I mean, of course, she told me what she was doing, of course."

"Yeah, she was worried about you. Still is."

"When did you buy her car?"

"Oh, she gave it to me."

"That was good of her."

"She's the best." Candy lowered her knitting. "Now you want to tell me what this is all about, or do you want to keep playing these games? And I'm sorry I haven't been by to see you at C.P.'s spread, but I was told your immune system was shot and visitors were not really welcome — also, no offense, but that house always freaked me out. It's like a fucking mausoleum. You want coffee? Breakfast?"

He thought of the bagels in his pocket.

445

"No, I had something before I left that freaky house."

Up on the mountain, in a hidden cave with a natural spring-fed pool, Lydia sat on a trunk and stared across a crackling fire. She was back in the red robe from the night before, and across the way from her, stretched out on a pallet, was the male who had been shot at.

"You look so much better," she said.

"Indeed." He glanced down at his bare chest. "By nightfall, I should be back to normal."

"I thought you were going to die." When he didn't reply, she exhaled and went back to fixating on the flames. "So . . . Xhex is your sister."

"If you don't mind, I'd like to keep the chatter about my family to a minimum." Even though his tone was sharp, his eyes were soft as he stared over at her. "I'd rather talk about you."

"I'm happily married." Fine, that was technically a lie. But it was also a truth. "My husband . . ."

"Is dying." As her head snapped up, he nodded. "My sister mentioned that last night. Often. While they were taking the bullet out of me."

446

To avoid his stare, she looked over at the medical supplies that were stacked neatly in the corner. The cave was furnished with trunks and equipment, more of a hideout than a home, but then the wolven who had used this refuge hadn't intended it to be much more than a transitory pawed-à-terre, so to speak. Lydia hoped that he didn't mind them borrowing it for a day.

"How did you find this den?" she asked. "It's well hidden. The wolven up here had to show it to me."

"My sister knew where it was. She said the guy who used to live here — well, it doesn't matter."

How did she know Callum, Lydia wondered.

"They brought you a doctor, then."

"Yes, the female healer took care of me. She was efficient and kind."

Lydia got to her feet and paced around. "It was you, the night before last. Who was up here when we came to meet Xhex."

"What a happy coincidence, is it not? I was here for another reason. I stayed . . . because of you."

Shaking her head, she faced off at him. "It's not going to be like that between us."

"Because?"

"I'm married." God, she wished she had a

ring to point to. "Happily married."

"And afterward?"

As pain lanced through her heart, she looked to the passageway out. "You know, I think I'm going to go —"

"I'm sorry," the male said in a rush. Then he tried to sit up and couldn't quite manage the vertical. "I'm rude sometimes."

Putting her hands on her hips, she felt the need to correct him. "That's not rude. That's cruel."

"I apologize." He moved his hand off to the side, as if he were wiping his comment away. "Last night, how did you know I was there?"

Lydia touched the side of her nose. "I smelled you, from where you were standing. You're not just a vampire, are you."

"No, I'm much more dangerous than they are."

"Is that a flex?"

"It's the truth."

She studied him objectively. With his dark hair and his fine features, he was handsome in an aristocratic kind of way, particularly in the fire's restless light — but he was muscular as well, and he was right about the dangerous thing. She could sense the predatory nature of him, the wolf in her recognizing the animal in him.

"My kind are not welcomed in mixed company," he murmured. "That was how my sister got into her difficulty."

"What kind of difficulty?"

There was a long silence. And then he spoke clearly. "She was sold into an underground lab. She was experimented on. It was hell."

"Oh . . . God."

"Our family put her in there. I watched her get taken away." He laughed. "You know, maybe it's the painkillers they gave me, but I will tell you quite honestly . . . that it has destroyed me, what happened to her. What was done . . . to her. It's become my life's work, as a matter of fact."

Lydia frowned. "That's why you're here on the mountain. You're looking . . . for the lab here. Do you work for the F.B.G., too?"

"In a manner of speaking . . . yes."

She started shaking her head. "You can't destroy the lab. They're trying to save people's lives."

"At the expense of vampires. And wolves just like you."

"Not C.P. Phalen's lab. My husband is dying from lung cancer, and the immunotherapy they developed could save his life if he tried it. But in any event, they will start treating people with the drug — people they

449

want to cure, not hurt."

As he frowned, Lydia talked even faster. "And the doctors who work there? They're good people. They're researchers who are ethical. I don't know what was done to your sister or where or by who. But what's being done here? It's going to save people's lives, and yes, it's developed for humans, but a vampire might need it."

"Vampires don't get cancer."

"Oh. Well. Still. But whatever, there are no vampires down there. No wolven. The subjects who will try it will be volunteers and they will be properly monitored."

In the silence that followed, she looked around again, as if anything in the cave could help her make her argument.

"After your husband dies," the male murmured, "you're going to come here and be on the mountain, aren't you."

"You don't want to talk about your family? Well, I don't want to talk about my future."

"All right. Then let's go back to you in the present." The male's voice got lower. "You're so beautiful, Lydia —"

"Well, isn't this cozy."

Lydia wheeled around. Daniel was standing in the entry to the den, his eyes ripping around and then locking on the male, who was clearly naked under the blankets on the pallet.

"Jesus . . . *Christ,*" Daniel barked. "You're fucking *him?*"

Lydia took a step forward. "What — wait, no. No, I haven't —"

"Don't touch me." He pushed her hands off of him. "And Blade, I should have known. You *fucking* asshole."

"Wait." She looked between the two. "You know him?"

"Yeah, I know him — and now I know what you've been doing while you've been lying to me about going to work. Kind of convenient that I didn't leave the house, huh. Easier to feed me the line of bullshit —"

"Daniel, this is not what it looks —"

"Oh, my God, a line from the movies. Of course, I only know that because I've been sitting on my ass getting ready to die for the last six months —"

"I am not having sex with anybody!" She started waving her hands, as if she could erase the conclusions he was jumping to. "Daniel, I —"

"I'm not even talking to you," he said to the male. "You sonofabitch. And you, Lydia, are you really trying to say you didn't lie? About the fact that the WSP closed down

451

months ago? About the shit about your car? If you'd wanted to give the damn thing to Candy, why the fuck would I care? Why lie about that? Or were you so busy lying about him" — he jabbed a finger at the male on the pallet — "that you just kept snowing me about everything? Fuck, Lydia. *Fuck.*"

"I didn't lie —"

"You did!"

"— for a nefarious reason —"

"There are no good reasons!"

"You are dying!" she hollered back at him. "And I'm dismantling my life because you're *dying*! Do you think I want to tell you that I'm pulling out of everything because you're going to be gone and I'm going to disappear into the lair of the wolven for a couple of years to recover? You're already dealing with everything, do you *really* want to hear about me giving up my job, my house, and my friends so I can help you to your grave? That I'm doing it all so I can squeeze out the last remaining days and months we have together —"

Daniel's flat voice interrupted her. "I don't believe you. I think you didn't tell the truth . . . because you were doing *him.* Don't you dare hide an affair behind my terminal diagnosis."

"That's not what's going on here," she

said with despair.

"You're naked under that red robe. He's naked under those blankets. And he just told you how beautiful you are." Daniel jabbed a hand into the pocket of his coat and took out some kind of bundle wrapped in a napkin. "Here. I brought a bagel for you. He can have the one I was going to eat — which is really apt, isn't it."

As Daniel tossed the food and turned away, she rushed forward, taking his arm. "You have this all wrong." She glanced back at the male. "Tell him. *Tell* him."

"He's not going to say anything," Daniel announced. "Not one fucking syllable is going to come out of his mouth."

Lydia looked back and forth between the two of them. "Do you know each other?"

"Oh, yes, we do. And if he's smart, he'll keep quiet about that. I may be half dead, but I'm in a really fucking bad mood and if he knows what's good for him, he'll stay out of this." At that, Daniel looked at her bitterly. "You know what the really pathetic thing is? I don't even blame you. I can't get it up, so why wouldn't you look for sex somewhere else. And I could almost have lived with it if you'd just copped to the truth."

He ripped his arm out of her grip. "Don't

you dare follow me. You're going to give me an hour to pack up my shit at the house, and then you can come back down there."

"Where are you going," she choked out. "Daniel, I'll leave, I'll be the one who goes, but you have to —"

"My future, however long or short, is no longer any of your business." He put his hands up before she realized she'd reached out again. *"Don't fucking touch me.* And don't you come off this mountain until I'm gone — that shouldn't be too hard for you, though. I'm sure you two have loads of ways to pass the time. She's all yours, Blade. Have fun — and Lydia, I'd be very careful if I were you. You may be confident about how special you are to him, but he's a helluvan operator. He's going to fuck you in ways you don't like and won't see coming."

"Daniel —"

"Stop saying my fucking name," he muttered as he walked off for the passageway. "I don't want to hear it come out of your mouth ever again. You two deserve each other."

THIRTY-SIX

"What do you mean, Daniel is gone?"

As C.P. sat at the side counter in her kitchen, the one where the cooks took their coffee breaks, she was utterly exhausted and clearly not tracking. After having spent the day in Houston meeting with her team, she'd just flown back and had no idea what time it was, why she had decided to end up here — or where Chef was, for that matter. The only thing she knew for sure was that she cared about none of the answers to any of that — and maybe not even to where Daniel Joseph might have gone to.

What was Lydia saying?

Bringing herself into some semblance of focus, she murmured, "I'm sorry, I really don't understand what you're telling me. Forgive me."

"He's gone."

Something in the woman's voice got through the screaming in C.P.'s own head, and as she looked at Lydia properly, a cold rush went down her spine. The amount of distress in that face was the kind of thing you saw around car accidents on the freeway.

"Sit down." She reached across and put her hand on the other woman's forearm. "Please, sit down and tell me what happened?"

Had he died —

"He's just wrong," Lydia babbled. "He's just — he won't listen to me. So he packed up and left."

"The program? The clinic?"

"Well, me, primarily. The rest of everything is just a . . . a side effect."

The woman was positively caved in on herself, her shoulders slumped, even her hair hanging limply: She looked as if she had been left in the wilderness to fend for herself in the middle of a blizzard.

And then something else occurred to her. "Lydia, he's not well enough to be out in the world."

"Do you think I don't know that?"

C.P. checked her watch. "It's ten p.m. When did he go?"

"This morning. He didn't want to see me again, so I didn't return until late afternoon. He cleared out all of his things from our room, just as he said he would, but I've hoped he'd change his mind and come back. I've been waiting out in front of the house ever since."

"Did he take one of my vehicles? Because they have trackers on them."

"No, he's on his bike."

"The *Harley*?" C.P. leaned forward. "Is he insane — I'm sorry, I don't mean to be insensitive, but has he had some kind of psychotic break?"

"I don't know. He wouldn't listen to me."

"Well, then we'll track his phone. Come on, we'll find him."

C.P. got to her feet and dragged the woman after her, going down to her study. Once inside, she went over behind her desk, called her computer up, accessed her contacts — and did a cut and paste into a phone tracker —

"Nothing." She sat back and looked across. "I'm not getting a signal. So either he's found and turned off the tracking on his phone or he's destroyed the cell."

As Lydia stopped pacing and they both went quiet, C.P. closed her eyes and rubbed the nape of her neck. What a day.

"How far are you along?"

C.P. popped her lids at the quiet question. "Excuse me?"

"You're pregnant." The woman touched the side of her nose. "It's evident — but it must be pretty early as I only just noticed yesterday."

"I, ah . . . I'm not sure what to say to that."

"I'm sorry. I should have kept quiet."

C.P. stared up at the woman, who was not really a woman in the conventional sense. Lydia wasn't meeting her eyes, which told her there were probably other things the wolven had sniffed out.

"Unfortunately, pregnancy is not compatible with my disease." C.P. smiled in a reserved fashion. "You must know that I'm sick, too, right? If you can sniff out a baby on board, surely you must be able to detect my cancer."

Lydia's face dissolved into sadness. "Yes, I'm so sorry. I didn't say anything because it is not my business, and you've never mentioned it to anybody."

C.P. lifted her chin. "I was going to be patient one. After Daniel declined the dubious honor." As the female became shocked, she nodded. "Yes, and that seemed rather fair to me given that Vita-12b was created at my behest. Now, though . . ."

"You can't."

"I've decided that I'm not going to terminate the pregnancy. I don't know what the future holds for me, but I will be doing whatever I can to stay alive until the birth."

"C.P. . . ."

"Do me a favor." She looked away. Looked back. "Call me Cathy. I'm really feeling a need to drop the bullshit these days."

Standing across the desk from the great C.P. Phalen, who was at the moment dressed in sweatpants and that fleece that smelled like Gus, Lydia fell silent. She had no idea what to say — about anything.

"Is it okay if I stay a few days?" she asked after a long pause. "In case Daniel comes back, you know."

"You can stay for however long you want."

"Thank you."

C.P. — Cathy, that was — nodded and seemed to get lost in her own head. Which was fine. Lydia had plenty to think about also.

After Daniel had left the den up on the mountain, the male on the pallet, Blade, had just stared at her without saying a thing — although she had felt as though he was reading her in some way she didn't understand, yet clearly sensed. When she'd demanded that he explain himself, he'd just told her that he wasn't feeling well and closed his eyes. That was it.

Frustrated, she had departed the den and then walked down the trail. Halfway through the descent, she realized she was still wearing the red robing. She'd ditched it and shifted, and spent much of the day roaming around, her mind full of recriminations that were only partially dimmed due to her being in her wolven form.

When she had finally arrived back at C.P.'s house, she had dressed in the clothes that she, as always, had left folded on the salt bag.

Just like she had been doing every day.

She should have told Daniel that she'd stopped working. But she had sensed all along he wouldn't be trying C.P. and Gus's drug — and she just hadn't wanted to talk about the future. She was living it with him; discussing the tragedy and all its implications had made her feel positively ill. And then there was the reality that her time away from the house and the lab was her sanity. Every weekday, from nine to five, she had coursed the acreage of the valley and the mountains in her wolven form. It had been the only way to stay even partially together under the pressure, and she had taken such solace with her kind, whether they were genetically just wolves or wolven like her. With her clan, in the lair of the wolven, she had reconnected with the side of herself that had been dormant by design, the practice of denial that her human grandfather had mandated for her survival no longer necessary.

Even before Xhex had told her that her future was on the mountain? She had known that to be true.

If she was going to survive at all after Daniel was gone, she was going to have to go there. And she'd been determined to start getting used to being in the lair.

"Thank you." Wait, what was she talking about? Oh, right, C.P.'s — Cathy's — hospitality. "I mean, well . . . I think I'm going to go check my phone. See if . . ."

But he wasn't going to call her.

"Daniel will show up," Cathy said. "Either because he comes to his senses — or because he's not going to have a choice."

A striking fear blew open Lydia's adrenaline system, and she struggled to control her panic. "I'm just . . . going to go check my phone."

"Do that."

"Let me know if you need me . . ." For what, Lydia didn't know. "And even though it's very complicated, congratulations."

C.P. — *Cathy,* and God, she was going to have to get used to the Cathy thing —

blinked quickly. "I appreciate that. It's a shock, as you can imagine."

"It's a blessing." Lydia put her hand on her own lower belly. "The father must be very happy."

As she let that drift, the other woman winced and said no more. So after an awkward parting, Lydia drifted back through the house's towering, black-and-white rooms and halls. Going along, she felt as though they were in the same place.

Lost.

THIRTY-SEVEN

Altruism was not the hallmark of a *symphath*. Not even close.

After night fell more than sufficiently, Blade finally got up off the pallet he'd spent the day on, and to burn a little more time, he immersed himself in the heated spring's gentle embrace. Just as the water reached his pecs, he heard an approach through the cave's passageway, the footfalls powerful and undisguised.

It was not who he wanted to see, although certainly someone he had expected.

"Sister mine," he said before Xhex strode into the cave, before he sank beneath the surface to wet his hair.

When he reemerged, he discovered she was not alone, her mate, John Matthew, standing at her side. The two of them looked good together, her so powerfully built and dressed in black, him the same. And though their bodies weren't touching, their connection was obvious, the kind of thing that was a second fire burning within the cave.

"Oh, I got both of you," Blade murmured. "How lucky."

"I came to see if you're dead," Xhex announced.

He lifted his hands. "Disappointed?"

"Yeah, kind of."

"At least that's honest." He smiled at her male. "John. How are you. Thanks for last night."

The Brother lowered his chin in a nod, but that was all that came back. Which proved he was a smart male.

"We need to know something." His sister glanced around the stark furnishings. "But first, I know Lydia's been by here, hasn't she."

The question was bullshit, nothing but a fishing expedition to light up his grid and test whether he'd been a good boy, whether he'd kept to his word.

"She stopped by this morning, but I haven't seen her since."

Well, that wasn't entirely true. He'd seen her in his mind all day long. The replay of her and Daniel shouting at each other, their grids glowing like forest fires, their voices clashing, had stuck with him in ways few other things could have.

"What is going on with you and her?" Xhex demanded. "I don't get it."

Wasn't that the question of the hour. And there was only one answer he could give: "Absolutely nothing."

"You've bonded with her. I could scent it last night — and it's still true as I bring up her name now. FYI, I don't think she knows what that means for a vampire male."

Blade said nothing. And as his sister's eyes narrowed on him, he sensed that it wasn't just the shift in his scent that told her where he was at with the female wolven. She was reading his grid, and why should he feel like that was a violation when he was doing the same to her?

And she wasn't doing well. Her superstructure was still all wrong. Was she even aware of it, though?

"Perhaps you'll move on to the real reason you're here?" he prompted.

Xhex rolled her eyes like she was sick of him, and he knew how that felt. He was rather sick of himself as well.

"That cyborg thing we took off the mountain last night." She nodded over her shoulder, like he didn't remember where the biomechanical soldier had been, out by the summit. "The Brotherhood and I — we want to know what it is."

465

"I would think that is self-explanatory to a certain point."

"The hell it is. It was part human, part machine."

"No, there is no human in them. Not that I've been able to find, at least."

"So you know what they are."

"I have encountered one or two in my time. But before you pepper me with inquiries, I will tell you quite truthfully that I know nothing of their origin. They are out in the darkness — working for some kind of master. Their larger, ultimate purpose, however, escapes me as of now."

"We're going to have to drill down on this. The Brotherhood doesn't like surprises in their territory."

"So they pay the taxes on this mountain? I was unaware that the land had changed hands. I rather thought this was a preserve."

"Don't be an idiot. You know exactly what I mean."

Blade debated on whether or not to further provoke her. And then lost interest and energy in such an escapade. "I am happy to share with the Black Dagger Brotherhood all that I know. And I just did. That's it."

Xhex glanced at her mate. Then returned her stare to Blade's. As her gray eyes narrowed on him, he was reminded of how deadly his sister was, and that made him respect her.

Then he thought of his wolf.

Ever since she had left him, an idea had been kindling deep within him, and he found himself praying he wouldn't decide to do the right thing by her. If he did, he had the sense he would be giving up the one true love of his life forever.

And really, why should he do that — especially, as a *symphath,* he was genetically engineered for self-advancement: There was nothing more antithetical to congenital narcissism than sacrificing yourself for another's happiness.

After all, Lydia would never know he could have interceded. No one would ever know — and he could show up here on this mountain in the wake of her mate's funeral, and drape himself in red robes and seduce her with some line of spiritual bullshit during her mourning period.

If Lydia chose him, honestly chose him — well, mostly honestly chose him — then Xhex would have no reason to ride him off the proverbial range.

He refocused on his sister, seeing her properly, and in the back of his mind, in the way back, he wondered what she would think if she knew that he had been *ahveng-*

ing her all these years. She must never know what he had been doing, however.

If anyone in the Colony ever learned how much he cared for her, she would become a target to be used against him — and she had spent too many years of her life already in danger.

He would not put her in that position, even though it meant that she would continue to hate him — and hate him she did.

"Forgive me, sister mine. My bath is concluding. You either need to shoot me in the head or leave me to my privacy. I am done talking — although I suppose you must be used to the silence with your mute mate."

Blade winked at John Matthew — and got bared fangs in response.

As Xhex snarled across the cave's rocky interior, Blade's heart ached. But that, like so much . . .

. . . he kept to himself.

THIRTY-EIGHT

The following day, the hours passed with an aching slowness for Lydia: dawn arriving, the sun drifting by overhead, night assuming prominence. Like every living thing on the planet, it was the cycle that she had always known, and yet now the components of minutes and hours were revealed as a very specific form of torture.

She spent most of the time in bed, staring at the door, hoping it would burst open to reveal Daniel's return. When she did get up, it was to go to the bathroom. Take a quick shower. Ghost down to the kitchen to pick up food and bring it back — as if he would somehow change his mind only if she were laying her head on his pillow.

The day after that was exactly the same. Well, except that sometime after noon, her phone went off. She all but lunged for it on the bedside table — only to discover that it was someone who wanted to talk to her

469

about the warranty on her car.

"You've got to call Candy for that," she muttered as she hung up on the telemarketer.

Back onto the pillow — and it was then that she finally fell asleep. She knew this because she was able to be present in a dream that repeatedly laid claim to her, her hyperawareness causing her to be awake within her subconscious's dance of delusions.

Naturally, it was about Daniel.

And he was dying.

The images, sights, and sounds were all based on memories. She had been present many times when he'd crashed. She had watched him turn blue and gasp for breath, or be unable to respond to simple commands. She had seen the medical staff rush in and had to jump back, jump out of the way. She'd begged and prayed for his survival. And naturally, all of that terror was where she went: She was at his bedside down in the clinic, and he was fighting for breath, clawing at the air in front of him for relief, nothing but a wheeze coming out of him —

Now is when you call for help, she told herself.

Straining with everything she was worth,

she called out to the closed door. Screamed for Gus, even though she'd been told he'd left, hollered for someone, anyone, to —

Her grandfather was the one who stepped into the room.

And abruptly, she traded places with Daniel: Lydia was now the one in the bed and she had no idea where he had gone — no, wait. That wasn't true. He had died, and now she was dying, too. Of a broken heart.

Her grandfather came up to her bedside. He was dressed in his tweed jacket and his wool slacks, his pipe in his hand, his bushy gray eyebrows down low, as if he were very concerned about her.

"Have you come to say goodbye," she choked out.

As always, he said nothing. He just stared down at her.

"Help me, Grandfather. What shall I do?"

Wordlessly, her grandfather's arm raised and swung around to the door, his knurled finger pointing out into —

Lydia woke up in a rush, the dim contours of the bedroom she had shared with Daniel familiar and strange at the same time.

"Grandfather? Are you here . . . ?"

When there was no answer, she wrapped her arms around herself and wept. She wanted to be mad at Daniel for misjudging her as he had, for jumping to a logical conclusion that nonetheless made no sense. Instead, she just felt like he had died, even though he was still alive.

And that dream was right.

She was in the process of dying, too.

In her soul.

About fifty miles to the north, not far from the Canadian border, Daniel sat outdoors in front of a crackling fire, his eyes lost in the flames that spit and hissed inside their circle of stones. From time to time, he coughed, partially from the cold irritating his shot-to-shit lungs, partially from the smoke, definitely from the dryness of everything.

The campsite he'd rented for the night had been free. Which was what happened when it was offseason and no one was monitoring their property. He'd just driven right around the flimsy arm barrier across the entrance to the campgrounds and kept going until he identified the most defensible position. After that, he had liberated some cordwood from under a tarp by the communal restrooms, and settled in for the night.

For two days, he had driven around upstate New York, memories of Lydia and his former boss in that cave version of a love shack burning him as if the images were acid on his skin, inside his veins, down his throat.

After he hadn't been able to find her at the WSP or at Candy's house, he'd guessed where she would go. Of course it was the mountain. Half of her was made for living up in those elevations, and he had always known she was happiest up there. He'd been seeking answers as he'd driven his bike up the broad trail, a violation of the WSP's stated rules, but hey, the goddamn organization was dead. Who the hell was going to enforce its standards and regulations against him?

When he'd gotten to the summit, he'd smelled the woodsmoke and followed the scent to an outcropping of boulders. A little walk around had revealed the passageway into the cave with its heated spring.

And the rest was history.

Funny how when you found your woman with a man you knew was a sociopathic killer, you kind of didn't think about your cancer anymore. Nope. And in spite of her betrayal, all he could think about was the danger Lydia was in.

He'd wanted to call Blade all day long. But what kind of threats could he leverage against the guy to get him to stop seeing her? And even if he had buttons to push, he wasn't going back to Lydia. There was no going back.

Groaning, he repositioned himself, stretching out even more against a rock and crossing his legs at the ankles. Then he linked his arms over his chest. It was going to be hellaciously cold tonight, but then he was numb all over. He wouldn't feel a thing.

He could kill Blade — he really could. The bastard had seduced —

"No, I did not."

For a split second, Daniel became convinced that he'd dubbed in the voice of the man he'd been thinking of — but then a long, lean figure stepped into the firelight.

Funny, it was kind of like what they had done before in April, when Blade had found him on the run and threatened him with Lydia's life if he didn't follow through and eradicate C.P. Phalen's lab.

Ah, good times, good times. And here they were again — and he was not surprised. Blade always knew where his men were, almost like they'd been chipped or something.

"I could shoot you where you stand," Daniel muttered. "I really could."

When the motherfucker didn't say anything, he looked up at his old boss properly. Blade's expression was remote, his lean face a mask of composure in the flames' orange and yellow flickers.

"If you came here to gloat," Daniel said, "don't bother. I told you, you can have her. You win. You taught me the lesson of disobeying an order — how long were you working this angle, by the way? I assumed you backed off bombing the lab site because you knew there was too much attention in the news already. Like, if there was an explosion, things could get too messy, what with all the press about the dead wolves and the red herring with that hotel site killing them. But no, you were playing a long game with me, trying to get me back through working her, weren't you."

Blade just stood there.

Like a statue.

"Oh, okay, you came to kill me, not have a chat." Daniel unlinked his arms and put them out. "Truthfully, this is great. Euthanize me. Put me out of my misery. You'd be doing me a favor —"

"I'm in love with her."

"What."

Of all the things Daniel had expected the man to ever say? That wasn't it; not about Lydia, not about anyone or anything.

"You heard me. I've bonded with her — not that you'd understand that kind of thing as a human."

Human? Daniel narrowed his eyes. "What the hell are you talking about."

Blade got down on his haunches and stared through the flames. "Your woman says the lab under Deer Mountain is working on drugs to save your life. Is that true?"

Daniel put up a forefinger. "Can we not refer to her like that, thanks. And yes, it is."

"But you haven't taken them, why?"

"Too much to lose. Or so I thought."

"You're already dying."

"Yeah, so time is really fucking important. Especially with the one I love — loved, I mean. Fuck." Daniel rubbed his face. "You any closer to putting a gun to my head? If we could move that along, that would be great, thanks —"

"You should try the drugs, Daniel."

"Like I'm taking advice from you about anything?"

"She'd be worth it. Time with a woman like her — it would be worth any risk." Before Daniel cut in, the guy kept going: "Fight for her, Daniel. You need to fight. Do whatever you can to stay with her. It'll be worth it."

Daniel sat up, the crackling of the fire

seeming to increase. Or maybe that was just his temper flaring.

"Don't tell me what I need while you're fucking the woman I love."

Maybe if he repeated the words enough times, he could jam everything about her into his past, make her something in his rear view — so that it didn't hurt as much.

"Look into my eyes," Blade commanded.

"Fuck you —"

The instant Daniel's stare was caught and held, the images started: He saw a progression of them, starting with the perspective of Lydia from a distance, through some trees — and Daniel felt an instant attraction, sure as if he were the one looking at her. Even though he wasn't. These were someone else's memories. Blade's.

He saw it all. From when Blade had first seen her . . . to later, when he'd become transfixed by her and one of the biomechanical soldiers showed up . . . to when she had protected him . . . to the moment his sister, Xhex —

"Alex Hess is your sister," Daniel breathed.

And then there were other memories. From inside the den with the hidden spring.

Of Lydia telling the guy she was happily married.

"Why are you doing this?" Daniel whispered as the man's face came back into real-time view.

"I don't know. It goes against my nature."

Blade straightened back up. And then he looked to the heavens as if he were searching for meaning in the stars that shone, bright and cold, above them both.

"Maybe it's because she was never mine to begin with. She's yours, all the way. Always has been."

"We're not married," Daniel whispered. "She lied about that."

That cruelly intelligent face shifted back to him. "Strikes me as the kind of thing you should rectify before the Grim Reaper shows up on your doorstep, but that's me. And I don't care what you do with what I showed you. Destiny has always been subject to free will — so if you want to complicate this by distrusting me or my motives, that's your prerogative. Frankly, I hope you do fuck it up. Because if you don't? That extraordinary female will no doubt live out the rest of her life as some kind of recluse, forever pining for her one true love."

Blade stepped back. "Be well, Daniel. Your business and mine end here tonight. I will not pursue any actions against that lab, providing they harm none of either of my kind. Or that of your wife's. I protect what I once failed to defend. It is the only way I've been able to live with myself."

With that, the man bowed —

And disappeared right into thin air.

Left on his own, Daniel stared into the darkness . . . and had to wonder whether or not he was dreaming.

THIRTY-NINE

Tap. Tap. Tap.

The sounds were muffled, and at first, Lydia dismissed them as the start of another dream, another descent into the madness that seemed to await her whenever her eyes closed.

But they continued.

Tap. Tap. Tap.

Sitting up, she pushed her hair out of her eyes. Then she looked over to the glass sliding door. At first, the shape on the far side terrified her — another mechanical soldier, sent to kill them all!

Except no. She recognized the bald head.

"Daniel," she cried out.

Scrambling through the messy blankets, she exploded across the room and fumbled with the lock. As she yanked open the plate glass panel, the cold air barged in as if it were sick of the great outdoors and looking to chill a new territory.

And there he was. Shivering, flushed — and looking at her as if he had been gone a lifetime.

It felt like he had been away that long.

"Daniel, you're wrong about everything —"

"I know —"

"What?" She stepped back. "Wait, come inside, it's freezing out there."

His teeth were chattering and his lips blue, and she wrapped him in the duvet before he could argue he didn't need it.

"Oh, God, Lydia . . . I'm such a fucking fool." He captured her face in his hands. "I was a terrible, terrible fool and I'm so sorry —"

"Wait, I don't understand —"

"Blade came to see me." Daniel wrapped the comforter more tightly around himself, took her hand, and drew her over to the bed so they could sit down together. "I'm so sorry. When I walked into that cave, my emotions got the better of me. I should have listened to you, but I just . . . I wasn't thinking straight. It's pretty goddamn unforgivable —"

"I swear, that wasn't what was going on. He'd been injured. Xhex brought a doctor to him, and I went there to see if he needed anything. I was naked under the robe because I traveled in wolven form out from this house for safety's sake. There was nothing sexual in any of it."

"I know."

Lydia blinked. And prayed she wasn't dreaming this all. But then she got pissed. "So he told you. And you believe him and not me —"

"He showed me." Daniel touched his temple. "He let me see inside his brain somehow, I don't know what he did or how. But you're right, I should have just listened to you, and I go cold when I think what would have happened if he hadn't come and found me."

"Where were you," she asked.

"At a campsite about fifty miles from here."

"But . . . how did he find you?"

"He's my former boss. He's the head of the Federal Bureau of Genetics. And I need to find C.P. He has a message for her. He's dropping her lab from his list of things to do."

"Your boss?" she murmured.

"*Former* boss. That's one of the reasons I jumped to the conclusion I did. It would be just in his wheelhouse to do something like that in retaliation for me not following through on my mission — not that it's any excuse. I was an ass —"

"I lied to you." She lowered her head. "So what you thought is not unreasonable. I lied first, Daniel. I shouldn't have done that."

"Yeah," he said softly. "I still don't really understand why you couldn't tell me about everything."

Tucking her legs up to her chest, she shrugged. "It was the start of my goodbye to you. Selling my stuff, closing up the WSP, giving my car away, getting out of my rental agreement. That was all part of your death, you see, and I felt like if I talked to you about it, I was starting the process — and I couldn't bear that. But I shouldn't have lied to you. I should have had more courage —"

"I love you."

Lydia looked over at him and wiped her eyes. "Oh, Daniel . . . I love you, too."

Sitting beside his woman, Daniel heard her say the words, but not with his ears. No, the magic she spoke resonated much deeper than that. And when she reached for him, he went to her like they were out of time: in a desperate rush.

Putting his arms around her, he drew her up against him, and she held him back, and they . . .

Kissed.

483

Their meeting of the mouths was the kind of thing that happened when you were trying to figure out whether the nightmare was over — and the truth was, he knew that this was just an intermission, at best. But he had learned something recently.

Don't argue with the gifts that you were given.

Maybe they weren't precisely what you wanted. Maybe they weren't even anywhere near what you'd prayed for. But to turn down a blessing just because your à la carte wasn't what you had demanded? What a way to disrespect fate.

Assuming this was all real — and it sure as shit felt that way — he was going to take this respite, this restart, and cherish it for as long as it lasted.

Daniel eased back and brushed a lock of hair off Lydia's cheek. "I'm sorry about all the drama."

And God, didn't that cover more than just what had happened in that cave.

They talked some more. Were silent some more. And spoke once again.

And then there were no words.

Just love.

Tucking her against him, so that her head was under his chin, Daniel stared across their bedroom. Deep in his chest, he had the instinct that this was the eye of the hurricane.

The storm was going to come back for them. Though they were reunited, the churning wheels of destiny were still grinding against them, and the winds of suffering were going to batter them once again.

But was anything more powerful than them being together?

No, he thought. Not even death.

It was with that conviction that he closed his eyes. "Shh . . ." he whispered. "We're safe."

"Yes," she said softly. "We're together so we're safe."

The next thing he knew, he was stretching out with her pressed against him. Soon, he was falling asleep, and so was she. Maybe they would meet in their dreams.

Practice for when he wasn't here any longer.

Forever, in the mind, in the heart . . . in the soul.

EPILOGUE

The next morning, Cathy Phalen sat at the desk in her study and watched on her computer monitor as Daniel drove Lydia off on his Harley. Neither of them were wearing helmets, so the glow on their faces, which had nothing to do with the cold, was easy to see.

Struck by the moment, she followed their progression as they passed in and out of the views of various cameras, the images shifting, the reality staying the same. Diagnosis: true love. And she was happy for them.

As her hand went to her lower abdomen, they passed through the final checkpoint at her main front gate . . . then they roared off. The last video she had of them was of Lydia turning her head to the side and laying her cheek on Daniel's back.

She hoped they would enjoy the good days ahead, however many of them there were. Whatever had happened, whatever conflict had occurred, had clearly resolved itself — and she wouldn't be surprised if she had to talk to Chef about a wedding cake.

Gus would have been great at that ceremony, as a best man, she thought. Maybe even the officiant. Then again . . . Gus was great at everything.

Tucking her feet under her seat, she pulled his fleece even closer to her. She had expected him to call her when he received the document she'd asked Daniel Joseph to witness and had one of her guards deliver, but he hadn't. Perhaps he was getting his own legal counsel to look it all over. That's what she would have done if she were in his position — that's what she would have advised him to do. If he'd asked her for advice.

She really wanted to hear his voice. One last time.

She really wanted to tell him that he'd been right. She had been too rich for too long, and had gotten in the habit of everything — and everyone — going her way.

And she really wanted to explain that she had taken care of Rob's ashes properly, and placed them in the back meadow in a very good spot — which was a strange confession, and maybe proof that she hadn't yet learned the full lesson of not using people to her own advantage. Why would Gus want to hear that she'd paid her respects to the father of her child?

God . . . she missed him. Somewhere, along the line, her business partner had become so much more to her, but she had been too busy being a created persona that the real person underneath had lost out on someone who had been one of a kind . . .

Her eyes were still on the monitor, on a static black-and-white image of the landscape across the county road from her gates, when her cell phone rang.

Reaching out without looking, she turned the screen over. And rolled her eyes.

But if she didn't answer, he was just going to keep dialing on his end.

Swiping to accept the call, she said, "I already told you, Gunnar. You need to talk to Gus. He owns Vita-12b now, not me. I even sent you a copy of the goddamn paperwork."

She thought again of that document. Gus had told her she needed to appoint someone to take over her business affairs — so she had. Who else could she have left Vita to? And the fact that he had accepted another job before he got the envelope she'd sent him had been a funny punch line, hadn't it.

"I would talk to Dr. St. Claire," that European accent drawled, "if I could. But he's missing."

Cathy frowned and sat up properly. "I'm sorry?"

"When I couldn't reach him following our conversation, even after many, many phone calls, I sent a representative to his address. His car was in the drive, but the back door was open. My agent went inside — there had been a disturbance in the front room. Blood and scuff marks on the carpet."

Cold terror tightened Cathy's throat. And then she felt an anger that went into her marrow. "Gunnar, so help you God, if you are fucking —"

"I want to buy that drug. You know this. Why would I harm the owner of record — and then call you to tell you about it? No offense, Phalen, but you are stupid if you believe that."

Her hand tightened on her phone. "I'll find him."

For them both.

"Good luck," Rhobes murmured. "Nasty business we're in. I've been a target myself of late, and it is not an enjoyable experience. Call me when you have him — or his body. If it's the latter, perhaps you and I have something to talk about again."

The call was ended and Cathy shot to her feet.

Her first instinct was to call for her guards. But she followed through on the thought that came after that.

Daniel slowed the speed of the Harley as he and Lydia came up to the side entry of the apple orchard. After a series of humps created by truck tires, and then a stretch of molar-rattling vibration over uneven ground, they hooked up with the road that ran down the eastern side of the field. Given the season, the leaves were all off the craggy branches, but he loved the view.

Then again, with the sun on his face, his bike on a roar, and his woman on the back with her arms around him? He could have taken them on a tour of a municipal sewage plant and still thought everything was beautiful.

When the road made a fat circle and changed directions to intersect with another route, he took them deep into the acreage, slowing to a stop when they could see nothing in any direction except for the apple trees.

After he cut the engine and threw out the kickstand, he tilted the bike and let it set itself on the packed dirt of the lane.

Lydia got off first, and as the wind caught her loose hair, the waves of blond and brown feathered over her features. He was the one who tucked them back behind her ears, and then she leaned in toward his mouth.

The kiss was not brief. And when they separated, he was breathing a little heavier. So was she.

"This is such an incredible place," she murmured as she looked around.

"Beautiful," he said as he stared at her rosy cheeks and her bright eyes. "Best view I've ever seen."

"You're not looking at the trees," she teased.

"Are there trees out here? I hadn't noticed."

Lydia laughed and wandered off a little, going over and bringing a branch down to her level. "I've driven by here a number of times, but I've never picked anything."

"Maybe . . ." He cut himself off. There wouldn't be a harvest for him next year. "I'm glad we're here now."

"Me, too."

Swinging his leg over the seat, he dismounted and put his hand into the pocket of his leather coat. He hadn't had time to get her a proper ring yet, but he couldn't wait. Here. Now. He was going to ask her to be his wife — and knowing his Lydia, the fact that he only had a zip tie that he'd trimmed the long end off of was going to be endearing.

"Come here," he said. "I've got something to ask you —"

The vibration started up in the inside pocket of his jacket, the one that was right against his pec, but as his woman turned to him with a smile, he forgot all about the phone call.

"What do you want to know?" she asked as she came over.

While his phone continued to ring on silent, he searched her face and saw nothing but simple curiosity. She had no idea what he was about to do —

"Is your phone ringing?" she said with a frown.

"No."

Brrrrrrrrrrr. Brrrrrrrrrrr. And then things went silent. Which was a good thing as he was about to take the fucking phone out, put it on the ground, and run it over a couple hundred times with his bike.

"Oh, I thought it was —"

Brrrrrrrrrrrrrrrrrrr. Brrrrrrrrrrrrrrrrrrr.

As Lydia lifted her eyebrow, he shoved his hand inside his pocket and took the thing out. When he saw who it was, he frowned and answered.

"Cathy?" he said.

He was still getting used to calling the woman by the informal name, but then she wasn't dressing like C.P. Phalen anymore — and she was going to be a mom. So yeah, big changes on the ol' house front —

"Something's happened to Gus," came the urgent voice. "I don't know anything other than he may have been abducted from his home. I don't know when, I don't know by who — but I need your help, Daniel."

Daniel's eyes shot to Lydia's. "Do you have his address?"

"I'm texting it to you now, it's about twenty-five minutes away. I'll meet you there."

Motioning for Lydia to come with him and get back on the bike, he remounted and said, "Bring backup with you."

"They're already pulling the cars around —" Cathy's voice cracked. "It's not Gunnar Rhobes. I just spoke to him. It's someone else, but I don't know —"

"We'll find Gus. No matter who has him — I will bring that man back home if it's the last thing I do on this earth."

"Daniel . . ." Cathy's voice broke. "I don't know what I'll do without him."

"You're not the only person who feels that way."

As he hung up, there was a *bing* as the text with the address arrived.

"What's going on," Lydia asked as she wrapped her arms around herself.

He got the location on Google Maps and made sure he knew where he was going. "Gus. Something bad's happened. We need to go to Plattsburgh."

"Is he all right?"

"I have no idea." Extending his hand out to her, he said, "We shouldn't waste any time, okay?"

Abruptly, Lydia's chin lowered and her eyes gleamed with a predator's menace. "If anyone's hurt that man?"

Daniel nodded. "It goes without saying. We take care of it."

Lydia nodded grimly, gripped his palm, and hopped back on the bike. As her arms came around him again, he gave them a squeeze. Then he started the engine with a jump, pumped the gas —

— and tore off down the lane.

For that physician? For everything the man had done for him over the last six months?

Daniel was going to find out what the hell had happened — and with Lydia's help, he was going to make sure if there were any wrongs to be righted . . .

The ledger was balanced.
The proper way.

ACKNOWLEDGMENTS

With so many thanks to the readers of the Black Dagger Brotherhood books! This has been a long, marvelous, exciting journey, and I can't wait to see what happens next in this world we all love. I'd also like to thank Meg Ruley, Rebecca Scherer and everyone at JRA, and Hannah Braaten, Jamie Selzer, Jennifer Bergstrom, Jennifer Long, and the entire family at Gallery Books and Simon & Schuster.

To Team Waud, I love you all. Truly. And as always, everything I do is with love to and adoration for both my family of origin and of adoption.

Oh, and thank you to Naamah, my Writer Dog II, and Obie, Writer Dog-in-Training, who work as hard as I do on my books!

ABOUT THE AUTHOR

J. R. Ward is the author of more than thirty novels, including those in her #1 *New York Times* bestselling Black Dagger Brotherhood series. There are more than fifteen million copies of her novels in print worldwide, and they have been published in twenty-six different countries. She lives in the South with her family.

The employees of Thorndike Press hope you have enjoyed this Large Print book. All our Thorndike, Wheeler, and Kennebec Large Print titles are designed for easy reading, and all our books are made to last. Other Thorndike Press Large Print books are available at your library, through selected bookstores, or directly from us.

For information about titles, please call:
(800) 223-1244

or visit our website at:
gale.com/thorndike

To share your comments, please write:
Publisher
Thorndike Press
10 Water St., Suite 310
Waterville, ME 04901